ALSO BY JOHN GARDNER

The Resurrection

The Wreckage of Agathon

Grendel

The Sunlight Dialogues

Jason and Medeia

Nickel Mountain

The King's Indian

October Light

The Life and Times of Chaucer

The Poetry of Chaucer

In the Suicide Mountains

On Moral Fiction

Freddy's Book

The Art of Living and Other Stories

Mickelsson's Ghosts

On Becoming a Novelist

The Art of Fiction

Gilgamesh (co-author, John Maier)

STILLNESS

and

SHADOWS

STILLNESS

and

SHADOWS

John Gardner

Edited and with an introduction by
Nicholas Delbanco

ALFRED A. KNOPF NEW YORK 1986

THIS IS A BORZOI BOOK
PUBLISHED BY ALFRED A. KNOPF, INC.

Library of Congress Cataloging-in-Publication Data
Gardner, John, 1933–1982
Stillness; and, Shadows.
I. Gardner, John, 1933–1982. Shadows. II. Title.
III. Title: Stillness. IV. Title: Shadows.
PS3557.A712S8 1986   813'.54   85-45592
ISBN 0-394-54402-1

Manufactured in the United States of America
FIRST EDITION

CONTENTS

INTRODUCTION

by Nicholas Delbanco

The cover illustration of John Gardner's collection of short stories, *The Art of Living,* shows a motorcyclist racing at the reader, straight ahead. His jacket is black leather, as was John's, and his expression is grim. It is as though he drives *In the Suicide Mountains*—another recent title—prepared to take that leap described on the final page of *Grendel;* there are fierce night rides throughout his work, and creatures everywhere at risk.

John Champlain Gardner, Jr., died of injuries sustained in a motorcycle accident on Tuesday, September 14, 1982. The afternoon was balmy, bright; the roads were dry. He was a cautious and experienced driver, a few miles from home; he swerved—to avoid another vehicle, perhaps?—and fell. John was forever trying to explain himself, but death is inexplicable; the coroner's report describes result, not cause. It is clear he was trying to make it, fighting to survive. We never will know what he saw while he fell, or felt when the handlebar dealt him its mortal gut punch. He maintained, repeatedly, he had no fear of death; he wanted the rider of *The Art of Living* to appear playful, not fierce. On September 16, two days after the accident, my wife and I received a letter from him full of future plans. He was to marry on the weekend of what became his funeral; he was immersed in a translation of *Gilgamesh*—"Fine pome!"; he sounded, as always, vividly alive.

John seemed somehow to have been born with a quicker ratio to the passage of time than the rest of us. He worked with a headlong, hurtling rush—at times, twenty hours a day. Each new home for him, I think, was absolutely home; each new set of friends was old and dear and gifted; his moderation was our excess and his excess brooked no containment. It's not so much a question of the forced march and furious pace, as if he knew he might die young and wanted to waste or miss nothing. Rather, it was

as if he decided that certain central matters demanded all the patient seriousness he had. He had no attention left to squander on sleep or table manners
or the IRS. . . .

What follows are two manuscripts: *Stillness,* a completed novel, and *Shadows,* a fragment. The first was written in haste, and shelved; the second was
a long-term labor, ongoing at his death. John handed me the manuscript
of *Stillness* in 1975 and, to my knowledge, left it at that; he salvaged a short
story of the same title from its pages. This is true of "Redemption"
also—though the story there related recurs in his work. "Stillness" was orig-
inally published in *The Hudson Review* and "Redemption" in *Atlantic
Monthly;* they have been collected in *The Art of Living.*

In 1980 I published a novel, the third of my Sherbrookes trilogy, for
which *Stillness* seemed the ideal title. I confirmed with John that he had
no intention of pursuing his own novel of that name. He shook his head;
he had put it behind him; it was not among his papers when he died.

Shadows, however, was present—some eight hundred pages of typescript, and many of those single-spaced. Although he could seem profligate,
he was in fact retentive; some of *The Art of Fiction,* for instance, comes from
notes taken twenty years earlier. *Nickel Mountain,* published in 1973, origi-
nates in work composed for Jarvis Thurston at Washington University in
1954. To anyone familiar with his method of composition, or with his accounts thereof, such accretion by bits and snatches will seem typical; Gardner
spoke of *Shadows* as a project since 1974.

The story of an alcoholic detective in Carbondale, Illinois, resisted him,
however; the manuscript includes a dozen stabs at starting it, getting it right.
Detective Craine kept shifting ground—as did, literally, his author: Gardner
worked on these sheets in Bennington, in Baltimore, at Binghamton, and
on the road in between. By February 9, 1978, he thought enough of *Shadows*
to mail pages for safekeeping to his friend and biographer John Howell;
in an undated letter thereafter he sent "part one of a perhaps five-part forthcoming novel" to his editor at Knopf, Robert Gottlieb. "Boy is it boring!"
he wrote. "However, I slog on . . ."

His projects of the period—principally *Mickelsson's Ghosts* and *Gilgamesh,* as well as the two books on writing technique, *On Becoming a Novelist* and *The Art of Fiction*—intervened. It is this reader's conviction that
Shadows could have proved a major novel, a worthy successor of and com-

panion piece to *The Sunlight Dialogues.* It resembles that book closely in ambition and donnée.

Others knew him longer and more intimately. I offer this account of friendship in the knowledge that it is representative—that many have been touched as I, and share in the general loss. We met on Tuesday, April 16, 1974. He came to Bennington, Vermont, on a reading tour; he and his wife, Joan, arrived for dinner at our house.

My first impression of Gardner remains: a short, pot-bellied, pipe-smoking man, with a high-pitched voice and rapid rate of utterance, pontificating splendidly and as if by rote. His eyes were red-rimmed, his white hair lank; he made his entry two hours late. It was not his fault, in fact; it was Albany Airport's, and the fog's. But somehow, in the ensuing years, there would always be some such disruption: a car would fail to start or end up in a ditch, a snowstorm would come out of nowhere, a wallet would be lost. Joan Gardner wore expensive clothing and fistfuls of jewelry; the novelist wore blue jeans and a black leather vest. He emptied a quart of vodka before he sat to eat.

I saw him often in such situations later; they are hard to avoid. Fame brings a constant, admiring assault, a request from civil strangers to be brilliant or outrageous or at least informed. It wears one down and forces one to substitute a mask for face; sooner or later, they fuse. This is doubly a danger for the writer, since privacy is the sine qua non of his work and he has had no training in the actor's life.

By midnight I had dropped my guard; by two o'clock he had too. Elena, my wife, went to sleep. Since I had to teach next morning, I tried to call a halt; I had to prepare for my class. Nonsense, said John, we'd have another bottle and he'd help me through the morning session—what was it on, by the way? "Virginia Woolf," I said, and construed his nodding to mean knowledge of her work. So we talked till four or five and met again at ten o'clock; I weaved my way to class.

In the event I did most of the teaching. Perhaps I knew more about Virginia Woolf; certainly I felt more responsible to the students than did their visitor. I lectured with a panicky inventiveness, stopping only for questions or breath. The session went well; I knew that. But Gardner assured me, with what I later came to recognize as characteristic hyperbole, that it was the best talk he'd ever attended—at least, on any author after

Malory. He knew something more than I did, maybe, about Apollonius of Rhodes . . . I was gratified, of course, and all the more so when his wife said he repeated the praise to her later; we had become "fast friends." The next night, after his reading, I asked if he wanted a job.

I was in the position to hire him but did not believe he'd accept. It was more an offhand courtesy, a variety of "If you'd ever care to come back through . . ." To my surprise he said yes. He was tired of his present appointment, possibly; his family hoped to move east. At the end of *Stillness,* he records the accidental-seeming sequence that brought him to Vermont. We were in his motel room; he was changing shirts. This completes my introductory image: a white-fleshed, full-bellied man with his pants legs rolled up, his pipe smoking on the coverlet, and papers all over the bed. Students clustered at the motel entrance, waiting to whisk him away. The last thing that he handed me was a drawing of himself as gnome, peeping out from bushes with the block-letter legend, "Should Nicholas require John Gardner, he can be reached at . . ." his number and address in Illinois. I did require him, and he could be reached.

For three years thereafter, we saw each other continually. Our families grew close and have remained that way. His presence was a gift. He ballyhooed my work in public and berated it in private. Day in, week out, we wrangled over prose. There was nothing polite or distanced about his sense of colleagueship; if he hated a line he said so, and if he hated a character he said so all the more loudly. At this remove it's hard to remember what we discussed at such length: profluence, *energeia,* walnut trees. I spent three days hunting through graveyards and telephone books in order to prove that Sherbrooke with an *e*—the surname of a character—would be more likely than Sherbrook without. He came up with a whiskey bottle spelled Sherbrook; I pointed to a Sherbrooke township south of Montreal. We cotaught classes and founded a summer writing program together. Out of many memories I will here cite two.

October Light was accorded the National Book Critics Circle Award for fiction in 1976. The presentation ceremony took place in New York, and John's publishers made it an occasion. They hosted a supper party afterwards, and a suite was reserved in Gardner's name at the Algonquin Hotel. He asked my wife and me to be his companions that night. He wore the dungarees we'd seen him wear all month; we, of course, dressed to the nines. He was tireless and generous—but most of all, and in a way that's difficult to pinpoint, he was serious. Where other writers would have rested on their laurels, he was busy lobbying for his present project—an opera. He was no good at small talk, too abrupt; he was busy all night long. This helps explain his torrential outpouring those years; he did not stop. His first question to me, always, was "What are you working on?" *October Light* was finished, therefore irrelevant.

The occasion was a success. There were important and beautiful people, good speeches, and fine wines. At night's end we repaired to the Algonquin, where they nearly refused him a bed. He had a typewriter and briefcase as luggage, no credit cards or cash. We somehow convinced the desk clerk that Alfred Knopf himself would foot the bill, and were escorted to the suite. There were flowers and fruit, bottles waiting on ice; we ordered brandy as well. As the bellhop left, John sat. The couch was vast. He sank in its plush lushness, and mice scrambled from his feet.

They were gone quickly; they scurried to some other section of the suite. But in that first instant I thought they had emerged from his boots. We laughed. We placated Elena and informed the bellhop on his return that he should make certain hereafter to clear away the cheese. Yet the image remains and retains its first power to shock: I saw his power in the process of collapse. The telephone rang. At home he had answered, "Hello, Gardners'." That was, he explained, a way of being noncommittal; it was a large family, and you never knew which one the caller intended. It was also a way of keeping celebrity seekers at bay; you didn't have to say, "John Gardner," and could therefore always say he wasn't in. It rang again. He answered, "Hello, Gardner." He seemed forlorn; the brandy and Book Critics Circle had no power to invigorate. He was white and tired and, for all our efforts at support, alone.

Within the year, he was operated on for cancer. His first marriage had ended; his second—to the Bennington graduate, the poet L. M. Rosenberg—was in the offing, and he had moved from Vermont. They took him to Johns Hopkins Medical Center for emergency surgery; on Christmas Day I flew down. At dawn on Christmas the airports are deserted, so I had an empty, easy flight and was in Baltimore by nine.

He had not expected me and was watching television. His usual pallor was more pronounced still and made the sheet seem colorful. When he saw me, he blushed. It was, I teased him, the first and only time he'd been caught in the act of watching TV; James Page, in *October Light,* had shot out the television screen in his house. So it would not have been pleasure but embarrassment that caused him to flush—but it was all right, I assured him, his secret addiction was safe. I blathered on like that until we felt at ease with silence; he lit up his pipe; all was well. I brought him Christmas tokens; he complained about the trouble he was having with a paragraph of *Shadows* ("Craine's work was a bore. His associates were bores, his clients were boring. . . ."). He had worked at it for three days now, but it wasn't right. The medicine tray held his IBM Selectric, and his window ledge was heaped with erasable bond. (The next time I visited him at Hopkins he was sitting up in bed and busily at work—irritable, almost, at the interruption. The third time Elena came too, and we could not find him; he was in the reaches of the hospital basement, having commandeered a Xerox machine. But that first instant when I watched him through the open door remains the image here.) I knew—to see him reaching for the TV monitor and then for his pipe, turning even this cell into a work space, disorderly, coloring—he would survive.

His work will. Novelist, poet, critic, playwright, librettist, scholar, translator, fabulist—at forty-nine years old, he had the exuberance and protean energy of men not half his age. He was involved in the theater, in music, woodworking, publishing, teaching, painting—any number of pursuits and none of them casual or slapdash. His paintings were intensely seen; his boxes and furniture served. I remember dropping by his house in Bennington to find so many bookshelves fabricated in one day that I thought the pipe smoke he stood wreathed in had caused my eyes to blur. He did seem, somehow, multiple. The first musical selection of the Memorial Service on East Main Street in Batavia—the town in upstate New York where he was born and buried—was a cassette of John and his son, Joel, performing on their French horns. They played "Amazing Grace."

But Gardner was a writer first and last; his motorcycle bag was stuffed with manuscript. Paper littered the road where he lay. He leaves a rich legacy of completed work. As his literary executor it has been my duty to decide—in consultation with his agent, Georges Borchardt, and his editor,

Bob Gottlieb—on the propriety of making public what was incomplete. That we have agreed to publish these two books is self-evident, but the process of so doing was neither simple nor brief. It may help the reader to know some of the problems we faced.

With respect to *Stillness,* the major issue is, of course, that of its creator's intention. He had decided to leave it alone. There are several other books—begun, abandoned, cannibalized—in his papers, and though an author cannot necessarily have everything he wishes published, the reverse is the general case: what he does not choose to publish is his choice. And the stories taken from this Ur-text ("Stillness" and "Redemption") were extensively revised.

That process of revision has been described by Gardner in his books upon the craft. Suffice it to say that he honeycombed his own texts with addenda, corrigenda, interlinears. A representative manuscript page of his "finished" work contains nearly as much handwriting as typescript. For some writers, revision is a process of reduction—of cutting, pruning back. His characteristic method, however, had to do with expansion: filling in the blanks. He planned to do so here. He spoke of his intention, how the "stillness" at the novel's center would connect to problems of particle physics, to tornadoes in the Ozarks, to Japanese theater—the Sarugakah No Noh. . . . Such matters are but adumbrated in this draft. The pages are open, a few corrections penciled in; he ended where the thickening would otherwise begin.

And *Stillness* was written in haste. Undertaken in part as a process of therapy, as an exercise of recall engaged in with his wife, the emotions recollected have scant tranquillity. The language feels spoken, transcribed. They would go to the porch, Joan Gardner remembers, ratify their memories—sometimes with a tape recorder, often with martinis. They took turns typing it out. Much of this book is autobiography. Many names are those of real people (William Dickey, William Gass, John Napper); many less public names have also been retained (Dr. Faris, the white-haired woman called Babs). He did have a brother Gilbert and an English sheepdog Bennington. The affectionate elegiac portrait of John Ferndean is a likeness of the sculptor Nicholas Vergette. Only perhaps with *Mickelsson's Ghosts* have readers come to recognize how much of himself Gardner put in his books, how strong a strain of reportage lay in the fabulist. That he changed his family's names and the color of their Mercedes was rudimentary protective coloration; this is personal, unmediated prose.

"I write for myself and for strangers"—so said Gertrude Stein. One of the paradoxes of the writer's enterprise is that we publish secrets—with the high hope that thousands will read them—we might hesitate to whisper to a friend. Time, too, is a form of distance; a decade after the composition of *Stillness,* the problems there confronted look less immediate. *("Life is fleeting,"* he wrote, *"even the worst of life is fleeting.")* And though it may be "Useless to inquire too earnestly what Martin Orrick meant," his intention seems as stated at his Prologue's close: "Therefore I write fiction, to make the beauty of change everlasting, unalterable as rock."

I think *Stillness* is important for more than biographical or bibliographical reasons. The passionate intensity of its central agon, the power of its language and unwinking inward glare—the values it espouses fairly leap from the page. One does not need to know the prototypes of Martin and Joan Orrick to know them prototypical and join in the struggle described. Passage after passage has the ring of truth. With all its flaws and excess—flaws *of* excess, principally, that mirror the characters' own—*Stillness* reads like the genuine article, a *de profundis clamavi.* Time does not mediate that. Some spelling errors have been corrected. We have changed nothing else.

Shadows is a different proposition. *Stillness* is complete and *Shadows* a fragment, technically incoherent and very much subject to change. Not one of its pages seemed "unalterable as rock." Though Gardner in discouragement might speak of shelving this enterprise also—and he did often—he returned to it for years. The stakes were higher, somehow, and therefore the anticipated yield. *The Sunlight Dialogues* deploys the conventions of detective fiction; "cops and robbers" appear throughout his work. As a medievalist he saw this hunt as quest; in *Jason and Medeia* he envisioned it as an epic journey; so, too, in *Gilgamesh.* The chase after authentic identity structures *The King's Indian;* the doppelgänger motif appears in "William Wilson," his libretto of Poe's tale. *Freddy's Book* and *Mickelsson's Ghosts* and a film treatment of a psychic professor all partake of such inquiry—the larger questions, really, of who we are and what we can know. I do not purpose here to write at length of Gardner's themes, but only to point out that *Shadows* engaged them again: this is the mother lode, the vein he most fruitfully mined.

His papers have been gathered in the Library of the University of Rochester. Two graduate students spent the better part of a year cataloguing what was left behind in his house in Susquehanna and his office at SUNY Binghamton. One of them, Jon Griffin, wrote an account of the process:

> I duly noted and filed . . . into acid-free folders: the student appointment sheets, grocery lists, addresses, letters from lawyers, accountants, the I.R.S., hospitals; the steady stream of correspondence with editors, admirers, disgruntled Jehovah's Witnesses or Mormons, supplicants of all sorts; the busted pipes and plans for a chicken house; receipts for two-by-fours or London hotels or motorcycle repairs; bounced checks, airline ticket stubs, snapshots, class notes, datebooks, maps, limericks; stage directions and directions to a friend's house; reprint permissions, publisher's statements, grant applications, flyers against dumping; postcards, business cards, bibliography cards, empty envelopes, horn music, a banjo string, a watch smudged with tar.

Making order out of the chaos of *Shadows,* however, has been my affair. None of the pages have dates. The first sheet of the manuscript, as filed "into acid-free folders," is numbered 350. Seven lines of double-spaced typescript, it has six lines of penciled corrections; the next page is single-spaced, on legal-size paper, and reads "344 cont." The next page, also single-space typescript on legal-size paper, is covered front and back with handwriting and reads 334. Six sheets later there is a page of "Acknowledgments." Then, in order, pages 345, 272, 301, 271. A representative twenty-page swatch is numbered as follows: 240, 101, 101, 100, 99, 98, 97, 97, 96, 96, 79, 92, 93, 92, 94, 93, 96, 93, 92, 91. The repeating numbers do not represent copies but revisions of pages, and every single one of them has substantial handwritten revision. The more or less clean copy of page 88 is followed by a handwritten 82, then handwritten 81, then 80 in a different typeface. Halfway through the manuscript, there is page 2, page 1, then 1 again, then 2, 2, "Prologue," 1, 303, 296. These are examples picked at near random, and they hold true for the whole. Gardner's script is spidery, intended for no second set of eyes . . .

The larger intention, too, stood subject to revision. One version of page 1 begins with the summarial statement: "Nothing is stable; all systems fail. Consider the case of Gerald B. Craine, detective . . ." That instability, germane to Craine's sense of self as well as his associates, governs the book; a drunkard and amnesiac, Craine finds himself, the watcher, watched. One title sheet reads simply, *Craine,* though the majority are *Shadows;* at an early point Craine's first name was not Gerald. As the book progresses, so does Gardner's interest in cancer and computers. The former is subjective—and the account of Craine's stay in the hospital seems as closely linked to personal experience as the text of *Stillness.* The latter feels concomitant with Gardner's later reading. A page of "Notes" may testify to that. They are worth reproducing in full—not so much for what they tell us of the book as of its author's restless questioning, the range of his concerns (Ira Katz, Elaine, and Hannah are secondary figures in the text):

Notes:

Idea of a novel as a huge computer product, routines and subroutines (given sub-themes recurrently plugged in to a larger program).

On hackers, is it "power" they love, or beauty (or some dream of beauty?) Are they artists, in fact. Does their behavior, or the compulsive gambler's, significantly differ from the artist's behavior? (How connected is the artist to the world outside?)

Ira Katz. His clocks call up the idea of removal from primary reality (not judging when to eat by hunger but by a system of marks on a clockface); his interest in linguistic reality (computable, he thinks, or at least plays with thinking), an interest which implies a mechanistic universe—played against his role as poet, always trying for linguistic precision different from that of a computer: whereas the computer tries to be precise in left-hemisphere or "logical" terms, poets try to be precise in RH terms as well, intuition and intellect interacting to create statements true to experience (the problem of private vs. universal experience enters here—the nominalist dilemma).

The uncertainty and impossibility principles.

The idea of computer irresponsibility and cancer. (Computers have old programs built into them, patches on patches, new features on new features; so the present programmer is dependent on the work of dozens, hundreds before him—doesn't understand what the computer is doing. Result, he's the victim or slave of the computer he manipulates. The irresponsible system, then—the computer process built of dozens of processes no longer visible—takes over the shape of society, even physical reality, for the human mind; is thus perhaps comparable to a cancer, that is, Craine's cancer. Raises fields of questions: cancer and faith-healing (psi activity, concentration, love and will); also the false hope of occultism; that is, the easy dismissal of physical (physiological) fact.

All the characters in this novel, as it's so-far planned and evolving, are men, discounting Elaine and Hannah, who so far haven't had their moments. Important to get to one or more controlling female intelligences, superficially to introduce RH factors, actually because (since RH-LH, intuition-logic analogies are oversimple) otherwise the dialogue will die, the power dim out.

How does one keep such a cumbersome system of thought (as this novel) alive? The question is not so much, Who cares? as Is it perspicuous? Maybe not important. Will or won't take care of itself.

Given such a range of possibility, and so much "planned and evolving," discretion seemed the better part of editorial valor. I have ventured neither to supply connectives nor to project the finished text. Seven "Fragments" have been added where the narrative leaves off. They may provide some sense of what the novelist called profluence—the story line's direction. But they act as vectors merely, and we cannot know for certain which line he would have followed to the end.

As with *Stillness*, no word has been added—but here many thousands are cut. We have been as ruthless with the novelist's material as he often was himself. One aspect of his prolixity was this willingness to shelve a draft, to start it all over again. As his books on fiction indicate, the process is continual and the writer must be chilly-eyed when looking at his work. "Maybe not important . . ." His legacy as teacher should, I think, include these tentatives—these examples of a less than finished text.

And the question of the final word must, alas, be moot. Susan Thornton, his fiancée at the time of his death, remembers Gardner telling her, "I've figured out how to fix *Shadows.*" He was standing in the garden, his pipe lit. "What is it, John?" she asked. He smiled; he cocked his head. "It's a secret," Gardner said.

Where drafts stand in obvious sequence, I have selected the last. Routinely, however, I have elected coherence. Book One, for instance (145 pages of typescript), is the clean copy submitted to Knopf and printed without emendation; the purpose of this volume is to let the reader read.

Someday—who could rule this out?—a coherent overview may surface of authorial intention. It is no small irony that his last protracted labor was on our literature's first fragment, *Gilgamesh.* What follows are fragments, disjunct. The interested scholar may consult the manuscripts at Rochester. But John Gardner writing at speed, or revising continually, wrote for an audience; his sudden extinction need not alter that. In a set of exercises devised for the apprentice (reprinted in *The Art of Fiction*), John has this to say: "To write with taste, in the highest sense, is to write with the assumption that one out of a hundred people who read one's work may be dying, or have some loved one dying; to write so that no one commits suicide, no one despairs; to write, as Shakespeare wrote, so that people understand, sympathize, see the universality of pain, and feel strengthened, if not directly encouraged, to live on."

Those who live on include his son and daughter. I wish to add one sentence to his work:

For Joel and Lucy: these books.

STILLNESS

Beauty is momentary in the mind,
The fitful tracing of a portal,
But in the flesh it is immortal.

—WALLACE STEVENS

PROLOGUE

"The people are like gnomes," Martin Orrick would write, "small and quiet, overmuscular, bearing overlarge heads. As your car drives past, just a few miles from town, they draw up from their work in the steaming bottom-lands and stand quietly dangerous, though intending no harm, as still as old stumps or fence posts or deer, watching without expression, their eyes like chips of steel. Toward noon, when the heat of the sun grows unbearable, they sink into the dark wooded hills from which they're sprung, fall back slyly into the shade of the past; and for a while nothing moves but the cir-cling hawks, an occasional eagle, the ear of a sleeping sow in a thick clump of pokeweed, and, always, the river. Oak trees, sycamores, and pines stand guard, and in the places where houses or trailers lie—or places where they once lay—maples, tulip poplars, cedars. Drive on, stranger, there's nothing for you here. If everyday humdrum life hides here, if men and women touch with years-old affection, or sing antique songs, or tell stories from their days of railroad building, when a few men made fortunes on apples or coal and the rest worked a lifetime for no better pay than their scars, crooked fingers, and shrewd, creased faces, you will not find it, you'll glimpse no smile not prepared with fearful calculation in advance. Here there is no trust. This is a harsh, inhospitable land: even those poor fools who love it are hardly at home on it, cursing its floods and tornadoes, its rust-red, eroding hills, cursing all those whom God saw fit to send more profitable land, yet cling-ing, for no reason, to this miserable tick- and mosquito-rich place, spawning ground of rattlers, cottonmouths, and copperheads, half the year drowned out by unrelenting rain, half the year dry as a biscuit. This is no place to pause, sink roots: here all things swirl and churn like the river, and the heart finds no rest, no peace, no stillness but the cyclone's core. This is a country for gnomes and madmen, a country for the living and dying, not the rich, calm dead."

Useless, as always, to inquire too narrowly what Martin Orrick meant. He was, obviously, one of those poor fools who loved the place—the southern Missouri Ozarks, where he'd fled from San Francisco in what his psychiatrist would describe, not long afterward, as a desperate attempt to shake the demons from his back, purify his sick heart by fire. That was not how it appeared at the time. He came, one who knew him at the time might have thought, in search of not life but a death worth dying, a death not wan and casual, unfelt. He would gallop his Roman-nosed black stallion through the night, when neither he nor his horse could see—his children in their beds, wide-eyed with fear, his beautiful wife indignant and trembling—and time after time he would fall and, drunkenly, crawl home. Twice he fractured his skull and, though his brain was his living, showed no remorse. Once, so drunk he could barely stand, he rode off on the bicycle his wife had bought him to keep him off the horse and made ten full miles before he tumbled, bicycle and all, down a twelve-foot embankment and came to rest in a stone-filled branch, where at dawn he awakened, guarded by his whimpering dogs. It was not, of course, the fault of the mountains. In their infinite patience, they could bear up any form of life at all: swift, light deer, sly coon, huge, thoughtful cows, squirrels, rabbits, wolves and foxes, skunks and groundhogs, cross-eyed, old-as-the-hills opossum, who murder young chickens for their sport. He would see the place later as gentle and beautiful, when his eye had changed. What he saw now—what he wore flared around him like a wizard's cape—was suffering, hunger for conclusion: life or death. "Old Man Death," in Martin Orrick's phrase, was evidently tempted. Again and again he sniffed the wind and came near, then miraculously drew back.

There was a party at the Orricks' high-gabled, pillared house, gray under starlight, the security lamp, and the shadow of trees—the roof and square tower surrounded like a graveyard by wrought-iron fence, and the hill on which the pretentious, severe old house stood (and the horse-barn, chicken house, smokehouse, and pump house) surrounded by low, shaggy mountains and, in the valley to the east, the silent, wide Mississippi. It was a party for one of Martin Orrick's students, who had that day passed her comprehensive exams. Though the house shook with music and light came bursting from every narrow rectangular or round-arched window—though cars stood everywhere, glinting like jewels, like the branches, the rooftops, the winter-darkened grass, all thickly cased in ice—Death would not be fooled, driven from the place by mere music and light—so a stranger with a taste for the gothic might have thought, and Martin Orrick would think before morning. Inside the high door with the fox-head knocker (firewood piled high to the left and right), the ceiling was low, like the roof of a cave, and the dark, crowded furniture sagged and bulged under the weight of slow-talking, slow-gesturing grad students, some of them asleep with their drinks in their hands, some noisily drunk, some asleep but still talking, smoking pot. Useless to try to drive home on that ice. (It had rained all day, then at sunset had suddenly begun to freeze.) It was five miles to town, over Ozark roads. Even the sober might never reach the foot of the driveway.

In the new room, the room that looked out on the pool, Martin Orrick, famous novelist, professor of classical and medieval literature, held forth like a blear-eyed prophet. Joan, his red-headed wife, watched in silence. She'd taken Demerol to kill her pain, such a dose that the world was like a landscape seen through blowing lace, and she suffered, besides, an odd dizziness not usually part of the Demerol high, and a ringing in her ears. She should go to bed, she knew, but she was afraid to. Martin grew, every day, more difficult. If she turned her back, he might suddenly attack some favorite student with cruelty and scorn he would refuse to believe himself guilty of tomorrow, or he might lure some young woman to the storm cellar or the barn or the tower. They would all know, these students who loved him and were always as embarrassed as she was, and helplessly they would watch, pained but not judging, big intelligent grown-ups baffled and hurt and struggling to approve, like children. She had no choice but to prevent it if she could, control him; and sensing her subtle, unspeaking control, he might at any moment turn on her in rage, say terrible things to her, and she, foggy, ringing with that damned, mysterious pain, would be defenseless. They must surely understand that he was mad, simply. Nevertheless it would be she, Joan Orrick, who would be guilty.

Baggy-faced, paunched, standing like a sumo, but icy-eyed, druidic—waving his martini and sometimes ferociously driving home a point with a stab of his pipe or the square index finger of his free, dark-red right hand—he spoke belligerently of the fall of man. "It's a three-part process,"

he said, or rather fumed, so mean of eye that one might well have imagined—or so it seemed to his wife—that the man to whom he spoke, half
asleep on his feet, his skin splotchy pink, his beard a mass of tangles, was
responsible. The ice-crusted trees on the lawn stood motionless, hungrily
listening—if Martin's weird theory of the universe was right—and the
black, silent river hurried on toward New Orleans, huge helpless mother
of animals and men, bearer of St. Louis and Chicago poisons, also treasures
of silt, generous feeder of bottomlands, smasher of dikes.

"First," he said, and cocked back like a horseman, "there's the fall out
of Nature, the fall that makes primitive bear cults and corn cults. We kill
to eat, and thanks to our consciousness we can't help but notice that in the
act of killing we take a step back from the general connectedness, the harmony of Nature, old Schopenhauer's universal howl of will: we've judged
and condemned brother bear to death, or brother stalk of grain—you follow
what I'm saying?—and however our intelligence may deal with the event,
the chest—the right lobe of the brain, if you like—calls it murder and shud-
ders with guilt." His eyes bugged, he spoke so earnestly. He stood with
his hand drawn dramatically to his chest. "We invent the Corn God, or
Artemis-Ursus, and do terrified obeisance, kill virgins to buy our way back
in." He was outraged.

He was talking loudly, but perhaps not as loudly as it sounded in Joan
Orrick's head. The bearded, pink-faced student nodded, sorrowful and logy,
keeping his eyes open and smiling politely by a mighty act of will. He stood
tipped back, the bottle of beer out in front of him for balance. In the shadows around them—a clutter of bottles and potted plants, a fog of cigarette
smoke, a thick stench of gin—other students listened, their heads thrown
forward, not so much from interest in Martin Orrick's theories—they'd
heard them all before—as in faint alarm at his drunken intensity. Martin
drank quickly from the glass in his hand and, before anyone could speak,
widened his eyes again, lifted his eyebrows, and plunged on, still more
loudly, shouting down a sudden swell of music from the speakers. "Second,
there's the fall from humanity," he said. The people around him nodded,
and to Joan Orrick's drugged perception it seemed they nodded in synchro-
nization, like puppets, like a Gilbert and Sullivan chorus. He said, swinging
forward dangerously, *"Gil*gamesh, for instance! He enslaves his own people—makes them build a great wall for their own protection"—his left
arm dramatically cast a wall up through the ceiling—"and thus rightly, nec-

essarily, Gilgamesh sets himself apart from his fellow men, and the people, rightly, cry to heaven for vengeance. Like the hunter, he's stepped out of the ring of the living. New rituals, some new kind of religion must be found. So we get, for example, Greek tragedy: we watch the hero raise his head above all others and we watch it blasted by the lightning of the gods, and in compassion and fear we at once admire him and reaffirm our common humanity. Ha!" He raised his hand in what looked like sharp warning. "Or consider Achilles and Priam in the tent, or Jesus on brotherly love." Again his eyes bugged, and his stance was an actor's pose: utter indignation.

"Or consider Martin Orrick," someone said behind him, and raised her glass in what looked like a perfectly serious salute. Martin didn't hear.

Bob Randolph, young poet in a fisherman's hat, trudging by slowly, as if watching a stream, saluted with his new glass of bourbon and said, "Whole point of *Moby Dick.*" He laughed as if to himself, for some reason—or giggled, rather—though the comment was serious, apparently, and walked on, out of Martin's range.

"Exactly!" Martin snapped, turning for a moment toward Bob, then back, blushing, glancing in embarrassment at his pipe. Then he said, "Third—" He hesitated, as if he'd lost his place, looked downright panicky, sipped his martini, then abruptly remembered. "Third—" He spoke still more fiercely now, trembling with emotion, for no reason she could guess. "There's the fall out of Self—the fall we read of in Jean-Paul Sartre: fall into nothingness, alienation of the eye." (Or perhaps he meant—she couldn't tell—"the I.")

The bearded, pink-faced student said, "Are there rituals to cure *that?*" and laughed loudly, like a bleating goat.

Joan Orrick was aware of something going by too fast for her drugged brain. For an instant she had an impression of herself as a child, schoolbooks in her arms, watching them in horror. "Buddy," she would cry—Martin had been "Buddy" when the two of them were children—"what's the *matter* with you?" She, Joan-grown-up, had no way to tell her, could hardly explain what had happened even for herself. And then the child's eyes swung around to meet her own, as she'd known they would, accusing and terrible—a beautiful child with hair like cut copper—and the older Joan shrank back, cheeks stinging as they would if she'd been slapped, and her mind cried through time, *I'm sorry!*

Perhaps the pink-faced student said it twice, or perhaps time snagged and she heard it twice: "Are there rituals to cure *that?*"

Martin looked as if he was about to have a stroke. So did the student he was talking to.

Martin laughed exactly as the student had done but looked sick with distress. "I don't know," he said. "There may be no cure but Jesus' mercy—'He that loses himself shall find himself,' or . . ." He shook his head, flashed a horrible grin, pushed back his long silver hair in fierce annoyance. "I don't know. No one does. 'Luck.' 'Amazing Grace'—whatever that is." He laughed again, grimly, nodding. "That's the price we pay for our sensible 'ungoded sky.' " He glanced up at the ceiling as if in anger. One could hardly believe that a split second ago he'd been laughing. She remembered that Hart Crane—ungoded sky—had killed himself.

Though no time had lapsed, or so it seemed, the people in the room were suddenly not where they'd been standing an instant earlier, and it came to Joan Orrick that, sitting upright among the pillows on the waterbed couch, she had fainted. Martin stood exactly where he'd stood before, like a smoldering fixed star, but Steve—the pink-faced, bearded student—was gone, asleep in the bathtub, probably, and it was the pianist, Joe Liberto, the one she liked best, at least among the men, certainly the one she was most willing to trust—he'd helped her hunt for Martin one time, when it seemed almost certain he'd drowned himself in the Sikeston sewer—it was Joe Liberto that Martin was lecturing. She could stand guard no longer, whatever might come of her abandoning him. *Where were you, Joe,* she heard herself thinking, *when I was ready to get married?* And she heard herself answering, sadly, but also laughing at the absurdity: *Not born.* She would faint again soon, and though the fainting so frightened her that she could hardly bear to think of it, much less wonder what it meant, she would rather be in bed when it happened.

She felt for the edge of the waterbed couch, one hand on each side of her, and carefully rose to her feet. The girl, Cezaria, who'd come to sit beside her, looked up, smiling, perhaps slightly puzzled, and she returned the smile, trying to think what Cezaria was saying, then moved, carefully balanced, toward the music room door. As if floating or dreaming, she passed the grand piano, the lounging students in the darkened livingroom, and drifted over to the square, sharp-edged newel post at the foot of the stairs. She paused a moment, steadying herself for the climb.

She'd said nothing to Martin about the fainting. She was sick to death of being always sick, always in pain, always drugged, and though no one could reasonably blame her for it, she was ashamed and angry and afraid it would finally drive him from her. How could he help but believe it was one more trick meant to keep him in her power? That was what he constantly accused her of—not without reason, she told herself bitterly, not without reason. She'd quietly stopped driving—he'd never even noticed that for nearly a month now she'd regularly evaded the steering wheel (she was secretly enraged that he failed to notice)—and she'd managed even to avoid ever mentioning the light-headed feeling. What was the use of telling him? she'd asked herself, and the question had filled her eyes with tears. There was nothing any of them could do. No use going to doctors either. She'd finally resigned herself to that. All her complaints were beyond their skill.

"Have you ever had anything like this before?" the one in San Francisco had asked.

"It's been happening for a long time," she said. "Off and on, I mean. No one's been able to figure out what's wrong."

"Hmm," he'd said, and had pulled at his moustache with the tips of two fingers. "Well, whatever you had before, you've got it again."

She was terrified all the time, day and night. She knew no psychology, but she knew it was important that all her dreams were nightmares. Yet she couldn't tell Martin. When she jerked in her sleep, she let him believe it was muscle spasms. To tell him the truth would be to make him more helpless, more guilty for no reason—more suicidal. Often she wished she could die and be done with it—but then what of the children? She knew well enough what would become of Martin if . . . something happened to her. And so she wept in secret, or secretly raged behind her mask of calm and weariness, pitying herself, hating herself, pitying and hating the world.

She took a deep breath, glanced over the bannister at the students in the room, none of them watching, then started carefully up the stairs. At the top of the stairway she could see the beginning of the wall with family pictures on it, her family, Martin's, their two blond children at various ages, the dogs, the horses, the houses they'd lived in in St. Louis, Iowa City, Oberlin, Chico, San Francisco . . . She stared hard at the wall of pictures as if it might draw her to the safety of the landing. She felt the stairway growing brighter, solider, and felt the lines of the picture frames, the door to Evan's room, the dented brass wall-sconce becoming sharper, sharper—unnaturally sharp—and understood too late that she was fainting.

Martin, in the new room, broke off mid-sentence. "Listen! What was that?" He stumbled toward the sound, up into the music room and into the livingroom's darkness toward the stairs. He found her at the foot, sprawled unconscious. She lay impossibly still and ghostly pale, with her eyes open, and where she'd struck her head on the newel post the blood gushed out like water from a hose. The pool of blood around her grew quickly as he watched, and though he knew about scalp wounds he was instantly certain that he'd finally done it, had finally killed her. (Why he should be guilty was a question that never crossed his mind. It went without saying that the fault was somehow his, however obscurely—and given the general complexity of things he was no doubt right.) "Christ," he whispered, and felt for her pulse. He could get nothing. He called for help.

In a matter of seconds they had the limp body loaded into Martin Orrick's car. It was then that the nightmare began in earnest. Because he was too shaky, he thought, to drive, he gave the keys to his Rambler to his friend the poet Bob Randolph, an easterner who might with luck get the car to town over the wet glare ice, as no one born here where ice was rare could do, and he himself took the keys to Bob Randolph's Volkswagen. Bob Randolph took the lead, Martin following in Randolph's car. They moved tortuously down the driveway, fences and trees on each side blindingly glittering, tires skating. Both cars made the turn, made the dip into the valley, and managed to snake up the winding hill that followed, then began, carefully, the second, much steeper, descent. Hunched over the steering wheel, watching the black car ahead of him—all around him the world aglitter like a diamond, everything white but the Rambler's two taillights—he saw the road's sharpest turn approaching, sliding toward them like a flaw in the dazzling, faceted brightness, and he knew—knew as if he'd seen it already, like the providential God Boethius understood—that Bob Randolph wouldn't make it. He slowed the Volkswagen almost to a stop and, as in a slowed-down movie, watched the black Rambler slip slowly, as if casually, toward the edge of the high-crowned, white-fire road, where it hovered a moment, as if thoughtfully, then gradually tilted up like a capsizing sailboat and fell, still slowly, thoughtfully, out of sight. He stopped the Volkswagen where the Rambler had left the road, got out too quickly, and banged down hard onto the ice. Trifling as the fall was, it knocked out his wind, and he lay straining for what seemed a long, long time before air would come. Then, rather than struggle to get up, he crawled to the edge of the shoulder.

The embankment was gradual but went down twenty feet. Below, the weedy field was ablaze with light, unearthly, ironically Christmassy, like a vastly magnified view from inside some exotic crystal, and at the center of all that light the Rambler stood sharply outlined, forlorn, coal black. Bob Randolph and the three who'd been riding with him were already climbing out, struggling to pull Joan from the backseat. She hung limp between them, like the figure of Christ in some descent from the cross. Their shouts came up to Martin as if from infinitely far away, and his friends' movements around Joan's inert form were like a clumsy dance. Martin was not himself, or at any rate not his best self. He simply watched, as one watches the northern lights (once, on their farm, his mother and father had seen perfectly clear angels in the northern lights, and a perfectly clear, unmistakable cross: they were not sentimentalists or religious fanatics and had simply watched, amazed, as he watched now, and later they'd wondered if they'd really seen it—a doubt he understood, because as a child, told to look for the Big Dipper, he had seen, not knowing what a dipper was, a clearly outlined frying pan as viewed from the top: it was the sharpest image he carried from his childhood except for one other, a frozen image of his cousin Joan, now his wife, when they were four), and even as they struggled up the glazed embankment, sometimes sliding back, her body sliding with them, his friends calling up to him in increasing anger, he hung suspended, outside time and space, watching as if it were a movie or a vision on which his life depended, though he himself was indifferent, until they managed to scrape and cut their way near enough that he could take off his coat and hold it out to them like a rope and help them to the road.

She still showed no slightest sign of life. He drove, took the wheel without thinking, though shakier than ever. He would not remember, afterward, the drive to town. His memory would go back only to the hospital corridor, where he stood, still trembling, drinking black coffee—"You're drunk," the nurse had said, crackling with hate—his hands bleeding from when he'd fallen beside the car, his student friends seated on the long wooden bench, ashen-faced, dishevelled, Dr. Crouse saying (distant, as if reserving judgment), "That's one more time you've been lucky as hell, whole lot more lucky than you deserve, that's the truth." Even after that violent letting, her blood pressure was dangerously high. If she'd made it to bed, the odds were close to a hundred to nothing she'd have died of a stroke before morning.

"What should I have done?" Martin Orrick said.

To Crouse his eyes looked defiant, hostile. His breath, his skin, his clothes, filled all Sikeston with gin-stink.

"Well I don' know," he said mildly. He was a soft-voiced Missourian with a private smile, obviously friendly, obviously noncommittal. For no good reason, he liked Martin Orrick—the novels, perhaps. Martin Orrick was a far better man in his books than in his life, God knew, yet he had a kind of madman's charm, some way. Charm like a tiger's. He was beautiful, powerful, the way mad poets were supposed to be, but he was also, in his madness, dangerous and stupid, burning up his life—everybody's life—like sunbaked kindling. Dr. Jimmy Crouse had no time for fools, but with Martin Orrick he kept putting off decision. He said: "The way you people live out there, Joanie sick as hell, and you behaving like . . ."

Martin nodded, a quick, ghastly jerk of the head, and for an instant closed his eyes, suddenly becoming more child than wolf or tiger. Crouse studied him, then put his hand on his arm and grinned, deciding, *Oh, the hell with it.* "You're crazy, boy, that's all's the matter. You gotta just sort of get on up and turn yourself around."

Martin laughed.

Crouse nodded, still grinning, though his eyes were solemn. "Well, cheer up. She'll pull you through, 'f you don't kill her first."

"Suppose," Martin Orrick wrote that year, "one could adjust optimistic Christianity and the gloomy facts of life—the universal banging of atom against atom, planet against planet, heart against heart. Granted, that is, that the whole thing's a river, mere blindly bumping chances, no prayer of rest—granted that the weather has a good deal to do with what I happen to love—indeed, with whether I survive to love at all—that my life is an accidental tumble of the dice, my ancestors' genes, my penmanship borrowed from a childhood friend (but strangely like my father's)—suppose one could learn, by the flick of a switch, to enjoy the bangings, celebrate the swiftly passing patterns as holy. Would that give stability? I hate idealists; no one hates them more or would sooner condemn them to execution. Sitting by the river, studying its refusal to repeat itself, the heavy yellow water never twice eddying in the exact same place, even the course of barges unpredictable, I grow anxious to dynamite Plato's museum, soft, comfortable home of my lean toward insanity. Process is all I care about. Therefore I write fiction, to make the beauty of change everlasting, unalterable as rock."

Useless to inquire too earnestly what Martin Orrick meant.

. . . but love can move mountains, love can burst all
bonds, even steel; nothing can stand in its way, as
we all know. It's our own mediocrity that makes us let
go of love, makes us renounce it.

—Eugène Ionesco

One

At a time when everyone who was anyone was plunging into her identity crisis, Joan Orrick became with a vengeance what she was. No one—certainly no one in her family—was especially surprised, and no one was sorry, though her husband told their friends he had moments of wondering if he'd survive it. She'd been a liberated woman since 1933, the year of her birth. She'd been a red-head (and was still), with a dimple and dazzling eyes and a dazzling wit, and her parents had soon discovered that she had, besides, "a really quite remarkable musical talent," as her first piano teacher said, with a frightened look. Her teacher, a Miss Huppman, had no talent at all—except for raising begonias—but Joan didn't know it and was flying, by the middle of her second year, through Bach's three-part inventions. Timidly, wringing her hankie at the door, Miss Huppman suggested, when Joan's father came after one of her lessons to pick her up, that perhaps Joan needed a teacher "a little more advanced."

"I see," her father said in his tentative way, with his hat in his hands.

He was a minor executive in the St. Louis Screw and Bolt Company—he would later be one of the company's two top men—but he was not yet (and in some respects would never be) a man bursting with confidence. He was, in fact, a farm boy who'd only reached fifth grade, and even that was partly fraudulent, since he had a brother, John Elmer, who looked remarkably like him and a Scotchman father who felt, perhaps rightly, that the farming couldn't spare them both. "I see," he said, somewhat alarmed, since he had no idea how to go about finding a piano teacher more advanced. He was, Joan's father, a handsome, broad-shouldered man, red-headed, like his daughter, with a Scotchman's pale eyes and brilliant smile, also a Scotchman's somewhat overlarge nose, which his daughter had inherited, but he bore it with such grace, as his daughter would do, that no one could ever take exception to it; indeed, years later, on his grandson Evan, that nose would become—elegantly harmonized with other noble features, a gentle disposition, and a splendid intelligence—a thing to make maidens weep.

"Is there," Joan's father said, "someone you could recommend?"

"Oh dear," said Miss Huppman, "these things are so difficult. Mrs. Wulker, I should think. She lives right near you, on Randolph." She looked at Joan's father as if she thought he might help her. "Perhaps someone in the city?"

Joan's father thanked her, paid her the fifty cents she charged, and walked, holding Joan's hand, to their square green Dodge.

Joan was, in her father's opinion, the most beautiful, most wonderful little girl in the world. Neither he nor Joan's mother would dream of expressing that sentiment to Joan, though they managed to communicate it, to some extent. Indeed, he sometimes called her—with what might have been a faint touch of irony—his princess. But the irony was really just his shyness—or his caution. She looked like a princess, and she ruled like a princess, not that anyone minded. (Thirty years later her daughter, Mary, would be exactly the same, an absolute—fortunately benevolent—despot.) When they could afford it, they bought Joan presents, pretty dresses, toys, books, a long-haired, cinnamon-colored dog named Flopsy (run over by a trolley car the first month she had him), and above all what was, for them, an enormously expensive spinet piano, a Story & Clark. They paid for a succession of piano teachers, including, finally, Leo Serota, the best pianist in St. Louis at the time, formerly chief piano teacher at Tokyo University; they bought her a twenty-five-dollar violin, later a fifty-dollar cello; they drove her, or rather her father drove her, to symphony concerts, where her father would fall asleep—not, as Joan imagined, because he didn't care for music, but because his day began at five, the music was soothing, the hall was dark, and he was an innocent, or at any rate innocent of false pride. He also took her, four times, to the opera—each time, by some fluke, the same opera, *Boris Godunov*—and innumerable times to what was then the glory of that wonderfully naive, ridiculous German city (as she would later remember it), the "Muny Opera," where she saw (and later played in the orchestra for, after she'd become a violinist and cellist) *The Red Mill, Desert Song, Springtime, The Student Prince, The Vagabond King,* and *An Evening with Gilbert and Sullivan.* (Though she was still in her teens, she could have told them when they put on that *Evening with Gilbert and Sullivan* thing that the Muny was finished, an epoch had ended; put your money on KSDF.)

Those were, naturally, wonderful times. The whole family would go to the grandiose, pseudo-Greek open-air theater in Forest Park—Joan had now two younger brothers—and sometimes her favorite aunt and uncle would go too, or the cousins from New York State. They would sit under the stars, hoping it wouldn't rain, or at any rate that was the hope all the grown-ups laid claim to if the smell in the air suggested doubt, though possibly they too took pleasure in seeing the huge set hurriedly rolled away, folded in on itself like a Chinese paper dollhouse, and the audience rushing out with programs held over their heads like housetops, and the huge old trees of the park bending, black against gray, and then the fierce Midwestern rain sweeping in, brightly lighted, like a theater curtain, and the low sky majestically booming, booming as if for joy.

Mostly, of course, it didn't rain, and they sat listening to the music, swaying to the dancing (swaying inwardly, that is; they were inclined to be timid), eating hot dogs or ice cream from the people who came selling them up and down the aisles like the vendors at a circus or a Cardinals' game. And then, very late (as she'd judged time then), her father would drive them home, going wonderfully fast, as he always did, the lights of the old houses flashing by like comets. Joan's mother, at corners or intersections, would suck air between her teeth and sometimes whimper, "Oh Donald, please!" and he'd pretend, for a time, to drive more cautiously.

Joan's mother was pretty and intelligent, the youngest daughter in a large German family even poorer than Joan's father's. The latter at least had a good-sized farm, an old, old place just off Sinks Road, Missouri, ten miles north of St. Louis, a fairly unprofitable farm at the time, cratered like the moon—except the craters were lush, filled with water, edged by trees—but a gold mine later: there was oil under those sinkholes, and huge caves where the Laclede Oil Company would buy rights to store natural gas; and besides, urban sprawl was hurrying north, so that in the fifties, lots overlooking the convergence of the Missouri and Mississippi rivers, of which the farm could offer several, would go for five thousand dollars an acre. One such lot, a large one, would be the site of Joan's father's large, modern house when he moved his family back home "to the country" from Ferguson. Joan could remember what it once had been like. When she was little the land was still heavily wooded, populated by wolves and cranes and her peculiar, black-bearded great-uncle Zack, who had a cabin with linoleum on the walls. Every spring he floated his mules across to the long, dark, vine-filled island and ploughed a little patch of it, where he grew horse corn and pumpkins and sweet potatoes. The place was infested with great fat rattlesnakes and copperheads. He'd sit on the porch and smoke his pipe and, he said, watch them play. She only saw him once or twice. He didn't even come out of the woods to go to church. Thankfully, as all the family said, he was long gone—his cabin in ruins, letting in light like an old broken crate—when the bulldozers came. The landscape would change beyond all recognition, and tony people would move in, or flambuginous-tony. Possum Hollow, where her great-uncle Zack used to hunt, would become "Castlereigh Estates."

Joan's mother's side was less fortunate, materially. They lived in a small house that—beneath the shingles on the outside and plaster on the inside—was a crooked old log cabin of a sort you might expect to find Negroes in. It went back to before the Civil War, but its antiquity gave it no particular charm. It was beautifully set, on a rise beside one of those rich, dense hollows one finds only in Missouri—a creek, huge old trees with crows in them, over by the fence a matched pair of mules—but the house itself was about as handsome as a tooth in a field. It was in excellent repair and always clean as a whistle—the family was, as I've said, German—but its only real glory was the people who lived in it, warmhearted, hardworking, good-looking people, of whom Joan's mother, Emmy, beyond a shadow of a doubt, was the nicest and prettiest of all. Her sister Cora, two years older, was also very fine; not as pretty, quite, but more relaxed, not inclined to have headaches. When Emmy married Joan's father, Cora would marry the brother who looked so much like him, John Elmer.

Joan's mother and father had been, of course, childhood sweethearts. They'd married during the Depression, but they were both working fools, energetic, tense people, though they mostly kept a secret of their nervousness—not that they were, in the bad sense, ambitious. Joan's father was handy; there was nothing he couldn't repair or build—in fact, later, he'd patent a number of inventions; and Joan's mother was a shrewd manager. They made a perfect team, as everyone said. They escaped to the city, then to the suburbs, then to better suburbs, and as their horizons widened, Joan became for them, increasingly, a creature to wonder at. If they doubted at first, they could doubt no longer: Joan did indeed have, as Miss Huppman had said, a really quite remarkable musical talent. At thirteen she had a weekly half-hour radio show.

Her talent was a difficult thing for her parents to deal with, to tell the truth. They were gentle, good people with no social pretensions; they hated snobs or, at any rate (since they hated, in fact, no one), felt extremely uncomfortable in their presence; and they saw overconfidence, even the slightest hint of it, as a dangerous thing if not an evil in itself. Joan was, alas, not as humble as she might be. People called her a genius and a prodigy, often people who ought to know. She was bound, her parents feared, for trouble, and they did everything possible to keep her from getting a swelled head. When people praised her piano playing, her mother said only (partly, of course, from shyness), "Well, *she* seems to enjoy it." When she brought home from school a report card with nothing but A's on it (in English, in science, in music, in phys.ed., in typing, in geography, in whatever she touched), her father would say, "Don't they give A pluses?" Joan would laugh, make some joke; but the truth was, she began to feel unsure of herself. Though it should have been obvious at a glance to anyone, even a total stranger, that her parents were so proud of her they were downright afraid—afraid that they might perhaps in some way fail her—Joan began to doubt that she was loved.

Also, at this point in her life she became, as old photographs show, slightly ugly. God moves in strange ways, and in the long run it was the best thing that could have happened to her, because it drove her to humor, added one more component of that splendid, living work of art she would later become. But it was a terrible thing at the time, for Joan. She had been, as a small child, beautiful. Years later, when she was a teacher, composer, novelist and wife of a novelist—also famous party wit—a friend would sometimes happen across, among other family pictures she had on the wall in the upstairs hallway, the picture taken of Joan when she was five, and would say, startled, "Is this *you*, Joan?" "That's me," she'd say and smile. And because she'd changed so, though she was beautiful now too, the friend would say, surprised into a childlike innocence exactly like that which the long-dead photographer had caught, "Why, you were *beautiful,* Joan!" To which Joan would respond, with just the right turn, just the right mock-sorrow (she was no longer one to take less than she deserved), "Wasn't I, though!" And the friend would glance at her, and though he or she might not put it into words, would notice once more that Joan Orrick was, in simple truth, more beautiful than any painting or valley or tropical bird that ever flew.

But between the ages of about twelve and sixteen, Joan was, to put it mildly, not as pretty as she might wish. She suddenly grew tall—taller than most of the boys in her grade. Her head became large, with far-apart eyes and a wide-bridged nose that was always slightly red and which frequently, for no reason, gushed blood. Her mouth, in the shadow of that mighty nose, was small, and—because of how the corners turned down—looked rather like the mouth of a shark. Her chin was small, her neck long and thin, her shoulders narrow, her breasts undeveloped, her hips oddly wide. She became pimply, and, mysteriously, her teeth, which were small, became misaligned, so that braces, Dr. Vogler said, solemnly nodding, were really the only prayer.

In unobvious ways, her parents reacted to the change. It was as if she'd betrayed a trust. They changed subtly, of course; so subtly that they weren't aware of it themselves, and even Joan, if anyone had asked her, couldn't definitely have asserted that things were different. The war was just over, the factory was making money, Joan's youngest brother was recovering from polio—a sweet, gentle boy who'd grow up to be the kindest, gentlest of men, plagued by a weak heart. What was wrong between Joan and her family, for all these reasons and for others, was hard to see. But it was nonetheless a fact that something had gone wrong, and it came down, finally, to this: she had been beautiful and brilliant; now she was only brilliant; and though her sense of humor improved—she was so funny, in fact, that she had to spend much of her school time in the hall: her remarks, though much quoted in the faculty lounge, disrupted classes—the humor had, her parents thought (and they were essentially right), a cruel edge to it. She had an eye for faults and for, worse, mere unhappy resemblances. Woe to the minister who had the chinless, triangular mouth of an elephant, the neighborhood pharmacist with a bunny rabbit's nose, the otherwise pretty beautician who had the eyes of a turtle! Her eye for types was so keen and merciless, and her dislike for certain types so fanatical, that no new style of dress could be successful in the schools she attended, no new student, teacher, or principal could be popularly accepted, no moneymaking project could be mounted by either her school or church until the word was in from Joan. Of a tiresome woman at the Methodist church, Joan's mother once said with careful charity, "Well, she's good at heart," to which Joan, then aged twelve, added quickly, with great innocence, "To make sure people notice, she wears light blue hats with white berries." One laughed, but one couldn't approve. (Her brother James, the eldest after Joan, imitated her humor and developed a harsh cynicism he would never get rid of. It would in the end nearly ruin his life.)

Yet however they might work to dampen it, her humor bubbled up, ever funnier, more cruel. Serious people told her, though they too laughed, that she was arrogant and mean and should be ashamed of herself. She half believed them. (Her father's mother was famous for cruelty.) Her younger brother's illness, and the attention he got, of course intensified Joan's self-doubt. And the obvious fact that she was different from other children, so that even with her friends she felt, or was made to feel, separate, abnormal, made her doubt even stronger. The idea that she was, in spite of everything, not what she should be became more or less fixed.

At least half persuaded that no one really loved her—with one important exception—Joan mugged and joked and earned a fair amount of money (she played for, among other things, a tap-dance studio on Olive Street), won applause on every side, and poured her unhappiness or anyway confusion into Mozart, Beethoven, Brahms, Debussy, Liszt, Chopin, and Bach. She played hour after hour.

For her mother, especially, it was a difficult period. It was impossible for her mother to ask Joan to stop practicing and do the dishes or clean house. What had they worked so hard for, she asked herself, if not this?—to say nothing of all that money spent. So her mother did the work, feeling persecuted, and even when she stopped to take a nap she got not a moment's rest. A serious pianist, as everyone knows, does not often play music straight through when practicing. Working up a piece by Mozart or Schubert, Joan skimmed with her eyes the parts she could play without difficulty, then went over, again and again, the parts that were hard for her, until she had them in her fingers. It's doubtful that Joan's mother heard once in her life a complete Beethoven sonata until she heard Joan play it on the radio or the concert stage. What she did hear, day after day, was five measures, or three and a half, endlessly, maddeningly repeated. It was impossible, of course, for Joan's mother to say, "Stop! You're driving me insane!" Instead, she would tense up her soul and wait like a painted Indian in the bushes, and at supper, Joan, eating salad, would close her teeth on the fork, then slide the fork out, leaving lettuce in her mouth, and her mother would cry angrily, with tears in her eyes, *"Must* you eat that way? You're driving me insane!"—a complaint Joan's husband would echo later, more sullenly, less dramatically, until he broke her of the habit; and then, without ever having seen her mother do it, their golden-haired daughter, Mary, would do it, and Joan's husband would sink his head into his hands and moan, "Jesus. Must be DNA."

But unhappy as she was at this time of her life, Joan had one great comfort: she was in love.

"Martin, don't you remember *any* of that?" she would rage, years later, clinging as he struggled to push her away. "God damn you, Martin, I *love* you."

"You love nobody, not even yourself. You *need.*"

"And you don't. You don't need a fucking living soul."

"That's right."

He was so cold he terrified her. His eyes, when he was drunk, became a paler blue, as soulless as the eyes of a dead man except for the hatred in them. It was incredible that anyone could hate her that much—hate anyone or anything that much. She would try to think, sometimes, what it was that she'd done wrong, but she'd be filled, immediately, with confusion and fright and would be unable to concentrate, unable to remember for more than a few seconds what it was she was trying to understand.

"Martin, come to bed." She dug her fingers into his arms, trying by sheer power to break through that wall of ice.

"No *thank* you."

If anyone had asked her why she wanted him, what in heaven's name she saw in him—as her psychiatrist would ask her a short time later—she could hardly have said. It wasn't the money: she'd have traded it all—the big, white pillared house with its towers, the Mercedes, the Essex, the trips to Europe and Japan—for a single day of the life they'd had when they were poor and he still loved her. It wasn't, God knows, because he seemed to her handsome, though she knew to her sorrow how handsome he seemed to other women—women who saw his neurotic unhappiness, his sexy arrogance and occasional childlike gentleness, his joy on a horse or a motorcycle—and had never seen that murderous glint in his bleary, ice-blue eyes, a glint like rifle bluing. But it would come to her, finally, what it was that made her cling to him, and she would know—then quickly forget again—that Martin's cruel accusation was partly right, that she clung out of need. He was her past, her whole life, and if he left her, as again and again he threatened to do—even tried to do, running to some floozy, some graduate student or girl from the past or colleague's wife—her whole life would be cancelled, made meaningless, would vanish in an instant without leaving a trace, the way the universe would do, he claimed, if Time should all at once be suspended. And so she would phone him at his floozy's house, would cry, would even use the children as a weapon, and he would finally come back, hating her and making her hate herself, and the children would move numbly through the big, cold house, gentle and beautiful and unquestionably doomed if she couldn't find some way to save them—save them all. Martin's father, at the time of his worst unhappiness, had been suicidal, had fought against the urge with all his might and had barely won. Now Martin was the same. She had no idea when he stormed off late at night, drunk and furious and full of that senseless, terrible grief, whether or not she'd ever see him again. If he killed himself, the odds against Evan's survival—hypersensitive and private as his father—were frightening. —And yet it wasn't just that, wasn't just concern about Evan and Mary or fear that her life would turn suddenly into waste, that made her fight to hang onto him. Once she had loved him more than anyone or anything, and though it seemed that the Martin she'd loved was dead, she knew it wasn't true. Sometimes, reading his big, gloomy novels, she would recognize with a shock of mingled pain and pleasure the Martin she'd long ago settled on for life. And there was a time when, waiting for her baggage at Kennedy Airport, she'd seen him without at first recognizing him—she'd had no reason to expect him there—and she had thought, in the flash of time it took her to adjust, *What a strange, nice-looking man!* Even after she'd realized that it was Martin, the memory of that feeling persisted like the next day's memory of a dream. For all the eccentricity of his hair and clothes—he was like a man who'd stepped out of a nineteenth-century American painting—he was a man you'd turn to if you needed help, a man inherently gentle and solicitous—to strangers, anyway—the kind who, even on the New York subway, would get up to give his seat to a lady, an old man, a child loaded down with packages.

"Martin, I *order* you to come to bed."

He laughed, and his eyes were so crazy she was afraid to press him. More than once he'd thrown her across the room when she tried to control him.

"What's happened to us?" she cried. "Look at us! For Christ's sake, what's happened?" Before she knew it would come over her, she was sobbing, and though she knew how he scorned her crying, convinced that it was one more trick, it was impossible to stop. When she loosened her grip on his arms he jerked back, and she instinctively covered her face, thinking he meant to hit her. But he was backing toward the door, fleeing again, though it was four in the morning and raining.

"Time," he roared, "that's what's happened. Ghosts. Dead people."

"Martin," she wailed, "I didn't *do* anything."

He stood with his hand on the doorknob, the lighted swimming pool behind him, and she stood perfectly still, as if precariously balanced: perhaps, drunk as he was, he would come to his senses if she made no threatening move, waited him out as he himself would wait out some vicious dog he was gentling.

"You never do anything," he said. He spoke as if she weren't human, as if she were all the world's evils squeezed together in an ugly imitation of human shape. "You do what the wind does, what falling bodies do. You plan ahead like a rattlesnake asleep on a rock."

Her anger was rising, impossible to fight. They were good at that, at least, good at stabbing each other. "What did I do? What started this?" He was too drunk to know, she knew, and her seeming control would make him still more furious.

His hand turned on the doorknob. She took a step toward him and said in panic, "Who are you going to? I'll kill her."

It was a mistake. The door was open now, rain blowing in. An image came to her, more real than the room, Martin in bed with some woman—white legs, dark hair, the face hidden—and she rushed at him in rage, but he was gone, the door was closed, and she fell. "Bastard," she said, weeping, beating the carpet with her fist. When she looked up, sometime later, her thirteen-year-old Evan was kneeling beside her, expressionless, patting her back.

Two

They first slept together, as they would both tell friends at parties later, when they were two—slept together in a drawer, in fact, when Joan's parents (and her Uncle John Elmer and Aunt Cora) drove east to visit the New York State cousins and help wallpaper the huge old faded-brick house the Orricks lived in. The Orricks owned a small dairy farm a mile outside the little village of Elba and were thought of locally as "old family." Exactly what this meant was never clear to her: her father's line went back to before the American Revolution, though west of the Mississippi such qualities weren't much valued. Like Joan's parents when they started, the Orricks were, despite their big house, as poor as church mice, and, except for their eldest son, so they would remain, though they might have claimed, if it had occurred to them, to be failed aristocrats: the family, a hundred years before, had been considerably better off. But very little concerning their social position occurred to the Orricks, it must be said to their credit. Like most people of their general class in the western part of New York State, they liked Indians, disliked Italians, voted Republican, put themselves down on official forms not as "Protestant" but as "Presbyterian," openly loathed labor unions and secretly loathed Catholics. The mother—Joan's father's cousin—was a devoted church worker and English teacher, a plump, short red-head with sparkling eyes, who loved ripe tomatoes and the color blue. The father wrote poems while working behind his horses or, later, while riding his steel-wheeled or (still later) rubber-tired tractors and sometimes delivered sermons in small country churches—sermons that were, everyone agreed, moving, in fact inspiring, and made no mention of either heaven or hell, though full of fine language and a curious deep current of woe.

He came from a long, long line of preachers, country lawyers, and school-masters, and would pass on his gifts as an orator to his eldest son.

Oddly enough, events from one of their first meetings would be the earliest memories either Joan or her cousin Buddy was to carry through life. She would remember, distinctly, how Buddy's grandmother (her father's aunt) had called from the bathroom, where she'd been giving Buddy a bath, "Everybody look out, a bear's coming!" At the warning, Joan fled to the bedroom door, then looked back in alarm, and lo, down the hall came running not a bear but a bare, Buddy with no clothes on. She had laughed and laughed, and he had stopped, hands clasped, and looked at her with four-year-old fury and alarm, and she, understanding his strange nature even then, had instantly explained the joke to him, and then he too had laughed, though somewhat doubtfully. He would all his life be suspicious, easily offended, difficult—as Joan's mother would say, "a dark one." As for Buddy—or Martin, as he would come to be called—he remembered one single, powerful image: Joan in a bright yellow dress with white trim, her red hair glowing, full of sunlight, her dimple strange and wonderful, so that he stared and stared at it. She'd laughed at him for that and had taken his hand and led him around the house—as she'd be leading him from one place to another all their lives—chattering, making him play games.

From then on, Joan's family and the Orricks would visit one another every few years—then oftener and oftener—and each time Joan and Buddy met they were surprised all over again by how much they liked each other. He visited her, as it happened—or rather, his family visited hers—at the time she had her appendix out, an occasion that would later prove grimly important for both their lives. Like all his memories of seeing Joan, that visit would have, when he thought back to it, a curious glow, a brightness of color, a heightened reality that made it like a dream or, more precisely, like a novel—he was, at that time, an insatiable reader, though he did poorly in school.

He sat on the side of her bed—she had a light blue nightdress and a light blue silk ribbon in her hair—and they made together a picture of a kind he'd never seen before. There was, in the book she had, a line drawing of a ship, and there was another page with glue on the back (as on a postage stamp) and, on the front, parts of the ship in brilliant colors—primary red, blue, yellow, bright green—which one was meant to cut out and paste onto the drawing. He listened in a kind of daze to her voice as she told him her adventures at the hospital, deftly moving the scissors around the colorful shapes. It was a voice that seemed to him unbelievably lovely—soft, light, brimming with that southern warmth that made his nasal western New York accent plain as a fence post. And as he looked at the colors, the warmest he'd ever seen on paper, he thought—as warm as the red Missouri roads, the great, curious Midwestern trees—cottonwoods, mulberries, sycamores—or Missouri's bright cardinals—and listened to the voices of her parents in the next room—the same sweet accents, the same warmth and humor—abruptly, he began to cry. No sound, only tears. But her red-headed brother James looked up from the floor where he was playing and cried out with what seemed malicious glee but was perhaps in fact just surprise and embarrassment, "Buddy's crying!" Buddy looked at Joan in alarm, not just ashamed but frightened, and saw that she was studying him, her face clouded. She said to her brother quietly, "Jimmy, you leave him alone." He was in love with her, in short, though the word was one he would never have thought of. In love with her whole family, her world. Despite the odd care she took of him, he had no idea that she was also in love with him.

The next time he visited Missouri, a year later, he stayed with another of the Missouri cousins—Joan's first cousin Betty Lou—who lived in the country. Both their families, Joan's and Buddy's, were always very careful about being strictly fair. No one knew at the time, including the children, that some of the Missouri cousins were for profound reasons closer than others.

At Betty Lou's, too, Buddy was happy, walking with her to the one-room country school where his mother had gone, and Joan's father and mother, a generation before, or feeding the rabbits Betty Lou's father raised, or simply sitting in a wide old dying tree, looking at the incredibly lush landscape, the blue, blue sky, and feeling all around him that special aliveness the Midwest always had for him and would have all his life, a "vast benevolent electric charge, a smell of the miraculous," he would write years later in one of his novels—an aliveness impossible to defend, he would find, to anyone not emotionally persuaded already, since it meant of course not only lush growth, pools of sunlight you could cut like warm butter, but also ticks, chiggers, and copperheads, rattlesnakes and cottonmouths, cyclones and devastating floods. He was sublimely happy, soaking up a summer warmth New York State could never know, and if anyone had questioned him at just that moment, he might have said that it wasn't his cousin Joan he liked, really, but the place.

That evening, however, he had an experience he would vividly remember all his life, in the sharpest possible detail, though it was one he would find, even after he'd become a famous novelist, impossible to put into words. Shortly after sunset, when the last of the whippoorwills were quitting and the heavy, wet midsummer air hung close, Joan and her family came driving out from town, piled out of their car shouting their greetings with voices that were like singing, and came rushing over to him, Joan and her two brothers, so wide-eyed, so charged with jubilant energy, sheer joy-of-life, that they seemed to be not of the same species as these good, slow country people, Betty Lou's family, with whom he'd been staying. Though Joan was at the moment in her unbeautiful period, he had time only to notice it fleetingly and forget again, because for Buddy that night it was as if the world's sound had been turned to full volume and its action sped up as in an old-time comic movie. She was the funniest girl he'd ever met. She amazed him. From the instant he first saw her getting out of the car (to borrow an expression from three decades later, but one which is here exactly accurate), he was high.

Despite her fears, it was not a time he forgot when their marriage was at its worst. Part of Martin Orrick's trouble, and no doubt part of his strength as a novelist, was that he forgot very little. He could drop back to almost any period of his life and run it through his mind like an old movie; he could remember, for some reason, the furniture in houses he'd visited only once when he was seven years old, and he could remember in imagery as sharp as that in any photograph not only the faces but also the hands, the clothes, even the shoes of people he saw only once or twice when he was nine or ten. But though his memory was extraordinary, he had no faith. He could remember loving Joan and believing she loved him, but he believed, looking back, that their love was an illusion. Stumbling through the rain, choking with drunken self-pity and rage, falling, laboriously getting up again, the three big dogs circling him in distress and bafflement, he thought the foul weather fitting, an appropriate symbol of his existence, the lot of poor idiot mankind. His chief virtue had been, once, that he was reasonable, fair-minded. He'd learned—so now he told himself—that the universe had no slightest interest in such things. Joan dismissed people for faults they could not help—dismissed them utterly and finally because their eyes were too close together or their ankles too thick. She imputed selfish or malevolent intent to acts harmlessly foolish, even generous; and her friends applauded her as if viciousness, cruelty, and cynicism were the healthy breath of truth. All very well to say that her views were not Martin Orrick's business, that she was one person and he another, and each had a right to his own identity. It wasn't true—not that he thought all this out at this moment. It was a part of him, a roar in his chest. She poisoned his life at the source, accusing him of evil motives when his real ones were nothing of the sort, and shifting the grounds of her attacks with wild whimsy, revealing what was obvious in any case, as it seemed to him, that she attacked not from conviction but for the sadistic pleasure of attacking. His best friend when he was an undergraduate—a young man as intense and neurotic as Martin himself, one with whom he would talk for hours, working out the structure of a Henry James story or a Shakespeare play, learning in the best way possible (he would have said) one of the essential ingredients of his art—was, according to Joan, a homosexual. Ah, what evil she could wring out of that stuffy, ladies'-mag word! Useless to cry out in righteous indignation, "That's not true!" because the next moment, according to Joan, Martin only liked him because, like all his superpious family, he had a penchant for sickies, and the next because he was Martin's "first Jew." In the end she'd made the friendship too painful to keep up. It was not that she didn't want Martin to have friends—he told himself in rage—merely that she preferred to choose them. It was a part of her character not likely to change. Martin, hating scenes—being, in fact, afraid of scenes, not overloaded at the best of times with self-confidence—had retreated to his study, putting his emotion where it was safe, into fiction; but it was inevitable that sooner or later he must emerge, and that the character of their war must change. He fought her with reason, but the battle was absurd: she would not reason, fired wild shots like a troop of circling, yodeling Indians, and he would drink and grow bold and full of hot self-righteousness and would try once more to fight her with reason and would be beaten to silence and crackling woman hate and flight. Running, slipping and sliding in the clay mud she hated as she hated everything on this farm he'd chosen as his place of retreat from cities—his battleground, pirate's cove, hermit's shack—stumbling and falling in erosion ruts, scratching his face on the branches of trees, he fled toward a place she'd never dare look for him, the creek, the pitch-dark caves along the farm's back fence.

The dogs ran beside him, whimpering as if they knew what stupidity he was guilty of, his children back in the house, probably awake, frightened, beginning to learn the hopelessness he'd gladly have protected them from if protection were possible in this hellhole world. He was not crying, as he would have done when he was younger, when there was, he thought, still a chance for him. It was as if he had seen one death too many, had lost utterly the power to feel grief—as if he had finally understood that this was the world's essential nature: idiotic conflict with no prayer of resolution—raving Arabs, raving Jews, raving blacks, raving whites; destruction of the innocent, Evan and Mary lying in their beds, listening. "Let's not drink anymore," he and Joan would say in the morning when they woke up and couldn't remember what had started it; but his hatred would still be there, burning like a coal, and her absolute insistence on her rightful ownership of his every emotion, and he would drink, yes yes yes, Christ yes!

He could hear the water now, deep and slow-moving, weighed down by silt, dragging dark masses and branches like the bodies of old men toward the Mississippi. He moved toward the sound, the dogs running closer now, perpetually circling, herding him back. He came to the caves, the smell of foxes, and he stopped, leaning on the slippery rock, panting. When he crawled in, the air was icy cold. The dogs came in after him, shook off water, pressed against him and settled. He listened to the rain, thinking of his children, thinking of his own childhood, the people who had shaped him and those who'd shaped Joan, or damned them, more like, though they'd meant no harm and though finally it was nobody's fault but his own, not even Joan's. He shivered, closed his eyes. The ground under him was smooth and cold, like a coin.

He couldn't remember, waking up shivering and numb in the morning, why it was that he'd come there.

Three

Both families were religious. Joan's went to church, did what was asked of them there and more, and never spoke, even in church, of religion. Someone who knew nothing of the lives of ordinary religious people—someone who knew only lapsed Catholics or lapsed fundamentalists, some unlucky member of that great unlucky class Martin Orrick would describe (with typical rancor and the plain injustice that served as his main form of irony) as "cynic-intellectuals, keen-eyed analysts of the interface subtleties of shit and Shinola, finger-wringing, foot-stamping, failed Neoplatonists," or, in another place, as "the gentle libertarian who curls up his lip when he says 'Wasp,'"—might perhaps have dismissed Joan's parents as hypocrites or trimmers, or—finding no disparity between their regular, seemingly mechanical and unreasoning attendance at the Ferguson First Methodist Church and their generally upright, warmhearted, and generous everyday behavior—might have put them down, simply, as two more credulous, pitiful ciphers in that vast majority whom Thoreau alleged to live "lives of quiet desperation." Nothing, in fact, could have been farther from the truth.

Though they were silent, both Joan's father and mother were more deeply religious than the official policies of the churches they'd grown up in. Joan's mother had been a Roman Catholic, and in a sense was still. When she settled her heart on marrying a Baptist, a boy she'd grown up with and loved from the beginning, whose virtues and defects she'd come to know like the back of her hand, she quietly scrapped the opinions of her church—not without some stress, even superstitious fright—asserting and affirming that the God she worshipped could not conceivably be such a narrow-minded fool as to despise Donald Frazier for the doctrinal persuasions of his parents. Religion for her had always consisted, essentially, of two

things: a timid but deep love of ritual—an appreciation, fundamentally aesthetic, of the gestures of the Mass, of music and vestments, of statues and
wide convent lawns (there was a convent in Florissant, not far off)—and,
secondly, an unostentatious devotion to basic goodness, the quiet morality,
fair-mindedness, and general optimism she observed in her parents and in
her older brothers and sisters, some of whom were grown up and had moved
away when Emmy—Emily—was born. Though she was by no means unin-
telligent, she had never especially concerned herself with theological questions—no more than had the rest of the countrified Catholic congregation
she grew up with, or the dirt-poor, absentminded priest who served them.
But she understood fairness: it was unfair to make a husband switch to Catholicism and break his mother's heart, and unfair to her family that she
shift to the camp of those who most openly denounced them. Forced to
leave the Church or else renounce Donald Frazier, for reasons not even her
father was sure of—as he all but admitted, turning from her sternly, pulling
at his beard—she quietly moved her Catholicism to another building, the
bland, friendly House of God as the Methodists understood him, and no
one was especially troubled except, of course, Donald's mother. Emmy was
robbed, in the Methodist Church, of ritual, and sometimes even here she
must sit through tirades against the religion of her parents; but even in middle age she would look over at Donald, who sat with his head tipped up,
as if politely listening, or sat with his elbow on the wall of the pew, the
inside of his hand across his forehead, eyes closed—he was fast asleep—and
she would decide again that she'd been right, that God was Love, simply;
it was as plain as the nose on Donald's face. In her later years she would
seldom go to church, but nothing had changed. She found her ritual in the
comings and goings of birds, the rise and decline of her roses, in sunrise
and sunset, the exactly punctual five o'clock phone call from her sister Cora,
and the ten o'clock news before she and Donald settled down to sleep. As
for basic goodness, her children were a great satisfaction to her—even James.
For all the unhappiness in his life, he was happy in his work, and good
at it. And Donald, with hair now whiter than snow, was an amazing man,
a saint. When you came right down to it, she asked herself—or meekly
asked God—how many parents (not that she'd dream of mentioning her
opinion to a living soul) had a daughter like their Joan?

Joan's father's religion—or at any rate so Martin Orrick would describe
it in one of his later, more unreadable novels—was "of a sort virtually

impossible to defend in a world which finds its fundamental verities in the *New York Times,* the *San Francisco Chronicle,* or the *St. Louis Post-Dispatch"*—the world Martin Orrick would howl at with all the volcanic rage of his convulsive, misanthropic soul (much to his profit, ironically, so that the rage would grow more fierce, more unjust and cruel, the prose more eccentric and bizarre).

Joan's father was a more or less classic Midwestern Protestant. He'd been raised in the Coldwater Baptist Church not far from Possum Hollow, a house of rabid Scotch-Irish fundamentalists where even those who were inclined to moderation must sooner or later be swept into the current of avid self-righteousness and cowering self-hate by loose talk of heaven and the slime of the earth, God's abundant love and wild-animal rage against all who offended his dignity or law. Martin Orrick would write: "Such churches have grown rare in America; not, one suspects, because people have grown wiser but because the weather has changed. Such churches thrive—not cynically, but in answer to ancient human needs—on extreme poverty, ignorance, and the unhealthy certainty that can come from living too far from books, too close to nature, whose laws are not ours; they thrive on a high rate of infant mortality—cholera, diphtheria, scarlet fever, plague—and a profound distrust of strangers. It is a curious fact that for the most part the warnings and admonitions of such a church, however dire, however vivid the imagery that engulfs and enflames them, are not aimed at the present congregation at all but at those who have stayed home on a given Sunday morning, breaking the community's phalanx wall, or the warnings are fired, like shots into a woodlot in the middle of the night, at the prowling, potentially dangerous unfamiliar—the German, the Frenchman, the Negro, or the sharp-eyed Injun boy over by the woodshed. It was the stranger, not the Baptist, who drank, swore oaths, and did no work. It was marriage to the stranger that led to madness or idiocy or the rolling-eyed human mule. It was only when they slipped into the stranger's ways, taking to drink, or taking into bed some gentile wife (as an earlier breed of intransigeants had it) that the wrath of the Fundamental Church came down like an axe on the heads of its own. When Donald Frazier set his mind on marrying a Catholic, the staddle on which his mother's church was built had already begun to crumble, the walls inclined to lean, the dark-stained windows were beginning to crack and let light in. In short, he understood what they were saying, but did not believe them.

His father, it was said, had been in his youth a happy-go-lucky, foot-loose man who might have come to no good; but he married Lulu Thompson, who seems to have been, judging by old photographs, a stunningly beautiful woman except that she had deep-set, evil eyes. (Joan and Buddy, when they visited—she was then over ninety—would hear from her stories of hammer murders and the lynching of "coloreds.") But photographs lie, and country wisdom is sometimes worth crediting. The children she reared, with John Frazier's help, were all secure, decent people. The eldest died a hero in World War I, and John Elmer, the least successful of the sons financially, was a man Martin Orrick would years later describe, borrowing from Homer, as a man "such as men were then and are not now." She was a religious fanatic, apparently; but she lived in harsh times. A central story in the family legend is that once they had a neighbor, a no-'count Frenchman, who would go on drunken benders and come shoot at the house with his gun, also at their chickens, sheep, and mules. According to one version—the version Joan Orrick was inclined to believe (her father wouldn't speak of it, would only chuckle and blush and look down and say, "Well, you hear a lot of stories")—the neighbor came one night into her grandpa's pitch-dark barn, and her grandpa was up in the mow with his rifle, waiting, and shot him through the head when he walked through the door. Then her grandpa took off on the horse he had waiting and rode to the house of William Burke, a mile away, who was sheriff at the time, and turned himself in. "What John," William Burke is supposed to have said, blinking the sleep away, rubbing at the roughness of his thick red neck, "you *didn't*, John! Aw *shit!*" and got out of bed and woke up his sons, and while John Frazier sat smiling, sipping at William Burke's whiskey (to calm his nerves), they rode half the night, to every neighbor for miles around, and they all congregated at John Frazier's farm and shot holes upon holes into the dead man. Though they might've lawed John Frazier, they could hardly law the whole county, so they left the thing lie.

It can be said in defense of Joan's evil-eyed grandmother that it was mostly thanks to her that Joan's father and his brothers and sister got whatever education they got, whatever feeling they developed for hard work and duty, and a good part of whatever notion, mostly generous, they got of God. Though Donald and John Elmer were as afraid of their mother as were Emmy and Cora of the Catholic Church, they put their fear behind

them with the same abandon their father had showed, the night he shot
the Frenchman, and turned to Methodism. Joan's father, all through the
years of her childhood, listened to the sermons with gentle tolerance and
no particular interest, viewing them simply as the opinions of one man (and
a man with the mouth of an elephant, at that). When it was time to sing
a hymn, he ran his eyes over the words, too shy to sing, perhaps a touch
ashamed of the noisy part-singing of the church that had raised him, a church
where Christianity was not always what it might be, where money was
gathered for foreign missions but no charity was left over for Catholics
like Joan's mother, to say nothing of Negroes, with whom he had all his
life a curious affinity, though he would never deny, looking back as an old
man, that he had a prejudice six miles deep; or he thought about the things
he had to do this afternoon—in large part chores an intelligent theologian
would describe as Christian acts: visits to sick friends and relatives, or to
lonely people whom no one liked but who were, in Joan's mother's phrase,
"real good people" (always based on evidence with which Joan was unac-
quainted); or he thought out problems—for instance, some necessary modi-
fication of the threading machine at St. Louis Screw and Bolt; or he would
wait for the hymn's too hurried "Amen" (as it seemed from Buddy Orrick's
Presbyterian point of view), so he could once more sit down and get to
business catching up on his sleep. When Emmy had things to do or felt
unwell and was unable to go to church, he went alone, a fact on which
neither of them commented, since they both understood it. It was in a sense
his salute to something he believed in; only an enemy, a cynic, a fool would
demand that he explain what it was that he believed. Though he slept
through the service as often as not, he loved it. To scorn him for sleeping
through a thing so holy would be like scorning a man for sleeping through
his daughter's twentieth recital.

His religion was obvious to anyone who looked. His company was one
of the first in St. Louis to insist that the union take Negroes in, though
Donald had no doubt that all Negroes are lazy. He stood at the top of the
main-shop stairs with a four-foot boltmaker wrench in his hands, saying
nothing (but everyone knew his opinion), and it cannot be denied—whether one calls it a good thing or a bad thing—that his intellectual
position and his position in the way of the shop's only exit had influence
on the Poplar Bluff poor whites who worked for him and did the voting

four times before he casually stepped aside, the vote finally having gone as he thought right, and allowed them to go on home. It's at the same time true that he thought of blacks as niggers (though more often, respectfully, as "coloreds"), tended to believe them transitional between the ape and man—so he'd many a time heard said in church, not that he believed all that churches told him; but he'd given it some thought, standing by the bars holding Joanie's hand, looking at the gorillas at the St. Louis Zoo: he could come to no conclusion, but though he dismissed the supposed similarity of a colored's nose and a gorilla's nose—a blind man feeling with a stick would see the difference—he was struck by the way gorillas' seats stuck out and by the pinkness of their palms. Once when he and Joan were standing there, watching the gorilla take listless swings at the truck tire that hung from a chain in his cage, a middle-aged black man who stood watching beside them smiled and shook his head and said, "He looks just like my mama." Donald giggled and blushed and looked down and said heartily, "Yea-uh!" On the authority of coloreds he'd known as a child, he believed firmly—until one morning when he was fifty and it suddenly occurred to him his leg had been pulled—that by some quirk of nature every colored child born was conversant with the language of mules.

Whatever all this may say of him, he was, like every true religious man, every man's friend and no man's judge. He joked with whites about blacks and with blacks about whites, not from hypocrisy but because in St. Louis one did not at that time—and does not now, except with great caution—make fun of whites to whites (except of course for Jews, who are fair game for everybody, especially Jews), though one might sometimes joke with blacks about blacks, since part of their charm was the fact that they seemed to encourage it. He knew his world, though he had no conscious systems, and could move around in it easily, safely, doing nobody damage. He was generous and trusting, though he locked his car doors and rolled up the windows in the darker parts of town and in Castlereigh Estates took precautions against burglars. Despite his Baptist raising, he did nothing from duty but acted by virtue of his fundamental love of life and the optimism, deeper than reason, that religion and parents who had loved each other—however they might snap or lash out from time to time—had built into him.

His religion, in short, was middle-class Protestant, a religion for the street. It contained no angels, no clearly defined heaven, certainly no hell. His chief pleasure, when he went to church, was picking up the gossip and seeing people dressed up in their Sunday clothes. Many years later his son-in-law Martin—no Christian by any stretch of the imagination—would defend Donald Frazier's religious nature with angry fervor; but Martin, for all the care with which he wrote, for all the precision with which he tried to think things through, would have no faintest inkling of the real secret behind his father-in-law's character. Donald Frazier remembered his mother in a way the old photographs in Joan Orrick's upstairs hallway neglected to record: as a fanatical idealist, a woman too intelligent by a mighty leap for her time and place, as cruel and misanthropic as Martin Orrick himself, but wildly optimistic, determined to kill the Devil, in whose existence she believed as firmly as she believed in her left foot. He remembered certain instants when his mother seemed to him a dazzling beauty: more such instants than a few. She had four sons, one daughter; and like all lively women who raise handsome, quick-witted sons in a house half governed by a handsome and quick-witted, playful man, she developed, quite unconsciously, ways attractive to men—a laugh, a glance, an occasional sudden gentleness, that softened for her children the bigotry, cruelty of tongue, and uncharitable suspiciousness that tainted her character. She loved music, especially the old Scotch songs and the more lively Baptist hymns (Joan and Buddy, when Lulu Frazier was in her nineties, would sing Irish songs, claiming they were Scotch, to tease her; whenever Joan played hymns and the assembled three generations sang, it was a rule that they must sing all the verses); she loved poetry, for the most part terrible poetry; and she loved fine clothes and festivities—a family reunion, a country Christmas with a huge tree and all the family around her, or every Sunday's dressed-up, chattering, wonderfully horse-scented buggy ride three miles over hill and dale, through dark hollows, past Negroes' cabins, past neatly kept fields of wheat and cane, to the Coldwater Baptist Church. Though her sons did not share her belief in the Devil, they had, at odd moments, her unearthly, eagle-sharp eyes. So, of course, had Joan. They could flash like sheet lightning if some affront, some slight to her pride made her furious, so that for many years Martin would be afraid of her, would even imagine she might someday kill him, though occasionally he saw that same flash in the eyes of his gentle son, Evan, and was unsure of himself, unsure of everything.

At the darkest time of his life, it must be said, he was at his feeble best when full of doubt and irresolvable confusion.

Again his pale blue eyes had the dead look, though tonight there was no sign of rage in them. He puffed at his pipe every three or four words, as if drawing what little life he had from it, his left hand closed lightly around the pipe bowl, his right around the rim of his martini glass. King Rolf, the Alsatian, lay beside him, his head on his paws; Evan's black-and-tan, as large as a lion, lay by the sliding glass doors that went out to the pool. You could hear the drone of the television coming from upstairs, where the children were watching God knew what—nothing worse than their life. He said:

"We've got to talk, you say. But it's futile to talk. There's no reason left in the world anymore, not even the illusion. It's like Johnson saying with the greatest sincerity, 'Let us sit down and reason one with another,' and lying about everything from Tonkin Bay to the price of a Job Corps T-shirt. Not that he didn't 'mean well,' understand. But it's over, that's all. No trust left, no faith. Why talk fairly with someone who obeys no rules, intends to destroy you? Better we trade insults, see if we can give each other heart attacks."

"It must be terribly painful to be the last honest man," she said. She lit another cigarette. Though her voice was calm as steel, her fingers trembled.

"You have a sharp eye. Yes indeed, my suffering's a rare and splendid thing."

"*We* don't suffer, of course."

" 'We' being, I presume, you and the children, the great united front." He rolled his eyes up, as if in brief prayer to some ferocious, bored god, no doubt some half-wit god jugged to the gills.

"You could *try* to talk," she snapped. "You're supposed to be this marvellous lecturer, the finest in your department, as you so frequently remark."

He pushed his chair back angrily and stood up, not to leave but to be farther from her, free to pace if he should need to. "When in *hell* am I supposed to have called myself a marvellous lecturer?"

"Except of course when you don't bother to show up."

His eyes widened, enraged but also baffled. He looked terrible—scratches all over his face from his rampage last night, bleary, baggy eyes. "Name one single time since I left San Francisco—"

"You've forgotten. You can't remember anything anymore. You drink and drink—it's a wonder you can sometimes still remember your name."

"God damn you," he roared, "stay on one subject for fifteen seconds, will you? What are these classes I'm supposed to have missed?"

"Plenty, Martin! Do you really think everybody doesn't know? I've tried to get hold of you a dozen times—ask Georges Fauré, ask John Porter. Nobody can find you. You're supposed to be in class, they say, but there's nobody in the room."

"That's impossible!" But he was staring at her, perhaps trying to remember, perhaps trying to judge whether or not she'd found something out.

"Does she massage your shoulders? Does she like to be fucked in grave-yards?" She smiled, mock-sweet.

He stared. His breathing was growing calmer; he was thinking something, she had no idea what. Finally he said, swirling his drink around and around, speaking as if to his glass, not her: "You fight with great spirit, but your stupidity beats you. Beats me too, in the end, but never mind; it doesn't matter." He raised his glass, extended it toward the darkness outside, to the right of the swimming pool, where the trees began to circle out, as if offering a toast to evil spirits. "Behold here the ruin of centuries of Nature's blind plodding. I give you, in this lady, the glorious culmination of a bold experiment, *homo non sapiens:* centuries of careful evolution in clans, selective breeding until the last trace of judgment was eradicated, nothing in the universe right or wrong but by virtue of its plaid and the loch it had the honor to get born beside; then a final bit of polish in the American South, magnificent Eden of noninterference, though black men turn on lynchers' ropes and trash eat clay: all argument abandoned, debate forsworn, no action permitted to the human mind but sad empty songs about love grown colder and heaven's six gates—oh *yeah,* my Lawd—"

"Martin, you're sick. You're really sick."

"That's true." He waved his glass. "And over here I give you this gentle-man, or rather this specimen, this noblest achievement of modern teratology, born with a gavel and *Robert's Rules of Order* and a bachelor of science in Talmudic law, no hasty construction, this monster of angular good sense, this tremulous howl in the wilderness of lies, this gibberish singer of decay-ing Truth—"

"You think this kind of talk makes *me* look stupid?"

He turned to look at her. "You remembered the subject! How'd you do that? You must've wrote it down."

Though he mocked her, there was no anger in his eyes now; even the dead look—or maybe possessed look was more accurate—had sunk away. She was suddenly aware of the pain in her right leg and midsection, from her pelvis to lower chest. It had been there, she realized, for a long time. She felt a touch of panic, as she always did when she thought about the pain, and got up abruptly to fix herself another drink. It was stupid to have another one—it meant Martin would, too—but she didn't care, tonight. Liquor was better than the drugs were, Dr. Crouse had said.

Martin said behind her, "You hurting?"

She dropped ice into her glass and glanced up at his reflection in the window. She saw her own there too. They didn't look like two people who would hate each other. How strange it was—how strange everything was, she thought fleetingly. People called them a handsome couple. The pain licked up sharply into her chest, then died down again. "I'm all right," she said. "It makes me mean, that's all." She carried the pitcher of martinis to him. He held out his glass and she poured. Smoke from his pipe spiralled upward. "Let's not get drunk tonight," she said.

He shrugged. "Whatever."

They sat down again, across from each other at the round formica table. She lit a cigarette, pushed the matches toward him. "You feel better when you're writing. You should try," she said.

"Tomorrow, maybe."

"What's wrong? Really, I mean."

He said nothing, looking into his glass.

"I love you," she said. "You don't believe it, but I do."

He smiled, politely scornful.

She said, more crossly than she'd meant to, "How can you stand it, not believing in anything?"

"Oh, I believe things," he said. "I just don't think any of them will help."

She watched him puffing gloomily at his pipe, following drops down the side of his glass with one fingernail.

"Do you want a divorce, Martin?" she said calmly, full of fear.

He pursed his lips, seemed to think about it. "Makes no difference," he said. "No."

"Because of the children," she flashed angrily.

"Partly that," he said. "Mainly because the whales are going extinct, and I don't have much faith in the life after death, and we haven't yet run out of gin."

"Jesus, you do rave on," she said.

"I do?" he said.

Four

Martin's parents, in contrast to Joan's, were noisily, articulately religious. Often, when Martin was very young, they would gather after sermons at his grandfather's house and debate the veracity of what was said by the man behind the pulpit. Martin's grandfather was a farmer and country schoolmaster with a brilliant, stubborn, morose mind (a child of Sagittarius) and a photographic memory with which he merely made trouble. At the age of forty-five he'd been tricked into marriage by the first lady lawyer in New York State, an Irishwoman (Protestant) as stubborn as he was, a determined red-head who by wily manipulation had put Luther Doane Orrick—such was his triumphantly gloomy name—into a position that threatened foreclosure on his two-hundred-year-old farm, but she offered (she was just twenty-eight at the time, a partner in the office of her father and uncle) the alternative of her not very noticeably gentle hand in marriage. He was flabbergasted, a confirmed bachelor, though a handsome man with coal-black hair that swept and curled out, edged with silver, fierce as his opinions, at his collar and around his ears. In his black top hat he was a man to reckon with (he was not, by any means, an advance-guard dresser), and the way he gripped his cane when just walking along—his arthritic knuckles bulging like the knuckles of an eagle at the moment of the strike—gave every living creature that stood within range of his eye or ear stern warning.

Caroline Slaine was by all this not greatly impressed. Though Anglo-Irish and a lawyer, she had no more scruple than a butterfly, no more fear of his bluster than a fox in a chicken house. Though she couldn't so express it in that sober time, not even secretly, he was a sexy old bastard and she wanted him. She summoned him therefore to her small, dark green, cluttered, book-and-map-filled office and, with a sweet imitation of feminine sternness, presented Orrick with her foreclosure threat. Luther Doane Orrick, breaker of horses, harrumphed twice, struck the floor with his cane, and denied her on grounds of principle, the principle being that he did not love her, not her nor no other Irishwoman, madam—no sir, by thunder, not even though she dared to declare herself of Protestant persuasion. From his positions, he told her, she would find him unmovable, no gilded rooster on a barn, that will turn with every wind. "Nonsense," she said, and at once set in motion the foreclosure proceedings.

When it appeared that the fool would rather give up his land than relinquish a principle, she trumped up an incredible criminal charge—yet was it so incredible after all, one wonders, considering the causes he was willing to support, the secret meetings he thought it honorable to attend?—at which point he said, or is said to have said, "Woman, what the devil are you after?" to which she is said to have responded—salaciously, considering the age in which they lived—"Children." She started, with easy Ram-child firmness, proceedings on the criminal charge against Orrick, and he hastily gave in. He could part with the ancestral estate (at the outside, nine hundred acres), but not with his good name. He was a ceremonious man, a high-ranking member of the Society of Freemasons (he would be buried with terrifying Masonic ritual, his grandson Buddy watching with wide, alarmed eyes), he was a titled officer in the local Grange League Fellowship, and he was, it would be discovered soon after his death, an officer in the Ku Klux Klan. What the Klan was up to in western New York in the late 1930s has never been certain. As an abolitionist and dedicated Yankee, Luther Orrick had nothing against the Negro race, of which Genesee County had then no representatives; but there were Catholics aplenty, a dangerous brood of drunken vipers, speakers of a wickedly ungrammatical English, suivants of a foreign potentate, the pope, hence a knife aimed directly at the heart of the American Experiment.

But mockery is always an easy thing; it brings down republics, schools of philosophy, and personal reputations without regard for truth or justice. "If the world ends in fire," Martin Orrick would write (though he was himself among the worst offenders), "it will surely be the arsonous fiery indignation of the stupidly self-righteous." Luther Orrick's hatred of the pope and all he stood for was perfectly earnest, perfectly sincere, and not a case of mere whimsical malice. He'd read certain accounts, some of which were true, about unruly Irish and Italian workers; he weighed them against the personality and character of that papist-deist Alexander Pope, who, though dead these centuries, was a man he might justly have said he loved, had *love* been one of the words he ever used; he considered the role of the Church in European history—the Children's Crusade and the Glorious Crusade of the Bishop of Norwich, the papal debasement of public morality which outraged Dante, the Vatican's making and breaking of kings, the cruel persecutions and mass exterminations—not that he entirely neglected the crimes of Protestantism; he considered the evil of idol worship, and the far greater evil of mindless superstition, with which even his own church had dangerously toyed in the days of Cotton Mather. He considered these things, weighed them, and made his judgment, characteristically severe.

As far as anyone who knew him could tell, and as Martin Orrick would remember him, he was an absolutely honest man, though one of strong opinions, most of them wrong. We may rightly scoff now at the sides he took, but his problem was the all but universal human problem, not that that wholly excuses him (as Luther Doane Orrick would be the first to grant): he understood only as much as he knew. He read more widely and a good deal more carefully than anyone else of the time and county he lived in. Though it may sound absurd to modern ears—yet in fact it is the case—he could quote much of Shakespeare, most of Pope, and all of Milton, not including the Latin, of which he could find no copy. He read both Latin and Greek with ease, though his education, he knew because he'd checked, was a trifle beside that of a twelve-year-old boy of the eighteenth century. For at least a week after closing it, he could quote to you all that had seemed to him of interest, sometimes whole pages, in the monthly *Rural Messenger*. But it is also perhaps true (discounting the rant) that, as Martin Orrick was to write of him later in the gloomiest of his novels, "for all his careful reading, for all his love of justice, he was a victim of the only press he could get hold of, which urges the reflection that we should thank our minimally lucky stars that so few people left in the world can read at all." Though he started late, he was an excellent father, a man who by word and example could inculcate the highest moral principles—though what his children would have done without their mother's affection, love of bad light verse, and ultimate moral laxity, God only knows. He had the largest and easily the most beautiful garden in New York State, or so he contended, and spent the best part of his last years planting trees. (Hence Martin's pronouncement:

"The chief mark of a decent man is that he occasionally plants what he knows he can never live to see.") He was a splendid orator who had political aspirations, but his positions, which his eloquence made very clear, were fortunately unpopular. He was a Yankee soldier to the day he died, who came to church late—because his chores took time and he lived seven miles from town—and always, with the greatest formality, would salute the flag when he came abreast of his pew, bringing the service to a momentary stand-still, before he would condescend to sit. He walked with a twisted cane of polished applewood, and when the minister said something he thought false, he would thump it severely.

After Sunday services Martin's family would argue, at his grandfather's house, about all the minister had said and foolishly neglected to say. The meals were such as meals were then and are not now—homemade bread, baked apples, mashed potatoes with gravy, sweet potatoes, squash, chicken, turkey, goose, pork, calf or cow from his grandfather's slaughter shed, or ham from the smokehouse, corn, peas, sweet pickles, cranberry sauce, elder-berry or apple or mincemeat pie, fresh milk and butter, the milk so cold no normal man would dare set his glass against his lip, such as men are today. The old man quoted Scripture, Thomas Jefferson, Shakespeare, or Julius Caesar, and banged his fist on the table; his sons shouted back at him, delight-ing in conflict but shouting with conviction—no one would have dreamed of cheating in the debate, or toying with the subject in the sophists' way, or speaking out merely to keep his hand in. The table was large, and though at least three sons and their wives would be seated there, the chil-dren—Buddy and his cousins—were there too, on scriptural grounds, listen-ing bug-eyed, spooning in food without looking at it, watching for Grandpa or Uncle Fred or Uncle Bill to bring his fist down again, or for Grandma to reach out as if casually and capture a fly. Like puppies who haven't understood rough play and snap at a heavy old shepherd in earnest, and go sprawling, yelping, knocked across the stubble by a huge, fierce paw, the wives of the uncles would sometimes mistake the loud shouting for anger instead of mere strong rhetoric, persuasion by a show of cannon power, and would cry tears of fury as they leaped into the battle, defending what was right. The husband himself was as likely as anyone else at the table to say, "Faddle, Louise!" or "Bosh!"

It was a game all old Yankee farm families understand, though to Buddy's uncles' wives and even to his mother it sometimes looked senseless.

"How can you *eat* with all that shouting?" Buddy's mother asked his father once, at their own kitchen table in the big brick house. "It makes my stomach upset!"

His father sat crooked, leaning like a milk can standing in a rut, waiting for the milk truck. He had a catch in his back—pain, he said, like some Indian had shot him in the kidneys with a flint-headed arrow—but it was haying time now (that was always when his back pains were worst) and if he meant to beat the rain he had no alternative, he had to keep a move on. He smiled as if apologetically, holding the cheap yellow plate with his left hand, forking with his right. "It's interesting," he said. "Helps you figure out in your mind what's true."

Knowing what was true and what was mere illusion mattered a great deal to Duncan Orrick, as it mattered a great deal to his father and brothers and would matter to his son—and as it did not matter in the least to Donald Frazier or to his daughter Joan, who played life's most difficult passages by ear and made none of the mistakes Duncan Orrick made, though again and again they stumbled where his kind moved surely.

He was a powerfully built, good-looking, shy man with a farmer's large belly as hard to the touch as a tractor tire. His voice when he sang hymns—or when, working around the farm, he sang "Redwing," or "Where have you been Billy boy, Billy boy?" or "I'll take you home again, Kathleen"—was a sweet, thin, high baritone, perfect in pitch and phrasing by natural gift, and so oddly, perhaps unconsciously sad that one paused a moment, looking at the ground, and listened. He had overcharged emotions, as his son Buddy would have: he cried easily at movies or when he heard music or poetry, a tendency that embarrassed him but one he could live with. We see in old photographs, especially one of his father's whole family, with Luther and Caroline Orrick seated and the sons and one daughter gathered around them, solemnly attired, the boys in knickerbockers, the girl in a long, oddly bunched white dress, that Duncan Orrick, then nine, had a faraway look that instantly set him apart from all the others, the look of a poet, or of a boy marked for suicide or drunkenness—not at all the unearthly, demonic look Joan's grandmother Lulu Frazier sometimes had, but a look otherworldly in a different sense, elfin, mystical.

He stood, in Buddy's childhood, five foot eleven, as tall as anyone in his family had ever grown. Five foot eleven was about average among western New York farmers at that time—there were men a foot shorter, like Walt Cook or Homer Gill, but there were also, for some reason, men like Jim Hume, Sr., or Sam Parise, who looked down on the world from where the air was thin, as Buddy's father would say, up seven and a half feet off the ground. Duncan Orrick's stature was of another kind.

Though he had overstrong emotions that might easily have led him into sentimentality—the same too painful, too easily triggered emotions that his father in his own life had hidden by bluster and an affected sternness—he was not swayed by his emotions to an espousal of wrong causes or misjudgment of men. Though he had a streak of boyish weakness, a timidity that amounted almost to cowardice, he would not be ruled by it but acted bravely, even courageously, standing up to dangers in a way that might bring credit to a man with twice Duncan Orrick's natural courage. As a representative to the National Synod of the Presbyterian Church, he spoke on the floor in opposition to church support of the Cesar Chavez California lettuce boycott, an action that demanded more courage than he would have thought he had. Though he was impressed by Chavez—despite the man's bullying arrogance—and was moved by his statement on the suffering of Chicano farm laborers, it seemed to him wrong that the church legislate the conscience of its members, supporting the destruction of a lettuce crop in a year of world-wide famine; and despite the cynical and monstrous crimes of California agro-businesses (like all small farmers, he hated agro-business in any shape or form with a murderous passion that brought tears to his eyes and made him stammer), he believed it wrong that the church should support one farm union against another and approve the ruin of small farmers whose nonunion help consisted, in California as everywhere else, of their unpaid or grossly underpaid sons and daughters.

"If the small farmer can't compete honestly, let him get out," said the man at Chavez's side. He smiled like a plump, sharp-whiskered cat, knowing well enough that the man in the aisle was himself a small farmer. The man on the platform was comfortable with these conflicts, in fact thoroughly enjoyed them. Duncan Orrick had no great distaste for a verbal fight himself, at the local Elba school board meeting, or at a meeting, back home, of the Board of Elders at his church. But here, he knew, he was out of place, outclassed. It was a forbidding, ultramodern auditorium that smelled of cigar smoke, seats like theater seats falling away—as it seemed to Duncan

Orrick's myopic eyes—like a restless sea. In the front of the room, the speaker's table, the chair's glowing gavel, the silver microphones on long, silver booms, filled him with awkwardness and apprehension.

No one rose to help him. He resisted the powerful temptation to sit down. Red-skinned and uncomfortable, his left foot hurting in its new black shoe, he said mildly, but with a trembling voice that rang through the hall, "Get out of business, you say. You and agro-business are on the same side there, with all your money and power and certainty you're right. Against odds like that, a small man's got hardly any choice but to stand up against you." There were shouts of "Hear, hear!"

The Synod talked, too, about women's liberation, about the Supreme Good as biblically male, about the need for rewriting the sexist hymnbooks—"Faith of our fathers, living still." He watched in anguish as furious, angry-hearted women read passages of Scripture that, it seemed to them, reviled their kind, or read, in shrill voices, lines out of hymns or standard prayers. From time to time the assembly laughed—when it was pointed out, for instance, that altering the hymnbooks would cost five million dollars, "assuming we make all the changes ourselves, instead of hiring an army of expensive lady poets." The laughter troubled him, filled him with distress and helpless confusion in the same way the anger of the women had done. He had difficulty breathing, all at once. He was old, at the time of this Synod meeting, and his heart was not good. He had chest pains more or less constantly, especially in winter, and sometimes when something upset him they flamed higher, became alarming.

His wife of fifty years sat beside him, listening, not laughing with the others except for an occasional "Mpf!" as if at something in her mind, and when she looked over at him now she did not at once see that something was wrong with him. "What will they think of next!" she said, and smiled her crooked smile—still pretty, still lively, though she was seventy-two. It was a fact that she did not like these young women, their strident voices, their extreme, intentionally abrasive opinions, above all their absolute indifference to what was for her (as for her cousin Donald Frazier) the central truth of the Christian religion, Love God, and thy neighbor as thyself.

"They're right," he said.

She looked at him, surprised and perhaps a trifle cross, but willing to consider his point of view.

"But they're asking for a whole new religion," he whispered. "They can't understand it's a historical process—the Virgin birth, the Apostle's Creed . . ."

She understood what he meant. Like all old, happily married couples, they'd been talking in a kind of code for years. She touched his hand. Hers was white and liver-spotted, his, dark red and rough, with cuts and scabs where he'd barked his knuckles prying a board loose or tightening a bolt with a wrench too large. "You should tell them, Duncan. You should raise your hand and tell them."

"No, I can't," he said. He tried to get his breath.

"You should. It's something they should think about."

"No, no."

She leaned closer to him, pursing her lips. "Are you all right?" she said.

"Perhaps I need some air."

They got up, with difficulty, their bodies old and stiff, and moved toward the exit, he slightly tilted, favoring his back, she walking with a great rolling limp, legacy of the time, a few years earlier, when she'd broken her hip.

The woman on the platform was reading angrily, ". . . and the glory of children are their fathers."

He was better, out on the street, walking.

She said, "I think you should have stood up and told them what you think, Duncan."

"I couldn't seem to get my breath," he said. "But next time."

Five

On two or three occasions when the two families met in Missouri, the reason for the visit was that Buddy's family had driven out to pick up his Grandma Davis—his mother's mother, Joan's father's aunt—who had been staying, for the past six months, with the Missouri cousins. She stayed with the Orricks normally, but it was in Missouri that she'd grown up—John Frazier's twinkling, hell-raising sister—and it was in Missouri that she'd met her Welshman husband, a carpenter, and raised her children. The house she'd lived in had burned to the ground many years ago, and the friends of her childhood and the days of marriage—those who weren't dead—were scattered now from coast to coast, living with relatives as she did, or at any rate most of them were. But even with her friends gone she loved Missouri and obviously belonged there. Though yellowish white now, her hair had once been red—like her brother's, like Buddy's mother's, like Donald Frazier's, like Joan's—and her complexion, though faded, still carried a hint, like a painting's undercoat, of the warmth that came from Missouri sunlight or the red Missouri earth. She could be happy anywhere, she always said, and it was true, no doubt; she loved to be with people, hear their stories, look carefully through their photograph albums, glance over at the children, observe their changes; but it was also true that whenever they drove across the Chain-of-Rocks Bridge, bringing her home for one of her visits, her face took on a mysterious peacefulness, as if she thought she was entering the Promised Land. She stayed sometimes with Betty Lou's family, sometimes with her brother for a day or two. She didn't get on well with her sister-in-law Lulu: against Lulu's fierce Baptist righteousness she raised the impenetrable, infuriating battlements of her placid, all-forgiving Methodist piety, proving in her brother's hushed, worried house that, though it may not be the case that "a soft answer turneth away wrath," it is certainly true that it can leave wrath speechless, fuming, and more terrible than before. Her brother, who had his own ways of dealing with things, would sit rocking on the porch, his narrow head tipping in rhythm with the rocker, his crafty, wickedly humorous eyes gazing off through the peach trees that edged his front lawn—his sister in the lumpy gray armchair beside him, Lulu in the house banging pots and pans as if seeing what it took to knock holes in them—and he would say, for instance, "Sis, I b'lieve you better move on into Donald's before Lulu gets so riled I got to shoot her."

Mostly, during her Missouri visits, she stayed with Joan's parents, Donald and Emmy. She was an even-tempered, generous woman who, little as she had, supported more charities than a man could shake a stick at. She would gladly mind the children, wash the dishes, dust-mop the floors, do whatever was needed, though it was not in her nature to notice, especially in a house as meticulously, inhumanly German-clean as Emmy's, that things needed doing. She would sit in the livingroom reading old copies of the *Reader's Digest* or taking a little nap sitting upright in her chair, her head supported by her goiter, and it would never occur to her to wonder what on earth had become of Emily (she was down in the basement, doing the wash, feeling persecuted); or she would sit in the kitchen, hands folded on the table, talking about old times or kinfolk, while Emmy washed and wiped the dishes, cut up celery and carrots, peeled potatoes, shucked peas, husked corn, sifted flour, made lemonade and tea, and Emmy would answer Grandma Davis's questions with seeming interest or would remark, "Well ye-es," or "I declare." Since, like most people, Donald and Emmy made abstract, general human virtues of the particular natures they happened to possess, they never dreamed of hinting to Grandma Davis that if she was going to live with them—eat their food, use their telephone, sleep in their bed, pile her amber hairpins on the dresser that was theirs—she should try to be a little more help. Asking her to work would have tried their basic timidity, and since they, in her place, would have seen at a glance what needed doing and would have done it, they could only feel she took terrible advantage of their hospitality. She would have been shocked and hurt if she'd ever had the faintest inkling of how they felt—if she'd known, for instance, that when she was well out of earshot Donald would sometimes call her, with a giggle and a blush, "the Queen."

For all that, she was in fact something of a queen. Much of the day she wrote letters in her room, keeping up with the friends and relatives she had left, or sending whatever little pittance she might have to needy Indians, orphans, southern Negroes, churches or medical stations in Africa and India, Oklahoma and New York. She was a preserver of traditions and rituals, telling the children stories of the family, how her father's people had come up from South Carolina to Kentucky and eventually to Missouri—you could walk in a straight line all day long and never leave Frazier land—or she would gather them around her chair and read the Bible to them, explaining the meaning of everything, explaining without rancor—with sympathy, in fact—how the Jews, despite all the warnings of the prophets, had betrayed Our Lord and had been forced, exactly as the prophets foretold, to wander the face of the earth all these centuries, despised by mankind, and had never been granted a home. "It's a strange thing, a terrible strange thing," she said thoughtfully, almost with distress, but never for an instant would she question her Maker's plan.

Buddy Orrick would remember all the rest of his life certain moments from those times Grandma Davis had spent with them, talking of Jesus and heaven's golden streets and angels. He would remember her reading of the story of Samuel, and how deeply impressed he had been by its message: if ever he should hear a voice call his name in the middle of the night, when everyone was asleep, he should answer, "Here am I, Lord." Joan would remember not the briefest flicker of those pleasant times—perhaps she'd experienced fewer of them; more likely she'd seen past Grandma Davis's opinions instinctively and, when the old woman talked, let her mind wander. What she remembered—not clearly, but with the greatest pleasure—was a book her mother had read to her, a large book with pictures that had a great deal of purple in them, the story of Mr. Mixiedough, a story that somehow involved the whole world's becoming dark.

Though most of her old Missouri friends were dead, Grandma Davis could count on seeing those who were left, or at least all those within driving distance of Florissant, Missouri, because they came to the meetings of the Cemetery Association.

Long before Joan and Buddy's time there had been, on an abrupt, sunlit rise in a hollow—a place unreachable now except by an overgrown farm lane—a square, white church with plain glass windows and a bell tower built like a wooden box with a well roof over it. In the yellowed photograph on Joan Orrick's wall, the church is a clean, well-carpentered building as sturdy and simple as a Shaker chair, so pure of line, so right in its proportions, so decorous—even the hitching posts as strong and direct as good sculptures—that the mind is teased toward wonder at the taste and common sense of the long-dead farmers, blacksmiths, storekeepers, and carpenters who built it. Two of the hitching posts remain, and the tree that in the photograph was a ten-foot-high sapling by the square front door is now a large maple, beginning to split and die. Around where the church was in former times, the high thin burial stones still stand, cocked this way and that by the shiftings of the earth, bearing the names—some of them mere shadows—of the people who were once Grandma Davis's kinsmen and neighbors: Patterson, Weimer, Jones, Hughes, Thompson, Frazier, Carrico, Davis, Kilpatrick, Burke. One finds there first names the world no longer hears, names Joan and Martin would jestingly consider when trying, years later, to think what to call their children: Lycurgus, Ezekiel, Asanath, Thester. Where the trees at the edge of the cemetery begin—some of them in among the trees, in fact, since the woods have begun to reclaim the land—stand the smaller, simpler headstones of family slaves. Though it's hard these days to get a casket in, people still bury there. The Cemetery Association pays the taxes and mows the grass, or did until Donald Frazier, who used to do the mowing, had a heart attack, and Joan Orrick arranged for the formation of a chapter of the DAR and got the hollow declared—rightly enough—"historic."

They would meet, Grandma Davis and her elderly friends, in the centrally located house of one of the most ancient of the members, in the heart of St. Louis. The pictures had oval, carved oak-leaf frames, the chairs were plush and wobbly, two loud clocks ticked, the glasses with ice water were dark, dark green or the deep red of candlelit blood.

"Pretend it's a roomful of ghosts," Joan whispered, and giggled behind her hands, sitting with Buddy on the cushioned window seat in the corner of the parlor—behind them, stiff, yellowing lace curtains.

They were receiving, no doubt, the same impression—the familiar faces of Donald and Emmy, John Elmer and Cora (the youngest in the room, but gaunt, transmogrified by the age-blackened wallpaper, the dark, cracked furniture, vases and mirrors, fringed table covers and piano runners), the more ominous faces of Joan's grandpa and grandma and Buddy's Grandma

Davis, and the faces of strangers, pale and liver-spotted, people in dark, strange-smelling clothes, with canes against their knees, or wooden crutches with rubber end-plugs, people who gestured or lifted their glasses with snow-white trembling hands. But though Joan was amused, pleasantly alarmed (if she let herself be) by the hint of mortality in every gleam of wood or old silver or glass, every dull, fading plane of upholsterer's cloth—she thought of shining caskets, the gray of old bone—Buddy was inclined to be frightened.

"I don't want to," he said.

Though both of them were ten, he was—thanks to his country background, his Grandma Davis, and his tendency to moon-gather—an incredible innocent, which made her laugh and feel, rightly, much older and wiser than he. She told him now of a funeral she'd been to, teasing him, delighting in her power to frighten or soothe him, exactly as she pleased. She whispered in his ear, "The *eyes* were open. People tried to close them, but they *wouldn't stay closed!*" She watched eagerly, waiting for his reaction.

He looked out at the sunlit street, a cat moving slowly toward a tree beside the sidewalk. It would be cool there. Here inside, the room was overheated and smelled strongly of kerosene. He sat perfectly still, wondering if the things she was telling him were so, his expression as solemn as an old man's. To Joan he looked that moment like her grandpa's old brown dog, sitting with his head tipped, waiting, sad as could be, for someone to pet him. He turned from the window, threw a worried look around the room, and said seriously, "I hope *you* never die," and glanced at her.

She laughed, and saw that her laughter had hurt his feelings. "Everybody dies," she said, and smiled, making up.

"I know," he said doubtfully, "and goes to heaven."

She smiled sadly. "And has to switch to harp."

Once when they went to Missouri to bring Grandma Davis home, Joan's parents showed home movies. They were, of course, the only people he knew who had a movie camera. They all sat down in the livingroom in Joan's father's house, Grandma Davis's armchair pulled up close to the screen, because her eyes were bad, Joan's mother and his parents in diningroom chairs along the side of the room, looking oddly prim, John Elmer and Aunt Cora against the wall behind Grandma Davis's chair, he and Joan by the back wall with her two brothers and his own brother, Gilbert, four years younger than himself. They were all talking, Aunt Cora leaning over toward Grandma Davis. Joan's father fussed with the machine, trying to get the square of light to hit the square of the screen—he had the projector set up on the piano bench and was poking magazines under the front, trying to get the right angle.

Joan's mother reached up for the lightswitch on the light green wall behind her, and Joan's brother James yelled, "Show the cartoons!"

Her younger brother echoed, "Cartoons! Cartoons! Felix the Cat!"

Buddy glanced over at his brother, who grinned.

"No cartoons!" Joan's father said, and laughed and blushed as if to say, "You little monkeys!" and started the projector. The lights went off. The projector whirred and clicked, and numbers inside targets showed jerkily on the screen. In burning summer light Joan's father's car appeared, halfway on the screen and moving across it. It stopped, and after a long time in which nothing at all happened and no one spoke, the doors opened, and Emmy got out of the driver's seat, while John Elmer and Cora got out of the back, followed by their son Bobby, and then Joan and her brother James, who'd gotten out the other side, came walking around the front.

"*There* they are!" John Elmer said. Everybody laughed.

They all waved, looking at the camera, and Joan's mother slowly put the back of her hand to her face. Suddenly the picture was of someone's backyard, much darker, and Joan's youngest brother, with white, white hair, was walking toward the camera, smiling from ear to ear, moving awkwardly, like a calf, his legs in shiny steel braces.

"Look at 'im go!" John Elmer said.

Before they could laugh, Joan was in front of a large building, wearing what looked like a Sunday dress and holding flowers.

"That's after Joan's recital," Emmy said, partly pleased, partly apologetic.

Joan walked toward the camera. The picture suddenly stopped jerking, as if the moment was important; but nothing came of it, she walked on out of the picture without once looking up. Instantly she was back, the same dress, the same flowers, but now she was looking at the camera, smiling.

"That's a mighty pretty girl," Buddy's father said.

His mother said, with conviction, *"Isn't* she."

"Looks like Sonja Henie," John Elmer said.

"Oh, John," Aunt Cora said.

And then, with mild horror, Buddy realized that he himself was in this movie. His parents' car was parked beside the curb, and they were all getting out. He remembered before his picture appeared on the screen that as they walked toward the house Joan's father was running the movie camera, and he remembered that as he passed he, Buddy, had made a face. Only now did he realize the implications, and the skin of his face began to sting. His mother and father went past the camera—Joan's father had made them come one by one—and then Gilbert came by, smiling shyly—he had dark, slightly curly hair and eyes like his father's, a little mysterious, as though, perhaps, he'd been a child once before and had not been happy, though he was happy now. He seemed wiser, gentler than the rest of his family—or was that, perhaps, a trick of Martin Orrick's memory, thinking back to that image on the screen long afterward? His brother Gilbert moved out of the picture and he saw himself coming, with none of his brother's confidence, though he was older, and he knew the stupid, obscene face must come, and waited, sick at heart, and it came—he stuck his tongue out, put his thumbs into his ears—and was gone almost instantly *(Life is fleeting,* Martin Orrick would write, long afterward, *even the worst of life is fleeting),* and everyone laughed. The screen was darkened by an image of Grandma Davis in a black dress. She seemed in the picture unnaturally large, somehow frightening. She moved very slowly on her heavy cane, smiling in a way that seemed not at all like her, and Joan, in the darkness beside him, laughed. As if the laugh had been a signal, her brother James, in the darkness just beyond her, said, "Here comes the Queen," and their father turned and gave him a quick look. Immediately, as if miraculously, the image was replaced by one of Joan in a white tennis outfit, white shirt, white shorts.

"That's a mighty pretty girl," Buddy's father said.

Her red hair swirled around her shoulders like fire, like copper, like a flying mane.

He glanced at his brother beside him, who caught the glance and grinned.

She was moving toward the camera. Perhaps her father, holding the camera, said something funny. She smiled.

John Elmer said, trying to be funny, "Here comes the Queen!"

They politely laughed.

The image went lighter, and still lighter, then froze, and suddenly she vanished like a ghost.

"Lights!" Joan's father said.

Her mother reached up to the wall switch and turned on the lights.

Six

It would be a strange thing, she often thought, to have second sight, as her Grandma Frazier was supposed to have had, and Martin's uncle George. It occurred to her, for instance, one day when she was forty, when Martin stopped the car to wait for a light at the corner of Olive Street and Grand, in St. Louis. What would she have thought—sometime in the late 1940s, standing on this corner, on her way to her part-time accompanist's job at the Duggers School of the Dance—if she had suddenly had a vision of what downtown St. Louis would be like just twenty-five years later? What would she have thought—what would she have felt—standing on that crowded, noisy corner—if the crowd had suddenly thinned to just three or four hurrying figures and the buildings had gone solemn, like prison or mausoleum walls? She imagined the vision coming as pure image, like a photograph or drab documentary film, with no hint of explanation—saw herself, in her 1940s schoolgirl's clothes, pleated skirt and short-sleeved sweater, a dark green coat and simple, light green head-scarf, bobbysox and loafers, her hair in a permanent, shiny and curly and a trifle stiff, books in her arm—since she came in directly from school on the bus, or on a chain of buses that shuttled her from Ferguson to Normandy to Wellston to downtown. There had been—was it on this corner?—a wonderful ice-cream place, the Park Plaza, where for a dollar you could get a parfait two feet high, and all around this section there were magnificent theaters, as colorful as circuses, with high, bold marquees on which yellow, red, blue, green, purple, and white lights (lightbulbs, she remembered, and even then some that had burned out weren't replaced) went racing around titles four feet high —*Rope, The Return of Frank James*—and inside, the theaters were like palaces: great gilded lions; red-velvet-covered, three-inch-thick ropes on golden posts; majestic, wide stairways that made everyone an instant king or queen; ushers in uniforms from the days of the Empire (God knew which empire); and in the great, domed theater itself a hush that was patently religious, the boom of voices from the people on the screen coming from all sides and from within, or so it seemed, oracular. All the great stores had been downtown then, Famous-Barr, for instance, glittering, high-ceilinged, ceremonious inside its towering, gold-framed revolving doors, the aisles choked with shoppers, most of them white, the counters and high walls vending wonders—coats and solemn-toned, stately dresses with the sleeves pinned out, far overhead, like hovering angels—and everywhere draped artificial-pearl necklaces or ruby-red or pool-ball-green or -blue or -yellow costume baubles, bracelets the color of copper in flame, and everywhere the scent of perfumes and talcums, newly printed books, the leather of new shoes, a smell as exciting and at the same time cloying as a vault of roses in one of the big downtown flowershops, or the thick, sweet incense in a Catholic church. Suppose in the twinkling of an eye, Joan imagined, that whole world vanished, and the girl on the corner, herself at fifteen, looked, stunned and afraid, at a city gone dark and empty, at least by comparison with the teeming, bright, jubilant city she knew: there came a silence, as if all the gay sounds of the world had been abruptly turned off, like the music and static on a radio; and there came the same instant a visual stillness, as if a heart had stopped—no motion but three or four hurrying Negroes, strangely dressed, dangerous, with hair grown long and puffed up like that in a Tarzan picture; nothing else stirring but two pigeons overhead and a newspaper blowing along the pavement. "I'm in the future!" the imaginary Joan would have thought, "and there's been some awful war, or a plague, and the world's been ruined." Who'd await the future if she could see it in advance? No use to tell the girl on the corner, "We're happy, Joan. Don't be afraid! There are beautiful places, though this one may be gone." She'd have backed away, frightened and betrayed—yes, terrified, of course, it came to her now. What else could she be, addressed by a strange, wild woman in dark glasses such as Negroes wore then in the most dangerous parts of East St. Louis, a fur coat that looked as if the animal had died at an instant of terror, every hair on end—a woman whose beauty was like fine cutlery, hair falling plain as an Indian's, except red, as brightly burnished and fiery as her own—leaning from the window of a dark blue Mercedes Benz driven by—how weird!—a sorrowful, baggy-eyed man with silver hair that swept down like angelhair past his heavy, hunched shoulders—a monster who was, she had a feeling, suddenly, someone she was meant to recognize. The girl would have stepped back in fear and anger, raising her hand to the braces on her teeth, and the real Joan would have called to her, shouting past the years in pity and anguish, "Child, child, don't be silly! We're as harmless as you are, we've betrayed nobody, nothing! *Look* at us!" Now the child did look, and recognition came into her eyes: the rich, wildly eccentric lady (who had beautiful teeth, Joan thought and smiled, feeling a surge of affection for the big-nosed innocent on the corner), the lady in the fur, with emeralds and a ruby and a diamond on her fingers, was herself—or her own "child," Wordsworth would say—and the driver was Buddy Orrick, grown sadder and crazier, but still alive, and married to her: so they'd made it, they'd survived! She came a step nearer, her face eager, full of questions *(we could drive her to Duggers,* the real Joan thought; *it's only a few blocks)* and her small hand came cautiously toward the real Joan's hand on the Mercedes' wing-window, both hands equally pale and solid, the child's and the woman's, until suddenly the child's hand was gone and Joan Orrick was gazing at cracked sidewalk, a piece of dirty cardboard.

Martin glanced over and saw her tears. "Hurting?" he asked.

And yes, she was hurting, as she nearly always hurt, these days, sometimes such pain that she passed out for a moment—hurting even when the drugs were at work, as now, causing visions—but she said, "No," and gave him a reassuring smile, "just thinking."

He reached over, touched her hand. The light changed, and the big car glided forward without a sound.

She said, "Duggers School of the Dance was just up ahead. Remember?"

"Which building?" He ducked down over the steering wheel to look up.

She pointed as the car came abreast of it. It had been gutted by fire, like most of the buildings in this neighborhood. He scanned the boarded-up, blackened storefronts. She could see he wasn't sure which one she meant.

Jacqui Duggers was tiny, the classic teacher of ballet but in perfect miniature, hair so tightly drawn back you might have thought from a distance that it was paint, as on a Japanese doll. She spoke with the accent all ballet teachers use, even those raised in Milwaukee or St. Louis, wiped her forehead with the back of her wrist like an actress, called Joan "dahling" with perfect seriousness and unfeigned affection, though one might not have noticed the affection at first glance, since she was always hurried, always slightly tense, as if she had to catch a plane for Munich or Paris in half an hour. She was—or so it seemed to Joan—a superb dancer, though Joan never saw her dance more than a few steps; and old photographs suggest that Joan's impression was right: the Jacqui Duggers in the pictures has that indefinable look—authority perhaps—that one sees at a glance in all real professionals, and she had danced with good companies of the so-called second rank in both the United States and Canada. "Ah-*wone*," she would say, and Joan's hands would move automatically on the keys of the piano.

Her husband, Pete Duggers, taught tap-dance in the mirror-walled studio below. He was nearly as small as she was, but thicker, almost stout, in fact, and he looked and moved like some Disney cartoon of a tap-dance teacher. He had a red face and wonderfully merry blue eyes, wore vests and old-fashioned arm-suspenders. If he ever touched the floor when he walked (and he did), it seemed at least to Joan that he did so by momentary whim. Jacqui's movements at the barre had a look not of lightness, the cancellation of gravity, but of majestic, powerful control, as if her muscles were steel and could no more speed up or slow down against her will than the hands of a clock could escape the inclinations of their mainspring. Rising on her toes in the middle of the room—a brief jerk and click as the heel and ankle locked, a brief trembling like a spasm, then the firmness of an iron wedge—she gave the impression that touching her calf or thigh would be like touching a wall. Pete's dancing feet moved, on the other hand, as if swinging by themselves, as if his body were suspended like a puppet's from invisible wires. His taps were light and quick, as if he never put his weight down with either foot, and they rattled out around him as gaily and casually—and as incredibly fast—as the fingers of his Negro piano player, a tall, flat-haired boy who sat sprawling in his chair with his head tipped far over so that he seemed to be always, except for his forearms and fingers, fast asleep. The speed and lightness with which Pete Duggers danced were amazing to behold, but what was truly miraculous, so that it made you catch your breath, was the way he could stop, completely relaxed, leaning his elbow on empty air and grinning as if he'd been standing there for hours, all that movement and sound you'd been hearing pure phantom and illusion. That was unfailingly the climax when he danced: the slow build, the elegant shuffles and turns, then more speed, and more, and more and

still more until it seemed that the room spun drunkenly, crazily, all leading—direct as the path of an arrow—to nothing—everything—a sudden
stillness like an escape from reality, a sudden floating, whether terrible or
wonderful she could never tell: the abrupt hush of a symphonic orchestra
dropped away, falling back from the soaring melody of a single French
horn—or then again, perhaps, the frightening silence one read about in novels when a buzz-bomb shut off over London. He stood perfectly still, the
piano was still, his young students gaped, and then abruptly reality came
back again as the piano tinkled lightly and he listlessly danced and, as he
did so, leaned toward his students and winked and said, "You see? Magic!"

Olive Street was already going down at that time, so the storefront was
shoddy, solo dancers and dance-class pictures on the windows, big, vulgar
stars, the glass around the pictures crudely painted dark blue, as if the Duggers School of the Dance were some miserable third-rate establishment not
worth breaking into or stealing from, though the door was not locked. But
that was a trick—the dancing Duggerses had trunkfuls of tricks: artists to
the marrow of their chipped and splintered bones. The scuffed, unpainted
door in front opened into a scuffed, unpainted entryway with a door to
the left and a knotty, crooked stairway leading upward. On the door to
the left, a sign said TAP DANCE STUDIO, and above the worn railing at the
side of the stairs, a sign, cocked parallel to the railing, said, SCHOOL OF THE
BALLET ☞ . When you opened the door to the tap-dance studio for the
first time, you did a mighty double-take: there were glittering mirrors with
round-arched tops and etched designs of the sort Joan would occasionally
discover years later in the oldest London pubs, and above the mirrors there
were walls of red and gold and a magnificent stamped-tin ceiling. It was
a large building, at one time a theater. The tap-dance studio (and the ballet
studio directly above it) took up the first thirty feet; then there was a railing,
also red and gold, from which one looked out at the long, wide ballroom
floor, at the front an enormous stage with ratty wine-colored velvet curtains, along the side-walls wall-candelabra between high painted panels—dancing graces, Zeus in his majesty, nymphs and satyrs, peacocks and
fat, reclining nudes done in highly unsuccessful imitation of the style of
Rubens.

She'd walked there with Buddy once, when he'd motorcycled in from
his school in Indiana and offered to drive her to work in her father's DeSoto.
He'd driven fast, as usual, his eye rolling up to the rear-view mirror, on

the look-out for police cars, and had gotten her to work much too early.

"Care to have an interesting experience?" she'd said.

Their footsteps echoed. The ballroom was fairly dark. They could just make out the carved figures on the ceiling, two storeys up, circling around the empty spaces from which once had hung huge chandeliers.

"It's like a church," he said.

She'd squeezed his hand and they'd stopped and, after a moment, kissed, then walked on, up to the front of the ballroom and up onto the stage, where the Duggers students gave their dance recitals. They looked up at the shuttered lights, ropes, catwalks—it was darker here, and spooky, as if the stage machinery belonged not only to a different time but to a different planet. Again they paused to kiss, and he put his arms around her and after a minute she moved his hand to the front of her sweater, then under the sweater to her breast. With his usual difficulty, for all his practice, he unsnapped her bra. She felt her nipples rising, and he pressed closer to her. With a grandiose sweep of his free arm in the direction of the dim, ghost-filled ballroom, he said, "Lady, how would you like to be fucked, right here in front of all these people?"

"Hmm," she said. After a moment, still with his hand on her breast, her hand keeping it there, she led him toward the further wing and the small door opening on a room she'd discovered weeks earlier, half-filled with crates, electric wire, old tools, and the rotting frames of old sets. There were a few old pieces of furniture—chairs, tables, couches—protected from the dust by tarpaulins. "Maybe we need a rehearsal," she said. They passed under a high window through which a single crack of light came and she glanced at her watch. Ten minutes. She stood looking around, both his hands on her breasts, until he finally noticed the couch and went over and pulled away the tarpaulin. As he came into her, huge and overeager, as always—but so was she, so was she—she said, "Isn't this an interesting experience?"

The whole left side of the building, as you entered from the street, was the Duggerses' apartment. It was the most beautiful apartment she'd ever seen, though not as original or even as spectacularly tasteful as she imagined at the time; she would see many like it in San Francisco, and far more elegant examples of the white-on-white style in London and Paris. Everything was white, the walls, the furniture, the chains that held the chandeliers, the wooden shutters on the windows. Against all that white, the things they'd collected stood out in bold relief: paintings, presumably by friends, all very curious and impressive, at least to Joan—smudges, bright splashes of color, one canvas all white with little scratches of gray and bright blue; sculptures—a beautiful abstraction in dark wood, a ballet dancer made out of pieces of old wire, museum reproductions, a mobile of wood and stainless steel; books and records, shelves upon shelves of them. Their record-player was the largest she'd ever seen and had a speaker that stood separate from the rest. Once when Jacqui invited her in, to write Joan her check for her week's work, Jacqui, leading the way to the kitchen, stopped suddenly, turned with a ballerina's step, and said, "Joanie, I must show you my shoes, no?" "I'd like to see them," Joan said. Jacqui swept over to the side of the room, her small hand gracefully flying ahead of her, and pushed open a white sliding door. Joan stared. On tilted shelves that filled half the room's wall, Jacqui had three hundred pairs of tiny shoes. She had all colors—gold and silver, yellow, red, green, some with long ties as bright as new ribbons, some with little bows, some black and as plain as the inside of a pocket. "Where'd you *get* all these?" Joan said. Jacqui laughed. "Mostly Paris." She gave Joan a quick, appraising look. "Dahling, Paris you are going to love. There is a store, a department store, Au Printemps. When you go there, blow a kiss for Jacqui!" She rolled her eyes heavenward. "Ah, the French!"

Years later, the first time Joan shopped at Au Printemps, she would remember that, and would do as she'd been told. And she would remember Jacqui too a few years later when, at Lambert Field in St. Louis, deplaning with her family from a European trip, a news crew of very cool, very smart blacks from KSDF-TV approached her with camera and wind-baffled shotgun microphones and asked if she had any suggestions for the improvement of services at the airport. "Way-el," she said, smiling prettily, batting her lashes, and speaking in her sweetest Possum Hollow drawl. She tapped her mouth with a bejewelled finger and gazed thoughtfully down the baggage area, then said pertly, as if it were something she'd been thinking for a long time and rather hated to bring up, "Ah thank it would be nice if awl these people spoke French." Her performance was included in that night's local news. Her parents missed it, as was perhaps just as well. Relatives called to tell them with pleasure that Joanie had been on television. No one mentioned that anything she'd said was funny, much less "peculiar."

"I wonder if I ever will get to Paris," she'd said thoughtfully, that afternoon in Jacqui's apartment.

Jacqui had laughed like a young girl, though she was then over forty. "Keep playing the piano and don't theenk twice," Jacqui said. "If you don't go to Paris, then Paris will have to come to you."

Where would they have gone, Joan wondered now, when the neighborhood had grown too dangerous to live in? Were they still alive? It came to her suddenly, for no apparent reason, that Pete Duggers had looked like the hero of her favorite childhood book, Mr. Mixiedough, in the story of the whole world's slipping into darkness. It was a book she'd wanted for Evan and Mary, but there seemed to be no copies left anywhere; not even the book-search people from whom Martin got his rare old books could find a trace of it. Had it been the same, perhaps, with Pete and Jacqui Duggers—swallowed up, vanished into blackness? She'd asked about him once at the Abbey, on 13th Street in New York, when she'd gone to, three times, a show called *The Hoofers,* which had brought back all the great old soft-shoe and tap men. On the sidewalk in front of the theater afterward, while she was waiting for Martin to come and pick her up, she'd talked with Bojangles Robinson and Sand Man Sims—they'd shown her some steps and had laughed and clapped their hands, dancing one on each side of her—and she'd asked if either of them had ever heard of Pete Duggers.

The Sand Man rolled up his eyes and lifted off his hat as if to look inside it. "Duggers," he'd said, searching through his memory.

"You say the man worked out of San Looie?" Bojangles said.

"I played piano for his wife," Joan said. "She taught ballet."

"Duggers," said the Sand Man. "That surely does sound familiar."

"White man married to a *bal*let teacher," Bojangles said, and ran his hand across his mouth. "Boy that surely rings a bell, some way."

"Duggers," the Sand Man said, squinting at the lighted sky. "Duggers."

"He used to go faster and faster and then suddenly stand still," she said. "He was a wonderful dancer."

"Duggers," Bojangles echoed, thoughtful, staring at his shoes. "I know the man sure as I'm standing here. I got him right on the tip of my mind."

Seven

"Change our lives?" Martin said, as if wearily amused, raising his eyebrows. It was Joan who had made the absurd suggestion, watching with narrowed eyes as Paul Brotsky stood stirring the martinis, around and around, looking at the carpet, thinking his own thoughts, or listening to the circling music. The suggestion wasn't really absurd, of course; more painful than that. He knew what changes he would make, if change were possible. But he, Martin, was fighting no more fights. Should he admire men stronger and braver than himself, destiny hunters who left skeletons in their wake like Melville's whalers—like Melville himself, when it came to that? He would accept what by chance and stupidity he had become: straight man to a clowning, half-wit universe, merry-go-round of Dame Fortune, stiff, groping zodiac. He would bury himself in events one more time, and one more, and one more, learn to breathe without air. He would write when he was able, patch up the age-old necessary illusions as painters repair old carousel panels, and would keep himself, the rest of the time, just slightly, not belligerently, drunk.

He looked over at his children, seated back to back with an oversize, woven Greek pillow between them on the waterbed couch beside the door leading out to the front lawn. Their long blond hair, the gentleness of their faces, the stillness with which they sat were almost identical—"Of *course,* my dear boy, two Capricorns, you see!" John Napper would say. Which suggested that they were there to see that all went well—Capricorn vigilance. *No need to fear, my beloved cautious watchers,* he thought; but they couldn't know that, after all they'd been through; nor could he. "Cancer and Leo!" John Napper had said, shaking his wild, majestic head, eyes twinkling merrily, standing away from his painting a moment to consider from this new, unexpected angle the miracle of life. "Makes for the stormiest of all possible marriages—high water and hell respectively, you know—but splendid when it finally settles itself!" He lifted his head, lips pursed, that strange, mad joy of his bursting from his eyes and hair like Blakean sunlight, or like the light that redeemed all memory in one of his own incomparable landscapes. "Splendid," he said, and hung fire like a conductor delaying for an instant the expected jubilant final chord, beaming with delight, divinely impish, then said it again, the universe from end to end his shining orchestra: "*Splen*did!" And Martin, for all his doubts about his marriage, had believed him absolutely. How could one doubt such authority? But he was now less certain of the things he'd believed that summer in England, in John Napper's sun-filled studio: remembered his feelings only as one remembers the feelings one had while reading, say, *Anna Karenina* sometime fifteen years ago.

Though it was true, of course, that his watchful Capricorns had influence. More influence, probably, than any to be found in the warring Crab and Lion. Loving his children, he could not help but be marginally optimistic; observing how they loved their mother, he couldn't help but see that his absolute distrust of her must be—in some way he couldn't yet fathom—a mistake. For that reason too he would bury his feelings, watch and wait. —Yet that was not, he would realize later, what he did. Mockingly, meaning to provoke wrath, he said—though he was unaware himself that his voice was mocking—"How in the hell are we supposed to, as you say, change our lives?" He held out his glass, and Paul Brotsky poured martini in from the pitcher he'd just mixed.

Stirring again, allowing the martini to water a touch more before pouring one for Joan, Paul said, "I don't know, I think change is possible." He spoke casually yet seriously, subtly avoiding confrontation by treating the question as essentially abstract, philosophical. He stood looking at the floor, stirring absentmindedly. He was black-bearded, short and heavy, stooped with what looked like weariness or too much thought, though he wasn't yet thirty. Without looking up he turned and carried the pitcher to where Joan sat, surrounded by large pillows, on the waterbed couch opposite the children's. He walked, as always, like a man slowly pacing, alone in his office. There were reasons for that. In Viet Nam he'd been separated from the company he'd trained with—temporarily drawn from the group for a desk job—and in their first mission every one of them had been killed. He wrote fiction now, or tried to. He had the necessary sympathy born of pain, the necessary intelligence and insight, even wisdom, and more than the necessary ability with words. But grief and self-doubt made his heart unsteady, undermined his purpose. He was still too close to that dramatic proof of the ultimate senselessness of all human acts to walk with much confidence on solid ground.

"Joan, you ready for more?" he said. She held out her glass, touched her throat with her left hand, and nodded. She wore a midnight-green Japanese robe with golden dragons, a plunging neckline, a golden belt, one of the many things she'd bought on their trip for the U.S. Information Service. Watching the two of them, his head tipped down, his two hands closed on his martini glass, Martin Orrick thought, coolly, objectively, what dramatic promise the scene would hold if one were to see it on a movie screen: a luxurious room overlooking a lighted swimming pool, an elegant wine rack—nearly full—across most of one wall, an abundance of standing and hanging plants, all furiously healthy, so that the place was like a jungle, and at the center of the shot a magnificently beautiful, tallish, slim red-head, and, pouring her martini, a brown-eyed, round-faced, elegant young man—he might have been a Polish officer out of uniform—and [CAMERA PULLS BACK, REVEALING:] himself, a strange-looking older man—he would seem, on film, much older than either of them, in shoulder-length yellowish-silver hair, his look of slightly too studied gloom intensified by the clean gold, red, and black of his Japanese raw silk smoking jacket. The music in the background, or, rather, coming from all around the room, is Mozart, so the drama is to be, of course, philosophical and tragic: *keenly intelligent, sophisticated people are driven by dark, secret passions to . . .* whatever.

"Yes, everything's possible," Martin said, speaking lightly, jokingly, because the children were listening. "But is it worth anything, this changing one's life? Shall we be astronauts? Barbers?"

"I shall be—" Evan said, looking up with a sudden smile from his book, "a fifteen-point master of Go."

"I thought you were going to be a shepherd," Paul said, mock-sternly.

"Only in the summer," Evan said, still smiling.

Mary said, not looking up from her book, "Vous êtes un schnozz."

In his mind, absently—watching Paul move back to the large, round white formica table where his own glass waited—Martin played out the dramatic possibilities. Young man falls desperately in love with red-headed lady; she returns his love; her husband, the man with the yellow-silver hair, is insanely jealous. Despite the terror and grief of the children, helplessly drawn on by their violent passions . . . A plot for fools, unfortunately, or at any rate a plot for a duller, therefore more dramatic cast. They were in love already, the red-headed lady and the young man now pouring a martini for himself. In love but as cautious and dignified as characters out of James. They talked to each other twice a week on the phone, when he had to be away at his office in Detroit. Nor was their love less scrupulous, less Jamesean, for the fact that when he could come for a visit they slept together from time to time, or sometimes the three of them slept together. Though it might have been shocking to someone somewhere, or excitingly kinky to some fool somewhere else, it was nothing you could make a movie of. They were as careful of one another, when the three were together, as the Flying Wallendas on the high wire; and their sexual pleasures were ordinary, mundane. Mostly, in fact, they sat side by side smoking and drinking martinis and told stories of their childhood or talked about books and articles they'd read or people they knew, or they simply joked, putting on accents and gestures like curious old coats at the Goodwill:

"Herman, how come you don't get in the whaleboat?"

"Have you considered, Captain, that from time to time when the soul looks out at the rough, anarchic sea—"

"Herman, the others are all in the whaleboat. If you'd join us, if you'd just kindly step into the whaleboat—"

"Aye, Captain, if I'd just! But what argument, I ask you, has the heart of poor miserable man with the mighty Leviathans of the deep? What cause for dispute, what unanswerable insult—"

"This particular leviathan is escaping, Herman."

"Go in peace, then, says I. Let 'im squint a while longer at the antique obscurities—bask off Calcutta, for all I care!—ponder with that half-ton brain for another three decades or so the malevolence of this world and its miraculous bornings. Little good it'll do him, that's my opinion, and maybe a good deal more harm than Mr. Kirk's harpoon."

"Please, just get in the fucking Goddamn boat."

"Hell no, Captain! How do I know it don't leak?"

"It's been inspected. —Mr. Barret, is it not the case that you inspected this boat just this morning?"

"Aye aye, sir."

"Exactly! And did it leak?"

"No sir, not to speak of."

"You see, Herman? Look, I'm a patient man. I'm the patientest captain—"

"What if I get sick?"

"Herman, we got *pails,* we got *whaler's hats,* we got the whole Goddamn motherfucking *ocean.*"

"Captain?"

"Well?"

"I quit."

If they hurt each other's feelings, Paul Brotsky and the Orricks, they did it because they'd drunk too much, and when it happened they apologized quickly and seriously and, as soon as possible, put it behind them. They were useless characters to prove theories by, or to stimulate pious shock or stir up pleasantly unwholesome titillation. For fiction they were, in short, worthless, like two somewhat moody old brothers and their mostly cheerful, mostly spritely old sister in some deteriorating farmhouse in New Hampshire. What Martin Orrick evaded or stubbornly refused to do or at best did ineptly, Paul Brotsky did easily and with pleasure—repairs around the house, shopping errands, above all, talk with Joan. She loved simply talking—talk about everything and nothing. Martin by nature made earnest speeches—noisy rhetoric to which he was only for the moment committed—or he said nothing, comfortably thinking his own thoughts or, more precisely, sinking into his own empty trance, his normal dull swing of alpha waves, his mind becoming like an abandoned airport in flattest Oklahoma with the slow-wheeling searchlight left running. He was glad to have her present—or the children or Paul—but quick to grow impatient and irritable when she or anyone just talked, that is, chatted idly, interested—like her father or her uncle John Elmer—in life's dwarfs and car wrecks, its diurnal trivia, all that Martin Orrick had severed his heart from long since. Part of what made Paul Brotsky exceptional was his gift for talking with either or both of them, drawing Martin out by casual mention of theories in which Martin had at least trifling interest, since they might prove matters of lasting importance—the universe as doughnut with holes leaking Time, or split-brain psychology, or Baxter's psychic plants—and keeping Joan in the conversation because, unlike Martin, he enjoyed her quips (Martin would for the most part simply register them, like a computer keeping more or less faithful count but rarely exploding into laughter) and because, also, Paul understood and partly sympathized with her indifference to the ultimate truth Martin Orrick had no faith in but was forever in quest of.

"Oh, come on, Martin," Paul said now, playfully, though with a touch of irritation. "You're always saying, 'Ah woe, life's worthless.' If you really don't take any pleasure in all this"—he waved, taking in the room, the big house behind it, the woods and hills, perhaps the stars—"you should give it to my brother Frank."

"That's true, you got me," Martin said, and smiled. "I like it all. I should be happy."

"Glanted, of course," Paul added, leaning forward—and suddenly his smile, his squint, his bow were to the last inch Chinese—"having nice house and good famiry is not rike getting Vradivostok back from filthy Russians."

"Exactry!" Martin said and bowed.

Joan smiled too, but she was in pain tonight, so that her mood was sombre, slightly cranky. "Martin, what *is* it you really think you want? What is it you think we're keeping you from?"

"It's not you," he said, and though even in his own ears the words sounded doubtful, he meant it, more or less. It was not her fault that, as he was noticing when she spoke, the color of the chlorinated water in the pool was an affront to nature, as repulsive as painted lips and fingernails, or worse in fact, since it was not only artificial but also phony pure. So should he pour in filth from the horse pond? Introduce frogs, dark sacks of mosquito eggs?

"Then what's missing?" she insisted. "What is it you think you want?"

He looked at her, pretending to be daydreaming. That was more and more his way, he'd begun to notice—more and more his stock evasion tactic. She was watching him with her eyebrows lowered, and it seemed to him for a moment that she was trying to make him explain what it was that *she* desired, why she, too, was dissatisfied. Perhaps even Paul, busily lighting his thousandth cigarette, his eyes on the match, was waiting, masking an unreasonable hope. Martin Orrick could have told them in an instant what they needed, in point of fact: a life of service, self-sacrifice. But they wouldn't have believed him, or, simple as it was, wouldn't have understood, would have resisted him on grounds of style, the grounds on which poor stupid human beings make all their most important choices, judging presidents by their grammar, philosophers by their gall; they would have thrown up reasonable, unanswerable objections—some unanswerable because too stupid and cynical to be worthy of an answer (however right the objections, from a computer's point of view, or an English-speaking spider's), some unanswerable because a trifle too profound, hinting at the central debilitator of the age, the dark, spinning hole at the core of things, the emptiness hurling all their reasonings outward, faster and faster, toward the final *fsst* of das absolute Wissen, the punchline no one would hang around for.

"My desires are simple," he said, too cheerfully, raising his glass. "Happiness, eternal life for everybody, an interesting adventure."

"These things we expecting next week," Paul said, Jewish. "Today we got fresh-baked bagels."

They laughed, including the children, looking over from their books. Martin listened to the laughter, his own and the others, and gazed out at the pool.

Paul blew out smoke, rubbed the ash from his cigarette on the ceramic ashtray, then quickly put the cigarette back in his mouth and drew on it, as if breathing without the cigarette had become difficult for him. He said, "I had an adventure once, when I was younger."

"Really?" Joan said.

He nodded, serious. "One time we were at home alone, and my brother Frank sucked my eye out."

Martin coughed up part of his martini, laughing. "You're kidding!" he said. Joan was laughing too, blushing as her father would.

Paul was solemn. "Nope. He really did. He ran over next door and got the neighbors and they pushed it back in."

"Jesus!" Martin said, laughing.

"Lucky you were in good with your neighbors," Joan said.

The scene leaped up before them and Martin became, instantly, the irritable neighbor. "Your ring my doorbell one more time, you kid, and I warn you, I'm calling the cops!"

"Please, Mr. Karinsky," Paul Brotsky whined, wringing his hands and cowering, "ya gotta help me! I sucked my brother's eye out."

"You got a big mouth, you lousy kid."

Joan said sweetly, playing Mrs. Karinsky, "You *sucked* his *eye out?*"

"We was just kiddin around like, and *fwupp,* out it came."

"You didn't swallow it, I hope."

"Oh no, ma'am, it's still hangin in there, like."

"How did it taste?"

"I don't know. Salty. Like a oyster."

"Ethel, you gonna stand here talkin with this fart? He sucks his brother's eye out, that's *his* business. Git home, kid, before I sic the dog on ya."

"But sir, *please,* sir, my little brother needs help."

"I ain't no eye doctor. Shit, I ain't even a fireman."

"I wonder what an eye would taste like cooked."

"God damn it, Ethel, you start goormay cooking people's eyes and that's definitely *it,* it's *over,* I'm movin in with my sister Claire."

"It was just a thought."

"Mr. Karinsky, if you help me I'll mow your lawn for you free. I'll wash your car. Also your storm windows, and put up the screens."

"Like hell you will. The first time you find me asleep in my hammock, *fwupp!*"

"Was it *very* salty? How big was it, exactly?" She leaned toward him with a witchy sweet smile. "Little boy, let me whisper in your ear."

"Ma'am?"

"FWUPP! FWUPP!"

They laughed a while longer, drunk enough that anything might seem funny. Then, except for the record-player, the room was silent. Steam hung over the swimming pool. When there was a pause in the music, Martin could hear the drone of the television the children had left on, hours ago, upstairs. *Ours but to reason why,* he thought all at once, for no reason.

No, no movie here, he thought, *no novel.* Maybe a photograph, a painting, a piece of music, since photographs and paintings dealt with isolated instants, not the dizzying swirl of all Time and Space, and music made mention of grandiose desires and glorious satisfactions, or tragic disappointments (equally of interest) without naming them. No such luck for the poor fool novel—or the brain's right lobe; a stupid art, in fact, from the spiritual point of view of those nobler arts. Unless, of course, one ducked the whole business of the novelist for wild-man characters with windblown beards and eyes like sapphires, people whose hearts swelled with love or rage or the hunger for revenge, with none of the usual ambivalence or dreary simple-mindedness, people who moved among towering crags or dark, antique, brown-fog-filled cities, creeping or brawling their way through plots hung thick with suspense and metaphysical implication, all hedged and fenced or hurled into the world like a Mississippi flood by mincing or bellowing rhetoric. He'd written such novels and would no doubt write more of them. But they left him angry, dissatisfied. Why *shouldn't* a man's life develop reasonably, like a plot, with choices along the way, and antagonists with names, and some grand, compelling purpose, and a ringing final line? But he knew, no one better, that the question was foolish. All art, even music, is invented from scratch, has nothing to do with birds or the rumble of thunder. The urge to make art discover truth was a childish, wrongheaded urge, as his friend Bill Gass kept crabbily insisting in article after article for *The New York Review,* as if hoping if he said it enough he'd at last grow resigned to it. Well, not Martin Orrick. It filled him with the rage of a hurt rhinoceros—though he'd admit it was true—that human consciousness had no business in the world, that the world was its relative only by accident, and a relative no more friendly than Joan's sunken-eyed, long-black-bearded, snarling uncle Zack. Writing his fiction, struggling for hours to get a gesture just right, or to translate into English the exact sound of the first large drops of an August rain on a burdock leaf, he would look up suddenly with a heart full of anger and a belly full of acid from too much black coffee, too many hours at his pipe, remembering again that all he so tirelessly struggled for was false from its engendering: he was tortuously authenticating by weight of detail, by linguistic sleight-of-wit, actions that never took place on this earth since Time began and never would, never could. Nature's love stories had nothing to do with those novelists make up; nature's suspense has no meaning beyond the obvious, that that which is mindlessly, inexorably coming has, for better or worse, not yet arrived. It was finally the same in all the arts, no doubt: all composers wrote country dances, all painters made their names on descents from the cross. If they broke with tradition, seized truth by the throat, they ended up mere oddities, bold revealers not of truth but of their personal quirks, painters of pictures at their best under black lights, writers of endless metaphysical novels in baby talk. Tradition doomed you, escape doomed you, and straddling the charging horns of a dilemma was a patently bad idea.

The children were asleep, their blond heads fallen toward one another, their books in their legs. Paul was mixing a martini in the pitcher. The music had gone off.

He carefully relit his pipe, then said, "Once when I was teaching at San Francisco State I had an interesting student. She was middle-aged or so, from New Orleans. It was a class in creative writing and I was talking

for some reason about astrology. To make my students wake up more to
differences in character, I think. Anyway, I was busy disclaiming any interest
in whether or not astrological theory was true, arguing merely that reading
descriptions of the various types would help them to notice more things
about people, and this middle-aged student said—her name was Myrtle
Payne—'You can always tell what sign a person was bone undah, you
know, once you've gotten acquainted with them.' I said, of course, 'Mm,
yes,' politely. Except for San Francisco hippies and teachers who wanted
to be their friends, nobody in those days would flat-out admit he believed
in astrology. Except my uncle George, maybe; but for his opinions I had
a special box. —But she wouldn't let it go. She was a very nice lady, an
ex-schoolteacher—dressed and talked like any other clean, middle-aged, intelligent southern schoolteacher—and I'd never seen a sign before that night
that she might be slightly bonkers. She said—we were halfway through
the semester at the time—'For instance, I b'lieve I could guess the sign of
almost everone in this room.' I thought we were in for an embarrassing
situation, but what could I do? I said, 'Really?' 'Would you like me to
try?' she said. 'You're a Cancer, of course.' And she told me what it meant
to be a Cancer.

"Crazy as it sounds, she went through the whole class—maybe twelve,
fifteen kids. I missed half of it, trying all the time to figure out how she'd
done it, that is, how she'd gotten ahold of all our birth dates—not that
she named the exact day. Anyway, I was wrong, I think now. She really
knew. John Napper could do it too."

Paul nodded. He'd stayed with them for a few weeks in London and
had seen John Napper often. He said, "And his brother Pat had that horo-
scope description of his son, remember?"

Martin glanced at him. "I'd forgotten you saw that." It had been made
a few days after the child was born, then put away, unread, in a bank for
six years. It was like witchcraft. He raised his drink, just tasted it, thinking.
Joan was leaning back into her pillows, eyes closed. He said, "I read about
you, my Virgo friend. Or Joan or the kids or—" He let it trail off; then:
"It's mildly uncanny. I know all the arguments against it. They read like
the French Academy's debunking of hypnotism. For instance, the argument
that what influences a child born in the northern hemisphere couldn't influence one born in the southern, which is sort of like saying that mustard
gas can kill you only if you're facing it. Anyway, I no longer resist it. I'm

as ruled from outside as any character in a book, and not just physically, like Newton's cannonball, but ruled where it matters most. I don't like it much, but it makes it hard for me to look at, for instance, the *Winged Victory* and solemnly resolve to change my life."

Paul Brotsky blew out smoke, tamping out his cigarette, and reached, mechanical as a German clockmaker's piano player, for another. "I don't know," he said. "I think people can change."

"Maybe," Martin said.

Joan opened her eyes, turned her head from side to side, then smiled. "I must've been asleep," she said. As she sat forward she winced, seemed to go pale. She took a deep breath, then got up. "Anybody hungry?" she said.

"Sure," Paul said, "always. I'll help you."

She shook her head—harder than necessary, shaking her hair out. "No, you sit still and let Martin talk to you."

They laughed. When she'd left them, turning on the light in the music room as she passed and moving on into the kitchen, they sat silent for two or three minutes, thinking, probably, the same thoughts. At last Martin said, "Not just the stars, and I don't mean, God knows, that there's some wonderful plan. But we're boxed in from every direction. It shouldn't matter, I know—only fools or drunks even talk about it. Decent people just live it out, like bees. Tell jokes, play games, go to work in the morning, get drunk again at night—"

Paul Brotsky said, careful and serious, scraping the ash from his cigarette, not meeting Martin's eyes for fear of giving offense, "If I'm in the way, Martin—"

Martin squinted, baffled, glanced over at the sleeping children, then back at Paul. "What the devil makes you think—"

"Well, you seem to be implying—"

Martin studied him. It was easy enough to see that he was hurt, but what Martin had done to hurt him he had no idea. He said, "You're not in the way. I'm glad you're here. You picked up something that wasn't there, or anyway something I didn't mean to put there. Because you're a Virgo, too sensitive to detail, or because neither of us can do anything for Joan, and helplessness makes us guilty, or because—who knows? The box again—or not a box, a cosmic spiderweb. The genes of your parents and your parents' parents back to Adam. Also the weather, the spinach in your stomach, the color of the carpet, a helicopter ride you took one time in Viet Nam—"

"It's strange the way you keep picking at it. I mean, the whole thing's so insignificant, so irrelevant. So the world's run by chance. So what's the *bad* news?"

"It's stupid, I agree."

"I don't mean it's stupid." He spoke more carefully than ever, avoiding Martin's eyes. "But you keep honing for this thing you imagine you can't have—freedom, or something. Freedom to do what? You make us all feel—" He glanced up at Martin, then down again, and reached out quickly to scrape the ash of his cigarette away. He said, "You make us all feel that *we're* the spiderweb. If you want to be free where I'm concerned, just try me, Martin, just say, Paul, get out. As far as Joan's concerned—"

Just that instant there was a scream and a crash from the kitchen, and they both leaped up. Paul put down his cigarette and started for the door, almost at a run, and a second later, Martin followed. There was another crash and another, and Joan's screams of rage. When Martin reached the kitchen door, Joan was in Paul's arms, her muscles tensed, her face dark red, not accepting the embrace, accepting nothing, crying, wild with anger. All over the floor there were pieces of broken plates, bits of bacon and lettuce. The kitchen window had been smashed out, also the glass on one of the cupboards.

"Jesus Christ," Martin roared, "we *said* we'd help you!"

Paul jerked his head around. "God damn it, Martin, get out of here."

Martin turned, outraged, planning to walk out on them all. The children were in the doorway, looking in, wide-eyed and pale. He did not notice—though he would remember it later—that they shrank back from him. "It's all right," he said. "Your mother's just . . . having a tantrum. Better go to bed."

They turned, moved away, and their helplessness stoked his fury higher. Evan—Christ!—was almost fourteen. What was going to become of them in this crazyhouse? "Good night," Martin said, and this time there was no trace of anger in his voice, only sorrow, equally poisonous despair—he heard it himself. "It's all right," he said—as he was always saying, to Evan's black-and-tan just after the car hit him, breaking his jaw, to his own big black horse when he shied from a deer that went bounding suddenly across the trail, to Joan when she lay in bed crying, saying, "Martin, what are we going to *do?"* He touched the two children's shoulders gently, absently, with hands like clumsy wood. "Go to bed. It's all right." And as they went silently up the stairs, he turned toward the new room looking out at the pool, went down the step and over to his drink on the white formica table. It was almost empty. He drained it and carried the glass to the bar to make another. His heart was beating fast and his face felt hot. Who it was he was angry at he could easily have said if he'd stopped to think, but he couldn't, that moment, stop to think. He would remember later, thinking back to that moment, that he'd done the same in London once. He and Evan were crossing a wide, busy street—Evan smiling and eager, looking up at the gables of the Parliament building—and leading him through traffic, not holding his hand, Martin had called back confusing signals, so that Evan had run when Martin meant for him to wait, and a car had almost struck him. The driver hit his brakes—a cripple in one of those state-provided three-wheel cars—and Martin had turned and had raged at the man, though the driver had done nothing, nothing whatever except stop with great skill in an emergency. But it was only after the poor man had driven off that Martin had understood that he, he alone, not the driver, not Evan, was in the wrong. So now. But his fingers shook and his heart beat violently, and when, after a moment, he heard Paul and Joan coming into the room behind him, he did not turn.

"I shouldn't have yelled at you, Martin," Paul said. "It was just—"

"No, it's all right." His hand was still shaking.

Joan said, almost finished with her crying, "I'm sorry I lost my temper. I burned myself on the fucking stove, because of the drugs—I couldn't think right—" At the memory she began to cry again. She brought out, "I wasn't blaming you. You should see what it's *like,* just once, Martin."

Now he did get up and turned to them, full of rage and grief, though not rage at them. "Look, I'm sorry. I'm *sorry.* For the love of God—"

"Martin," Paul said sharply, "you didn't *do* anything."

"I know, it all just happens. That's the *point."* Tears rushed into his eyes all at once, and his rage and helplessness increased, and as he fought the tears a whimper came out, childish, infuriating. Instantly, Joan came to him, put her arms around him, and pressed her face against his chest. "Joan, I'm sorry," he said, and was crying now in earnest. "We've got to change our lives." He half sobbed, half laughed.

Joan said, "Paul's told me about his psychiatrist in Detroit. I want to go to him, Martin."

Martin nodded, clinging to her, unable to speak. He brought out, "Do. Yes, do." He reached, like a feeble, foolish old man—or so it seemed to him—toward Paul's shoulder, bringing him into the embrace. Martin Orrick had, needless to say, no hope that a psychiatrist could help. She'd been to plenty before. But perhaps; perhaps. Paul's presence helped, certainly—helped them to break their deadly patterns, circle for a moment more like dancers than like fighters. So he told himself now. But he'd known from the first, and would know tomorrow, that when she threw those dishes, she threw them—in her mind—at him. And she was right; he should have noticed and helped.

Eight

Causes and effects are not neatly separable, as we sometimes find them in fiction. Martin Orrick's nature helped the accident to happen, and the accident helped to shape his nature, each feeding on the other as past and present do, or ends and means, or—as Orrick would say—the brain's two lobes. In any event, part of what Joan's mother called his "darkness" had to do with this: One day, in a farm accident, Martin—that is, Buddy—ran over and killed his brother Gilbert. It was an ugly and stupid accident which, even at the last moment, Buddy could have prevented by hitting the tractor brakes; but he was unable to think, or rather thought unclearly, and so watched it happen, as he would watch it happen in his mind, with undiminished clarity, again and again until the day he died. It was a shattering experience, needless to say, for all the Orricks. Buddy's father was almost unable to go on living. Sometimes Buddy would find him lying in the manure on the barn floor, crying, unable to stand up. Duncan Orrick was, as I've said, a good man—gentle and intelligent, a dreamer. He'd loved all his children and would not consciously have been able to hate Buddy even if Buddy had been, as he seriously imagined himself, Gilbert's murderer. But of course he could not help seeming to blame his son, though in fact he blamed no one but himself. Though he was not ordinarily a man who smoked, he would sometimes sit up all night or move restlessly from room to room smoking cigarettes and crying, or he would ride away on his motorcycle, trying to forget, or playing with the idea of killing himself, hunting in mixed fear and anger for reasons not to do so and coming down, always, to just one, the damage his suicide would unquestionably do his children. Sometimes, as his son would do long afterward, he would forget for a while by abandoning reason and responsibility for love affairs. He was at this time still fairly young, distinctly handsome, and so full of pain that women's hearts went out to him automatically. At times he would be gone from the farm for days, abandoning the work to Buddy and whoever was available to help—some neighbor or one of Buddy's uncles. A fool might have condemned Duncan Orrick for all this, but no one in the family did, certainly not Buddy, not even Buddy's mother, though it increased her sorrow. He had always been a good and faithful man; no one, whatever the pain he might cause, would dream of demanding that he do more than survive.

As for Buddy's mother, she cried all night, sometimes lying alone, and did as much as she had the strength to do—so drained by grief that she could barely lift a pot or pan—for her husband and children. She comforted Buddy and his younger sister, and herself as well, by embracing them almost ferociously when the waves of guilt and sorrow swept in, or by thinking up work that would distract their minds, or by prayer. And because she had great strength of character, and because, also, she was a woman of strong religious faith, she kept the family functioning. Her children would have no real sense until long afterward just how much strength that period demanded of her or how heavily she depended, for her own survival, on Duncan's sister Mary and Mary's husband, Buddy's uncle George.

But for all his mother could do for him, Buddy Orrick had suffered psychological damage that would take a long time to heal. He had been, before, suspicious, easily hurt, self-absorbed. He became now more withdrawn, more self-absorbed than ever. The accident had happened in early spring. He'd seen, the day it happened, the first light-blue wild flowers blooming along the road. Working the farm, ploughing, disking, dragging, cultipacking from morning to night, he had plenty of time to think—plenty of time to replay the accident in his mind, against his will, his whole body flinching from the picture as it came, his voice leaping up independent of him, as if perhaps a shout could drive the memory back into its darkness. Driving the big Farmall F-20 over rocky fields, dust rising behind him or, when he turned into the wind, falling like dry rain until his face and hands were as dark as a Negro's and his hair was thick and stiff—the hills all around him greener every day, the spring wind endless and steady and sweet with the smell of coming rain—he had all the time in the world to cry and swear bitterly and hate himself. He had not loved his brother—or anyone—as much as he should have, he thought, as much as he now helplessly and for the most part without showing it loved his father and mother and sister and, a short while later, his new, red-headed baby brother. He was basically incapable of love, he thought. He was simply a bad person, a spiritual defective.

He had always told himself stories to pass the time when driving the tractor, endlessly looping back and forth, around and around over a twenty-acre field, fitting the land for spring planting. He told them to himself aloud, taking all parts in the dialogue—here where no one could see or overhear him, half a mile or more from the nearest house—gesturing, making faces (exactly as he'd do in the study where he wrote his short stories and novels, some fifteen years later). Once all his stories had been of sexual conquests—always very chaste; lasciviousness was not one of his weaknesses—or of heroic battle with, for instance, escaped convicts or kidnappers who, unbeknownst to anyone, had built a little shack where they kept their captives (female and beautiful) in the woods beside the field where he worked. But now they were all of self-sacrifice, pitiful stories in which, as in Dickens' *A Tale of Two Cities,* he made something, at last, of his worthless life by throwing it away to save some other, fit to live. At some point in these stories he would confess his worthlessness, naming all his faults and giving numerous examples, granting himself no mercy; and, absurd as it may sound, he would weep honest tears of remorse as he angrily denounced himself. If on some unconscious level he hoped he might in this way ground his guilt and sorrow, the trick did not work. The foulness of his character (as it seemed to him) became clearer and clearer in his mind until, like his father, he began to toy in earnest with killing himself. As it would do all his life, his chest would fill with anguish, as if he were drowning or bleeding internally, and his arms and legs would grow shaky with weakness, until he had to stop the tractor and sit for a few minutes sobbing. But he lacked even the strength of character to kill himself, as it seemed to him. He was finally indifferent to the agony his mother and father suffered—otherwise wouldn't he have killed himself long ago? Once at night his father found him up in the pitch-dark silo, lying in the corn ensilage, crying, and he climbed in through the silo door and felt his way over to him and took him into his arms and tried to speak to him but couldn't, since now he too was crying; and Buddy was aware—though he could do nothing about it—that whereas his father's crying was real, his own was self-conscious, false. Bits of ensilage had gotten under Buddy's collar, cold and tickling, and his mind would not ignore the unpleasantness, would not, whatever his wish, abandon itself to grief.

Thus it seemed to him that everything in the world condemned him, and condemned him in vain, since he lacked the nobility of heart to feel pain as he should. When the wind was high outside his window at night, making the screens and pinetrees groan like sorrowing ghosts, he wanted to feel horror, recognition of his state of damnation; but he felt only unloved and afraid, felt above all, perhaps, a tawdry embarrassment over the fact that, day after day, his family must see him, strangers must see him, knowing what they all must know, that he had killed his brother. That was the heart of it: he was tawdry—though the word was not one he knew at that time. That was what he hated most in his innumerable faults: they were tawdry.

He was forever telling lies—for no earthly reason, not to hide things, not to make himself seem better than he was, not even to hurt people, though sometimes the lies did turn out to do harm. It was an astonishing thing, and even more astonishing that he could do nothing about it. He made up story after story, things he'd seen, people he'd met. He told friends at school that his family was Polish and had changed the family name. (In later years he would claim and even to some extent believe that he was Welsh, though the only Welsh blood he possessed was that of his carpenter grandfather, who was only half Welsh himself.) He told his art teacher, merely to make conversation—he had at the time a great, sad crush on her—that a cow had died last night. When she ran into his father the following day she asked about it, with great sympathy. Buddy Orrick, thinking of his stupid habit, would grind his teeth and clutch his head in both hands, or sometimes jerk angrily at his hair. Also he was lazy. He simply couldn't make himself do his school assignments. He would swear at himself aloud and order himself to work with furious indignation (he would all his life be one of those people who talk to themselves); but it was useless, the very sight of the printing on the pages of his textbooks filled him with a drowning sensation like sorrow or perhaps anger, though the work was not hard. He would get out his French horn to play for just a little, and the next thing he knew, his father would be poking his head in at the door, saying wearily, with red-rimmed eyes, "Buddy, it's after midnight." Also he was a fool, and a dangerous one. He once walked five miles with his closest school friend, completely forgetting that the boy had a heart condition. The following day the friend nearly died.

Buddy Orrick's faults hounded him, or when he slept rushed over him as nightmares. At times he would abruptly stop brooding on them and, instead, would struggle for oblivion. To avoid the nightmares, he learned to get by on less and less sleep; in school he became a troublemaker, a tiresome smart aleck; at home, when not working for his father, he learned to concentrate so intensely on his horn playing, alone in his room, or his writing, or composing at the piano in the livingroom, that nothing at all could break in on him, from within or without—except that picture, the replay of the accident. He would be known, years later, as one of the most prolific "serious" writers of his time, despite a heavy schedule as professor, scholarly editor, and public reader. His secret was that he had learned all too well, during those painful years, to concentrate totally, dropping out of ordinary reality as a ghost sinks down through the stones of a castle floor. Lying beside him, racked with pain, Joan would never cease to be amazed by how, the moment his head touched the pillow, he was fast asleep.

He had various means of avoiding painful feeling at this time, his early adolescence. He would do endless trigonometric identities, mindlessly driving on like a circling atom, using up great swatches of butcher paper; he began at this period to write poems and stories, to draw and paint in oils, and to compose music; but his chief means of escape was playing the French horn.

It was odd that he should be at all good at it. Though he'd taken piano lessons for seven years, he'd never gotten past the John Thompson fourth book, could play a Bach two-part invention only stumblingly, and had an idiotic and infuriating habit (in Joan's opinion) of holding the pedal down. But on the horn, luckily, he turned out to be less inept. He was soon studying on Saturday mornings with a man who was at that time one of the best French horn teachers in the world, Arcady Yegudkin—"the General"—at the Eastman School of Music; and owing to a scarcity of decent French horn players in the area at that period—and owing, too, to Yegudkin's influence—he was soon sitting in at concert time with small civic orchestras throughout western New York and southern Ontario.

There are no such French horn players left as was Arcady Yegudkin. He had played principal horn in the orchestra of Czar Nikolai, and at the time of the Revolution had escaped, with his wife—dramatically. At the time of their purge of Kerenskyites and supposed sympathizers with the older order, the Bolsheviks loaded Yegudkin and his wife, along with hundreds of others, onto flatcars, reportedly to carry them away to imprisonment. The Bolsheviks' intention was of course somewhat darker. In a desolate place, a forest hundreds of miles from the nearest city of any size, machine guns opened fire on the people on the flatcars; then soldiers pushed the bodies off into a ravine and the train moved on. The soldiers were not careful to see that everyone was dead—they believed in the Revolution, but they were not to the last man bloodthirsty maniacs and did not relish their work; besides, they believed that in a place so remote, a man or woman only wounded, not yet dead, would have no chance against the cold and the wolves—and so they cleared the flatcars, averting their eyes from the fellow Russians who stirred or groaned or whimpered for mercy, washed away most of the blood from the flatcars, and fled. Arcady Yegudkin and his wife were among the very few who survived, he virtually unmarked, she horribly crippled. Peasants who hated even politics ostensibly undertaken in their behalf, and who were outraged that any government anywhere should raise its monstrous, idiot hand against poets and musicians (four famous poets were killed in the massacre) nursed the Yegudkins back to something like health and smuggled them to what had been, until lately, St. Petersburg, and thence into Europe. There Yegudkin played horn with all the great orchestras, all the great conductors, and received such praise as no other master of the French horn has ever been given with the possible exception of Dennis Brain, who was at least approaching Yegudkin's power when his car crashed in 1957.

He was, this Yegudkin, a big-bellied, solidly muscular man who, for all his age when Buddy Orrick knew him, still had black hair and a black moustache, with a few bits of silver and touches of white, especially where it grew, with majestic indifference to the narrow-minded taste and opinion of the common herd, from his nose and ears. The sides of his moustache were carefully curled, in the fashion favored by nineteenth-century European dandies, and he was probably the last man in Rochester, New York, to wear spats. He wore black suits, a huge black overcoat, and a black hat, and his wife, who came with him and sat on the long maple bench outside his office door, never reading or knitting or doing anything at all except that, sometimes, she would try to speak to his waiting students—mumbling questions and remarks in what the student could not even recognize, at first, as broken English—Yegudkin's wife, shrivelled and twisted, though according to Yegudkin she had once been the most beautiful woman in the world, wore long black dresses and black gloves. They would come, early on a Saturday morning, down the long marble hallway of the second floor of the Eastman School of Music, the General as erect and imperatorial as some benevolent, sharp-eyed Slavonic king, moving slowly, favoring the old woman who crept along beside him, clinging to his arm; and seeing Buddy Orrick seated on the bench, his books and French horn in its tattered black case on the floor beside him, he would extend his left arm regally and boom, "Good morning!" like a genial but not-to-be-ignored command.

Buddy, who had risen at first sight of Yegudkin, would say shyly, "Morning, sir."

"You haff met my wife, Mrs. Yegudkin?" the old man would say, taking the great black cigar from his mouth. He asked it each Saturday, month after month.

"Yes sir. How do you do."

The old man was too deaf to play in orchestras anymore. "Hvatt's the difference," he said. "Every symphony in America, they got a Yegudkin. In Hollywood at the movies, my boys play horn for twelve dollars a minute. Who teaches them to make so much money? The General!"

He would sit in the chair beside Buddy's and would sing, with violent muscular gestures and a great upward leap of the diaphragm to knock out high notes—*Tee! Tee!*—as Buddy read through Kopprasch, Gallay, and Kling, and when it was time to stop, give Buddy's lip a rest, Yegudkin would speak earnestly, with the same energy he put into his singing, of the United States and Russia. The world was filled, in the late forties and early fifties, with Russophobes, and Yegudkin, whenever he read a paper, would be so filled with rage at the stupidity of man he could barely contain himself. "In all my age," he sometimes said, furiously gesturing with his black cigar, "if the Russians would come to this great country of America, I would take up a gun and shot at them—*boof boof!* But the newspapers telling you lies just the same. You think they are dumb fools, these Russians? You think they big fat-face bush-overs?" He spoke of mile-long parades of modern, terrifying implements of war, spoke of Russian cunning, the beauty of Russia's oldest cities, spoke with great scorn, a sudden booming laugh, of Napoleon. What it all meant Buddy Orrick could hardly have told you, at the time, and since he never answered, merely agreed politely with whatever the General might say, the General probably had no idea at all of where Buddy stood on these matters of such importance. Nevertheless, he raged on, taking great pleasure in his rage, sometimes talking like a rabid Communist, sometimes like a rabid anti-Communist fascist, sometimes like a poor citizen helplessly caught between mindless, grinding forces. Then abruptly he would stop, and Buddy would raise his horn and they'd go back to work. He put Buddy in the Eastman Junior Symphony (Howard Hanson would remember him years afterward as having always played sharp) and got him paying, though not very well-paying, jobs with small orchestras.

The General rarely played for his students, though even at the time Buddy Orrick studied with him, when Yegudkin was in his seventies and no longer performed in public, the old man claimed he practiced six, seven hours every day. Buddy heard him once. A new horn he'd ordered from Germany, an Alexander, arrived at his office—a horn he'd ordered for a graduate student. The old man unwrapped and assembled it, the student looking on, and the look in the General's eyes was like madness, or at any rate lust, perhaps gluttony. When the horn was ready he went to the desk where he kept his clippings, tools for the repair of French horns, cigars, photographs, and medals, and pulled open a wide, shallow drawer. In it he had perhaps a hundred mouthpieces, of all sizes, shapes, and colors, from raw brass to lucite, silver, and gold, from the shallowest possible cup to the deepest. He selected one, fitted it into the horn, pressed the rim of the bell into the right side of his large belly so firmly that the horn was more a part of him than the limb of a maple is a part of the tree, clicked the valve keys a moment to get the feel of them, and played. In that large, cork-lined room, it was as if, suddenly, some awesome creature from another sphere of reality, some world where spirit is more solid than stone, had revealed itself. The sound was not loud but was too big for a French horn, as it seemed to Buddy Orrick. Too big for a hundred French horns, in fact. It fluttered and flew crazily, like an enormous trapped bird hunting wildly for escape. It flew to the bottom of the French horn register, the foundation concert F very few among even the best can play, and went below it, and on down, as if the horn in Yegudkin's hands *had* no bottom, and then suddenly changed its mind and flew upward in a split-second, absolutely flawless run to the horn's top E or concert A, dropped back to the middle and then ran once more, more fiercely at the E, and this time crashed through it as a terrified bird might crash through a skylight, and fluttered, manic, in the trumpet's high range, then lightly dropped back into its own home range, and abruptly, in the middle of a note, stopped.

"Good horn," said Yegudkin, and put it in its case.

Buddy Orrick stared. Timidly he said, "You think I'll ever learn to play like that?"

Yegudkin smiled, beatific. "No," he said.

Nine

One of Buddy Orrick's virtues—though he was then unaware that he had any virtues—was that he couldn't be discouraged by the knowledge that he was destined never to be the greatest French horn player, or the greatest anything else, in the world. Nothing in his background demanded anything like greatness of him. His Grandmother Orrick had been a good, honest lawyer, as some of his cousins would be the best country or, later, city lawyers they knew how to be, but with no strong urge to become flashy trial lawyers who defended rich murderers in spectacular cases, or to become famous and powerful politicians, or even to become rich. His grandfather and father were merely careful, honest farmers who kept their animals fed and sheltered, saw to the general upkeep of their land, kept the fences patched, and never sold a bushel of apples that wasn't a firm, honest bushel. Neither his father nor his grandfather saw virtue in working harder than was necessary, violating the Sabbath, or neglecting the non-material needs of their families. Buddy's Grandfather Davis, whom he never saw, was in a sense emblematic of what they all stood for. He was the best possible carpenter, which in his day was merely to say a good carpenter. His prices were fair, he understood his tools, he left no gouges, cracks, splinters, loose pegs, badly sunk screws, or carelessly unbeveled edges. The idea of greatness was inherently foreign to a family so firmly and even proudly middle class. Nor was it in their nature to pick and choose what kind of work, in their chosen professions, was worthy of them and what work not. When Charles E. Davis, carpenter, was hired to put the roof on the tower of the St. Louis railroad station, he looked up and sadly shook his head, thinking what a hell of a ways it would be if he happened to fall, then gathered together his tackle and went up, with his helpers, and put the roof on. The houses he built were square and true and had no foolishness in them except what some fool demanded and paid good money for. His sheds and barns were as steady and firm as any in Missouri, though no one could tell which barns were his and which ones were built by Clarence Rogers, his partner, or by Odell Crow, from across the river. He was a craftsman who worked by medieval standards, to whom it would have seemed a sacrilege to introduce some clever, original detail, some cunning device that might serve as a signature. Only time, he would have said, can determine value. In both style and structure, he approved what had been tested, what had proved inoffensive after years of looking at. When he fished he used cane poles, cotton lines, and corks made of cork, and made no concession to machine technology except metal fishhooks and lead eargrip sinkers. (As Martin Orrick would write, reconstructing his grandfather's character on the basis of old letters and family talk, "He might have been persuaded, by the passage of an acceptable number of years, to give his tentative approval to the precision and intricacy of an Ambassadeur reel, the smooth hardness of monofilament line, but it would not have been within the twentieth century.") With conservative care like a carpenter's, with the determined, step-by-step diligence of a farmer in the days when men still ploughed with horses, Buddy Orrick—or rather Martin—would write his long, complex novels, constructing, half a page a day, his incredible interlace of literary theft and original labors of imagination, leaving drafts constructed from the center outward, intricate and messy as the confused, enormously serious web of a black widow spider, drafts so cluttered by cross-outs, inserts, and erasures, balloons and parenthetical questions or remarks, that no one but the author could figure them out, and not even he when as much as a day had passed. One looks in vain through the early drafts for any sign of brilliance or even common wit; one finds only corrections aimed at getting colors more exact, or changes in the estimates of a building's height, or revisions of the weather. Surely any other writer would have quit in disgust a dozen times, but Orrick labors on, so that one begins to half believe—at least with regard to his own writings—his famous remark on literature, that "genius is one percent inspiration and ninety-nine percent obdurate stupidity." In his teens, when writing poetry and fiction was still for him a casual hobby, he put this stubborn, almost mindless doggedness into playing the French horn. Yegudkin had of course been right, he lacked the true musician's gift; but he had, as he would always have, amazing persistency, and playing allowed him not to think. On a summer evening after chores, he would sometimes walk out past the barn with his horn and climb the steep hill to the apple orchard and play—his father's cows watching from the far side of the electric fence—until his lips felt flabby and he could hardly keep his eyes open. He would play scales, lip trills, open-horn arpeggios, études, fragments from concertos, orchestral snippets. Sometimes on clean-smelling warm summer nights he would walk farther, to the wide, high hill at the back of the farm from which he could see all the houses and villages for miles around, and there, in sight of his neighbors' lights but as safely remote from their judgments and opinions as from the stars overhead, he would play his emotions without daring to name them, without even directly feeling them, lightly distracted—as once he had been by ensilage in his collar—by the exigencies of horn technique. He became in those moments, as he would become in his writing long afterward, a sort of human conduit, a spokesman for the ordinary human feelings coming up from the scattered lights below (and from his own chest) and a spokesman for the ice-cold absolutes in the black sky above him—though he felt himself separate from, rejected by both his neighbors and the stars; and because he was only a musician, not a philosopher, he had no real idea what it was—if anything at all—that his music was expressing. It would be the same when he was a famous novelist, years later. The stories he told would be intricate, elaborately plotted, complex; his characters would have the depth, the ambivalence, and the ultimate unpredictability we encounter in real people; the world he created would seem, in his best work, more solid than the world of the reader's chair; but Martin Orrick, moon child—born, that is, under the sign of the Crab—would have no more idea what his novels meant than did the shelves on which they stood. He built them of carefully recollected emotions set side by side or one against another—the emotions of characters, the emotions implicit in particular kinds of language, the emotions embodied in particular acts—and he tinkered with the thing he'd brought into the world with an old-fashioned carpenter's stubborn, unambitious concern for workmanship, until he could feel his creation beginning to resist him, beginning to be itself, at which point, like any benevolent god, he would abandon it, wishing it good luck.

Thus the French horn, though he would never be a really first-rate player, nudged Buddy Orrick partway back to health. For all his self-hatred and self-pity, he couldn't help but see that he was better on the horn than most people his age—easily better than anyone that year in the All-State Orchestra, for instance, where he played principal horn. His emotions were still too raw, his insecurity and fear of discovery still too great for him to be anything but generous—defensively shy and friendly—toward players less well trained than himself; but he was improving. Before long he would think himself much better than he was and would hurt people's feelings by showing them, more or less gently, all they were doing wrong.

Needless to say, when he saw his cousin Joan now, she accompanied him on horn concertos. They were by this time writing to each other regularly and had even joked of marrying, though they hadn't yet held hands. When the time for his Eastman Preparatory School recital came, on which his scholarship depended, he wrote and asked her to come to New York and accompany him. She agreed to come. The visit would turn out to be one of considerable significance in their lives, both for better and for worse, though part of its significance they wouldn't understand for some time.

They played the Mozart third concerto and the relatively easy Beethoven horn sonata, and he played well, as she had known he would. To Joan—and no doubt to his mother and Aunt Mary, beaming in the first row—he looked wonderfully handsome, playing the horn. He was dressed very formally in a suit and tie, as she'd never seen him except perhaps once or twice at church, and he had that touching scrubbed-farmboy look, comic and poignant (a word she pronounced at the time, only having read it, *pwagnant*). He missed, at most, only two or three notes in the whole performance, which she knew was remarkable on that slippery instrument, and he had, there in the paneled auditorium, a beautiful, soulful tone. It couldn't really be said of him, as people had said of her (and would say all her life), that he had remarkable talent. In fact in certain ways, she was prepared to admit—though her heart crashed wildly at sight of him—her cousin was musically stupid. Though his technique—result of pure diligence—was impressive, he sometimes went sharp, and he couldn't even hear it when you pointed it out; and he rushed his sixteenth notes and, when you told him so, stubbornly insisted it wasn't true. His stubbornness really was amazing, in fact. *She* was the one who was supposed to be from Missouri. But she found ways of tricking him into slowing down—without his even knowing what was happening to him—and as she told him, brightly smiling (so that he, too, smiled), he played in tune much more frequently than not.

Her unbeautiful period, it ought to be mentioned, was by this time behind her. She'd grown into her nose; by some mysterious process her mouth—in fact, everything about her—had changed, become all one could wish. She even noticed it herself. Though Buddy didn't mention it, she knew, much to her delight, that he too had noticed. Running to meet her on the platform at the Buffalo train station, he'd stopped suddenly, a few feet away, and had blushed bright red, as her father would do, so that she too had blushed. Then he'd come to her quickly, for fear he'd lose his nerve, and had given her a quick hug, as he always did when they met again after months apart, and she'd turned her face just slightly, so that her cheek brushed his, and she'd smelled his country after-shave and felt the coldness of his ear. He snatched up two of her heaviest bags to hide his embarrassment and said, "It's really neat to see you."

She smiled, watching him, wondering if he'd look up, and feeling, as always, much older than he, though she was in fact one month younger to the day. "You too," she said.

When they practiced he worked with an earnestness that amused her. She did not guess—though it would come to her much later—that what made him play so carefully, so tensely and therefore awkwardly, was not fear of the recital but fear of looking bad in front of her. (During the recital his nervousness would make him forget about her and he would play lightly, easily, no longer thinking of the music note by note.) All the time they practiced his family hovered near, his mother leaning over her left shoulder to watch the notes fly by, his ten-year-old sister leaning over her right, his red-headed baby brother standing at Buddy's knee, watching with an expression of awe and loving admiration, though he must have heard Buddy play like this a thousand times, and often from that same position, standing by the bell of Buddy's horn. Sometimes his mother would say "Hmpf" with interest when Joan picked her way more or less successfully through a difficult passage (it was all difficult, when it came to that; the piano reduction had been done by an idiot), but though she was watching the notes, Buddy's mother didn't think to help out by turning pages. In short, it should have been a miserable business, Joan leaning forward toward the music not really in order to see the notes but because Buddy's mother and sister were crowding her from behind; yet it wasn't miserable, only funny and exciting, the cluttered room, completely unlike anything you would ever have seen at her mother's house—the piano top so crowded with pictures of friends and relatives, including a large, colored picture of herself, that you could hardly find a place to put a pencil down—the clutter of emotions—the family's pleasure in the music and delight in her cleverness, Buddy's nervousness, his slight embarrassment at the behavior of his family, though it was obvious that he also felt affection for them, and her own confused feelings of pride, love, embarrassment, claustrophobia. When they finished the first movement Buddy's mother and sister clapped and cried "Bravo!" and Buddy was more embarrassed than ever. Then his father came in, smelling of the cow barn, and came to the doorway, smiling as he always did at sight of her, and said, "If music be the food of love, play on!" Buddy looked down, and Joan studied him, then said, "Ready, baby?" He glanced up and, after an instant's hesitation, nodded.

After the recital they all went out to eat, Joan and Buddy's mother and his aunt Mary—after whom, years later, their daughter would be named. They ate in the high-ceilinged, dark diningroom of some old hotel, and Buddy's mother and Aunt Mary spoke over and over of what a beautiful recital it had been and what a shame it was that Buddy's father and Uncle George had had to miss it. While they were eating Joan felt a sudden sharp pain, a pain so fierce she went white and almost fainted. It was exactly like the time her appendix had ruptured, and she was so frightened she couldn't even cry out. She managed to say in a whisper, "Aunt Mary, I—" and Aunt Mary, who was a nurse—head of the maternity ward at Genesee Memorial—looked at her and said, "My dear!" and got up so quickly she almost knocked the table over. The next thing Joan knew, they were driving very fast to the Rochester hospital in Aunt Mary's car, Joan lying in the backseat with her head on Buddy's lap, and he was bent over her, looking white and frightened, touching her face gently, brushing away her tears and saying, full of concern, "You'll be all right, Joan. You will." As if because his voice was magical—that high-tone, flat eastern accent she loved—the pain shrank away and, after a moment, vanished. She was about to tell him, then changed her mind. Outside the car windows, streetlights and snowy trees flew by. She felt a flurry of panic at what she was about to do, then whispered, "Buddy, kiss me." His eyes widened slightly and then, timidly, he obeyed.

At the hospital, as at so many hospitals later, the doctor found nothing wrong. It was impossible, they told her, that her appendix could have grown back. "But it must be *some*thing," she said. Did they think she'd made it up?

The doctor, who had a round head and a large brown moustache, merely smiled and looked at the middle of her forehead. "It seems to be just one of those things," he said.

"Just thank the dear Lord it's gone and pray it won't come back," Aunt Mary said, and took Joan's arm, severe as a sergeant—her normal way of showing affection. They returned to the room where Buddy and his mother were waiting.

"Nothing?" his mother said, incredulous, prepared to be annoyed at the doctor.

"Nothing they can find," Aunt Mary said, with such finality that Buddy's mother shook her head and said no more.

As they walked back to the elevator, Buddy took Joan's hand.

Ten

His uncle George was a short, dapper, big-jawed, quick man who wore gold-rimmed spectacles and three-piece suits, usually brown ones and fairly conservative, though his nature made them seem merrier than they were. (In no corner of his jubilant Scorpio soul did George Preston wear checks or flashy bow ties or a moustache; though he was a teller of stories and a first-rate salesman, he was serious about life, ready every day to be called to some delicate, important work, or a friend's marriage, or a funeral.) He was full of pleasure and darting curiosity; there was nothing decent that he wouldn't try his hand at, from butchering cows to leg-wrestling a Seneca Indian, and nothing he tried was he bad at except for English grammar, for which he had no flair. His house on North Lyon in Batavia, New York, was atoggle from end to end with ingenious devices he'd run across in his *Popular Mechanics* magazines—he kept a great stack of them by the toilet in his bathroom—strings, pulleys, and levers for turning lights on and off again, or for opening or closing or starting or stopping things. When his basement flooded, as basements in his part of the city did each spring, regular as the mail, he had a steamship's pump that he'd built, himself, to empty it. On every door and window of his house and garage and potting shed, he had clever devices he'd constructed himself to keep burglars and mischievous children out. The arches he wore in his wide brown highly polished shoes were of his own design and basement manufacture.

Given his talent and boundless energy, George Preston might have been anything; but his father died when he was still a young man and, though he wasn't the eldest and thus wasn't, by a certain line of reasoning, responsible, he threw himself into taking care of the family and sacrificed, pretty much without a second thought, whatever chances he might have had as an artist, engineer, or who-knows-what. He'd driven ambulance during World War I and had a thousand stories, most of them so funny that people laughed until they cried, sitting around the table in his crowded, brightly lit diningroom, or at the picnic table he had in back, behind his garden, by the horseshoes court, or at some other man's table, for instance the long one in the high-ceilinged room in Duncan Orrick's house. Dozens of those stories would show up in Martin Orrick's novels. He had also, in certain moods, darker stories—and a darker streak in his character—stories of atrocities he'd seen at first hand, half-crazy Americans who drove tanks in to finish off wounded boches or took shots at the drivers of the German Red Cross. Though late in life he would come to believe he'd made a sad mistake, he resolved to bring no children into a world so bleak and dangerous, a world in which even the best of men, if the cards were right, could revert in the twinkle of an eye to murderous gorilla.

After the war he'd bumped around for six months, then worked for a while in the family dry-cleaning establishment, the Sunshine Cleaners, a long, airless place sweet-smelling as a bakery, except the smell was of starch and warm cloth and soap and cleaning fluid—a small establishment just off an alley across from the furtive back entrance to a bank and next door to a farm-implement repair shop. The rooms behind the cheerful, plant-filled front lobby were as filled with steamy windows as a winter snowstorm has flakes of snow, the walls between the windows painted dead-man gray, all the rooms crowded with bagged and loose laundry with yellow or blue tickets, and antique machinery, workers without faces, and the noise of the equipment—the woof and hiss of the big steam presser, the *clush* of washers, the rattle of hangers as they slid along their long wooden bars.

Later, though he still kept an interest in the place, he took on various selling jobs—as a Watkins man serving the local farmers, small-townsmen, and villagers from Rochester to Buffalo and from the shore of Lake Ontario to the hill towns of Warsaw and Perry; then as an independent "grocer on wheels" serving, among others, the people of the Tonawanda Indian Reservation, with whom he learned to speak a little Seneca and whose virtues he would admire, and whose stories he would quote, in sombre imitation of the Seneca manner, for the rest of his life; still later as a furniture salesman in one small-town furniture store after another.

Everyone liked him and he was famous for his honesty, though that was not true of the people for whom he worked. He read books about salesmanship and personal magnetism, whatever came to hand, also books that might help him judge the character of his customers—books on phrenology, palmistry, and astrology—and if he made a mistake in attempting a sale he made a careful note of it in a ledger he had, and made an effort never to repeat it. (He had once chanced upon a book about calligraphy and wrote, even when he was seventy-two and could barely hold a pen, in an elegant, tasteful hand. He used the slanted, hyperlinear *and* of a nineteenth-century professional scrivener.) He was not, for all that, a hard-sell salesman but a man who believed that business was an honorable and responsible profession and, indeed, in a democracy of ordinary men, as noble a profession as a man could turn his hand to. He wouldn't sell shoddy goods to any man if he could find him something decent for a price he could afford, nor would he lie about the value of the goods he sold—wouldn't even lie by keeping silent. To his bosses' displeasure, he resisted selling what he knew in advance the customer would have trouble making payments on: he would talk with the man in his merry, joking way, trying to make the man see sense and perhaps, incidentally, selling him something else he had equal use for and could more easily afford and might someday be glad he'd gotten hold of. Not at all that he was a pious moralist who delighted in butting in on other people's business. His judgments of the customer—however merrily he talked, ducking and weaving and feinting like a boxer, rubbing his hands like a man undecided about what to eat first at some splendid potluck—were complex and serious-minded, and he understood that, when a family buys furniture, practical considerations are not always of the first importance. Occasionally people have urgent need of what they cannot afford, and the salesman's just business is to get the sale made in the way least likely to do damage. It was not from arrogance or the wish to play God that he drew that opinion. He saw business as a service, and even used the word. Though he did not believe and would not say—except jokingly, after he'd lost a sale—that "the customer is always right," he saw the customer as his only true employer, himself as the customer's agent and faithful servant. He believed that if he proved himself a trustworthy servant, the customer would return when he needed George Preston's services again, and would mention the name, or pass on the card, to people they knew who had need of him.

As a general rule, the stores for which he worked didn't share his philosophy—not surprisingly, of course: it was late in the day for an old-time

Yankee peddler. The stores for which he worked were owned by people interested in making money quickly, people who knew about interest rates and inventory shift, but nothing about gluing or angled joints or fabrics. They were in "business," not "furniture." They were strangers who came to the hardware-store and tourist-court villages of western New York from the high-pressure clip joints of Syracuse, Rochester, or Buffalo, where volume was the not very carefully guarded secret and where the customer expected to be cheated and was. Personal relationships between salesman and customer were unheard of in such places, if only because the customer was forever on the move, chasing down leads on the American Dream in Cleveland or Pittsburgh or Philadelphia, leaving in his wake a great flutter of unpaid bills. George Preston hated his employers and made no bones about how he felt; but he was easily the best furniture salesman in the area, and after a little unpleasantness his employers invariably let him go his way until, despite his efforts, their shoddy business failed and another stranger bought up the inventory and the battle began again.

He was a fiercely energetic salesman, one who would drive miles after the store had closed to look at a piece of furniture reported as failing to hold up—he would do a little carpentry or tacking or sewing and then a better sales pitch than he'd offered the first time, this time for free—and he would personally look into the problems of a customer who couldn't pay the installments, yet he had abundant energy left over for other things. He had a vegetable and flower garden that was the envy of all who knew him—a picket-fenced, rose-gated square of land behind his ordinary house, a garden with pebble paths and neatly lettered signs, flowers and vegetables arranged to suit the markings on an intricate map he kept in what he called his den. He had at one time done beautiful pencil and charcoal sketches, mostly pictures he'd copied out of books and magazines; and though a professional artist would eventually have noticed that he'd never had a lesson, no ordinary eye could have discerned the fact. In their small, thickly over-furnished house, he and his wife, Buddy's aunt Mary, had charcoal sketches of hunting dogs, landscapes, horses, old mills, barns, cattle in a pasture, forests; and though they were amateur, and some of them copies, they were the work of a man who had an eye. One sees the same thing in the photographs he took. He'd begun because, working in his garden evenings—with his sister Hattie, who lived with them—he had loved sunsets, the special green light that came over the garden and the vacant lot behind, the cloud formations and depths of red, yellow, blue, orange, violet that would blossom for an instant and never be repeated. He worked up to a two-hundred-dollar 35mm Kodak with all the trimmings—tripod, lenses, lens brushes, carrying case—and took hundreds of pictures of sunsets and roses, later boxes and boxes of pictures of the Grand Canyon, Mount Rushmore, and the South Dakota Badlands, wherever he and his wife chanced to spend their once-a-year two-week vacation; also hundreds of pictures of places in Pennsylvania and New York State that they could reach—sometimes with Buddy and Joan—on a weekend. He took the usual photographs, trying for the world, not artistic innovation—the arches at Watkins Glen, the Bridal Veil at Niagara Falls, the waterfall and trestle at Letchworth Park—but the photographs he took had unusual power. He understood light—understood the single beam that comes slicing through the darkness of a vine-hung grove, the ripple of light in a brook as it emerges from an overhang of roots, the polychrome haze above a factory. Toward the end, he took photographs only of people, always people he loved and understood. Some of them would hang on Joan Orrick's upstairs wall.

Despite the fact that he read all he could find about astrology, phrenology, palmistry, and the rest—and tried to make practical application of what he learned—he was never a credulous, superstitious man. As he explained to Buddy Orrick once, leaning toward him, taking his arm in his right hand, the way salesmen do, and gesturing with his left, "Pontius Pilate was right: 'What is truth?' That's the question. Yet it exists, we all know. The real moral of that horrible story is, Pity the bastard that guesses wrong!" He had no use for organized religion. He'd once been cheated in a business deal by a minister at the Batavia Presbyterian Church, and it was a thing he could never forgive or even be persuaded to try to understand. He could have forgiven almost anything—fornication, sacrilege, theft, even murder—but never dishonesty in business. Business was precious; its laws were the holiest laws he knew. A man who could defile the laws of business could do anything, and the fact that such a man could occupy a pulpit put God's special interest in churches in the gravest doubt. "God was a businessman," he used to say merrily when ministers came to call. "Big funny-lookin brown-eyed Jewish fella. Matter of fact he was in the furniture business. Did cabinetwork." He didn't scorn churches; he dismissed them with a wave, as he dismissed flying saucers. His wife was a faithful churchgoer, and that was fine with him, but as for himself he'd never again darken a church door, or rather, brighten it, since everywhere he went people smiled and traded jokes with him, mostly off-color ones, or spoke of their families and latest strokes of luck, and thinking back later to his wonderfully beaming bald head, they would smile again.

Though he was not credulous or superstitious, he was interested all his life in magic and psychic phenomena and had in his library, which later went to Martin Orrick, books ranging from the works of W. W. deLaurence to those of Swedenborg. Both his father and his father's brother Bill, who lived with them, had been turn-of-the-century amateur magicians who attended experiments of the notorious Dr. Luther Flint, witnessed escapes by the incredible Houdini, and bought every magic book or illusionist's device they could afford. Like Flint himself, they were fascinated by the possibility that, despite the certain fraudulence of nearly everything they saw in the theaters or the upstairs séances of sharp-eyed old Rochester ladies, something in all that mumbo-jumbo might be true. It was, perhaps, the safety valve of their rationalism. George Preston's father was, by profession, an animal trainer: he broke horses for the coach or wagon or "the ladies' pleasure" and, on the side, trained dogs, cats, and mice. Men had at that time fewer books on the training of animals than we have today, and a trainer earned his reputation by learning to analyze an animal problem and solve it. Though "behaviorism" was a word that had not yet been perpetrated, all nineteenth-century animal trainers were behaviorists, and those who were religious, as was George Preston's father, sooner or later confronted the greatest and oldest of philosophical problems.

Men had of course special reasons, at that time, for suspecting that there might be more to the occult than the ordinary skeptic would admit. Mesmerism was still new and shocking, and though the Académie Française had denounced Mesmer as a charlatan, anyone who troubled to learn the technique knew that "animal magnetism" was real. George Preston's father and uncle Bill learned the art and were soberly convinced that the only reason they couldn't mesmerize people who were miles away was that they were doing something wrong. They had long discussions of these mysteries and attended every experiment they could get to. Also, on the side, less for simple pleasure than as insurance against the chance of bunkum, they learned tricks with cards, goldfish, rabbits, nickel-plated pistols, and mirror boxes. Many of these George Preston learned, some only when his father and uncle were dead and he inherited their books. At his own death he passed them on to Buddy, through whom they reached Evan, who made them the back-bone of his wonderfully skillful, ridiculous act. ("Goldfish?" he would say, raising the handkerchief behind which he was supposed to find the ace of hearts. "Oh well," he would say to the audience, smiling and blushing with pleasure, exactly as his grandfather would do, "it could be worse. Once I got chickens.")

In their search for something beyond mere illusion, George Preston's father and uncle Bill gave psychic tests to George and his brothers and sisters. They would deal out, for instance, a pack of ordinary playing cards, face down on the table, from which each member of the family was to select one without looking at it, and was to sit with his fingertips just touching the card until he believed he knew the card's value. It was a foolish game, George's mother thought, more tiresome even than guessing thoughts or Ouija, and no one in the family would have played it if George's father and uncle Bill hadn't been salesmen as clever as George Preston was to be. They would play this "game," as they called it, hour after hour, on the brothers' theory that psychic power was a thing that required developing, like a muscle; and time after time the members of the family would, after much thought, name the cards they thought they had, and the cards would be turned up, and everyone would be wrong.

One night, according to family legend, an odd thing happened. Buddy Orrick's uncle George, who was six at the time, fell asleep in his chair while the game dragged on. When his father called his name, he looked around, confused, realized what was happening, and named a card at random—the four of clubs. "Turn it over, Georgy," his father said, a touch impatient, and he was already turning to the next player when George's small fingers turned over the four of clubs. According to George Preston's story later, the family whooped with delight and hugged him, overjoyed because in this game for loonies and idiots someone had finally won. His father and uncle were eager to deal the cards and try again, but it was late and George's mother—she was a pinched-looking woman who wore her hair in a bun and, judging by her photograph, had no good to say of anything—put her foot down: the children must get some sleep.

The brothers agreed at once, but they were unscrupulous mad scientists and had their plans prepared. Half an hour later they crept furtively to little Georgy's bed, candles in their hands, their flickering shadows towering be-hind them, looking over their shoulders, half wakened him from sleep to give him a playing card, keeping the face from him, and asked him what it was. "The queen of diamonds," he said. It was, indeed, the queen of diamonds. He would remember years later how, looking up into the two men's crazily eager, candlelit faces, his father holding another card to him, he'd felt a wild surge of excitement himself, a sudden conviction that in some way he couldn't put his finger on, he knew how he'd done it and could do it again. But he knew the next instant that he'd been wrong about that. He had no idea what the card he was touching now might be.

"I don't know," he said.

"Come, come," his father said, smiling, the candlelight glinting on his teeth. "Make your mind a blank."

Their heads were tipped toward each other, and their smiles, their slightly lifted eyebrows, the way the fingertips of their right hands gently touched their beards, were identical. It seemed the intense reality of *their* image that blocked his vision of what the card might be. The room was becoming more solid by the moment: the wallpaper, stained where the roof had leaked, the commode with its shiny, cracked pitcher and chamber pot and washbasin, the scratchy curtain, every thread more precise than usual—as if the two men and the room were a startling, unreal vision, so that his ordinary knowledge of the value of the card had been driven from his thought by the intensity of the strange dream risen before his eyes. "I don't know," he said again. "I'm sleepy."

"That's right," his uncle said, and tilted toward him like a huge automaton. "You're sleepy . . . very sleepy." He raised his hand, moved it slowly from left to right. George slept.

He could never have proved, he would readily admit, that it had been anything more than luck that night. His father and uncle had continued to force the game on the family—also other games of the same kind: for instance, one with painted matchsticks, where one was supposed to guess what color had been picked from the painted, round tin box. He was not especially impressed by the fact that, according to his father's careful records, his guesses were right with surprising regularity, particularly those he made when, as he played the game, he was so tired he could barely keep his eyes open. What did impress him—though he knew it was of no scientific use and could find in it no meaning beyond its pure facticity—was the feeling that sometimes came over him that he was in curious hands. Once, driving his grocery truck, he was suddenly overcome by extreme fear that had no apparent cause—such terror that he was forced to pull off the road. The terror turned to nausea, he had to vomit in the weeds. Coming from the family he came from, he looked at his watch and wrote down the time on the back of one of his order blanks. The terror had come, he discovered later, within one or two minutes of the death of his uncle Bill.

Years later, when he met Lulu Frazier for the first time (George Preston was then fifty), she stared at his face for a long while with her deep-set, malevolent-looking eyes and finally said to him—they were seated at the dinner table at Joan's Grandpa Frazier's, and loud conversation was going on all around them, but the old woman seemed unaware of the noisy laughter and talk—"Second sight comes from the Devil. Beware of it."

A chill ran up and down everyone who heard, and the talk died down. She was a frightening woman, those last few years. George Preston made some joke, but her staring eyes bored into him.

"Lulu, you hush," John Frazier said, and he made no pretense that it wasn't a warning. If she troubled him again, maybe he'd get up, in front of all the company, and hit her one.

But the warning was wasted. Staring straight at George she said, "This man you brought here has second sight."

"Then it certainly doesn't come from the Devil," Aunt Mary said. Her blue eyes flashed.

Eleven

Anyone could have predicted that Joan and Martin's marriage would be a stormy one, and not just because, as the painter John Napper took such pleasure in discovering, years later in London, he was a Cancer, she a Leo. In fact her mother, at the wedding, just before Joan went down the aisle, had said jokingly, "Just remember, it's a good *first* marriage." It was of course the last thing in the world she'd have said in earnest, not only because she was still essentially a Catholic but also because, when you came right down to it, she loved him almost as her daughter did. She was in a certain way in love with his father too, as a matter of fact, though it was not at all the solid and serious love she felt for Donald. Duncan Orrick had sad and beautiful eyes and a shy tenderness that made him abnormally vulnerable but also able to write and speak poetry, and these virtues or defects his son had too.

It seemed to Emmy very risky, their marrying at nineteen, neither of them ever having seriously considered anyone else, though she and Donald had done everything in their power to encourage Joan to go out with other boys. Buddy and Joan were very different kinds of people, that was what frightened her—different in a way she and Donald, or John Elmer and Cora, or even Buddy's parents, had never been. She was brilliant and lively, wonderfully funny, she kept things hopping. Buddy was, well, morose. Emmy understood, of course, and she didn't like to be critical, but he really was, as she'd said once fretfully to Donald, an odd one. He'd come roaring in on that motorcycle from his college in Indiana, two hundred and fifty miles away, having driven straight through, no doubt as fast as his horrible, noisy machine would go, and he wouldn't even have shaved, though he was coming to see his fiancée, and he'd have on jeans and that grizzly leather jacket and boots with holes in them, and dark circles under his eyes because he never slept, and when Joan persuaded him to take a bath he'd leave such a ring around the tub you'd think he'd been working all month in a coal mine. He never brought a suit, brought not even a toothbrush, brought only his French horn and a book or two and the machine he rode on. (Emmy was terrified by motorcycles, always had been. One of her brothers had been killed in a motorcycle accident.) He would sit in the livingroom and smoke and smoke until the whole house reeked, and long after she and Donald had given up and gone to bed, he'd still be there, sitting on the couch listening to records with Joan, or lying beside her (to call a spade a spade), as they'd been doing now for years—though just *what,* just how *much* they'd been doing she wasn't quite sure and would rather not know. The kinds of music he listened to were gloomy, morbid, not at all the light, sparkling kinds of music Joan always played. Some of it presented no discernible melody, or if it did have a melody it was the kind that made you cry. There they'd lie—or lay?—listening half the night with the lights off, hardly ever speaking. It was all, she said to Donald, "so unhealthy." But they'd of course done the same, she and Donald, riding in his father's car, Donald's arm around her, his hand near her breast, she subtly encouraging him. And then once—well, never mind. If they loved each other as she and Donald had loved each other, and if their love would grow as hers had grown, and Donald's, then she had no objection, was glad for them, in fact joyful—but did they? Everything was so different now. What was a parent supposed to do?

Lying in the darkness, Donald's arm around her waist, both of them listening to the record playing and thinking of Joan on the couch beside Buddy, she felt as if her insides were bleeding, she was so worried, and from time to time she would ask Donald, really not knowing, herself, "Should we tell them to go to bed?" She suspected, naturally (and rightly), the worst. "It's just the sex thing that draws them together so," she complained to Donald one night. "Those two just look at each other and *boom,* it's an explosion." But Donald said wearily, sorrowfully, "No, they was like that before they ever heard about sex." And that was true, all right. She'd known it herself, had merely wanted Donald to say it. She ought to be reassured but, like Donald, she was worried just the same, worried sick. She would smile, long afterward, when poor Buddy—that is, Martin—had to suffer the same thing, when it was his own daughter, Mary, that was in love. And she would smile, too, at how needlessly they'd worried, though that was what life was all about, of course. They had their troubles, Joan and Martin, but thank the Lord they made a great deal of money, and their children were wonderful, which must be a sign that the marriage was better than anyone back then could have hoped it would be—though Cora and John Elmer, she must admit, and Mary and George Preston had had no doubts at all. When they came back to visit, when they were middle-aged, Martin a famous novelist now, with silver hair falling down his back like a woman's ("That's expected of famous writers," she told friends, though she had, of course, her doubts), and Joan a composer who'd had her music recorded by some orchestra in New York—pots and pans, it sounded like, or planets in collision, though Emmy was the first to admit she wouldn't know (she liked it, secretly; was it supposed to sound childishly funny, full of joy?)—when they came back, anyway, or when they invited Donald and her for a visit in England, while they were living there, it was not like seeing one's children but more like, well, bumping into old friends. No one would dream they'd been through what they had. "She's turned out to be a nice-looking girl," Donald said. Though she was usually more careful, Emmy had laughed straight at him, the understatement was so ridiculous, and he'd blushed and laughed too. Their grandson Evan was an absolute jewel, as saintly and gentle as Donald and as, well, pedantic as his father, but not gloomy, not crabby or misanthropic—not that there was anything wrong with Martin, she added quickly in her mind. He was good at heart. It took some getting used to, the way Evan's hair fell past his shoulders, like a girl's, or like his father's. But he was a wonderful boy, he really was, doing those magic tricks with his tailcoat and top hat, acting as if he never knew himself what miracle might happen next, cunning and innocent, exactly like Joan. She'd laughed until she thought she might fall out of her chair.

In London everyone was a magician of sorts, or at any rate everyone at their party was. The great, tall silver-haired painter Mr. Napper did mind-reading tricks, and his brother who was some kind of television director did tricks with cards and forks, and finally they'd all prevailed upon Evan to do his show. She'd really been fooled by his bumbling at first—as why shouldn't she be, a gangly yellow-haired twelve-year-old claiming that before he could do his tricks he had to find his rabbit, and hunting foolishly behind doors and under chairs until Mr. Napper, the one who was the painter, said (they must all have been in on it), his face lighting up—and his eyes so wonderfully, beamingly sneaky she should have guessed that very instant—"It's coming to me!" Evan stopped and looked at him, smiling in a way that was supposed to be innocent but was as obviously crooked as the smile Donald had when he'd skinned somebody out of a five-thousand-dollar machine for, say, two hundred dollars; and Mr. Napper said, "Sh! The spirit's speaking! Yes, spirit? Yes? (This is very difficult, he's speaking Swahili . . .) Come in, spirit! Ah!" And then, with a wildly mischievous look, "If my translation's correct, it's in a large black purse." Innocently they all looked around for a purse, and one by one they ended up staring at the purse in her lap. She blushed, feeling very strange, as if the laws of the universe had altered, and tentatively opened her purse. Out peeked a rabbit. "Oh," Evan said to Mr. Napper, "gee, thanks."

He was also a wonderful musician, as Joan had always been, but played French horn like his father—except better than his father—though she didn't like to say it—and of course she might not know. He was really more like Donald than like either of his parents, a mathematical whiz. As for his younger sister, Mary, well, she was a joy, simply. She too had that unreal-seeming yellow hair—in the summer almost white. She wrote poems and stories like a little professional, acted in plays, took lessons on the harp . . . It was wrong, Emmy knew, to brag on one's grandchildren, but she was too old, had seen too much, to pretend she wasn't proud. It made her see her own past in a whole new way, made her see the world in a whole new way. She had, now, Parkinson's disease. She'd learned to understand very simply what things made her happy.

Yet their worry at the time Joan and Martin were getting married was natural, inevitable. At his college in Indiana he rarely went to classes, rarely left his room—"writing a book," he said sourly, daring you to challenge him. When he came to visit Joan, he would glumly put on the suit she'd bought him and kept in her closet for him to wear when he came, and he'd go off with her to concerts or the Institute's dances, and he'd stand around all evening hardly speaking to her friends, and not just from shyness: Joan had nagged him about it once in Emmy's hearing and he'd answered, "What's to say?" He'd often talked like a Jew or an Italian, in those days. Why it hurt her feelings, Emmy didn't know. He had a cruel, vulgar streak. Joan liked nice things—clothes, furniture, houses. He was utterly indifferent, even scornful. He hurt her. Emmy saw it, but she was helpless. Joan was beautiful and lively, eager for life, and she'd fallen into the oldest trap in the world, or so it seemed to Emmy: she'd fallen in love with a handsome, gloomy-souled misanthrope. He could be funny when he wanted, and there were things he took pleasure in—how often she'd wished people who didn't know him as the family did could see him at his best!—but no mistake, he was a dark one.

Nonetheless, they were married; there was no preventing it. Donald and John Elmer made an apartment for them upstairs in Donald and Emmy's house. Buddy—or Martin, as Joan now called him, to his regal disgust—transferred to Washington University and took a part-time job in the Pine Lawn Bank. Joan gave up her chance to tour with the Symphony again—so willingly that Emmy couldn't help but wonder if there hadn't been some trouble—and took courses in music education to help Martin through graduate school. It was a strange two years. Sometimes they—the family—would sit up late playing bridge, or he and Emmy would have talks in the kitchen about the meaning of things, such as the value of religion even if it was false (he had strange ideas, and it was a long time since she'd played, except by herself, with strange ideas), and it seemed to Emmy that everything would be all right. But at other times she couldn't help but think, however she fought it, that the marriage was nothing short of a crime, a shameful waste—a girl of Joan's ability enslaving herself to a young man whose idea of a worthwhile life was writing stories and novels full of crude obscenities. Emmy said only, cautiously, "If you get your novel published, will you use your own name?" But Martin was at least attending classes now—doing well in them, in fact. For graduate school, to everyone's amazement, especially Martin's, he got a Woodrow Wilson Fellowship. It paid what seemed to her a great deal of money.

They moved to Iowa and were happy, apparently, Joan teaching a great flock of Bohemian-American musical naturals (so she wrote), Martin sometimes helping, more often studying and writing every day, all day long, far into the night. Her letters were full of happiness and there was really no question that everything was wonderful, except that they couldn't manage money. They were of course not the kinds of letters that encouraged you to read between the lines. Emmy would learn only long afterward that (as she'd suspected) they had their trials. They had fights sometimes. They had violent tempers, both of them, and Buddy—Martin—was selfish, prickly, he wanted to do nothing but work in his room. He was also resentful. He didn't like it that Joan earned most of the money, didn't like, ever, to be told what to do, hated even her gentlest suggestions, even hints that he might possibly clean his fingernails or buy new shoes when the soles were flapping when he walked. (On the other hand, of course, her "wit's cutlery," as Martin called it, was not always her best friend.) Martin was also secretive, sullen, and occasionally dishonest—he'd sometimes pretend he'd been at school all day when in fact he'd been home writing. He was a mess, really, though at times when they weren't fighting that wasn't Joan's opinion. Beautiful, sunny Joan loved her sad-eyed Martin more and more. Partly she pitied him—held him when he had nightmares, soothed him when his black depressions got frightening. But also they had a good time together. The fiction he was writing now seemed to her fairly good, and he had cheerful moods when he would actually, as she put it, come out and play.

They collaborated on musical comedies, which earned them money and praise, and Joan, who'd never before acted, played comic parts and was an immediate sensation. When he met her after the first night's performance, Martin was smiling, looking straight at her—he rarely looked straight at anyone. "You were funny," he said. "As a matter of fact, you were fantastic." Hard as both of them were working, there were numerous other things they did just for fun. They played in various little Czech village bands, both of them switching from instrument to instrument, when Joan wasn't conducting. They gave summer music and painting lessons and threw parties where Joan's teaching friends and Martin's student-writer friends played games, from charades to volleyball, and no one got drunk, no one slipped away with someone else's wife—in short, they were happy.

Only twice during those graduate-school years did she suffer that mysterious, searing pain. At the university hospital the doctor said, "Mrs. Orrick, we simply can't help you. There's really nothing there." She knew, as Martin did, though they weren't quite able to believe it yet, that whatever the X-rays showed or didn't show, he couldn't have been more mistaken.

Twelve

Though he was cranky and odd, arrogant, even insubordinate—as an instructor in the sophomore poetry course, he threw out the course plan for one of his own making, which lost him his job—Martin did well in graduate school and was even well liked by his professors and fellow students. He had a curious, small-boy innocence that sometimes made Joan love him till she thought her heart would break and sometimes made her want to stove his head in. Everything, with Martin, was principle. He might attack some classmate or professor without mercy, but never for an instant—as it seemed to him—could anyone imagine it was personal. No one, as he thought it must go without saying, could be more ignorant, more cowardly, more base than himself. Often he'd leave the victim of his attack in psychological shambles, and he wouldn't even know it. Often, unfortunately, the victim was Joan. It began to emerge that the difference between them was serious, perhaps dangerous. He had none of her brilliance, none of her wit, but studying endlessly, with mind-crushing orderliness, reading some one poem again and again until every little nuance was clear to him ("The hourglass whispers to the lion's paw" or "Hugh Selwyn Mauberley"), or reading some one book over and over—Plato or Blake or Roger Bacon's *Opus Majus*—until he was sure he understood every sentence in it, he developed a background of authority she couldn't match or deal with. She had no wish to know the kinds of things he knew—certainly they didn't make him a more lively conversationalist, it seemed to her—but all the same, she felt intimidated. Even about music—incredible irony!—he could make her feel stupid. She began to attack him more frequently—flash out at him, with her light, quick wit, some insult he would get only tomorrow in the shower.

Why she'd attacked he would have no idea, as sometimes even she had no idea. He began to be occasionally impotent.

They had other problems. There were certain things that were obviously his responsibility, not hers (as Joan at that time understood the world)—responsibilities he refused to deal with: the car, things around the house that needed fixing. He was becoming more than ever before a drudge, moreover; he never wanted to go out, and when they did he frequently embarrassed her. Or friends would come over and he would sit smiling politely, witlessly, never saying a word, obviously not listening. It was even worse if he was feeling cheerful. He'd talk at endless length of things no one cared about, stories of famous chess players who'd gone mad, for instance. Half of them he made up. He'd still be holding forth, laughing loudly, fully persuaded he was the life of the party, when she finally gave up and went to bed. Sometimes she'd wake up, hours later, as it seemed, and she'd hear them all laughing in the livingroom, still there, as if the things he said really were of interest. She would be all at once terribly lonely, seeing with icy clarity that, for all her early promise, her supposed beauty, she was already, at twenty-three, a failure. Tears filled her eyes and she wished bitterly that she'd never grown up. Princess my ass, she said, and wept at the loss of her innocence.

Yet when she looked back at them later, they seemed to her good years even so, those years when they were making it. Martin got exactly the kinds of jobs he wanted—good schools, first Oberlin, then San Francisco State, where the pressure was not so great he'd be prevented from writing fiction, yet the quality was decent; and wherever they went, she taught, concertized, took an occasional course, began composing a little. (He too composed. He was unbelievably bad.) Their fourth year in California, she taught in what was known, inaccurately, as a ghetto school and won the California Teacher of the Year Award. Martin was proud and had a party for her—unspeakably embarrassing. He got obscenely drunk and read the citation and the whole *Chronicle* article aloud. It actually crossed her mind that she might leave him. But mostly it was better. They went to plays, met painters and sculptors she admired (Martin had never heard of them), met doctors and lawyers everyone had read about (Martin had never heard of them), and newspaper columnists, even movie stars (Martin had never heard of them). It was the life she was born for. They had, by this time, a large old house in pre-earthquake San Francisco, in the Mission District, and Martin was doing well. Reviewers said of him, "A brilliant new writer has arrived upon the scene." Of her they wrote, "Few pianists now at work can match the articulation of Joan Frazier's right hand," and "her sheer joy in performance recalls technicians like Levin." "Who's Levin?" Martin asked. "Character in some old fable," she snapped. Martin was, in short, the same old Martin, gloriously handsome, with tragic, soulful eyes—though not as tragic or soulful as he imagined, she sometimes irritably thought. At three in the morning, getting up and going into his study, she'd say, "Are you *ever* coming to bed, Martin?" He'd be sitting at his desk, the room full of pipe smoke, an untouched martini glinting like a diamond beside his typewriter. He'd turn his head, stare at her like an owl, or maybe like E. A. Poe's ghost, jugged on visions, perhaps not even noticing that she was naked. The windows of his study were high, round-arched; they looked out across the city. "What you need is a black panther, like Lord Byron," she said. "Pardon?" he said. "Oh, fuck yourself," she said. From sheer misanthropic perversity he defended Lyndon Johnson and the Viet Nam war, argued in favor of capital punishment when all San Francisco was talking of Caryl Chessman, and in print described John Updike as "mentally disabled." "Martin," she said, "how can you *think* such things?" She spoke cautiously, like a welfare worker uneasy about prying. "The time has come," he said, "for thinking the unthinkable!" Then, more like himself, "Come on now. They argue like maniacs, all on the same side. I try to give their pompous rant a little dignity." "Dear Martin, you're such a *kind* man," she said. He bugged his eyes out and waved his arm like a Shakespearean actor. "A little less than kiss and more than cunt," he said. "Oh Jesus," she said, and rolled her eyes up, and closed the study door.

"How," people asked her, "did he get to be such an old curmudgeon so young?" She would laugh, though she was embarrassed, not so secretly, and they too would laugh. What Martin said at parties was of no importance, she might have told them, even to Martin. Halfway through the party he'd sometimes go up to his study and write or go play with the children, or if the party was at somebody else's house, he'd drive home early, leaving Joan—without even telling her he was going—to get a ride with some friend. He was a pain in the ass. But on the other hand, antisocial as he might be—and now, when she got him to go out with her, often drunk as well—his huge, slow novels had a kind of gloomy beauty; they were better than most other people's novels, it seemed to Joan. When he gave readings women students fell in love with him and asked her, breathlessly, what it was like to be *married* to such a man. "You have no idea," she said, and flashed her wicked smile. When he gave readings—dressed like a silver-haired peacock (she and Martin were now in their thirties)—she too could gladly fall in love with him again, though she thought herself something of a fool for it. But she never really thought, in those days, about whether or not she loved him. When they were with people he liked, of whom there were fortunately two or three, like the poet Bill Dickey, he talked eagerly, happily, and it was a joy to be around him. The rest of the time—except now and then when his indifference to going places filled her with rage—she was too busy to pay much attention to how she felt.

Then quite suddenly, as it seemed to Joan, everything came apart. She found he'd been having, apparently for some time, an affair with a large, untalented, peasant-faced friend of hers. He'd written her a letter and forgotten to mail it. Joan stood by the diningroom table, the letter in her trembling hand. "She 'understands' you, I presume," she said to him, wild with rage. He merely looked at her, cowardly, miserable, loathsome, but also superior, as usual; she was talking cheap clichés, revealing again her worthlessness. She grew wilder yet. "God damn you, Martin, defend yourself."

He looked down at his glass, then turned away and went to stand by the window with no expression on his face at all, like a tired old man waiting for a bus. It was dark outside, raining. "Martin, what about the *children?*" she wailed. Evan was six, Mary four. Beautiful, bright children, Evan like Joan, outwardly at least, Mary like her father, and they both loved those children, as anyone could see, with all their hearts. "You bastard!" she said, "you ugly, slow-minded, unwashed, filthy, arrogant, selfish, neurotic, drunken *bastard!*" It built like a magnificent arpeggiate crescendo in Brahms, and at its peak, exactly as she burst into tears, she hurled a cut-glass candlestick from the table—it had cost them plenty, and it did not escape her, even as she threw, that in throwing something expensive she proved she was serious. Incredibly, he let it hit him, stood like some big, half-wit Frankenstein monster, as if mournfully asking to be killed, and, to her horror, the candlestick crashed into his face. Blood splashed out across his nose and forehead, and he turned like a stunned animal toward the kitchen. She ran after him, calling, "Martin!"

"Stay away from me," he said, and looked at her. "I warn you." His eyes were, she thought, insane.

She hesitated, frightened, saying, "Martin, it was an accident! I didn't mean it! Please!"—still sick at heart because he no longer loved her—how obvious it was, how obvious it had been for months, she saw now—and with his hand over his face, blood rushing through his fingers, he walked out through the kitchen door into the darkness and rain. She ran to get her raincoat, still trying to decide what to do even as, awkwardly, she pulled the raincoat on, then ran after him. There was no sign of him now. She ran around the side of the house to the front. No sign of Martin on the street, either, only a few splashes of blood on the sidewalk, blurring in the rain. She called to him, then began to run, striking out blindly—she had no idea which way he'd go—toward the lights of the closed-down business section, the all-night Mexican restaurant, or toward the park—and that struck her, suddenly, as tragic. There had been a time when she could anticipate his every flicker of emotion. She stood on the shiny, steeply rising street, the lights of a car coming slowly toward her through the darkness of trees, the broad, empty lawns, and she screamed his name. The echo rang around her, clicked off brick and stone walls, concrete steps. After a moment a light went on, high above the street, and someone opened a window. A stranger came toward her, an old man, head tipped. "Martin," she whispered in terror. The same instant, everything went white. The pain that hadn't troubled her for more than a year was suddenly rising inside her, all around her, like an explosion, more intense than it had ever been before. The city went spinning, sucked away toward darkness, she heard a mumble of voices, then nothing.

Thirteen

Martin told her, sitting with his head tipped back, his eyes closed, beside her hospital bed, that he was leaving San Francisco. He'd taken a job in some unheard-of new university in the Missouri Ozarks. She wept, assuming he meant to go there with that woman. It was partly pride, she would admit later, when she was able to think about anything at all. Paul Brotsky would read to her, fondly and teasingly, years afterward, "The Leo tends to have too much false pride and may be boastful and snobbish. Since he always wants to be at the head of things, he must be made to realize that others like to be leaders too." Yes, all that was true. One of the things most horrible to her when she'd believed Martin was abandoning her was the shame, the unspeakable embarrassment she would feel in front of friends when it was known that she had been a "bad wife"—to say nothing of how she would feel before her parents. And it was no doubt true too that she had wanted too much "to be at the head of things." That was always Martin's chief complaint, that in everything she did she sought to dominate him—and it was his chief defense for having fallen in love with Neva, the big, slow-moving, guitar-playing friend who'd betrayed her. Neva accepted, demanded nothing, or so it seemed to Martin, and perhaps it was true. (At every thought of Neva, her mind winced back, enraged. Some people were *born* to accept, demand nothing, she thought brutally. Some people were born without rights. Joan Frazier was not one of them.) —But if pride was part of what she'd felt that day in the hospital, it was only part. Though the day was bright outside the hospital window, the white and cream-colored buildings glittering like cubes of sugar, falling away toward the heart of the city, the bay beyond, nothing was light or beautiful inside her: she was full of pain and sorrow as loud inside her head as a waterfall, and it was as if all the people and places and things she'd ever loved were being crushed, ground to bits in that churning, falling torrent of pain. She was haunted by memories, one after another—they came over her in a great clattering confusion when she slept—images of sorrow and failure that she'd misunderstood. She remembered with a sudden and terrible vividness Jacqui Duggers' three hundred pairs of shoes, brave colors, brave hopes, and the way Jacqui's eyes lit up with eagerness when she spoke—in her defiant white apartment there in dingy St. Louis—of Paris. She remembered angry-eyed, black-bearded Uncle Zack, his broad, lean back turned squarely on the world, his shotgun cracked over his hard, skinny arm—"kin to vipers," his own sister, Lulu Frazier, called him. And then into her mind came the image of her father, and the sound of his voice, and her anger and despair were baffled, driven back, leaving only her sorrow and confusion. She'd seen him cry rarely—once when, before they were married, she'd thought she was pregnant. He would cry again now. She couldn't stand it.

Martin said, "I can take the children east with me if that's what you want. Whatever."

She leaned up on her elbows, turning on him wildly. "To live with that whore? Not on your life, Martin Orrick. I'll see you dead first!"

He looked at her as if puzzled, his face slightly tensed, like that of a man forced to look at a wound. "There's not gonna be anybody with me," he said. "I'm going back alone."

Her mind fumbled with it, still full of pain but at the same time rising with foolish eagerness toward a hope too humiliating for her to admit just yet. "You'd like that, wouldn't you—get rid of all three of us. You could grow a little pot on the back forty and fill your whole tarpaper shack with teenage pussy."

He said nothing. She closed her eyes, crying again. Every morning she left at seven for the school where she taught, to give the kids extra lessons, lay out the day's work, grade papers she hadn't gotten to, and fill out reports or repair broken instruments, and often she wouldn't get home at night until well after six. It was Martin who got the children up, dressed them, fed them breakfast, typed or read with them playing on the floor beside him. ("The heart of a Cancer," Paul Brotsky would read in the new room, years later, "may be painfully divided between his family and the sea. They are wonderful providers and can turn a cave into a paradise, but they also like employment with shipping lines and sea travel.") It was Martin who, as the children grew older, took them every day to nursery school—walked with them down to the trolley-line M car and rode, one arm around each of them, through the long spooky tunnel—and at the nursery school played with them for half an hour (the other parent helpers were women with frosted hair) until it was time to walk the half mile to the college and meet his classes, talk with students. And it was Martin who had time to take them on excursions—to the Pacific, to the zoo, to Chinatown. So she knew, really, that it was not the three of them he meant to be rid of. She opened her eyes and said abruptly, looking at the ceiling:

"Can we go with you?"

He said nothing. She was afraid to see what his expression was, but when he got up from his chair and moved toward the door, she did look, ready to strike out. But he was shrugging, standing half turned away, as if undecided between two lives. As if wearily, ultimately indifferent, he said, "Of course." The circles under his eyes were darker than she'd ever seen them, and he looked as if he hadn't had a bath in a month. She would be amazed, later, that she'd failed to see, that moment, the truth, that he was sick—"had troubles," as her mother would say, apologizing for him, perhaps for everyone, the whole universe to the last scorpion "good at heart." But plain as his sickness was, she hadn't seen it. Even when she said softly, "You're crazy, Martin," it never for an instant crossed her mind that what she said was true.

"I have to go, Joan," he said. "Have to pick up the kids." He moved toward the door.

"Would you kiss me good-bye?" she said. "Out of pity, I mean, because I'm sick."

He almost smiled, hesitated, then decided to obey.

"I love you, Martin," she said, searching his face.

He nodded, noncommittal.

She had an image of him, all at once, living with Neva, growing weirder and weirder, dirtier, smellier, wilder of eye, and she had a flash of understanding, as if from outside herself, that she did not want him to destroy himself, and that finally it had nothing whatever to do with her own desires. "So you imagined," he would say later, scornfully, when she told him of the feeling, and there was no way she could prove it was the truth. But she knew. It was like the free will argument he was always on about. For all his reasoning, for all his fancy logic, all his long-winded quotes, you knew when you were free and when you weren't, it was as easy as that. Some things were certain—many things, in fact—and if reason undermined those certainties, it was best not to listen.

"Nevertheless," she said firmly—she could not know until he told her later, that her tensed cheeks, her sternness made it seem like tyrannical assertion, an attempt to command his feelings—"I do love you."

After he'd left, she asked herself in panic, "What in hell am I going to do in the godforsaken Ozarks?"

That night, because of the drugs, perhaps, she had a brief, frightening memory of the man she'd seen coming toward her through the rain, just before she'd fainted. He had his head slightly tipped, his arm stretched toward her as if he was greeting her, had been looking for her. His skin was gray, and for a moment it seemed to her that she remembered seeing Death. She toyed with the idea, knowing all the while that he'd been only an old man, perhaps an old man alarmed by her cries and hurrying to help her; and she remembered something she hadn't thought about in years, that her Grandma Frazier was supposed to have seen Death many times. She'd seen him one day when she was a child, in church—or so she claimed and obviously believed. They were singing a hymn, and a stranger came into the back of the church—an elderly country man in a shabby black Sunday suit, his hands folded limply in front of him, his head just perceptibly moving, as if with palsy, his lips touched by little involuntary tremors—and he'd come timidly down the aisle, no usher noticing him or coming to his assistance, and he'd come to a bench where there was room to sit and had stopped there. He didn't join the hymn, merely looked, with a somewhat curious, intent expression at a cousin of hers, a girl named Dora McClaren. When the congregation sat down, he too sat down. Then the sermon began—the message from the Lord, they'd called it then—and she'd stopped watching the man, though she could still feel his presence, still feel the oddity of no one at all's having noticed him. Whenever she happened to glance over at him, he was still gazing as if thoughtfully at Dora. And then once when she glanced over, he was gone. She started as if from a dream and looked all around her and back down the aisle behind her, but it was as if the boards of the church floor had opened up and swallowed him. That night Dora McClaren took a fever; three nights later she was dead. No one believed Lulu Thompson's story of the man she'd seen in church.

Joan pushed all that away, as she'd always done, or had always done at least since the age of twelve. She would never understand those misty times, she'd decided long ago, the days when Missouri was like a tropical jungle, full of snakes and vines and rich, dark green grasses, Indians, riverboat Negroes, dour, bushy-bearded Germans, lanky Scotchmen with eyes like flint—a time when every voting day meant murders and riots, when the Mississippi River had no bridges, only ferries, and the houses, like palaces, in downtown St. Louis were centuries apart from the cabins where country people chopped down trees and sank ploughs into the land and shot snakes. It was possible, perhaps, that her grandmother had told the truth about what she saw in plain daylight, walking along Halls Ferry Road, or sitting half asleep under a shade tree near Coldwater School. Looking at the faces in old photographs, the buildings sharp-edged, as if cut out of paper, the sky oddly luminous, she had the feeling, sometimes, that things might have been visible then that were visible no longer.

But what she mainly felt now, and only partly because she'd remembered again the stories of her grandmother's second sight, was revulsion at the thought of returning to that place. It was a feeling she could never have explained to Martin—he demanded logic, reason, possibly because if she worked by those rules he could always win—and her feeling about Missouri was the very opposite of logical. She loved the place, loved her family, and did not want to be there. She could say no more. Where was it, then, that she wanted to be? That was the kind of question Martin would ask. Paris, perhaps. Geneva. How was she to know? For now, San Francisco. He would think it immoral that she had no idea where she wanted to live, what she wanted to become. It wasn't immoral, it was *good*—but what was she to say? When he told stories of adventures he'd had with the children, things they'd said or seen, she felt cheated of a natural right. That too she wanted, to play with them as Martin did, let the hours slip by as a child's hours do. She wanted everything, all of it—but not return, not roots, not a life she'd lived already.

She would learn, later, a metaphor for the helplessness she felt, when Martin and Paul would talk of the right and left lobes of the brain, the left one intelligent and verbal, tyrannical, the right a poor ignorant woman-ish thing, too stupid to say *pencil* when the hand it controlled had a pencil in it, but a lobe that understood music instantly and totally, without words, and took paintings to heart, without knowledge of perspective or schools or strange jargon like "pointillism." Though their thoughtful, intellectual conversations almost never got through to her, almost never penetrated her defensive wall of jokes and suddenly remembered chores—escapes from the room in which the talk went on—their talk of the poor, sad, miserable right lobe had stirred her to attention. It was the lobe that controlled the left side of the body, the *sinestre,* the lobe that had to do with intuition, mystical leaps, with her own ability—or so she translated their talk—to guess the first names of people she'd never met. She'd discovered it first at her father's factory. She could look at a man who worked for her father and know immediately that his name was Ray, or Virgil, or Ben. She'd probably been wrong more often than she remembered, she realized, but that wasn't what mattered. Often she was right. And in the same way she could look at a woman and know what kind of house she lived in, what the furniture was, what kind of children she had. Martin had been telling her since before they were married that she ought to be a novelist, and for all his own novels he got her to help him with what people should be called, what their houses should look like, what games they should play. They talked of the right and left lobes of the brain, Martin and Paul, soberly reasoning, saying to each other that what both of them needed, as writers of fiction, was a more highly developed right lobe of the brain, and they would hold out their hands to the light from the fireplace in the Vermont house she'd lately gotten Martin to buy, observing to each other how both their left hands were blotchy and poorly defined, weakling in comparison to their deeply lined, muscular right hands, proving that their right lobes were sickly, unable to assert themselves; and she'd realized they were talking, without meaning to, about her. She'd felt a partisan's sadness for the sickly right lobe, and she'd realized, sitting in the flickering light in that huge Vermont house without furniture, that she was all both Martin and Paul were not, could do all they futilely demanded of themselves; and she'd realized, in the same flash of insight, that like the right lobe they spoke so admiringly of, she was mute, inarticulate, couldn't possibly make clear what she was and stood for, because as soon as they gave her the freedom to speak she would forget what it was she'd intended to say, would laugh and blush, like her father, and make some joke.

All that was in the future. What she knew as she lay in the Kaiser Hospital was that leaving San Francisco to return to Missouri was like a death. Why was she doing it? —There had never been any question about her not doing it. But for all her pain and sorrow and confusion, the question was locked into her flesh like some medieval instrument of torture: *Why am I doing it?* It would present itself even more dramatically later: he would beat her senseless, chase like a vacant-lot puppy after bitches, and though she was the proudest woman in the world, she would cling to him. Why? Neither the stupidest woman she'd ever met, a faculty wife for whom all the world was a sorry comedown from Lincoln, Nebraska, nor the shrewdest and most powerful woman she knew, one of her two closest friends in San Francisco, the Beckett scholar Ruby Cohn, would have put up with such nonsense for an instant. The longer she endured it, the more she saw of salvation by divorce, the more her pride should have pushed her away from him. But it was never a question. It wasn't reasonable, and at times she would admit it was hard to call it love. But she'd decided. Why? She had decided.

I'll go with him, she thought. *I'll take him for every fucking penny he ever earns.*

Then the pain struck again, and she forgot her rage. She rang for the nurse. No one came. She became frightened and rang again, then again. Still no one. The pain came out of nowhere, possessed her in a flash, and then was gone again, leaving no trace but a rawness, a feeling exactly like a skinned knee, but inside, and everywhere. A shadow fell across her, though there was no one in the room. "Martin," she cried out, "don't leave me here!" Then the nurse came, fat, stupid. Joan couldn't have a shot for at least another hour. "Doctor's orders," she said. "I've got to," Joan said, but the nurse shook her head, sublimely boss. "No use to playact. That's the doctor's orders." Joan saw at once what she was dealing with and threw the pitcher across the room, screamed with all her might, raised the hospital roof. They at once called the doctor, who told them sternly that they should have called him sooner. She got her shot. She slept.

To Martin she said nothing of her horror at the thought of returning to Missouri. Her father had had a light heart attack; that was one of Martin's reasons for wanting to return, or so he told her now. He wanted Evan and Mary to know their grandparents and cousins. What could she say? He was telling the truth about his reason for wanting to go back, though not all of it.

She remembered fishing with her own grandfather, in one of the sink-holes on his farm. He'd sit on the log that ran down into the water, in a patch of leafy shade, yellow sunlight all around him, and he'd give her advice on baiting the hook or casting toward the middle, or he'd tell her stories of mules he'd had, or his odd Dutchman neighbors, or stories of barns that had burned, or crazy fellers—there'd been one that lived right behind his place, used to come and steal eggs, same as a fox—and all at once, while he was talking, Joan would get a bite, and she'd jerk the pole upward, and he'd yell, "Thar ye go! Haul in now!" and out of the still water, glittering and flashing in the air like something dangerous, or anyway startling, after all that quiet, would come a sunfish with an eye like a frightened mule's, and her grandfather would tell her if the fish was big enough to eat.

Meanwhile the hospital tests dragged on. A month passed, then two. There was nothing they could find.

"Mr. Orrick," the last of the neurologists asked Martin, "has your wife ever experienced psychological problems?"

"Not that I know of," Martin said. "You mean you think her pain's—imaginary?"

"That's a possibility we're inclined to consider," the doctor said.

Martin looked at him thoughtfully, looked up at the ceiling, then once more looked into the doctor's eyes. "You're wrong," he said.

Fourteen

They moved to the Ozarks, a stupid university, a stupid little town, or so she thought at first, though she found a nice house, miraculously—a large old farmhouse with pillars, five miles from the village. It rained all winter long. The roads turned to gumbo, occasionally glazed with ice. Martin bought wormy old horses for himself and Evan and Mary, then wormy old dogs, and he tried to make the children learn to ride, though they were afraid of riding, and his yelling made them cry. The so-called university had no buildings yet, though construction was in progress, huge box-shaped horrors towering above weeds. He had his temporary office, with six other people, in a small, white house, the kind poor people live in in drab Ozark towns, a partly fallen chimney, a rusty porch glider on the sagging, peeling porch. Hippies with squeezed-shut hillbilly faces came and smiled and hunkered on the ground and talked, asked to borrow the horses, fucked their pale-eyed, long-haired girlfriends in the woods, the mow, the garage, the bathroom, and if no one was looking stole hayforks, grain, even lightbulbs speckled with whitewash from the barn, and drove up in their vans, when Martin's Rambler wasn't there, and emptied the gas tank by the barn. When Martin came home from work, if that was where he'd been, he would saddle up one of the wormy horses and ride off by himself into the gray, cold woods, and the wormy black-and-tans would run behind him. She couldn't go with him, couldn't ride at all. Either she was in too much pain to sit up, or she was light-headed with drugs. She tried again and again, stubbornly, but it was useless; as soon as they'd begin to go fast, she would fall, cracking her ribs, wrenching her back, bruising herself from head to foot. There was very little she could do, in fact, except sleep and hate herself and read. The children came up to her bedroom sometimes, trying to cheer her, and they partly succeeded, sitting beside her, reading or drawing pictures, or playing with stuffed animals. Evan was beginning to learn card tricks now. She hated card tricks with a holy passion—she wasn't sure why, perhaps it was because of the kind of people she'd known who'd done them when she was in high school and college—but Evan was funny, his hands small and clumsy, so that complicated tricks that went smoothly in his mind came out through his fingers with a charming clunkiness, as if done by a small clown in gloves. Mary would watch him admiringly, sometimes playing straight man or accomplice, and she, Joan, who was supposed to be watching very carefully, would close her eyes and be glad they were beside her and would wonder what was to become of them. They never seemed to fight—as she and Martin did constantly, the little he was home, not teaching or riding or sealed away from reality in his study. She should *do* something, he kept telling her. She laughed, furious. What a fool he was! She had too many years of experience to get a teaching job. The state had made a law against the schools' exploiting her, with the result that the schools, miserably poor and hopelessly backward, could afford to hire only inexperienced, young teachers. They might not have hired her in any case. The one time she'd mentioned to the county superintendent—she'd been driven by desperation into bringing it up—that she'd once won the California Teacher of the Year Award, he'd looked up at her over his spectacles with undisguised loathing and said, "You don't say. Well I declare." She knew his kind—maybe they were all his kind, here in southern Missouri. Crooked politicians; not educational dimwits, worse than that: indifferent, even hostile to schools and teachers and children. He'd fussed with papers, waiting for her to get up and leave, and so at last she'd stood up. At the door she'd said with a Missouri drawl and a sweet smile she knew he would understand, "You ought to get some *air* freshener in this office, Mr. Creed. Ah b'lieve they sell it in the dimestore." —It didn't matter, of course, that no one would hire her. She was on drugs all the time now. She frequently wondered if she'd ever again be able to think clearly, clearly enough even to write one really good, funny letter to her San Francisco friends.

Every Saturday that year he drove her the ninety miles to St. Louis, to see her psychiatrist, though neither of them believed for a minute that the pain was psychological. At the end of the year the psychiatrist was convinced that Joan Orrick was as sane as anyone, except perhaps for that peculiar devotion, even now, to her long-haired, cave-eyed husband. The psychiatrist shook his head, pursing his lips. He was young, and in a weak way, good-looking. Joan had changed his life. When she'd begun her sessions he wore dowdy clothes, talked pompously, like the Oklahoma boy he was, and never read a novel, sent back bad food at a restaurant, or attended a concert. She'd given him advice on what he ought to wear, what he should read, where he ought to go. Toward the end of her year of work with him she discovered—or rather Martin pointed out to her—that the notes he took during their long, rambling sessions were all on phrases she'd used that he wanted to imitate, musicians she'd mentioned that he wanted to hear, or interesting art shows, places to eat. On her psychiatrist's advice, she checked into Barnes Hospital for more tests. The bill was enormous. They found nothing.

Martin kept writing, as he'd always done. It was the one thing in their lives that was stable, invariable. He would get up before dawn and would write until it was time for him to go teach his classes—he'd have no breakfast but coffee and would hardly notice either her or the children—and he'd write when he came home, far into the night. Those were the only things he cared about, it seemed sometimes, his writing and his teaching. But that wasn't quite true. He cared about the place. It was the one way the children had of reaching him. The three of them would walk through the pasture, holding hands, or would explore the woods, finding caves and waterfalls, learning where the foxes and skunks kept their dens, where the beavers had dams, where the rattlesnakes crawled out onto rocks to get the sun. Whatever he loved, they loved, automatically, without question. They learned the names of birds—far more names than he knew, born and raised in the east, where one never saw a cardinal, a purple waxwing, a prairie chicken or mockingbird. They learned the names of trees—Evan brought home books from the school library, and they'd search through them together, or huddle around them in the woods, trying to make out what kind of tree it was they stood under. And circling around the farm with him, talking about things, they learned his ridiculous, tortuous way of reasoning about things, judging, weighing, pondering what-ifs, until the supper table became what it had been at Martin's father's house, an endless debate of—nothing. Once in St. Louis he bought an old French horn—he'd sold his long ago, when they'd needed money in graduate school—and he began to play it a little now and then. Evan too began to play, though only casually, tenta-

tively, as if testing to see if his playing the horn was what his father really
wanted. And again and again, though they were terrified, they tried to learn
to ride the horses. It broke her heart, watching them, their lips pressed together, their eyes full of fear, their blond hair streaming out behind them
as they cantered around the yard. Couldn't he see that they were terrified?
She tried to tell him, begged him to wait till they were older, but the children pushed as hard as he did. Once when he had Mary on the green-broke
Arab he'd bought for her, a rabbit jumped up in the path and thundered
off, and the horse bolted. Mary clung to the saddle horn screaming with
fright, Martin galloping behind her, unable to overtake her, and she made
it all the way from the bottom of the pasture to the old peach orchard behind the house before she finally fell off. She could have been killed, even
Mary must have known it, but that very afternoon they'd caught her luring
the horse to the high wooden gate, so she could get on again, and that same
night, in spite of everything, there the three of them were at the kitchen
table, studying once more the books on horsemanship they'd inherited from
Uncle George, things he'd gotten from his horse-trainer father. Paul Brotsky
would say years later, lying beside her, smoking a cigarette, Martin on the
other side, "It's a strange thing to think about. We keep the dead alive.
We carry on the things they cared about whether we like it or not. They'd
be nothing without us—that is, nothing but dead—but on the other hand,
without them, we'd be nothing. I guess if you like that means we're determined—you know, chained by the past. Or you can look at it another way:
the things they were interested in, the things they were, give us our possibilities." Martin said nothing—she could feel him smiling, gloomy in the dark.
He understood though, she knew. It was Martin who'd brought it up. She
said, "Do you realize William Shakespeare never heard a Mozart string
quartet? Isn't that incredible?" Paul groaned in mock-agony. "Jesus, Joan,
must you keep screwing up the syllogisms?" "You keep telling me to stick
to the facts," she said, "and I tell you a fact and you yell at me." They
had walked in the old Vermont cemetery that day, reading the names. It
was interesting that you could know without anyone's telling you what
a man looked like, even how he thought and talked, if his name was Nathan
Harwood. "Course, you have to bear in mind the date of birth," Paul said,
gently making fun of Martin's thoroughly uninformed and slightly too
fashionable interest in astrology (but it was Paul who had memorized the

zodiac characteristics, Paul who knew that, born November 5, 1804, Nathan Harwood was a Scorpio). "Exactly," Martin said. "Also helps to know if his mother was an Indian."

The children picked up, too, Martin's freakish love of violent Midwestern weather. When tornadoes came—first a blanket of terrible, swiftly moving clouds and then, in the lightning-filled distance a funnel, pitch-black and swaying, rushing toward them—she was so terrified she could hardly move, but Martin would stand at a thudding, rattling window or even out on the windswept, rain-drenched lawn and would watch in awe and a kind of crazy joy. If he would condescend to go down with them into the storm cellar, he would stand near the foot of the stone steps listening, and as the roar came nearer, the boom-boom-boom of colliding, warring mountains and skies, his mingled excitement and welcome fear would make his eyes demonic. *"Listen* to it!" he would say, and the children, one on each side of him, would take his hands, thrilled and terrified, and would stand, knees bent, as if prepared to run for the darkest corner of the storm cellar, their white faces peering up the stairway at the crack of greenish light. She remembered that her peculiar uncle Zack used to stand—so people said—on the listing porch of his shanty in the woods and fire his shotgun at cyclones when they came near. And she remembered that once when someone spoke of it, her Grandma Hughes—her mother's mother, who'd lived with them a while when Joan was four—had said, making everything strangely clear: "He likes cyclones." (Grandma Hughes was tiny and wore floor-length skirts and a Mother Hubbard bonnet. Joan's father had cut her toenails with hedge clippers. She rarely spoke and made very little sound when she walked. She got up early and worked steadily all day long, endlessly circling with her dust mop or broom, or patching at whatever little chores she could find to do. Sometimes she would suddenly smile.) And now, watching Martin, Joan happened to remember that her Grandpa Frazier, too, for all his gentleness and playfulness, had loved storms. How strange and complicated everything was—as if everything in the universe was secretly connected, tending toward some meaning too large for human beings but sure, just the same, and final, and perhaps serene. Then the cyclone was past, leaving nothing but a wide, sweet stillness, and she felt that in a moment something would come clear to her. Martin held out his arm to her. He said, "May I escort you back into the world, madam?" She smiled. The children were smiling too. Had she imagined all those fights? Imagined the drunkenness, the fear of her that showed in his eyes, or hatred? "Wah, mah *good*ness," she said, "yo so kind, suh!" They waltzed toward the stairs.

One afternoon, almost by accident, Dr. Crouse, their general practitioner in Sikeston, made a discovery. If an X-ray was taken when she was standing up, it was strikingly different from one taken when she was lying down. He ordered an exploratory operation at Barnes Hospital in St. Louis, by a Dr. Saul Krassner—"not much of a bedside manner, I'm told, but he's one of the best in the business," their Sikeston doctor said—and what he'd suspected proved true: she was a mutant, her internal organs weren't anchored to her body walls, and, partly because of that, she had a malrotated colon. All that could cause discomfort, but it wasn't the reason for the mysterious pain. She was one of those fairly rare people who grow adhesions, Dr. Krassner explained—delicate flesh tubers that begin in inflamed tissue—after a fall or an operation, for instance—and grope out through the darkness of the body—potato sprouts—tentacles of an octopus—thousands of little strands, completely invisible to the X-ray camera, feeling their way like timid snakes through the maze of her workings, closing around bone or intestine or liver, wrapping around the tiny electric switches of her nerves, locking her pain signals into the "on" position, so that from her knees to her shoulders she was one great howl of pain. When she was unusually tense, or went through a period of unusual exertion, the adhesions, like her muscles, tightened, closed like a fist. It had all begun, apparently, when as a child she'd had her appendix out—it was around the scar on her abdomen that the adhesion growth was thickest—but she'd suffered, since then, many falls, many blows. There were signs of those flesh weeds everywhere, groping through her body.

"What can be done about it?" Martin said. He sat absolutely still, pale.

"Well," the doctor said, rubbing his hands, "periodic operation can keep tearing 'em out, or tearing a lot of 'em out, that is—"

"And starting up more—?"

"That's the hooker, of course." Dr. Krassner shook his head, one brief, hard jerk, as if marvelling at nature's destructive cunning.

Joan and Martin waited.

"It's something we have to live with," the doctor said. "No use lying to ourselves, it's a losing battle in the long run, but at least you get a good, long run. It's not like being told you've got inoperable cancer. People can live years and years with this thing. But it hurts a lot, of course. Aye, there's the rub. Makes life no bed of roses. We have to try to learn to ignore it, that's all."

Martin stood up, went over to the window. "We," he said acidly.

He couldn't see, as she did, the doctor's look. He was a man of maybe fifty, very tired, for all his false heartiness. He was not personally to blame for the world's illnesses, though that moment he seemed, despite the bluster, willing to accept at least part of it. He took her hand and squeezed it a little roughly. "I'm sorry, Mrs. Orrick."

She nodded. "Yes, thank you."

He said, "The reason I say we have to learn to ignore it is there's really no hope of getting rid of that pain, anyway not all of it. Kind of doses that would take, the drugs would get you quicker'n the other thing. You grasp my meaning?"

She nodded, just perceptibly, the faintest possible stirring of her head against the pillow.

"You'll be feeling, by the way, a whole lot less pain for a while now—that is, after you've mended from the cutting—the operation. You may have—who knows? We never know about these things. Everybody's different. Takes all kinds, they say." He flashed his grin, then glanced over at Martin, who was staring out the window. Forest Park lay below them, where she and Martin and their families had gone, long ago, to those silly, tenderhearted musicals at the Muny. She remembered suddenly, and tears filled her eyes—useless to say it was stupid, sentimental: the human heart has no taste, no sense—

Springtime, Springtime, Maytime,
Will you love me ever?

Dr. Krassner said softly, his hand on her wrist, "You need a pain shot, Joanie?"

She nodded. "Yes, please." She was thinking, *Buddy, kiss me.* Tears ran down her cheeks.

When the doctor was gone she said, more to the room than to Martin, "What he's telling us is, I'm dying."

"Not exactly," Martin said.

"No. No, of course. Not exactly."

Fifteen

She learned to live with pain and the idea of a shortened life, though she didn't exactly swear off all drugs, except at first. It helped that after the operation wound had healed she had—as Dr. Krassner had predicted she would—a long period when she was almost completely free of pain. Though she waited nervously, knowing it must come back—watching her insides with the blank expression of an Ozark hunter watching leaves in a woods—she would sometimes go for days at a time without remembering her condition. In spite of herself, she began to find herself hoping that the doctor had been presenting only the darkest picture possible, that in fact the adhesions were gone for good now, the whole thing was over. She was not therefore happy, though she had periods of such happiness that she was shocked and baffled when her troubles with Martin flared up again. A thousand times they were at the edge of divorce, and now there were magazines and women's groups to make her feel stupid and guilty for so stubbornly clinging to him, or, rather, to their life. Often it seemed to her that for Martin she was dead already. He bought a huge old motorcycle and wrecked it the first week, grew his hair much longer, had passionate affairs one after another, and even when he tired of them or she somehow managed to bring them to an end—it usually meant some drunken scene and sometimes she and Martin would nearly kill each other—he'd go on writing to the women or phoning from his office, go on liking them as if they were dear and harmless old friends. He insisted, when she could make him say anything at all, that there was nothing wrong in it, insisted that she had no hold on him—love not freely given was not love, he said, but mere socially convenient slavery, and he refused to be socially convenient or anybody's slave. They'd been married for nearly half their lives; they were neither of them the same people, he said, who'd taken those pious, wildly optimistic vows. "Martin," she said, "don't you *remember* us?" "Characters in some old fable," he snapped. She tried to understand it, accept it. She had affairs herself, but it was never the same. She loved Martin, only Martin—perhaps it was, as people hinted, a sickness—and Martin accepted, approved of her affairs, even when they made him slightly jealous, because he had this theory about love, and he would rather die than abandon a perfectly good theory.

It was true that he'd changed radically. He'd never been her slave, whatever he might think—such was her opinion—but since they'd moved from San Francisco he'd done exactly as he pleased in everything, independent as some new Jesse James, or maybe Genghis Khan. It was he who bought the house they'd been renting, without consulting her. (He paid far too much money. Scornful of dickering, even when he knew he must lose by his scorn, he took the seller's first offer.) He went through, in fact, a period of real insanity, as she learned when she finally got him to a psychiatrist. When they'd first moved from San Francisco, he was turning off his hearing, even his sight, at will, psychotically withdrawing from anything that "bored" him—that is, the doctor said, threatened him. Whenever they had parties he'd get so drunk he could hardly stand, and he'd go sleep in the barn, or reel crazily through the woods, singing or ranting Shakespeare, waving his arms, falling sometimes, bellowing at the stars:

> "Yet know, my master, God omnipotent,
>   Is mustering in his clouds on our behalf
>   Armies of pestilence, And they shall strike
>   Your children yet unborn and unbegot,
>   That lift your vassal hands against my head
>   And threat the glory of my precious crown . . ."

The children, at such times, were afraid of him. So was she, for that matter. Though he ranted against "mindless, self-pitying existentialists," he'd developed a conviction that he was a Nietzschean superman. The kinds of rules she lived by, the kinds of rules her parents had always lived by, were moronic. They led to happiness, yes; a happiness of circling insects. All rules were moronic; all happiness was finally insect fodder. He threw away her psychiatric bills, threatened hunters with violence when they came onto his land, though the land wasn't posted, parked his old Rambler where he damn well pleased. He no longer paid attention to traffic lights, merely looked, somewhat casually, to see if anyone was coming. But terrible as that period had been for them all, his psychiatrist claimed it was in a certain sense healthy. In his sickness as a child, he'd lost confidence utterly, fled from pain and conflict and from emotional attachments, leaned entirely on Joan, who seemed so competent, so willing to do the work—even the emotional work. Yet he'd always hated what seemed to him his weakness. And now suddenly, however crazily, he was choosing to run his life. She needn't be surprised if he seized the reins fiercely, looking angrily over his shoulder, spoiling for a fight. He was determined—unconsciously, so to speak—to grow up.

Joan listened, squeezing her hands together, occasionally raising her Kleenex to dab at her eyes. The psychiatrist was fat, square-bearded. He looked like a cartoon of a psychiatrist. The way he leaned forward, studying her as if paternally, made it seem as if he thought it had been all her fault. For some reason, God knew why, she'd worn a suit to this meeting with Martin's doctor, and had pinned her hair up in back. She felt now for all the world like his mother, some domineering bitch a man would have every reason to resist. She thought of telling the psychiatrist she didn't always look like this, there were people who thought she was Goddamned beautiful. In a dress with a plunging neckline, with her hair falling free . . . She started to say it, and then for some crazy reason changed it in the middle. "I don't always look like this, Dr. Bern. Sometimes I look really horrible." *Silence, exile, cunning,* Martin had said once, quoting something. It came to her that that was what she too was up to, just now. Why? But she had no time to think.

He took off his glasses, leaned further toward her. His vest had a stain of some kind on it. Food perhaps. She hated him. "My dear," he said, "this has all been unbelievably painful for you." He reached toward her. There was hair on the back of his short, fat hand. "Let me ask you just one question. Is it worth it?"

She started, realizing what side he was on. "He's my husband," she whispered. No doubt her hatred showed. "I'm his wife. Nobody understands that anymore. It's crazy."

He patted her hand. He'd been hated before. It was nothing to him. "You are a very brave woman," he said. "Make no mistake." Then, drawing his hand back, he told her more about Martin's rebellion. He spoke not to her but to his glasses now. Small, steel-rimmed glasses. Fashionable. Martin's wish to grow up, face life squarely at last, admit his weaknesses but also assert his rights as a man—a decision encouraged, undoubtedly, by his success as a writer—was the reason he'd moved, abruptly, ferociously, to the barbaric Midwest he'd always loved—whatever the consequences for her and for the children. "You see," Dr. Bern said, "he is a fanatic about truth. A problem of his Christian upbringing." His decision, not quite conscious, to confront life head-on was the reason he was writing more darkly now—and, it might as well be granted, writing more beautifully, letting his pain in—than he'd ever done before. The wish to be himself, grow up, face the truth, was the reason why, when other women showed the slightest interest, he fell violently in love with them, or imagined he did.

"You understand what I'm saying?" Dr. Bern said, glancing up.

"I understand you think I should divorce him," she said.

He smiled and shook his head. "Not at all, Mrs. Orrick. I am saying he has no sense of you. None whatever. To your husband you are a symbol of evil and repression. He may grow out of this, though the odds are not good. He may well become an artist of some stature, and he may become a healthy and confident man, but his attitude toward you—not to put too fine a point on it—" He paused, considered, put his glasses on. "You are an exceedingly beautiful woman, Mrs. Orrick, and, I understand, a very talented one. The risk to you personally, in this whole affair—"

It came to her now that she'd been wrong about Dr. Bern. She said, perhaps only to see how it would sound, "Yes. I understand. I've been wrong. I'll divorce him." She was sick with grief and fear.

He was embarrassed and took his glasses off. "Perhaps," he said.

For all his scorn of shrinks, Martin admitted ruefully that what his doctor had told her was perhaps true. But what of her, what of the children? she asked. "I'll get to that," he said, so grimly that she was frightened.

That year he accepted a one-semester position as Distinguished Visiting Professor at the University of Detroit, and they met Paul. Paul wrote beautiful fiction, though it went nowhere, trailed off into a sorrow that made the plot unfinishable, the theme unresolvable. There seemed nothing he didn't know and nothing that was of use. He could talk easily, brilliantly, of science, music, literature, art. He could tell, with dark humor like that of Martin's uncle George, of things he'd seen in Viet Nam—how captured Viet Cong were pushed out of helicopters so that the one left would tell

whatever trivia he knew, how joke-telling, freckle-faced kids became inhu-
man—a helicopter pilot with pink sunglasses with a piece of tape across
one lens, another with a bushy black beard grown halfway down his chest,
human bones for a bracelet, another who flew in a derby and tailcoat—could
tell of small Buddhist girls in the hire of the U.S. Army, whose families
had been murdered, no one knew by whom, and who sat, expressionless,
typing out fraudulent reports of heroism, their faces expressionless, though
sometimes, coolly, mechanically, they would reach up and wipe away a
tear as other people wipe away dust or sleepiness. Paul Brotsky knew, in
his own view, nothing, believed in nothing. Even to Martin his nihilism
was frightening.

She said, "I'm in love with him, Martin. It's insane. He's just a child."

"It's all right," he said.

She began to believe something was changing, it would perhaps be all
right.

Sixteen

"There are no individual causes, no discrete effects," Orrick wrote.

Martin Orrick had fled—"half unconsciously," as his doctor said—to the only solid truth he could remember: the stormy, humid, narrow-minded, murderously potent Midwest. If it was an act of self-assertion, the first real act of self-assertion since his life had gone off orbit, it was also an act of self-resignation: as people capable of believing in God can resign themselves completely to the will of God, throwing away the compass, abandoning desire, acting spontaneously in response to a call as clear, if not as literal, as the one that came to Samuel in the middle of the night, so Martin abandoned himself to a place—a set of emotions, principles, if you like, translated into the solidity of red earth, low, angry mountains, huge, slow-moving rivers, cyclones, birds and snakes. The place—"wasted heart of the country," Joan called it—did not fail him. The woman who would awaken him to the truth about his wife was inevitable there, and he would find there, also, the Ferndeans, who would recall him to himself.

When he moved from San Francisco to southern Missouri, the Ferndeans were away on sabbatical—actually one of the work-leaves John Ferndean took from time to time, just as Martin did. Now the Ferndeans came back to their farm just a few miles from Martin's—John Ferndean, famous sculptor, his pretty, wildly energetic wife, and their beaming, noisy son, a year younger than Evan.

The first time Martin Orrick met them at a party he picked a fight with the sculptor, scoffed at him for riding to the hounds in a red coat because fox hunting, to Martin, was snobbery and fakery. (In all his life Martin had known only one person who'd ever ridden to the hounds—a tall, elegant lady who borrowed large sums of money which she never returned, and painted large pastel pictures of toilets.) But the sculptor, who'd grown up in England, was real, and he was a marvellous horseman—far better than Martin, who had the seat of an Indian but had never been trained—and he was also a truly extraordinary sculptor, teacher, husband and, perhaps above all, father. Like Martin, he'd come to this place because he loved it. (To be precise, he'd come for one semester as visiting artist from the Royal Academy of Art in London, and had at once bought a farm and settled in.) "Far as ye can see, lad, this land's all mine—though not on paper, me attorney claims." Though he stopped for red lights, he was no more than Martin a man bound by trivial rules. If his life was stable, conventional, "moral" (to use a word Martin Orrick describes in one of his novels as "obscene and despicable"), it was all those things by his free and conscious choice. In the life of John Ferndean, to put the matter briefly, Martin Orrick found rules he could approve of.

They rode together often, and sometimes Joan and the sculptor's wife and all the children rode with them. (Ferndean took a month to get Mary and Evan riding like dragoons.) Temporarily freed from pain by Dr. Krassner's operation, Joan Orrick could ride with pleasure now, and she learned, with some amazement, how beautiful the countryside was—fog in the hollows, deer poised like listening spirits on the hills, groves full of dogwood trees and waterfalls, and suddenly, when you least expected it, the wide, rolling river, circling eagles overhead. They counted rare species of butterfly, sang what they called horse operas, and after they got back ate lamb or wild goose, and Joan told stories that made everyone roar with laughter, or the sculptor's wife told stories of life in South Africa (with many an *"Achh, Huttt!"*), or Martin and the sculptor talked earnestly, boomingly, of the principles of art, told jokes, played loud games, fiercely argued politics or education or religion, always both of them on the same side. The world grew warmer, healthier, it seemed to Martin—became, mysteriously, more beautiful. The two families took trips together—Mexico, England, Italy, and filled their houses with memory-packed junk. They all became, quite literally and quite perceptibly, more handsome. Even when they were tired, the children almost never fought. They made rambling, magnificent sand castles looking out at the Mediterranean, Martin and John Ferndean working alongside them, inspiring them to greater intricacy and nobler scale, and as they worked through the long, hot afternoon, the people around them—first children, then adults—Italians, Yugoslavs, and impoverished Englishmen—joined the effort one by one until for half a mile the beach was fortified. ("Look, Daddy," Dennis Ferndean said, "that man's peeing right into the Mediterranean!" "Nothing strange about that," John Ferndean said, grinning, his shaggy eyebrows lifted, "standing so close like that, 'ow could he miss?" The children played bobby in Regents Park, built tree houses at home, painted, made clay figures, began learning to play musical instruments, held kite parties and badminton tournaments, played endlessly—though a stranger might have thought them too old for such things—with their innumerable stuffed animals and Legos. The two families, with all their friends, made an endless slapstick movie, in which the sculptor played the dashingly handsome hero and the dogs and horses (Joan Orrick observed) had all the best lines.

Time passed—a year, then another and another—and the Orricks were, much of the time, happy. If Martin Orrick didn't actively love his wife, he could forget, sometimes for weeks at a stretch, his conviction that, essentially, she hated him. Joan blossomed, even fell in love with Martin's mountains, as she called them, though there was something more suitable to her nature somewhere else, she knew, though she did not pine for it. Besides, now that Martin was making so much money—he'd had, by this time, three best-sellers—they could take off a semester for writing and travel where they pleased: the mountains were no longer a trap. She could sometimes believe for weeks and weeks, even though she was now in pain again, that the world had grown healthy, buzzingly alive, charged with that deep, jungle-rich Midwestern light she'd known in her childhood. She persuaded Martin that they should spend six months in Geneva, the next year six months in Paris, and the next full year in England. There Evan became a magician in earnest and it was there, too, that he began his work on photography—learning by the book, as he did everything, photographing not people or landscapes—except, of course, when his mother insisted—but mainly dead leaves, cigarettes against a curb, the nostrils of a young giraffe at the London Zoo. Mary began playing the cello and writing poems and stories, sitting opposite where her father wrote, at the kitchen table in their Regents Park apartment beside the canal. When the music teacher at her school was taken ill, Mary went at once to the headmistress and said, with great seriousness and—after six weeks in London—an English accent as impeccable as any English child's, that her mother was an excellent music teacher, in fact she'd once won the California Teacher of the Year Award.

"Is that *so,* Mary," the headmistress said, tilting forward with interest. She was a spiffy lady who wore slacks and bright chokers and fine old rings which suggested that her family was well off.

"California is one of our largest states, actually," Mary said.

"That's very impressive indeed, I must say," said the headmistress.

That afternoon the incomparable Mr. Lyman, second in command on the music front—ha *HAH!*—in flamenco boots and black trousers so tight he could barely bend his knees, his hair silver-white, though he hadn't yet reached forty, his fingers aflutter in a way that in America would instantly have pegged him a raving homosexual (he had, in fact, not the slightest inclination), arrived at their apartment with a huge bouquet: "I have come, my dear lady, to seduce you if I can. —Oh, excuse me. I take it you're Mary's father? —Ah, madam!" And away he flew toward the livingroom, and Martin Orrick, unshaven, papers in one hand, a bottle of Whitbread's Ale in the other, gazed after him. "Mrs. Orrick, I presume?" Mr. Lyman said, and bowed grandly and handed her the flowers. "I have come, my dear lady, to seduce you if I can." In short, she was hired to teach music.

Winter came, and snow. Evan rode the underground to Rutherford School in a tailcoat and top hat, practicing card tricks—in his vest, a magic wand. Mr. Pringle came, mornings, in his horse-drawn milk cart to leave milk in glass bottles. When Mary spoke American it sounded like a clever but distinctly English imitation. Martin, climbing in through an upstairs window when he was so drunk he could hardly have stood on solid ground, fell two storeys into a rock pile and broke his leg. Spring came. He walked with a cane. Joan was composing now, as well as teaching. String quartets for children; then, as she grew confident, music for older people. Martin sat writing in the sunlit kitchen, hour after hour, for all the world like some smooth-running, bleary-eyed, and shaggy machine. Sometimes he would turn and stare for a while at the grass and flowers or the dark mirror-surface of the Regents Park canal. Sometimes he'd go walking, late at night, and would stare, heavy-hearted as a caged bear in rut, at the girls on passing buses. For the first time in his life he attended a pornographic movie. It made him sad, merely. Joan would come in from her work sparkling, that long, red glistening hair electric, tits high, as if she were in a perpetual state of arousal, as perhaps she was. "Baby," she would say, kissing his bewhiskered cheek as he sat at the typewriter, "come fuck me." He would obey.

Paul Brotsky came to visit and stayed three months. She became still more beautiful, more terrifying. He—Martin—would stand, big-shouldered, long-haired, baggy-eyed, slightly fat, morosely watching as they went briskly down the sidewalk, Paul and Joan—and frequently Evan and Mary—on their way to Harrod's to get groceries and flowers, and he'd be so filled with sorrow he could barely get his breath. Not jealousy, not the faintest flicker of that, or so he told himself. He loved Paul Brotsky very nearly as he loved the other three. But loss, the loss of his whole life. He remembered how, when they were young, when he was teaching at Oberlin, he'd looked at her as if from an enormous distance—as a ghost might have looked at her, incapable of making himself known to her—had studied, feature by feature, her beauty, and had wished in a kind of agony that he could buy her fine clothes, beautiful jewels before her beauty passed. Lying beside her, touching her breasts, the splendid hollows on each side just above her pubic hair—as fiery red as the hair above: he could not touch it, ever in his life, without seeing its miraculous color in his mind—moving his hand lower, closing his fingers on her crotch, magnificently firm and as square as a box, he had wanted to weep at the waste of such beauty, such nobility beyond his means. She slept on. She'd been concertizing then, flying in and out, making just enough money to pay for the plane trips but loving what she did, and getting good reviews. Except at parties, he almost never saw her when she wasn't too tired to talk, or else asleep. He couldn't write when she was practicing, so she practiced over at the music building—went there early in the morning, before he was awake—and if they met for lunch, there was nothing much to say. He had never been talkative, and her talk was anecdotal, and no anecdotes are formed in a concert pianist's practice room. So he would lie beside her, touching her as she slept, and when she grew moist under his fingertips he would gently part her legs and make love to her, hungry and sorrowful, wondering if she was really asleep. Sometimes, sitting in a concert hall in some city near enough that he could go too, watching her play—her head thrown back as if defiantly, striking the keys with such controlled violence you'd have sworn it was a powerful man you were hearing (but her hair flowed down her back, dazzling, and the sheath she wore, metallic blue, split open to show the sweet cleavage between her breasts)—or her head lowered almost to the keys of the piano, tipped sideways, listening as if hungrily to pianissimo notes flying by like summer rain—he would feel, besides pride—oh, unspeakable pride!—a kind of horror at the thought that that woman was his wife. He had thought all that would change, once he himself grew famous. He imagined himself getting letters from adoring readers in Dallas or, say, Binghamton, New York, imagined college girls coming up to him after readings, Joan looking on with timid love. But it was the dream of a fool. He would indeed get the letters, and college girls would indeed come up to him and make love with their eyes; but she was the strong one, and would always be. She was, as some fool would at some point say to him, learning that he was the husband of Joan Frazier—she was, as the fool said, "dynamite." As he would write, in one of his earlier novels, only slightly disguising his dire situation, "Have you tried making love, my friend, to a famous violinist? Your member, though so grand you sometimes step on it, can be nothing in comparison to her trembling, plunging bow. Though you touch her with the gentleness of the Angel Raphael, Mendelssohn was there before you, and Mozart and Bartók, and, my friend, you will never compete." He watched them walking down the sidewalk toward the bus stop, Paul Brotsky swaggering, full of youth and good humor, almost comically square-shouldered and mighty of chest ("Shall we speak, tiresomely," Martin Orrick would write, "of beautiful noses? Philip Baratovich had a beautiful nose: exactly the right size and shape and color, so perfect one almost didn't notice at first, and arching out above it on either side, with Russian abandon, two perfect black eyebrows on a forehead worth more than all Shakespeare's sonnets, or Beethoven's quartets, or—let us speak recklessly, for Art is Art—the Wisdom of the Bible. He also had large, yet elegant feet. His teeth, however—for which I thank God—had imperfections."), Joan glowing in his company—there was some ad Martin Orrick had read one time in the *New Yorker,* which, needless to say, he hated—an ad for shirts or ties or something—that said, *"Your man is your most important accessory"*—and Paul Brotsky was that, and not just physically. The children were laughing at some joke of Paul's, Evan with his blond head majestically thrown back, his camera swinging from his shoulder strap, Mary laughing in a way that made her suddenly American again.

And he felt, on one hand, that his work, his passions, his sickness had made all this possible, and it was good, supremely beautiful; and felt, on the other hand, utterly, tragically separate, cut off. He felt in his bones Camus's image of the man who sees the world through a glass, through which no sound can pierce. On the street, marching gaily toward the bus stop, the very Platonic image of joy, vitality; in his heart, suicidal blackness. (Once, downtown, he met his former love Neva. She was fat now, but still, in his eyes, beautiful and good. They embraced, clumsily, and had tea together. She gave him, furtively, her London address. That night he went walking, intending to go to her, but instead, for some reason, he went into a pub. He awakened the next morning in his own garden, his crutches beside him, his face scratched and bruised. He had a feeling—but he couldn't remember—that he'd tried to kill himself.) They had said, "You want to go to Harrod's, Martin?" "No, you go," he'd said. "I sort of feel like working." They reached the bus stop, and Mary stood with her head cocked, pointing her finger at Paul, saying something that Martin couldn't hear. Joan made a swooping rush at her, like an eagle or a witch, and everybody laughed. Tears filled Martin's eyes and he whispered in the doorway, "Dear God, somebody please help me."

Two weeks later the Ferndeans arrived in England. Martin Orrick quit writing and spent all his time going to museums, studios, parties with John. All he would remember clearly, afterward, was that one afternoon, sitting in the apartment the Ferndeans had rented, a jazzy little place that made you laugh at first sight of it—Victorian grandiose in a ten-by-ten room—he'd said, "Damn it all, John, that cough of yours is really disgusting. You've got to quit smoking those cigarettes. Take a pipe." And he'd given him the pipe he was smoking. "Pipe?" John Ferndean said, with that wonderful cockney innocence he could put on. "Say now, *there's* a bitta class!"

They learned at the end of their stay in England that John had lung cancer. Back in southern Missouri, they saw each other almost every night. They never talked about death unless John Ferndean brought it up. However, they talked about it regularly, because, in a way, it was a rare opportunity: Martin Orrick was a writer of the first rank, and John Ferndean an artist so good he could never be tricked by the faintest breath of sentimentality. It became, between them, an unspoken pact that John would tell Martin every flicker of feeling that came over him. What they learned was, finally, that there was nothing to say: that the single most striking fact about dying was that it was embarrassing. People behaved strangely toward a dying man, and the dying man became—with full awareness and humor, in the case of John Ferndean—paranoid. "One of the things ye do, lad, when yer dying, is you worry about money." And grinned. And: "It's like dogshit ye can't get off yer shoe." And: "It's a curious thing. I'm the healthiest man I ever knew, except for this cancer."

When he learned that he had cancer, already metastasized, he still had the rippling, overdeveloped muscles of a sculptor and horseman. His voice was a little rough, and his cough was constant—dry, casual, more like a mannerism than like a serious cough—but no one would have dreamed he wouldn't live to a good ninety. Or rather, no one but Evan would have dreamed. Evan read, religiously, the books handed down from Martin's uncle George. Who knows why—(there are no individual causes, no discrete effects)—he believed absolutely what he read in those books. The books about horsemanship had been true to the last word; the books about magic had proved infallible—even he, the most helplessly clumsy incompetent in the world, as he viewed himself, could do tricks that amazed his family and made even John Napper, who was *really* a magician, beam with pleasure. And so he had accepted without question what he read in Uncle George's books about palmistry, and when he read, for the first time, John Ferndean's palm, one afternoon in London, he looked at the lifeline and felt suddenly dizzy, terrified, as if the earth had swung off course. His eyes flushed with tears, and he couldn't think what to say. Nadine Ferndean said, leaning hard toward him, a Taurus, a woman of mysterious psychic energy—as he knew because once he'd held a coin suspended from a string above her head, and it had spun wildly, exactly as it did when he held it above Dennis Ferndean's head—"Tell us about the lifeline." He'd sucked in his breath and said laughing, scared to death, "According to his lifeline he should be dead by now." All of them had laughed, but Nadine had leaned hard at John Ferndean, saying—who knows what it meant?—"You *see,* John, you *see?"*

John Ferndean said to Martin: "I can't help feeling I *asked* for it. It's hard to believe you got no control whatever. I read these Indian mystics, and when they tell me a man dies by choice, I believe 'em. But ye know, it's peculiar. I wake up in the mornin, and the sun's shinin in, and I jump out of bed like a cockerel off 'is roost. I never knew anybody that liked getting up more than I do. I run out and feed the horses, and ye'd think I got some kind of electricity in me pants." He grinned. Dying had no effect on his grin. *"You,* now, lad, if ye woke up dead some mornin it'd make you a Christian. 'Praise God's mercy,' ye'd say."

Martin Orrick would remember, mainly, one image. The Ferndeans came to supper, and Dennis and his mother came blazing in, noisy as a cyclone, faces shining, eyes wide. Martin walked out onto the pillared front porch to meet John. He wasn't there yet. It was a night without stars, no light but the yellow light coming from the house and, out by the barn, the bluish white light of the security lamp. Then, in the darkness around the huge old maple, he saw John Ferndean coming, slowly, carefully, like an old, old man. He had the huge sculptor's body he'd always had, the same wildly, generously curling hair; but cobalt treatments had made his stomach bad, and his muscles, for all their size, were no longer in tune. He came through the darkness cautiously, sadly, and it seemed he might have come to Martin Orrick's views. But then, coming out of his absentminded daze, he grinned and said, "Hey, lad," as if they'd all survive.

It was a ghastly time, and not the least of its horror was that Martin was soberly, desperately, in love, and much as he'd have liked to have kept that fact from his dying friend, it was a secret impossible to keep. Joan, recognizing a threat more serious than any she'd ever had to deal with before, fought more ferociously than usual to hold him. The scenes at the Orrick house became monstrous. Once, when he was so drunk he couldn't walk ten feet without lurching and falling but insisted, all the same, that he was going to Sarah, Joan hit him on the head with a fireplace log, hoping to save him by knocking him out (also, as she'd readily admit, she was furious, half-crazy with jealousy). The sharp edge of the split log cut deep, but Martin chose, that night, to be indestructible. He turned and slugged her in the face with all his might—her cheek, the next day, would be enormously swollen, so that her eye was squeezed shut, and the whole right side of her face blue-black—and then, in a daze, blood rushing down his face and the side of his head, he ran out to the truck he'd bought just two weeks before and headed it down the driveway, the big Alsatian on the seat beside him. Because he was dazed, he couldn't remember where Sarah Fenton lived—couldn't remember her name in fact, though his heart ached for her kindness, her strange, all-forgiving reasonableness—and so he simply drove, urgently, on and on, crazily hunting. When he came to himself, he was in Indianapolis. Perhaps it was his parents in New York State that he'd meant to run to. He stopped for gas—he'd no doubt stopped before, but he couldn't remember—and while the attendant filled the tank, Martin went into the men's room and saw, in amazement, how he looked, caked blood on his forehead and running down the sides of his nose, his hair stiff and messy, his chin darkly stubbled. He washed the blood off, as well as he could, then grimly marched back to the truck, paid for the gas, and turned around, heading back toward Missouri. He'd reached his decision. He would end the marriage, choose Sarah; but first he would wait out John Ferndean's death and would take John's family and his own to Spain as he'd promised to do. It would be a fitting conclusion, a natural breaking point. He had no doubt that the decision was right, though the thought of losing his children made the tears run gushing down his cheek. As for Joan, he had no love left for her, he thought. It had finally happened, what he'd expected for years: she'd tried to kill him. "That's not right," Joan said hours later, weeping, "I was trying to knock you out. I was trying to save you." And he realized in guilty confusion that no doubt that was true. Nevertheless, he told her his decision. "Martin," she said, "don't do it. Please." He said dully, icily, "It's done already."

Joan searched wildly for a way to defend herself, make him see sense, make him understand that she still loved him. She knew well enough that Sarah had the odds. Sarah was "reasonable," "instinctively just," he said. Oh yes. Terrific. "She can afford to be," she snapped. "She's not your wife." But with every word she spoke, though it was all true, she knew she was burying her chances more deeply, because Sarah *was,* in Martin's experience, gentle and reasonable; steadily, ploddingly, unfailingly. With her every attempt to save the marriage, Joan made the contrast between them, she knew, more obvious.

"She's cunning, Martin," she said. Then, trying to be fair, knowing his childish and unreasonable love of fairness at any cost, she added, "Maybe she doesn't even know it herself, but she's cunning: she's after you, seducing you with talk and that horrible macrobiotic cooking, talking about only the things she knows you like—"

That, he could have told her, was not true. Sarah talked endlessly of health foods and exercises, which bored him to tears—though he was inclined to believe her theories about eating; at any rate, the nervous stomach that had plagued him all his life no longer troubled him when he stopped eating meat. Neither was it true, as Joan insisted, that he loved her because she was younger, prettier. She was only five years younger than Joan, and in everything she did she was as slow as an old woman. Sitting in her small house watching her cook, or watching her type one of his manuscripts, he was driven wild by the deliberateness with which she did everything, as if she expected life to go on forever. But he could put up with that. She was not, certainly, prettier than Joan; but her fundamental goodness and gentleness gave her a beauty Joan could not at that time match, in Martin's eyes, and she commented on his fiction in a way no one had ever done before, naively treating his characters as actual people, urging him to see in them virtues he'd missed, persuading him to be kinder about their faults. She was uninterested in possessions—she owned practically nothing—but she had taste, an innate sense of what was solid and good, that Joan, in his opinion, lacked. She gave him a beautiful hundred-year-old clock, the most beautiful he'd ever seen. It made everything in his house seem to him trashy, quick and easy. He did not, of course, tell Joan where the clock had come from; but Joan had an infallible sense for these things. For all its beauty—lovingly fashioned; firm, heavy wood; antique, wavy glass—the clock lasted just three weeks. That she could destroy such a thing astounded him. It was more shocking than her hitting him on the head with a log. He remembered what he'd put out of his mind for years, that when they were first married she'd "remodeled" a beautiful old chest his parents had given them—had sawed off the legs and put on idiotic handles. He was surer than ever that he must leave her right after the trip to Spain, start his life all over. He told Sarah his intention, as he'd told Joan.

"If it happens, I'll be a good wife," Sarah said.

"It will," he said firmly.

She kissed his hand. She wanted it to happen, wanted to believe him. But it was a fact that when he went on reading trips, it was Joan he took with him, and the children. Under her mask of serenity, she was annoyed, timidly suspicious. Because he was honest when he talked about Joan—honest about her humor, her fears, her talent—Sarah understood she wouldn't get him without a fight, for all his protestation. She hesitated—characteristically. It would be enough, she told herself, if they could just be lovers. But lying on the pallet beside him, moonlight streaming in, she would study his sleeping face, puffy from too much drinking, and tough under her fingertips—like the face of anyone who drank too much milk, ate too much meat—but nevertheless a good face, well constructed, phrenologically the face of a man who would die old if he could learn moderation, learn to slow down, and she knew it would not be enough for her merely to be his lover. She wanted him as, so far as she could remember, she'd never wanted anything, and wanted children by him. "Yes, she will make me fight for you," she said. He opened his eyes and she smiled. She hadn't meant for him to overhear. But she saw that he was still asleep, even though he looked at her. "Well then," she whispered, and her eyes slightly narrowed, "I will fight."

She cooked for him, when he came to her, as she'd never cooked before. She'd been well trained, and at each new taste she introduced him to he would say, staring at his chopsticks, "That's amazing!" She typed for him half the night, not very accurately, but working till her fingers ached and she could hardly see. She massaged him, taught him Do-in, convinced him that he was magnificent, drunk or sober, happy or sad, played him her tapes of gypsy music, sometimes played piano or guitar for him, and again and again, though when they'd first become lovers he'd occasionally been impotent, made love to him. She was an artist on the pallet; she could make anyone believe he was the world's greatest lover. But she knew, also, how to talk to him, usually, or so she believed, and it was partly true. It was by talk, in fact, that she'd attracted him in the first place, when she was sitting in on one of his English classes. She talked mostly about the things he cared about. That was as it should be, in Sarah's opinion. The whole idea of women's liberation made her sad, made her laugh. She had been liberated all these years—in the sense, at least, that she'd gotten every job she'd ever cared about, had traveled as she pleased, had made money, had lived with men. She was ready to be a simple, devoted wife. Tentatively, at least. Though she loved him so hard her heart would leap when she heard the crunch of his tires on the drive, she knew, with a tiny corner of her mind, that love was still an experiment for her, she was prepared, in the end, to fail—not that she was planning on it. She would fight for him, and if she won, his love for her would take care of her faint reservation.

Joan Orrick needed no formal announcement that the fight was on. When Martin told her his plan to divorce her immediately after the trip to Spain, she flew at once to the most powerful weapon available: the Ferndeans. She told them on the phone of Martin's love affair and of hitting Martin with a log and of his terrible, dazed drive to Indianapolis. The Ferndeans, shocked and grieved, asked them to come over. Then, fierce-eyed as her grandma Lulu Frazier, but with no evil in her heart, nothing in her heart but a violent longing for a loving, absolutely faithful marriage like her parents' marriage, or that of Martin's parents, she told Martin what she'd done.

"How *could* you?" he said, and by his horrified look she knew it was as bad, in Martin's eyes, as her smashing of Sarah's clock.

She had no answer to give him. It had not been a conscious act of self-defense, and it hadn't been at all that she wanted them to see how he treated her, wanted them to see that gross, black bruise. She had acted, simply. And now, seeing through Martin's eyes how painful it would be for Nadine and John—because what could they do?—she thought, like Martin, that what she'd done was wretched, inexcusable.

But they went, Joan's bruise grotesquely covered by white cream, Martin's head misshapen, and sat crying in the room where John Ferndean lay, crying with them, breathing with difficulty—beginning to drown—his wife puffy-faced on the side of his bed, crying as she'd been doing since Joan Orrick phoned.

"We love you," Nadine said. "Why must you kill each other?"

Martin could remember none of it afterward, except their sorrow and helplessness and his huge load of guilt. He watched Joan talking to them—he himself said almost nothing—and couldn't even hate her for having done this thing. She was like a child, a child he'd loved. He thought of how all her life she'd ruled him, led him around, guided him to dark rooms or groves for their childhood love-making, thought of how he'd loved her voice when she called him at his father's house from St. Louis, how they'd laughed together, holding hands, when his uncle George told stories, or played French horn and piano together, under Yegudkin's sharp black eye. Why *couldn't* they have been like her parents? he wondered. But they'd been similar kinds of people, her mother and father, just as his parents had been similar kinds of people; and all their lives he and Joan had been deadly opposites. He remembered how he'd loved going to church as a child—loved the singing, the responsive reading, the long pastoral harangue. Joan was indifferent to all that. If she went at all, it was for the organ music. She was so little interested in the ideas and myths that she used "heaven" and "Armageddon" interchangeably. (He would learn much later that he was wrong about her there. She was in fact interested, but her ignorance made her shy of asking. Every time she went to her psychiatrist in Detroit, she would go with Paul to the cathedral, now attended mainly by blacks, and she would bask in its beauty—and the merry, chatty, holy foolishness of the congregation, shaking hands on all sides, wandering up and down the aisles, putting up colorful signs: JESUS IS NUMBER ONE—as her mother had once basked in the order and dignity of the Mass, the warmth of grass and flowers on a convent lawn. Joan Orrick was in fact, like her mother, profoundly religious.)

"We just wish there was something we could do," John Ferndean said. "We feel so helpless."

"I know," Martin said. "Look, we're grateful—"

"I know, I know." John Ferndean touched his wife's hand, and the love in the gesture made Martin sick with grief, thinking, *Why you, not us?* And: *I'm sorry. I'm sorry.*

John died within a year. Martin and Joan watched, visited nearly every night, took care of his family as well as they could, given their own desperate situation, and went to Spain and southern France with them afterward to stare at famous ruins, Martin looking helpless and stable as a wall, no longer mad, though more eccentric than ever, and full of sorrow. Nadine Ferndean spoke to him as he'd heard her speak to her husband, in the trips they'd taken before, saying, "Hannibal *couldn't* have crossed the Alps." John would have answered, "Of course he could! Look there!" But Martin could say nothing. Even if his eyes were not blurred by tears, what did *he* know of Hannibal? They went down into the dark and frightening cave where people had hidden at the time of the Inquisition. "Reminds you of Stonehenge, doesn't it," she said, "—the feeling, I mean." He had never been to Stonehenge. *Johnny, lad,* he thought, *I forgot to tell you. I hated you for dying.*

At the end of the Spanish trip, Joan began to cry, hour after hour in their stateroom, not asking for sympathy or attention, simply mourning her marriage, her children, Martin, and the beautiful, talented child-Joan wasted and betrayed. She had decided to kill herself. Martin, when he learned, squinted in disbelief, then said, helplessly, "Don't. I'll stay."

"Will you really?" It was a plea. She was beyond shame now.

He nodded.

Seventeen

Sarah Fenton was small and thin. Like all macrobiotics, she had an Oriental look—large, mournful eyes, straight, lively hair (it was as black as coal), and the dry, pale mouth of someone who has lost blood. She was thirty-five (Martin Orrick was forty) and had been everything—a teacher in Brooklyn, an off-Broadway actress (she was then twenty-five, but in the photographs one can discern no difference between Sarah at twenty-five and Sarah ten years later), a teacher of yoga on 24th Street, a translator from Spanish, Italian, or French, whatever was needed, at the United Nations. She was a fair actress, judging by her reviews, but she had no faith whatever in reviews—indeed, had no faith in herself at all. She was (Martin Orrick pointed out to her) a Pisces, a back-stabber whose knife went unfailingly into her own slim back. She had done—what else? She'd lived for two years in Spain, with gypsies—it was there she'd learned guitar. Though she never played it well, she played it in the long-fingered gypsy style, and never in her life was she guilty of hillbilly hammer-ons and pull-offs. She'd also lived for two years in India, in the courtyard of a temple, where she'd divided her time between meditation and watching healings. She would become, herself, a sort of healer. She had no explanation of what she did, and could achieve no miracles, but she could change people, simply by her presence, could make them receptive to whatever restorative powers time and chance might afford. Both her mother and father were southern Missouri doctors, general practitioners, sad, intelligent people who'd been divorced for years. They both loved her and were baffled and disappointed by her strange way of life, never settling down, living with riffraff, cranks, and gurus. But if Sarah was home, they'd sometimes send her their hopeless cases, and she would massage them and talk with them and make them imagine they felt less pain.

Except for quirky theories about diet, she had no code, no beliefs, or at any rate none she had words for. She'd lived comfortably for a year in Arizona with a professional thief, a good poet, she believed (Martin Orrick, when he saw the poetry, agreed and wanted to promote the man, but Sarah claimed she had no idea where he might be by now: it was not in her nature to keep track of such things), and she'd studied and later taught Tibetan sexual exercises which aimed at spiritual transcendence. Like all her rare and beautiful kind, she wore large hats, long purple or wine-colored dresses and curious-looking shoes, as if her beauty were a secret to be carefully guarded. She spoke very little, never without carefully rehearsing what she would say, and never unkindly, even when she was angry. She watched people as a child does, and soon knew all there was to know about them, none of which she minded. If she had faults—or such was Martin Orrick's opinion—most of them were faults of style. Having lived so much of her life with untouchables, God's children in India, gypsies in Spain, Mexicans, American Indians and blacks, her laugh was too loud for polite society. And in her thirty-five years she'd found nothing yet to give absolute commitment to. Martin Orrick might have changed that. She loved him as she'd never loved anyone before, but unfortunately—as she at last saw, more clearly than he did—he loved his wife. She lay weeping in his arms, unable to tell him yet what made her cry, because he wasn't yet ready to understand that it was Joan, always, only Joan that he loved. And in the morning she got up and washed her face and, mentally, changed her life.

She still had not told him when he visited her in Boston, where she was taking, partly out of idle curiosity, partly from a romantic wish to believe, a course on the raising of the dead. The class took place in a large upstairs room in downtown Boston, and she could see, slyly watching him, that he had assumed from the first instant that the students were all insane. Some sat stiff-backed on their Japanese mats, spines absolutely straight, so that the power of Ky could come rushing down into them from the universe. ("Sit up straight, Martin," she would sometimes tell him, "think of your poor miserable electrical system.") Others lay sprawled out, fat and splotched, with lifeless, frizzled hair—she knew them and was fond of them and could have explained so that even Martin would forgive them: they came to this place because they were incurably sick, or lost, or hungry for religion, and those who came out of loss or hunger would almost certainly be helped, and those who came because medical science had given up on them would either get better, half by accident, or would die. ("Martin, Martin, be *gentle*," she would say, subtly controlling his every move, and would kiss his fingers, "they don't hate you, they aren't even *looking* at you.") Still others leaned miserably against the wall, unwashed and hairy, big tall pimply-faced boys who were always angry and trembling at the edge of tears. They needed to be made love to, needed their cocks sucked, needed to be told, hour after hour, how *strong* they were, what beautiful, mysterious *eyes* they had. There was no irony, no cruelty in Sarah Fenton's thoughts. That was what they needed, and if she could have found girls for them, she would have done so.

Martin studied her, affectionate and curious, and observed that her hint of a smile was smug, as if she was proud of these people, these specimens, whatever he might think. He looked at the people in the room again, then back at her. She touched his knee with her gentle, emaciated hand. Then the teacher arrived, one Michio Kushi, and greeted his strange class without seeing it. They all prayed, silent, sometimes clapping their hands smartly. The lecture on the raising of the dead began.

Martin watched and listened in awe and not unfriendly disbelief, his thick, dark meat-eater fingers laid on Sarah Fenton's translucent hand. It was insane but also fascinating, this sober-minded talk of raising the dead. Crazy as he might be, the man was no charlatan. He demonstrated the breathing, ten thousand years old, he mildly claimed, that would suck down the powers of the universe, and spoke of how first one must revive the brain.

"Blain die first, you understand?" If a man had been dead for as much as fifteen minutes, his mind, when you brought him back to life, would be like a child's. But between fifteen minutes and fourteen hours—the maximum—there would be very little difference. "Next we must levive the pancleas." Next the heart. In his black suit, black hair, thick plastic-rimmed glasses he looked like a Japanese monk. After every important pronouncement he bowed. He spoke of yin and yang, the earth's rotation, the cycles of the moon, spoke of sodium and potassium, the powerful electrical charge in the earth—the reason people sometimes come back to life in the grave. He spoke at length, thoughtfully and carefully, of the moral considerations involved in the raising of the dead—how it was a sin against nature to raise a man who had not died by mistake, to raise a man who must die again tomorrow or next week. He demonstrated the orthodox modern method of starting up the heart by pounding violently on the victim's chest, spoke of the orthodox revival of the heart by electric shock, and showed—strange—a badly taken photograph of an old Chinese painting of a corpse being struck in the chest by a physician. As Martin listened, expressionless—not tempted to laugh: crank or not, Kushi was a holyman—he was aware all the time that she was watching him out of the corner of her eye, from the ambush of her long, dark lashes. At the end of the session—it closed with a prayer—she whispered in his ear, "But he's a good man, mmm?"

Immediately afterward, there was a session advertised as "The Cure of Cancer." She wanted him to hurry back to the fine old dark house and make love to her, but he wanted to attend. "You goon," she said lovingly, "I'm not signed up for that. It costs twenty-five dollars for six weeks, and the way this place works, one session costs the same as the whole lot."

"I've got twenty-five dollars," he said.

"OK," she said, and smiled and shrugged. "I'll wait for you."

"No," he said, coming out of his trance, "I've got fifty dollars. You stay too. I'm a rich and famous novelist."

"You're crazy," she said, and raised his hand to her lips, then lowered it, and with the fingertips stroked her own breast. He remembered with a shock how it had been with Joan, when they were kids. He remembered the next instant that fifty dollars was more than she spent, living in her macrobiotic commune, in a month.

Kushi had left the room. Though the class was supposed to begin at once, he was gone for half an hour. Outside the high, bare, round-arched windows, the sky was red. It would soon be dark. Martin's seat was numb. He hadn't sat cross-legged since God knew when, and the class in the raising of the dead had taken two full hours. It was surprising, in fact, that he felt as well as he did. The leg he'd broken, that time he fell in London, was throbbing slightly, but it wasn't really painful. Nevertheless, he decided to give up his dignity and sprawl. If fat, teenaged girls could do it, and bearded freaks, why not the great Martin Orrick? What would Joan think, he wondered, if she could see him here? But his mind flinched away from it in something like fright. She would say, standing in the eight-foot-high doorway, her face alive, as theirs were not, her attire immaculate, her eyes as bright as jewels, whereas theirs were dusty—except Sarah's, he thought: Joan would have liked Sarah, in some other world, some other time—a world and time that would never come, now—Joan would say, standing in the eight-foot-high doorway, "Have we time to exterminate these people, Paul? What time's the concert?"

He sprawled on his side, and gently, shamelessly, Sarah snuggled up beside him. How simple and reasonable it seemed. *I love you, Sarah,* he thought with all his heart. —But at dinner, in the big, dark-beamed house, when someone had asked Sarah to pass the God-knows-what, he'd nudged her out of her trance saying, "Joan, would you pass the . . ." She hadn't seemed to notice that he'd called her Joan, though surely it was impossible to miss a thing like that. If she did notice, she instantly forgave him, as she forgave everything. But it preyed on him a little, that slip of the tongue. He and Joan had been married more than half their lives, their habits were like rock; yet even that wasn't what struck him, troubled him. Calling Sarah Joan, he'd said it with affection, and the feeling that had slipped out for an instant from the darkness of his mind or, maybe, heart—the absolute identity of his feelings for Joan and Sarah, and the reminder of Joan's priority—shook him. The more he thought of it, the more suspicious it looked that Sarah had not blinked an eye—had expected it and didn't mind. He had dimly planned, ever since the Spanish trip—without quite daring to think about it—that one day, like some character in an Updike novel, he would muster up his courage and break with his family, sometime when Joan was strong enough to take it, and would settle for the rest of his life with Sarah. It dawned on him now that it might never happen, and not, as he'd imagined, because he was afraid.

Kushi arrived, bowing and apologetic, blushing like Joan's father, though his skin was dark. He had with him a man who claimed to be a Harvard medical professor, and a woman with, he said, metastasized cancer. It was no doubt true: she was wasted and gray. With a little start, Martin came awake: it was all not as innocent as he'd all this time imagined. The Harvard professor was going to certify that the woman was, yes, dying, and then Kushi would demonstrate . . . He touched Sarah's hand. "Let's leave," he said. She glanced at him and nodded.

They walked through snowy Boston streets, holding hands, looking into stores, admiring brightly lighted window displays—clothes, books, jewelry, paintings, furniture, television sets, things for which she had not the slightest desire. She owned, in all the world, a piano, one beautiful hand-made tablecloth, four books, a record-player and eleven records, a magnificent hundred-year-old Spanish guitar, two dishes, a cup, one spoon, one knife, enough clothes to fill her large leather suitcase, and one pair of chopsticks.

"Martin, there's something I must tell you," she said. He studied her face but could see nothing, except that she'd carefully arranged it. He remembered that she'd been a schoolteacher, because that was the way she was looking at him now, exactly: as if he were a child who'd done something very wrong, and though she was fond of him, and not angry, she must bring it to his attention.

"Are you sure this is the time?" he said, not knowing what it was she had to say but knowing most certainly that he didn't want to hear it.

Her composure broke, her gaze flicked away from him, and she said, "Perhaps not."

They walked on, with more purpose now, moving toward the trolley that would take them to Brookline and her house, her room, her pallet laid out on the wooden floor on a line that went exactly north and south.

I must tell him in the morning, she thought, and suddenly knew she wouldn't, hoping against hope.

He returned to southern Missouri looking rested and well fucked and loaded down with bags of mysterious junk he insisted would be good for them. Joan said, not crying, looking bleak and abandoned, "She gives you something you need. I wish I knew what it was, I'd give you the same, and more, more than anyone could possibly give you."

"It's the health food," he said, and his smugness, though it should have made her furious, made him handsome, sexy.

"I wish you could love me too," she said.

"I do," he said.

She flew to Detroit, and said to Dr. Behan, "I want you to help me change myself so that Martin will love me."

"Is that all?" he said, and smiled.

"I'm serious," she said. She told him about the fights—he'd heard at least something of that from Paul Brotsky—about how Martin, when he was drunk, became, as it seemed to her, a different man, how he called her awful things, hit her sometimes, or worse yet, stormed off in the middle of the night, sometimes in the car. What frightened her most of all was that some night, driving a hundred miles an hour and so drunk he couldn't see, he would kill somebody. That, if he lived through it, would break his heart, drive him crazier than he was.

"You're sure your perceptions of this aren't a little distorted," he said. He was silver-haired and lean, so good-looking one thought one might have seen him in some movie or on television. Paul had been right about him; she could tell already. She'd been to enough psychiatrists to know he was extraordinary. If he had any method, she would learn over the next few months, it was simply to listen carefully, catching the little lies—for instance, if you said "one" when you really meant "I"—and saying exactly what he believed, as an ordinary, decent human being, a committed physician. He would suggest often that her perceptions were distorted. Frequently she would have no idea, after a session with him, just what it was he'd said; but she began to move through the world as if Dr. Behan were watching her, began judging her behavior as he would judge it; and she felt herself changing, changing quickly.

"Maybe my perceptions are distorted, I don't know. But I know he doesn't care if he kills himself. It may be he's secretly trying to kill himself, or it may only be he doesn't think; but either way, I know for certain it doesn't matter to him."

"And you think he doesn't love you—after all these years."

"He's told me he doesn't. Often. He's told me again and again the only reason he stays is the children, and . . . I believe him."

Dr. Behan frowned, as if she'd done something slightly wrong that he would get back to. He said, "You really believe, Joan, that if you get rid of certain . . . faults"—he waved vaguely, as if thinking about her faults, then finished—"he'll suddenly love you again as, you say, he used to?"

She nodded.

"Isn't that a strange thing to believe?"

She nodded again, and her eyes filled with tears.

Behan winced, glanced down at her hands. At last he said, "Hmm. Well, perhaps it would help if you brought him with you next time, so I could speak to him, get a better idea. Will he come?"

"Oh, he'll come," she said. "He hates it, the way things are now."

After the session she went with Paul to a Detroit Symphony concert, then home to his apartment, where they cooked a huge dinner and made love. As she was just drifting off to sleep something startled her awake—the pain, perhaps, though it seemed to her there had been something else, someone in the doorway, studying her—and she whispered urgently, "People can change, save themselves."

Paul said, "*I* said that. You keep ripping off my best lines."

Eighteen

Behan liked Martin immediately, and understood almost as soon as he saw them together what was wrong. She too, in fact, quite suddenly understood, though she had no idea what to do about it. Behan said, in his simple, physicianly way—exactly as he might have asked about an ulcer or a skin irritation—"Do you love Joan, Martin?"

"I feel . . . affection for her," Martin said. "Sometimes when I'm lying beside her at night I feel a great, helpless tenderness, a wish that I could make her life better. But . . . it's difficult. She insists on dominating, absolutely controlling, and I feel like I'm suffocating. For instance—"

She leaned toward him, tears running down his face. "I *don't* dominate. *Some*body has to take charge. All you want to do is write. If you'd once try acting like a husband—" She broke off. Martin had gone into his icy shell, his arms hanging limp, fingertips trembling.

"That's what I mean," he said. There was a quaver in his voice, as if in a minute he would cry, but he wouldn't, she knew; he would merely become more withdrawn, fall silent. "I say anything at all and she strikes out, or changes it, and I just back away, give up."

"But why does it all have to be *my* fault?" she asked.

Behan had said nothing all this time, merely watched Martin and occasionally glanced at her in a way that made her feel left out, disapproved; but now he said a little sternly, "Joan, why do you insist on dominating this conversation?"

"I'm not, I only—"

"Yes you are," he said. She felt spanked, like a child, and covered her face with her hands, crying harder. "Who's idea *was* this," she wanted to say. "Who was it that said in the first place that I was going to change, become a nicer person?" *(Nothing is fair,* Martin had once written; *thank God you're one of the winners, or, if you're not, come out shooting.)*

Martin said, "I gentle dogs sometimes—you know, dogs that have been mistreated and have turned vicious. I feel about Joan as I feel about some of them—affectionate but . . . she bites."

"I see," Behan said. Then, after a moment, "Is there anything else you'd like to tell me?"

"I don't think so," Martin said.

"You might mention your hatred of women," she snapped.

"That's true," Martin said, without feeling, without any trace of embarrassment or hurt. "I wasn't aware of it until recently, but I've been, all my life, afraid of women. Not my mother, my aunt Mary, maybe one or two others. But generally . . . That is, I fall in love, or something like love, but I'm afraid."

Matter-of-factly Behan said, "It makes you impotent at times?"

"Until recently."

Behan glanced at Joan, guessing something and deciding whether or not to pursue it. He decided not to and got up. "Well, good. That's enough to get us started. Would you mind waiting outside while I talk a little more with Joan?"

By now Martin too was standing. "No, fine," he said. They moved toward the door, Behan saying something she couldn't quite catch. Not about them. The weather, maybe, or "How long are you planning to be in town?"

When Behan came back he said, "Don't cry, Joan. It's going to be easier than you think."

They began on her slightly cruel humor. She was a fast learner, and within a week she had learned to keep silent, think twice, and she discovered a surprising thing about herself: she liked becoming, as she jokingly called it, "a nicer person." Within a month she had learned not only to hold her tongue but even to reconsider, think again about the person who roused scorn in her. That was better yet, more mysterious and exciting. People she'd never really noticed before—people she'd dismissed, wiped out with a quick little thrust of wit—turned out to be interesting—not, heaven knows, that she wanted them to tea.

With her visits to Behan, something else changed, too. Martin and the children, alone while she was away, began playing instruments together. Evan was beginning to be quite good on the French horn and violin, Mary on the cello and Irish harp. "Why don't they play instruments with *me?*" she asked Dr. Behan. *"I'm* the musician."

"Maybe it's not as much fun," he said.

She decided to change that. It was the hardest change she was able to make. She'd never minded wrong notes when she was teaching school, had never minded inattention, disorganization, had not even minded, particularly, when in the middle of a piece one of the players wandered off into some other song, as if he'd forgotten that the others were there. But she minded terribly when her children played badly, and minded even more when Martin made, God help us, suggestions on interpretation. She would rather have been thrown into quicksand, would rather have been eaten by wolves, crawled over by spiders and snakes, than contend with their perpetually and individually changing beat, their forgetting of flats and sharps. She'd look over at Martin, nodding ferociously to keep him in rhythm, and she would think—because he was growing handsomer now, beginning, tentatively, to believe that something really had changed, perhaps finally—she would think, *I love you, you son of a bitch, but how you ever held down an orchestra chair is more than* I'll *ever know.* She didn't notice until suddenly it was an accomplished fact, that they were all getting better, and by leaps and bounds. She tried to write music for them to play together, but it was impossible, she was unable to concentrate. She also began a novel, because when the pain made her stay in bed all day she could at least, she thought, write; but that too proved impossible.

He tried to make her eat nothing but vegetables and fish, because the body can do wonders about curing itself if not pumped full of poisons. *Man ist was man isst,* he said. She knew whom he was quoting, and it filled her with panic and anger that he hadn't yet forgotten. When the U.S. government offered him a chance to lecture for six weeks in Japan, he snapped it up. She couldn't understand why, at first, since he hated to leave his writing for that long at a stretch; but when they got there she understood: Japanese food. She liked it, in fact—and would learn to cook all the famous Japanese delicacies—but the best thing she found in Japan was Kobe steak.

All their time in Japan they had only one fight, and even that was brief and trivial, a matter of her jealousy. Though it hurt her to think of Sarah, she no longer hated her, if she ever really had. As she would understand more and more clearly as time went on, Sarah had worked a miracle in Martin: had made him sexually well, as probably no one but a stranger could have done. It hadn't been pure charity, of course. What she'd done, as Joan finally got Martin to describe it, was exactly what the California sexual therapists were supposed to do for impotent, self-hating and woman-hating men. She'd done it so exactly in order, stage by stage, if one could believe what one read about sexual therapy in magazines, that Joan Orrick couldn't help but suspect that Sarah Fenton had worked by plan, putting him through a program. When she got him to read the article, Martin looked thoughtful and said nothing. It was important to him, of course, that Sarah should have loved him, not merely helped him. But if he had doubts there, he was a fool. Nevertheless, they never spoke of Sarah now, Martin because he had quietly abandoned his promise to her and was ashamed of himself, Joan for another reason.

It was a rainy summer night, dark as pitch except for the lights of the Mercedes and the yellow light in the windows of Sarah's small house. As the car drove up, Sarah came out onto the porch, smiling, imagining it was Martin. But when Joan got out in her glistening black raincoat and made a dash to the shelter where Sarah stood, Sarah's face went suddenly pale and showed a brief struggle between fright and a decision to be brave. At the top of the porch steps Joan stopped, put her hand on the railing as if tentatively, shyly, and with the other hand pushed back the rain hat. "Hello, Sarah," she said. Her voice was friendly, and though she herself was surprised, it was not a tone she had to fight for.

"Hello, Joan." Sarah stood perfectly still, distant, her thin hands folded in front of her, arms straight.

Joan took a step nearer, gave a slight laugh and said—foolishly, as she thought the instant she said it—"It's raining."

Sarah said nothing, merely looked at her, solemn.

Joan looked away, feeling somehow as if she, not Sarah, was in the wrong. But no one was really in the wrong, she knew; or anyway so she'd told herself, again and again, before she'd started out. Sarah knew only what Martin said, that she, Joan, did not love him, and if what he said were true, Sarah might be right to try to take him from her, even at the expense of . . . She shook her hair out, wiped the rain from her face. "Can we talk, Sarah?"

Sarah thought about it, then nodded and glided in her long, faded robe toward the door. She opened it, still without speaking, and Joan went in. The room smelled of cooking oil, incense, and kerosene; Sarah used lanterns.

There was no furniture, only flat Japanese pillows and one low table. Sarah came in, closed the door softly, and after a moment they both sat down. At last Sarah asked, "What did you wish to say, Joan?" Her words sounded carefully planned, rehearsed. Her expression was impossible to read. Guarded, perhaps beaten, withdrawing.

Joan tried to think, listening to the rain, then brought out without plan, "You love Martin, and you think I don't, but you're wrong." Her eyes filled with tears; she ignored them. To keep from crying she made herself cold, efficient, and she continued: "You've made him love you. I don't blame you for that, but I *do* love him, so you're wrong to try to take him from me. He loves you partly because you're so fair, so reasonable. If that's true—"

"Why should I believe you?" Sarah said quietly. It dawned on Joan only now that Sarah was scared to death of her.

"I'm not here to hurt you," she said.

"That's not what I asked."

In panic, she tried to think what Sarah had asked, then abruptly remembered. "But you *do* believe me. *Look* at me."

Sarah did, then looked down. "Very well, perhaps I do. Nevertheless—"

Joan said, "Martin and I grew up together. We've been married more than half our lives. We're like the same person. That's the truth, Sarah. Though it's also true that . . . something's gone wrong. I can't please him, I frighten him. But I'm trying to change. I *am* changing. There are things I have to save—not just myself, not even just myself and Martin and the children. There are things—" Before she knew she would do it, she found herself telling about their parents, their friends in San Francisco, Uncle George's books.

Suddenly, like an actress—but it was real enough—Sarah turned away. "Please, don't do that."

Joan kept still, watching her. Though Sarah's face was as expressionless as ever, tears ran down her cheeks. She sat motionless, as if hoping to ward off attack. At last Joan said, "There are things you do for him that I don't know about. If I knew what they were, you couldn't compete, you wouldn't have a prayer."

Sarah laughed, a sort of groan.

"Tell me what they are," Joan said.

"Why should I? What about how *I* feel?"

Joan Orrick closed her eyes a moment, concentrating. She had the feeling she sometimes had with Evan, playing checkers: there was a way to win if she could just stay wide awake, not let her mind wander for even part of a second. "He loves you because you're fair, honest." She spoke quickly, softly. "If I knew exactly what you do together—what I do that's wrong, without knowing I'm doing it—"

Sarah's eyes widened. "You're asking me to tell you—"

She refused to be distracted. "It would be fair then, wouldn't it. If there are things you know, that I haven't learned, and you keep them secret, and if after that he marries you because you're fair and honest—in other words because you've tricked him—" Relief flooded in, exactly as when she managed to set up the winning move in checkers, and she watched like a spectator, enjoying the beauty of the move as poor Sarah squirmed. She could be sorry for Sarah if she let herself, could even ruin the move for compassion's sake; but she resisted the temptation. Let Sarah sacrifice. Somebody had to lose.

Sarah stood up, retreated toward the window. "Joan, this is crazy. Please, I'd like you to go."

"I want you to tell me everything you do." She saw that in a moment Sarah would be crying, and she was tempted more strongly than before toward compassion, but again she held firm, thinking, *You're beaten, Sarah. I know why he loves you, but somebody has to lose.*

"I can't tell you. It would hurt you. I know you, Joan. I know you better than you think."

"Yes. It will hurt me. But we have no choice."

Sarah swept her hair back and pretended to gaze out the window at the rain. "I can't tell you. But you've won. I'll stop seeing him."

Joan stood up, moved toward her, then paused, six feet away. "It's not enough, Sarah. There's someone else like you, somewhere."

There was a long silence. At last, crying, Sarah nodded.

It had not been by Sarah's techniques that she had won him, or if it had been, Joan Orrick would be the last to admit it; but she knew now, beyond a shadow of a doubt, how to keep from hurting him, how to show the love that had made her cling to their life.

"Am I becoming a better person?" she would say. He would look at her, shaking his head as if in wonder, and she was happy. She began to feel confident. She was never afraid of him now, and not often afraid for him. For no reason that she could exactly explain, he no longer drank, or, rather, drank only now and then, at a party, and even if he got himself so drunk he couldn't walk, he never turned on her—never in icy rage called her "catshit," or stormed off to walk or gallop like a maniac on his horse or, worst of all, drive crazily off through the mountains. When he was roaring drunk, he did impersonations of famous men, and often, as in the past—but more joyfully than in the past, it seemed to her—he and Paul Brotsky did famous conversations, for instance between Czerny and Beethoven, or Shakespeare and Marlowe, or Wilbur and Orville Wright:

"It won't fly, Wilbur."

"It'll fly. Now just get in the fuckin airplane."

"No. My shoe's untied."

"Never mind your shoe's untied, get in the airplane!"

"I think we should've made it of aluminum."

"Aluminum's not even invented yet. Just get in the—"

"Wilbur, I've got an idea."

"Yeah."

"Let's invent aluminum."

"Orville, you Goddamn clown, we spent two thousand dollars and nine years of work and—"

"Wilbur?"

"Yeah?"

"You fly it. I'm too young."

Even Evan and Mary began to grow confident, began, that is, to believe that the changes were permanent. "Daddy's different," Mary said one night, and had a cautious look much like Martin's.

"How?" she said, knowing, wondering if Mary would dare say it.

"His eyes crinkle. His mouth never smiles, but—"

"We're all of us different, honey," she said.

She refused to think about the fact that her insides were changing too. Sometimes, when the pain was really bad, so that all she could do, despite the drugs, was lie in bed and cry—Martin would come and lie beside her and hold her, telling her he was sorry, wishing there was anything at all he could do—she would be frightened, so frightened that she'd begin to sweat, though she refused to think what frightened her. ("Have you noticed, Mr. Mixiedough, that the world is becoming increasingly dim?") When she slept, she had nightmares: Sarah came with word that Paul Brotsky was dead, and when Joan went sobbing to find Martin and tell him, he was gone, no one had been in his study for what looked like years—his leather chair was rotten, there were cobwebs on the typewriter. She called out in terror to Evan and Mary. The house was empty, silent except for the ticking of a clock. Even the dogs were gone, had left no trace. When she looked out at the mountains, gray, unstirring in the winter rain, she knew her family was not there either. The clock ticked on. *"Martin!"* she would scream, and would wake up shaking violently, and he would be holding her, out of breath from running, telling her, "Joan, it's all right, it's all right."

Life is fleeting, he wrote, *even the worst of life is fleeting.*

"Martin," she whispered once, "it's *not* all right." And at the look that came over him, she knew she must not mention that again.

Once Evan frightened her as badly as she'd ever managed to frighten herself. They were in a restaurant in Japan, at the New Japan Hotel, the four of them eating and laughing, a picture-book family no one would believe—and as Evan was telling some endless story, Martin smiling politely, looking past him with glazed eyes, waiting for it to finish—Evan suddenly stiffened and gave a faint cry of terror and reached toward Martin as he'd have done if the floor had suddenly dropped from under him. "Evan, what's the matter?" Martin said, and caught him in his arms.

"Daddy, I saw something!" Evan said, white.

"What did you see? There's nothing."

Evan was looking around the room as if lost, the way you look around a room when you wake up and don't know where you are. "I saw something," he said again. Mary, too, was looking around, afraid.

"It's all right," Martin said, and held Evan tighter.

"You were looking at me," Evan said a little later, "as if I was dead, or invisible, and then—" But he couldn't remember what happened next.

She remembered her grandmother, and Martin's uncle George, and she clenched her hands into fists to make the trembling stop. She remembered that Martin had said one time, "I'm as ruled from outside as any character in a book." *That's not true!* she thought—and it came as a revelation: *I've proved it's not true in my life.* Paul had read to her from his astrology book: "The Leo child is daring, unflinching, and unafraid." She said: "Are you aware, Martin, that I am daring, unflinching, and unafraid?"

"I am indeed," he said, and actually grinned, so that even Evan grinned and drew back, slightly embarrassed, out of his father's arms.

She remembered—guiltily, for some reason—that Paul had read of the Pisces—Sarah Fenton—"The Pisces child is a mystic and self-sacrificing seeker of harmony." Anger flashed up in her for an instant, and she thought, *I can run circles around her mysticism and harmony,* then remembered: "The Leo is proud and jealous." Abruptly, with pleasure, she laughed. She *was* proud. She *liked* herself, and the whole world loved her, and they had better keep it up or by God there was going to be hell to pay.

Though brilliant, Joan Orrick was not a woman who often had ideas. She had one now. Perhaps Martin was determined by outside forces, like a character in a novel—perhaps Cancers and Pisces and Virgos like Paul Brotsky, even Capricorns like Evan and Mary—were determined and, because they were determined, needed the subtle, medicinal influences of all Time and Space to heal them, save them. Leos were free. Even though she never did concerts anymore, the metaphor for her life was the concert stage. These people she loved—these beautiful blond children rushing toward adulthood, and even Martin Orrick, famous novelist—were not her equals, though she couldn't move a finger without them: they were her audience. *For you, my loves,* she thought, *I wear this golden dress, these diamonds and rubies, flashing them up and down awesome chromatic scales. For love of you I resurrect the dead of Vienna, also St. Louis dancers, black-bearded hermits, crazy-eyed old women, the bullet-ridden bodies of no-'count drunken Frenchmen. Sit up straight and listen, and God damn you if you cough! This is a love song you're hearing! No praise will be too great, but there will be, please, no applause. A silence will be sufficient, such a hush as would give the frail mystical Pisces a heart attack.*

Mary said, leaning toward her father, "Why is Mommy wearing that wicked grin?" (Wicked was one of the words she was using in her fiction lately.)

"Wicked?" Joan said. "Your gentle, sweet mother? Wicked?"

Nineteen

One night, toward the finish of one of his tours, he did a reading at Bennington College in Vermont. It was a cheapie, as she called it. For readings, these days, he got a thousand dollars a night. But Bennington supported young writers, and Martin had a messianic passion for backing promising beginners, now that he had clout. He had several young writers he wanted Bennington to invite up for readings from New York. She went with him, as usual, and it was the usual great success. He read the kind of thing he was famous for, poetic and dark, a tragic piece that made human existence seem senseless and useless and, by virtue of its very waste, or perhaps by virtue of its redemption through art, worth clinging to. She remembered some critic's having written of him once—and it was truer now than ever—that "his characters move terror-stricken, adrift in a universe grown wholly unfamiliar." She remembered the words because she'd wondered at the time why people were always so impressed by such things—why they thought him a great artist when he made everything seem sad and hopeless. Yet it was beautiful writing, there was no doubt of that, and not shapeless, self-regarding like, say, Mahler when he tried something heavier than a song. All the same, it was a view of the world that Joan Orrick did not share. How incredible, she thought, that intelligent people should find misery and pain, even at one remove, in fiction, so attractive!

It was a pleasant place for a reading—a small, comfortable hall in what had once been a barn, wooden floors worn smooth and shaped by generations of students, small-paned windows of a kind she'd found common in the east, the whole thing totally unpretentious, which was precisely why one felt here so real, so classy, so solidly connected with the past and therefore the present. The people gave her the same feeling—their clothes, the way they sat, the structure of their faces. They might have been sitting here, calmly listening—without intense Midwestern hunger or squinting fascination, without mulish reservation or timidity or gall—as long as the low, accommodating mountains of Vermont had been listening, as long as flat eastern voices like Martin's had been speaking of life's steady sorrows and hurrying joys.

He was reading in a black robe with a great, silver chain, as he often did lately. He was such an eccentric it looked natural on him, very handsome, in fact, his prematurely silver hair flowing down his back, his English-Irish-Welsh voice singing through language as the voices of his preacher teacher lawyer ancestors had done all those years, or centuries rather, calling in vain for heaven's mercy. People wept, listening. She could have wept herself, but against the power of the story, against the "dark vision" his reviewers absurdly, perversely praised, her pleasure in his looks, his power to move strangers, triumphed. He was now distinctly fat. She liked him fat. And it struck her that, whatever his faults, he had never lost that childlike fairness: principles were evil, never people, in his fiction. He created no bad characters, and if he'd seemed not to love her, from time to time—the complaint was behind her—it was nevertheless true that all through the years, every heroine he'd put on paper was recognizably herself. All but one of them were red-heads. In fact in one of his novels—he was obviously unaware of it—*all* the characters were red-heads. It startled her to notice that just now, here in this roomful of "Bennington girls," also talented and handsome eastern woman-teachers—musicians, novelists, scientists, painters—she felt perfectly at home—in fact queenly. She recalled that her father had called her "princess" when she was little. (Her mother, because of the Parkinson's disease, now trembled, no longer drove a car, wrote letters in which the penmanship was so small you very nearly needed a magnifying glass. But she seemed wiser than she'd seemed when she was pretty and young. When she and Martin visited her parents now—and the same was true when they visited his parents—they all talked like friends, like adults. They were all, of course, proud of him, and he was properly grateful; he would mention in interviews all they'd done for him.)

He was coming to the end, building toward it like a Russian composer, turning the lights out one by one, unostentatiously, forcing nothing, offering no opinions, the music speaking for itself. She was startled by an odd discovery, and though no one sitting near her would have noticed the change, she came suddenly wide awake, thinking, *He* believes *all that!* It was, she would write in her own novel—the one she began in her mind that night—the most important discovery she'd ever made about him. She saw him all at once as different from herself—after all this time with Behan, trying to learn to see people as essentially like her, encouraged or wounded by the same kinds of things—saw him as a completely separate human being with separate problems: nothing was her fault. He was simply *like* that, and her love, or her failure to love him as she should, had nothing whatever to do with it, had only to do with how things stood between them. She found herself loving him, pitying him, admiring him with absolute detachment. It was as if the room had suddenly grown enormous, as large as the universe he was forever bringing into his stories and novels, and he was a star at the edge of it, rushing outward from the calm, hushed center, and it was not her fault.

When he finished reading his typically mighty final line, there was a moment of stillness while the usual chills ran up and down the people's backs (not that she meant to be unfeeling; it was wonderful, wonderful; but she'd been through it many times): then applause, intense and prolonged. He was instantly transformed to his ordinary self, shy, slightly suspicious that they couldn't really mean it, unworthy of this frightening honor. When the crowd of adoring maidens thinned she went up to him. "You were terrific!" she said. As they were leaving, going to the party, he took her hand.

Casually, over drinks, someone asked if he'd be interested in teaching at Bennington College for a year. He grinned and asked her what she thought. She said, "Certainly!" "Really?" he said, surprised. "I like it," she said, "—not that I want to boss you, understand." "Boss me?" he said, and actually looked blank. She smiled, radiant, for the benefit of the others, and Martin, looking slightly baffled, said, "If Joan thinks we should come, I guess we should come."

No one doubted for long that she'd been brilliantly right, as usual. In Bennington the children could go to good schools that offered interesting courses not available at home, and they could play in the Sage City Symphony—she and Martin as well. The man who taught strings and conducted the orchestra in the Mount Anthony Junior and Senior High schools turned out to be Daniel Antoun, as fine a teacher and musician as anyone in the east, knocking off concerts, one after another, that few civic orchestras could have touched. Evan would turn, overnight, into a really first-rate horn player, and Mary would begin taking lessons on the harp in Schenectady. Joan, one afternoon, found a house for sale, a splendid old place with leaded windows, a hanging staircase, a third-floor ballroom (which they would immediately turn into a theater). It cost half what their house in Missouri cost, and it was right next door to the oldest house in Vermont and the most beautiful church. "Could we?" she said. "We could live here six months and in Missouri for six months. The children love it, Martin." Which was true. He called his publisher, got an advance on a new novel. They signed the papers.

She met, at one of the Bennington parties, a New York City anesthesiologist who made some use of hypnotism—or mesmerism, as Martin stubbornly insisted on calling it, in memory of his uncle George. He could teach her autohypnosis, he said, and at least to some extent get her off the drugs. She could kill at least part of the pain and still compose, perhaps teach. (She had no immediate need of a job. She was doing psychotherapy, on those days when she was well enough, at the college. She imitated Dr. Behan's method, but added touches no one but Joan Orrick would have thought of. She gave students the words to "When You Walk Through a Storm" and "Climb Every Mountain" and urged them to sing them with feeling whenever depressed.) Though both Martin and Paul Brotsky had been urging her to try autohypnosis for years, the hypnotist's suggesting it made it suddenly a concrete possibility—in fact, she knew at once that it would work. She had to do something, she knew. She was working as much as possible on her novel now, and it was infuriating that she couldn't think clearly.

"If I could only concentrate," she'd said to Dr. Behan, "I think I might turn out to be, you know, really *good.*"

He'd smiled. "Does it matter?"

"Oh, very *much,*" she'd said.

And he: "If you are, what will Martin think?"

She'd said without an instant's hesitation, knowing it was true, "He'll think it's wonderful." Then, a second later: "But he'll hate it if it's bad. It won't be anything personal—nothing to do with whether or not he loves me—but oh my God will he hate it!" And then suddenly, exactly as she'd done as a child, she'd laughed: "So let him hate it! Fuck him!"

Dr. Behan smiled, looking her over. "That should do it, yes."

The minute the hypnotist suggested he could help, she excused herself and went to find Martin—he was talking to a dignified gray-haired lady named Babs—and dragged him back to where the hypnotist sat. She told him what the hypnotist had recommended, and said, "Could we try it, Martin?" "What's this 'Could we'?" he said.

She began the lessons, flying down twice a week to New York. It was at first disappointing, and she would soon learn that her hopes had been too high; but the hypnotist insisted that her progress was miraculous, considering the dosage of drugs she was on. "Serious pain isn't easy to talk yourself out of, Joanie," he said.

"He just wants to get into your pants," Martin said.

She kept trying and began to have a little success. She began to go for days at a time without drugs. She could drive again, at least sometimes: she knew when she could make it without dizziness or fainting.

She said to the hypnotist, leaning forward in her chair, that what he'd done for her life was astonishing. He asked her, timidly, if she'd be interested, perhaps, in having an affair. She thanked him but declined. "I've been thinking," she said, "what I'd really like is a dog." She'd seen one advertised in the Bennington *Banner*.

"A dog?"

"I haven't had a dog since I was four," she said. "When he was run over, my mother was heartbroken, and all I ever had after that was cats—and a pig, one time, and a pony that bit."

"Dogs bite," he said, trying to be helpful.

She said, "My husband and children have dogs, but not me, not my own." She looked out at the buildings, the dirty snow. "What I was thinking I'd like is an Old English sheepdog. A boy dog." She grinned.

She said the same thing to Martin, and after she'd mentioned it four or five times he surprised her with an Old English sheepdog, male, which she named Bennington. She'd made a mistake, she realized; an Old English sheepdog wasn't what she meant, she'd had in mind some other breed, a whole lot smaller. But Bennington (Bennington the Dog, as they called him, to keep things clear—and for some reason they spoke to him only in French) was a joy and fell madly in love with her, though he was almost impossible to housebreak.

She was happier than ever. "Look, it's *snowing!*" she would cry out, every time it snowed. Evan would look up from his paperback of card tricks, or the photographs he'd developed and was now trimming with scissors, or from his French horn études, and would grin at her. "Neat!" She went skiing and skating; she bought tap-dance shoes and started practicing in the back room with Bennington the Dog, who barked at her like crazy. Mary would roll up her eyes and moan, exactly like Martin, "Culture, culture, culture."

"This," Joan said, "is a buck-and-wing."

The house shook, the dog barked insanely.

"But is it Art?" Mary said.

When she was caught up with the schedule she had for her novel, she composed horn duets for Evan and Martin, harp pieces for Mary, string ensembles for them all—including Paul, when he came to visit. They all went, every Sunday night, to the rehearsal of the Sage City Symphony. Martin growled about his students, the dogshit, the cost of food (he'd always been cheap; now that they were rich he was downright stingy). He complained about the endless paperwork Bennington College required of him; wrote half the night ("Genius, unmitigated genius," she would say, looking over his shoulder, and would kiss him on the bald spot), and often lay in bed late with her mornings, holding her in his arms. She drove through the mountains in the big blue Mercedes, with Bennington the Dog on the leather seat beside her, buying curtains, carpets, furniture. Every other day she was asked if she was interested in having an affair. She wore, everywhere, except when she visited Dr. Behan in Detroit, where display could be dangerous, her rings: a big diamond, two emeralds, a ruby in an antique setting from Cartier's. (Deep down, Martin too was an absolute snob.) Also one of her enormous fur coats (not endangered species except for, possibly, she wasn't sure, her second-hand lynx; anyway, Martin apparently didn't notice: he was still on whales). "Who's that woman?" strangers asked. She decided to see if she could improve on the effect. She went on a diet, made a habit of the Canadian Air Force exercises. Martin refused to diet. He liked himself fat, thought it made him look more mature, more significant. Some interviewer asked her if success had "spoiled Martin Orrick." "Oh, horribly!" she said. "Unbelievably!" Martin of course denied it. "It's not success," he said, "it's simple recognition, as when one remarks, 'Ah ha, there goes a camel.' " She suggested that if he were to go on a diet he would look even more mature and significant, like a trim little London banker. He wasn't fooled. "Loveliness is not my bag," he said.

Her self-confidence increased. Even Martin was impressed, was almost, in fact, regularly cheerful. "Maybe all women should be issued adhesions," he said. She laughed. She had learned to hide from him almost completely the fact that she was in pain, except, of course, when it was so bad she had to turn to the drugs again, and could no longer manage full control. Pain or no pain, she laughed a lot, these days, and made other people laugh. Once when they stopped to buy fish at the fish truck that came over the mountains every Thursday from Maine, bringing lobsters, clams, crabs, and bluefish, a big burly man in a lumberjacket dared to step in front of her in line. She was wearing a black leather coat and beret and leather boots and looked, more than usual, like a high-priced Girl Commando. She at once stepped around him and in front of him, reached up and poked him in the chest, and said, "Watch yerself, buster, or I'll push yer face in." His eyes widened, his mouth opened, and then he bent over and laughed, slapping his knee, and couldn't stop. The fish man laughed too, and she had to stand there, leaning on her elbow, waiting to be served.

Her doctor said, in his dingy little office in Shaftsbury, "You realize, Joan, this hypnotism's all very well, but that stuff's in there working. You're going to have to face up, before long, to another operation."

"I know," she said, "and another and another."

"Well—" he said.

She smiled, listening to the ticking of his clock. "Not just yet. But soon. I promise."

He shook his head, chewing on his pipe. "What's your secret?" he said.

"I'm in love," she said.

"Does your husband know?"

She leaned toward him confidentially. "My husband is a fool."

Dr. Faris was nonplussed and looked at her forehead. "It doesn't seem to bother you much," he said.

"Well, you see, he's rich."

Driving home down the mountain afterward, she thought about it. They *were* rich—not that, in point of fact, they had all that much money. But his sad, hopeless stories made people who heard them or read them come alive, made them gentle, made them notice their compassion for one another. His readings had the effect of a really good funeral: they made people come together and defy that age-old horror of things, the restless churning of sudden births and deaths, a universe of clumsily bumping bits of force, a cry out of the grass—and they were better than funerals, because the horrors he wrote of were all made up, mere airy might've been. (She knew what horror was, knew in, excuse the expression, her guts. "Watch yerself, buster," she said to Death, riding, sadly watching her, in the wide blue real-leather seat behind her back.)

As she walked into the house, Martin was shouting as if in Euripidean rage, defying the gods, cursing the gray earth that so patiently bore him, "God *damn* Bennington!" Either the college had sent him more forms or he'd stepped in some dogshit.

"Hi, Martin, I'm home!" she called.

"Hi, Mom," Evan said, grinning, looking up from the carpet where he was reading a great, fat paperback, Martin's last best-seller. A sign of their progress was that Martin's mad rages no longer frightened Evan at all. Mary waved hello from the couch, where she was writing, not bothering to look up.

Martin hadn't heard her call of greeting, still howling his anger like a Midwestern tornado. She poked her head in at the study door. "Bennington the College, dear, or Bennington the Dog?"

"You're home," he said, staring with murderous, icy eyes. But he loved her, it wasn't personal.

"Mmm," she said, nodding. "I'm home."

SHADOWS

The external world of physics has become a world of shadows. In removing our illusion we have removed the substance, for indeed we have seen that substance is one of the greatest of our illusions . . . The sparsely spread nuclei of electric forces become a tangible solid; their restless agitation becomes the warmth of summer; the octave of aethereal vibrations becomes a gorgeous rainbow.

—Sir Arthur Eddington

BOOK ONE

One

Something poked him on the shoulder, and a soft voice whispered in Craine's good ear, "Detective, you're being watched!"

He jerked his sharp nose and thick glasses from the book, heart leaping, throat constricting, just in time to see Two-heads Carnac's blue choir robe go flying around the end of the bookshelf. Craine glanced left and right, trembling and blushing, half in rage, half in embarrassment, black eyebrows lowered, cheek muscles twitching, but so far as he could tell, no one had seen. The gloomy old bookstore—Tully's Tome Shop: Used Books & Maps—was practically deserted, as usual. There might be browsers among the floor-to-ceiling stacks that ran the length of the store, butted against the brown cracked plaster wall on the street side, but in the area he could see—the dim central cavern with its map-cluttered tables, astrolabes, and faded, illegible old globes—no one had looked up. A white-haired professor, soft-featured, large-eyed, like a wise old white Tom in an expensive gray suit and spectacles, stood leafing through a dictionary, bent over the pages with a round, brass-framed magnifying glass—he was a man Craine knew, though the name now escaped him; a doctor, member of the medical faculty—and over by Wilbur Tully's desk a young woman in a shabby black floor-length cape with a collar that went up into two sharp points stood picking through paperback books on the occult. Her hair had a dead look; maybe she was pregnant. Except for Tully himself, hunched over his ledger in his usual gray cardigan, frameless spectacles gleaming—behind him his grizzled brown bulldog waiting with infinite patience beside his dish—there was no one else in sight.

Craine stepped carefully to the end of the bookshelf where the choir robe had disappeared. At the nearest of the tables that now came into view,

Carnac sprawled as if he'd been there for hours, engrossed in a map of the Holy Land. "Maniac," Craine muttered, and lowered his nose toward his book again, then pursed his lips and, with a curt little nod and a cunning look, as if someone had suggested it, moved back to where he'd been before, out of Carnac's view. It was too much to hope that Two-heads would forget him, mercifully go trouble someone else. The whisper was still in Craine's ear, like an itch: *Detective, you're being watched.* He glanced to the left, past his shoulder, then quickly to the right. It wasn't true; no one was watching him. "Maniac," he whispered again, angrily. He spoke sternly, but, listening, he wasn't convinced. He was by nature a suspicious man—it had saved his life on more occasions than one—and his years had taught him it was best to suspect the worst. As a matter of fact he'd been feeling all morning a weird impression of eyes following him, tacked to him like buttons, some observer single-minded as a cat. A light shudder passed over Craine's shoulders and down his back, and he thought momentarily of the whiskey in its brown paper sack in his trench coat pocket, but he did not reach for it. He ran his tongue around his mouth—dry as dust from too much smoking—bent closer to his book, and, for an instant, squeezed his eyes shut.

He got an image, in the movie-house blackness inside his mind, of a face, bearded, bespectacled, as expressionless as stone. He was so startled by the sight—memory or vision—that he opened his eyes at once and, to his consternation, lost it. When he closed his eyes again all he saw was the image of Carnac sprawled at his map table as if he'd been propped there since time began. The books and walls around him had the dried-out, slightly rotted look that sooner or later came to everything in Carbondale, every line clean but moldy, like the wood of old pilings, or like deadmen at the rim of a swamp—the look of things submerged and then salvaged again, as if the Mississippi River had come boiling over the hills like a cancerous eruption, death-yellow in the sun, and had lain on the town for a week or so, dropping silt and gray slime, then receded at last, leaving behind it, when the dirt was washed away, that deep-down, ancient, decayed look. Oak boards, one imagined, were as soft as daddock, and one might have believed that even the concrete of the sidewalks was in secret sprouting seeds. It was only an impression; Carbondale had never been flooded in all its long history, or anyway not by the Mississippi River, twenty miles westward, beyond the county seat and walled off by wooded blue hills; but it was often enough soaked by torrential rains, storms of a kind Craine would have associated only with the tropics, before he came here: fat warm drops out of a black, roaring sky—it was tornado country—flash-flooding rains that turned the streets to yellow rivers and made the grass, the pokeweed and trumpet vines in vacant lots and the edges of people's lawns shoot up lushly, obscenely, made althaea shrubs and redbud trees hang heavy as overgrown animals, hogs too fat to walk or obese, shaggy calves penned up at slaughtering time. Surrounded by all that churning vegetation, thousands of humming insects and hurrying birds, the town's old oak trees, above buckling sidewalks, glowed darkly, like pensive observers full of gloom. After each rain the sun would come out and burn hot as a furnace, charging the world with muggy dampness and making huge, roiling clouds overhead and, soon, more rain.

The whole town smelled musty, Tully's Tome Shop more than most places—not that the smell was one Gerald Craine disliked. The mustiness made him think (standing with his eyes closed, chin lifted above the book) of compost heaps, mulch in a greenhouse, attics where a man might explore for a week without exhausting the debris of some stranger's past—old *Collier's* magazines, crockery, stuffed trunks. That was the one real pleasure he got out of his work as a detective. The past—any past, or any but his own—even the history of some thin-lipped ex-mailman—had a spirit to it, a mysterious aliveness that could pull him up short every time. A childish pleasure, or "childlike," rather, as his neighbor down the hall at the hotel had said, correcting him—not judging or condemning, simply observing, getting the facts lined up, accurate and precise, in his compulsive, poetical way; should've been a policeman. "I just record things," he'd said one time, speaking of his poetry. Craine had watched him, not perfectly certain he understood. Maybe it was this: that poems were, to Craine's neighbor—so Craine put it to himself—like the proofs of their existence effeminate, instable people put in journals. The weather, the temperature, sensitive impressions. There was a line in one of the books he'd published: *Autumn, clear as the eyes of chickens.*

Craine had paused over it, interested, but after that the poem had gone nowhere, no story, no characters—nobody home—just more sensitive impressions. He'd glanced warily at his neighbor, thinking—or toying with the possibility of thinking—"Sick mind"; but he hadn't felt sure of himself. What an ordinary person, some objective observer, would have said, he knew, was "Craine, that's ridiculous. Lots of perfectly healthy people write poetry." That might be true and then again it might not. Mental aberration was an interesting business. Nine times out of ten most people missed it, but in Craine's line of work you developed a careful eye for possibilities. What kind of grown-up, healthy person would go around noticing that a clear autumn day, especially in the late afternoon, was like the eyes of chickens? No harm, the objective observer would say. Live and let live was their motto, these objective observers—till somebody started to find bodies down under the house.

Eyes of chickens. It showed a kind of fixity—obsessiveness. Hinted at a kind of self-absorption, subtle hedonism, a curious detachment or withdrawal from the ordinary serious concerns of humanity that could make you uneasy, once you thought about it. Craine would keep an eye peeled, wait for more evidence. The man had a thing about chickens, possibly. His cat was called Rooster.

Yet he did seem harmless enough, Craine's neighbor, and no doubt some people thought well of what he did. He'd published three of those skimpy little books—Craine had not read them, though he watched for them now, whenever he was in bookstores—and he taught English at the university. He was young—thirty-two—and bearded. Jewish. He wore suspenders and arm-garters. City boy's hankering for the country, no doubt. Another mistake, and not without dark implications: potentially dangerous desire to live more lives than one. Except for the cat he'd taken in, and sometimes a girl-friend for the night, Craine's neighbor lived alone. His room ticked and clicked. He was a collector of old clocks, also hourglasses. Sign of dissatisfaction, reactionary snobbery, faint-trace hatred of his fellow man. An alien, then: a kind of Martian in our midst . . .

Craine gave a sudden little jump. Watched!—Watched by whom? he wondered in brief, wild panic. Watched by the police? His right hand began picking at the front of his coat. His eyes teared up. It was monstrously unfair, like everything. There were dozens of them, only one of him, and they were young, clear-headed; no memory blanks. *Ah son, my son, step off the straight and narrow for one little ball-ball-shuffle-shuffle-hop—mark my words, my boy . . .*

And if not the police, since why should the P.D. be interested in him, in these days of cutbacks and tax revolt, the Age of Accountability, and election year at that, if he wasn't mistaken (he had no idea what year it was; it was all pure rhetoric, games, games, games) . . . He clenched his fist as if to hit himself.

If not the police . . . Again the shudder passed over Craine's shoulders, and he abruptly changed his mind, snapped his eyes open, drew the whiskey in its sack from his overcoat pocket, tucked the book under his elbow, and unscrewed the cap from the bottle for a quick restorer. As he drank, quickly and furtively, his Adam's apple lunging, he glanced right, along the book-shelf.

Carnac was at the end of the aisle, as Craine had somehow known he'd be. He stood making a face with the half of his head still movable, his thick lip lifted, pink underneath, from the huge yellow mule's teeth, his right eye wide open, tumulose in the shadow of his top hat. As Craine accidentally took a step in his direction, jolted and thrown off balance, trying to get the bottle recapped, trying to wipe his mouth with his overcoat sleeve, Car-nac bent forward as if in shocked surprise and made his knees knock to-gether, playing horrified darkie—maybe a little mongoloid idiot thrown in—and waggled both large, pink-palmed hands. "Lawdy!" he mouthed without a sound, "oh Lawdy Jesus!" Still holding the whiskey sack, Craine jabbed one finger toward Carnac, warning him, furiously stabbing in the general direction of the black, misshapen jaw. Whiskey splashed out as the bottle jerked. At the last minute, Craine remembered not to shout and, blushing, filled with righteous indignation, got the whiskey capped and back into his overcoat pocket, both hands shaking, then turned his back and bent closer to his book.

. . . *rationalized in 58 B.C.,* he read. He nodded thoughtfully, angrily.

It would be lunacy, of course, trying to talk sense to Two-heads Carnac, and more lunatic yet to shout at him, here in the stillness of Tully's book-shop. That was no doubt what Carnac wanted. For Craine to shout, make himself appear to all the world a drunken lunatic. It was like an old movie, some slapstick comedy in which Carnac had cast him as the stuffed-shirt donzel who in secret took nips; the music teacher, maybe, who liked to touch little boys, or the self-righteous moustached policeman in the whore-house, representative of lying society on its fat, white horse. Nothing could be stupider; Craine was nothing of the kind. A drinking man, maybe; but he put on no airs. Look at him!—baggy old overcoat, hat down half over his ears, knotted shoelaces . . . But you'd have better luck arguing with

Jehovah than with Two-heads Carnac. What he really ought to do, when Carnac pulled one of those antics of his . . . Craine frowned, staring hard into the open book, mechanically wiped his mouth with the back of his hand, then smiled, malevolent.

The white-haired professor, or rather doctor, padded by, behind Carnac, carrying the dictionary and magnifying glass, holding the glass out in front of him as if looking for clues. He glanced at the choir robe, then over at Craine, but showed no interest or surprise. That was the usual response, these days, and, reminded that Carnac was no more important than he let him be—like a roar out of the earth, or a tornado in the distance—Craine turned away again and once more lowered his nose into his book. As the print swam into view, four inches from his eyes, he began lipreading, forcing himself to concentrate. *In the view of the Vedic priests,* he read (the gray type waggling on the page like minnows), *each sound in Sanskrit corresponded to some natural force in the universe, so that in theory at least, if one correctly pronounced the Sanskrit words meaning "Mountain, move," the mountain ought to move.* He read the sentence twice, uncomprehending, his mind on the black man who stood watching.

"Maniac," he said again, decisively. Tears squirted into his eyes—eyestrain, partly, and partly a touch of the usual midmorning drunkenness. It couldn't be emotion; he was feeling nothing whatsoever, numb-hearted as a stone.

It was a fact, Carnac's mania. Carnac was Carbondale's one authentic lunatic, if you didn't count Craine, and Craine didn't. (He lowered his nose toward the book again, eyes sliding left, then right.) Carnac read tarot, when he was able to speak English—he had fits of glossolalia—and since he read neither shrewdly nor tactfully, he was sometimes beaten up by his customers. The long dark blue choir robe and black silk top hat were only the more obvious signals of his lunacy. He claimed he was a dowser, an alchemist, an astrologer, and to prove it he walked with a long, gnarled staff, like Moses. Sometimes, depending on the company, he claimed he was the living voice of Christ or Mohammed. "Penny for Al Khem?" he'd say, running up to Craine. It was merely to torment him. He'd learned long ago, if he ever learned anything, that Craine would give him nothing. Yet the mad little black man would follow Craine for blocks, shuffling along drop-foot, waving his top hat as if to drive away some stench, begging and spitting, wickedly imploring Craine's mercy with his one good eye. The two sides of Carnac's face looked in different directions. He'd been hit by a train. He was not an intentionally troublesome man, just playful and crazy as a loon; all the same, he was trouble. He'd be arrested every two, three weeks or so, once for begging with a sign that said STOP CHRISTIANITY! And to Gerald Craine he was especially trouble. He'd elected himself Craine's devil. He'd dart from some entryway, drooling and gibbering, picking as if at Craine's clothes, but from six feet back, sometimes making sudden passes, like Mandrake the Magician. Meeting Craine on the sidewalk he'd stop, throw his arms out, strike the ground with his stick, and cry, "Whang!" Craine had once caught him by the neck and yelled, shaking him—at the time flashing panic at the rage that had come over him—"Two-heads, why are you *doing* this?" Craine's voice went up an octave, like the voice of a child about to cry. "Whoo-ee!" Two-heads yelled, as if joyfully, snatching off his top hat. "We making contact, brother! The spirits say, 'Two-heads, don't you mess with him, baby! That dude in the service of St. Cyril!'—but I mess with you anyways." "Saint who?" Craine had yelped, but Two-heads had managed to wriggle free and had run from him, swinging his rear end obscenely and shimmying all over, making shocks and waves fly up his choir robe like light off a pigeon. Craine had not pursued and had never again touched him. Two-heads' neck was as muscular as an adder's. Ever since, the very thought of that flesh under his fingers made Craine's skin crawl.

Carnac's whisper came through to him from the other side of the book-shelf. *"Hssst!* Look down by your belly, Mr. Craine! Quick!"

Before he had time to think better of it, some thought of the scar on his belly in his mind, Craine raised the book and looked down, below it and between his lifted arms. Carnac's black fingers came poking out, reaching through from the far side of the bookshelf, holding fanned-out red and white bicycle cards.

"Pick a card," Carnac whispered. He waited. Then, as if the police might swoop in at any moment, "Come on, man!"

Craine lowered the book with his left hand, slowly, then after a moment reached forward with his right, his mouth turned down grimly, and drew a card from the fan. He tipped it over slowly. "Ace of hearts," he said. His voice was thin and jarring, even in his own ears, like an iron wheel on con-crete. He put the book down—slid it, opened to his place, onto the books on the bookshelf—then slowly, deliberately, tore up the card, glanced at the floor, then put the pieces in his pocket.

"Pick another," Carnac whispered, as if everything was exactly as it should be. His smell came through the bookshelves, sour as medicine.

Craine picked another card and slowly tipped it over. "It's another ace of hearts," he said, and methodically tore it up.

"Two aces of hearts!" Carnac whispered as if in astonishment. "There's some mystery in this! Pick another!"

Craine picked another, tipped it over—another ace of hearts—and tore it up.

"Man, you lucky I caught you when I did," Carnac whispered, and drew his hands and the remaining cards back in through the bookshelf, out of sight. "Strange forces is converging. No question about it!" The cards and the tips of his fingers reappeared, the cards face up. They were now all twos of diamonds.

Craine lowered his head to look over the tops of the books into Carnac's eye. It was wet, as if tear-filled, and unnaturally wide, staring as if trying to pin him where he stood. Craine glanced down, and instantly, as if reading his mind, Carnac jerked his hands and the cards back out of sight.

Craine leaned closer to the bookshelf. "You don't fool me, Carnac," he said, too quietly for anyone else to hear. "I know what you're up to."

The wet eye closed. "God bless you for saying that, brother! You got a heart of gold!" The eye popped open, very wide, as sober as the eye of a myna bird. "You the only one in this universe understands me, that's why I takin good care of you. I lose you, Craine, and I'm 'onna sink into hopeless confusion. You hear about St. Peter, trine walkin on the waves?"

Craine laughed sharply, then scowled and abruptly turned away. It was his usual experience with Carnac; everything just at the edge of making sense. His madness was surely studied, like that of a fool to some old-time king. But also he was crazy; he'd been diagnosed. Sometimes he would sit on the sidewalk and cry. As if guiltily, Craine's mind flicked away from the thought, and his right hand, unbeknownst to him, moved to touch the bottle in his pocket. He glanced at the watch on his left wrist—ten a.m., too early to be as drunk as he was, he thought, unaware that he was thinking it. He retrieved his book, still open, from its shelf.

As Craine started down the aisle, retreating, Carnac called softly, "That's a interesting point you make, tearin up my cards. I guess I never looked at it that way before." He sounded hurt, and, again for no reason he could think of, Craine felt guilty. He glanced at his watch.

As he emerged into the central area of the bookstore, where the tables were, Craine stopped abruptly. The doctor from the university stood six feet away, gazing at the floor, slightly smiling, the dictionary under his arm. There was someone else there, Craine believed for a moment, or rather someone else standing not far off, toward the back of the store, motionless, hidden among the stacks. He got a sudden mental image—as if the person in the stacks had beamed it at him—of a huge winged bull carved in stone. He would have known, if he'd thought for a moment, thought hard, that it was a memory from his childhood, a visit to some museum with his aunt Harriet; he might even have worked out why it was that he thought of just that, just then; but Gerald Craine did not believe he retained any memories from childhood; plagued by blanks, he shrank in distress, with a thousand excuses, from the very idea of memory; and in his tingling alcoholic panic—a chronic state at the moment grown acute—he did not think at all. The doctor glanced up at him, lifting his head with the elegance of a prince so that he could see through the lower lenses of his bifocals, and smiled still more brightly, nodding. He stood with his head thrown slightly forward, like a man looking into a fire or across a vast desert or out at the sea. Craine approached. The person in the stacks—person or snake coiled to strike; he was suddenly uncertain—did not move.

"Morning, Doctor," Craine said, trembling, mustering all his courage. He raised his right hand toward the brim of his Stetson, then, because of the violent trembling, reconsidered and, attempting to disguise the gesture, reached into his inside pocket, got his pipe out, carefully not disturbing slips of paper there, and with almost imperceptibly shaking fingers stuck the pipe between his teeth.

The doctor seemed to notice none of it. "Well, well! Hello there, Detective!" he said. "Any progress on those murders?"

"Murders?" Craine said, giving a jump. Then, seeing what the man must have in mind, he grinned and bleated, "I'm not in on that." He let out a bitter laugh. "No doubt the police are doing all they can." In the flood of relief, he nearly remembered where it was that they'd met, what it was they'd talked about, but then at once the memory slipped back into shadow, out of reach.

They shook hands, an easy, automatic gesture on the doctor's part, awkward on Craine's—partly because he had to shift the pipe to his left hand, partly because the doctor had stumbled onto one of Craine's oddities: like a raw-skinned old farmer, he disliked shaking hands. He squeezed hard, as if to make up for his reluctance, then quickly drew the long, skinny hand back and wiped it on his coat. The rough cloth grated against the numbness in his fingers.

"It's a terrible thing," the doctor said. "Right here in Carbondale! What is it, five now? Five, I think."

"You might be surprised," Craine said, pedantic. "Murder's very common in Carbondale. Been that way for years." The conversation was academic, one of those tedious labors of politeness. There hadn't been a murder in three, four months. Chances were it was over, like the Hollywood strangler thing.

The doctor nodded. "Yes, that's so, so I've heard." He looked at Craine with interest. "One of the highest murder rates in the nation, right here in Little Egypt, as they say. Mine wars, lynchings, slot-machine wars . . . But five young women in one year—"

"Everything's old hat in Little Egypt," Craine said. He realized at once that he'd sounded impatient. He added, "One of them was up in her sixties—the professor's wife."

The doctor nodded, and, with a look of distress, putting his pipe in his mouth, Craine nodded too. The professor—some man in economics, Craine recalled; computer expert—had come home to his house out on Lipes' Ridge Road at five o'clock—that was his story—and had found the house strangely quiet, as if empty. He'd gone down cellar and there was his wife, stark naked, tied up in a chair. She'd been beaten, then stabbed in the neck and chest. On the floor there were twelve empty beer cans.

"You suppose it's all one man?" the doctor said. His concern was personal, not ghoulish. He had a wife of his own, no doubt. She'd be home alone right now.

"No telling," Craine said.

"No, no telling," the doctor agreed.

It was not quite true. Craine could narrow it down, he had a feeling, if he put his mind to it. The twelve beer cans, the woman beaten and stabbed and tied up *after*ward . . . But it was none of his business. The police had all the help they wanted; even hired a university specialist, it said in the paper. They'd stumble along as usual, trying this and that, following false leads—maybe even shadowing poor miserable Craine, if what Carnac said was true—and possibly sooner or later, by accident . . . Craine scowled, trying hard to concentrate, but abruptly, as if shaken loose by the shudder that now rocked through him, the whole thing fell out of his mind.

He drifted with the doctor toward Tully's desk. The girl in the cape was gone now. Light shot in through the transom above the door, tinted green by the glass, giving the room a kind of underwater look, the light shaft aswirl with motes. The grandfather's clock behind the desk read one fifteen. The pendulum wasn't swinging. On the glass of the pendulum chamber a chipped, ornate golden legend read *Time Lost Can Ne'er Be Recaptured.*

"Don't forget what I tole you!" Two-heads Carnac called from behind him. "They watchin you, brother—gettin ready to jump—so mine your p's and q's!"

Craine's jaw tightened, cracking the pipe bit, and his mind flashed an image of chipped, ornate *p*'s and *q*'s. Except for the tightening of his jaw he showed no sign of hearing. *One fifteen,* he thought, gazing fixedly at the clock, which gazed fixedly back at him. He tried to remember if he'd had lunch.

"Fascinating mind," the doctor said, and smiled again, tentative, as if meaning to imply some question. He cocked his large head sideways to see the title of Craine's book. Craine, misunderstanding at first, held his arm up so the doctor could read his watch, then, seeing his mistake, tilted the spine of the book so the doctor could read it.

"Sanskrit?" the doctor said, and briefly met Craine's eyes.

Craine nodded vaguely, only now registering the doctor's observation—"fascinating mind"—and scowled, thinking about Carnac's wrecked brain. Raising his left hand, book and all, he took the pipe from his mouth. "Sometimes you'd swear he's as sane as you or me," he said. He shifted the pipe to his right hand.

The doctor glanced at him to see if the irony was intended, a smile flickering at the edges of his mouth, then nodded. "It's fascinating to watch him," he said at last. Again he spoke a little tentatively, watching for Craine's reaction. He was a handsome old man, broad-shouldered, smooth-gaited, his teeth white as snow. No doubt he'd been an athlete, fifty years ago. All the well built and good-looking were athletes in the doctor's day. Health nuts. Bernarr MacFadden, if that was the fellow's name. Sun baths, air baths. The world was innocent; honest work for honest pay. Not that Craine remembered. He remembered nothing—on principle, he liked to say: "Reality is what we say it is, correct? Language is our prison." "Why not our walled garden," his neighbor the poet had broken in, but Craine had hurried on, pleased with his opinion and unwilling to be disabused of it: "Only those who remember the past are condemned to repeat it! He he! Ha ha!" His neighbor had grinned, shaking his head. "I'll say this about you, Craine, your craziness runs deep." But though Craine refused to remember the past, and for the most part couldn't anyway, he'd read about it, even read MacFadden. Five leather-bound red books, with anatomy cutouts in various colors. No photographs.

Still the doctor stood head forward, like the sphinx. If his snow-white teeth were false, there was no way of guessing it. Craine's teeth, Craine remembered, closing his mouth, were gray.

"They think like lightning, these people," the doctor was murmuring confidentially, "but sometimes it's difficult to translate." Craine nodded, a quick jerk. (There were words in Choctaw, he'd read somewhere, that had no equivalents in English. Indians did badly on IQ tests, he'd read. Lived in a whole different world.) He nodded again. The doctor's face was pink—benevolent and serene. Though he'd been handling books, his hands were as clean as if he'd just finished washing them. Craine did remember now where it was that he'd first seen him: they'd met at the AAUW Book Fair and had a long conversation—more like a lecture by the doctor—about Roman baths and lead poisoning. Dimout of the Empire through idiocy; the rich and powerful were all either half-wits or crazy. "Pollution is the Number One threat against humanity," Craine had read. Especially cigarettes. Only ten percent of the people who get lung cancer were never habitual cigarette smokers, he'd read. On the brighter side, however, there was scientific evidence for life after death. "I saw a white light, and I knew at once it was Jesus," someone had said, brought back to life. Craine smiled wryly. He remembered the doctor's name now. Dr. Tummelty.

"They work by instinct, that's the thing," Dr. Tummelty was saying. He swung his chin toward his shoulder, indicating Carnac, behind them. "They say the first thing that comes into their heads, and so—theoretically at least—they're never wrong." He slowed his walk a little, his light blue eyes on Craine's neck. "Fascinating, the way they work." His nostrils flared and narrowed, and he shifted his gaze to Craine's forehead. Perhaps he'd only now caught the whiskey smell.

"Never wrong?" Craine said. He strained to make his mind focus, nailing his gaze to the grandfather's clock, and stopped, partly to let Tummelty go ahead of him to Tully's desk, partly to put distance between his breath and the doctor's nose, but Dr. Tummelty stopped too.

"I'm not a specialist in these things," Dr. Tummelty said softly, "it's just a hair outside my field, but it's a theory I've been, so to speak, toying with." It was clear that he was ready to abandon the theory if Craine had good arguments against it. He studied Craine earnestly, his head once more thrown forward and slightly tilted, his faint smile encouraging, assuring Craine that an honest opinion would not offend him. His hair was snow-white, perfectly combed, exactly the same white as his manicured cuticles. White with blue shadows, like the shadows in bone. Carnac had dropped out of sight again, vanished utterly into the darkness of the stacks. If there was anyone else there, Craine could see no sign of him; but then, Craine had bad eyesight. Tully glanced up, then returned his attention to the ledger, his jaw working furiously, chewing. Craine looked again at the legend on the clock, *Time Lost* . . . The universe, if physicists were right, was fifteen billion years old. So he'd read. He shook his head just perceptibly to clear it. The bulldog lay perfectly still, as if dead, beside his dish. Waiting for one sixteen, Craine thought, and smiled grimly, as if enraged.

"There's an idea medieval theologians had," Dr. Tummelty said, studying him. "They took the view that the angels never stammer—the way humans do—because they never tell lies." He grinned. Craine's eyes narrowed and, quickly, apologetically, Dr. Tummelty went on, "It's not the opinion about angels that interests me, it's the opinion about stammering. Not that I generalize about stammerers—not at all!" He glanced around, smiling, slightly blushing, then back at Craine. Again, he cocked his head, princely, the gesture of a man about to make a terribly important, though tentative, point. "But it got me to thinking about how quickly these people like Carnac there can make leaps from thought to thought—the swiftness and ease of their, so to speak . . . so to speak . . . gibberish. The unconscious is wonderfully intelligent, you know? That's the great point the Zen Buddhists make. A woman walks down the street, for instance—" He waved the magnifying glass, showing where the hypothetical woman was, suggesting the dignity and indifference of the woman's walk. Craine nodded, pondering it, his mind darting off to the complexity of the human walk—two legs. Strange process, when you thought about it, two ungainly projections we balance over, hurrying here or there, or teeter on, pausing between backward or forward falls . . . And the human eye even stranger, heaven knows!—a single cell, he'd read, stretched and ingeniously adapted. All those centuries of ex-periment, hit-or-miss development, millions of years of Nature's tinkering with an eye that for most of that time couldn't see, and then, clink, "Snake eyes!" Who in his right mind would believe it? In fact he didn't believe it. No, he was with Einstein, not that Craine was a religious man.

The doctor was rambling on, oblivious, urgently concerned with his own speculations, objective as a philosopher, but quietly insistent—even desperate, a disinterested observer might have said—the doctor's head tipped and thrown forward still more, as if to see more deeply into the queerness of things. "She doesn't seem to look at the strangers she meets, but all the time a part of her mind is, you might say, 'scanning'—watching for signs of, let us say, let us say, *danger.* Scanning like a computer, I mean. I don't suppose you work with computers much?" He saw that Craine did not, and nodded, apologetic. He hurried on, "She judges our eyes, our clothes, our walk, all without consciously knowing she's doing it, and the first little sign that something's wrong"—he made a quick jab with the magnifying glass—"she's suddenly all attention." Craine leaned, startled, in the direction of the jab. He was thinking again of the murdered women. Did they know, right from the first instant, what was coming?

Dr. Tummelty bent closer and lowered his voice to show that he was serious, dead serious in all this, though of course it was all just a theory, he might be mistaken. His snow-white hair was blow-dried but nevertheless perfect, every hair in place. He wore a wedding ring. "We add and subtract, make up sentences, and so on, with the slowest, most trivial of our facul-ties—the part of our minds we're normally most aware of, the part we most value in our . . . value in our, so to speak . . . everyday affairs. But all the while, these more ancient faculties, things closer to the brain stem, are scanning the world for us, quicker than instinct, or one with it perhaps, though for the most part we're scarcely aware of them. We block them, doubt them—that's partly what makes us civilized, so to speak—but they're always there, ready to assert themselves, too simple and pure to lie to us—too primitive. By some accident—some severing of a nerve, some al-tered synapse, conceivably even some conscious choice—a man like Carnac there, a man who occasionally connects with the timeless, or so he be-lieves—the 'bioplasmic universe . . .' whatever . . . You follow what I'm saying?" He moved the reading glass slowly toward Craine's arm. The movement struck Craine as obscurely ominous, like a cat's paw slowly reaching.

Craine smiled in panic, scanning for faint sounds of life behind him, his eyes narrowed, sharp as needles. His head was drawn back, cheeks twitching, as if prepared to jab out and bite. "Interesting," he said. Now they drifted again toward Tully's desk, slowly falling toward it on their flesh and bone stilts, gauging and subtly controlling the fall with the swollen cells in their skull holes.

"There's no greater mystery than the human mind," the doctor said softly, his head tipped, trying to see into Craine's eyes. "Some fascinating things came out of Viet Nam—severed lobes are the least of it. I wrote a book on the subject." He blushed. "I don't mean to bore you. If I'm talking too much—"

Absentmindedly, Craine nodded. He could feel the unseen stranger's eyes on him again, drilling into his back. Was it possible, that theory the ancients had, vision as a stream of particles? Physics, he'd read, knows of no one-way events. Then could looking at an object disturb the object?—provoke some infinitely subtle response, a prickling of the thumbs? Could the atoms of his body—that was the point—could his atoms, just perceptibly molested by particles beamed from an observer's eyes . . . He must try to remember to think about that, he told himself. He'd write himself a note—he had pockets full of notes, and back at the hotel whole drawers full of them—but it was impossible just now, he had the book in one hand, the unlit pipe in the other, and moreover the doctor had his hand on his forearm, or rather the brass rim of his reading glass, pinning him where he was . . .

The doctor was still speaking, a curious scent like mint, maybe catnip, on his breath, one more brute obstacle in the way of concentration. "You've read about severed lobes?" the doctor was asking. Then, giving his head a little lift to get the lenses of his bifocals right, he smiled and corrected himself: "Yes of course. I'd forgotten. You read everything. Ha ha!" He tapped Craine good-humoredly—a fellow culprit—with the magnifying glass. "So where was I? Ah yes, Carnac! Fascinating mind. You're good friends, I take it? I've noticed the way he keeps an eye on you."

"Carnac?" Craine said, starting awake, indignant.

"A man can't have too many friends," the doctor said, and smiled again, more warmly than ever, as if to comfort him. For all the smile, he was watching Craine shrewdly. Judging his health, perhaps. Yes; he would have heard about Craine's operation.

The bell above the door clanged and a fat young man in an oversized red sweater came in, opening the door just enough to slip through it, more timid than furtive, or so it seemed to Craine on reflection. A college student. Small, neat features in the middle of an oversized head. Large hands and feet. He affected a bored look, as if his coming to the bookstore was someone else's idea, not his. Closet intellectual? Pervert in pursuit of dirty books? Poor devil wouldn't find them at Tully's—not a chance! Tully was a Baptist. Maniac on the subject of perversion, or such was Craine's suspicion. He knew the look. The squeezed-shut face, the anger that drove Tully's everlasting grinding of nothing between filed-down teeth. Tully's dog opened one eye, then let it fall shut of its own weight. The young man looked at Tully's sign, a piece of cardboard tacked above the shelf by the door, PLEASE DEPOSIT BOOKS AND PACKAGES HERE—THE MANAGEMENT, glanced down at his canvas bookbag, and then, as if the bookbag were a bomb, or infected with plague germs, slid it, touching it with only his fingertips, onto the warped gray shelf below the sign. He shot a look at Craine and Dr. Tummelty as if the offense were theirs—whatever the offense: the sign, the increasing smell of winter in the air, the tall, stopped clock—then ambled, hands in pockets, rear end rolling, toward the stacks.

They had arrived at Tully's desk now, and Craine again stepped back to let Tummelty go first. The bulldog looked up mournfully, then down with a weary groan. "Opera," he seemed to say. Craine slightly widened his eyes. Out on the street a truck passed, making the door rumble. "Oh! Oh, thank you!" Dr. Tummelty said, glancing at Craine as if he'd spoken. He laid the dictionary on the desk in front of Tully, who opened it without bothering to look up, read the price written in red pencil inside the cover, and wrote it down on a sales slip.

"Lovely weather," the doctor said, holding out a twenty-dollar bill.

Tully frowned and continued to frown, chewing hard, as if thinking it over, checking the truth of the statement from various angles, by various calculations, including Scripture.

"The magnifying glass is my own," the doctor said.

Now Tully did look up, the creases growing darker around his button chin. Light sparked off his spectacles, and his mouth pursed more tightly, still chewing. Again Craine's mind tricked him, for it seemed to him that Tully said, just audibly, "Ye think my damn place looks like a pawnshop? Ye think I'm in the Goddamn an*tique* bidness? I'm in books and maps, mister, or doctor, whatever ye call yerself. I'm in the *readin* bidness. History! Works of the *soul,* doctor!" But Tully's mouth wasn't moving, except to chew. Craine bent closer, making sure. No, no question about it. Whatever he was thinking, Tully was keeping it to himself. Craine should have known, of course. They rarely spoke, these old crocodiles. "Warm ott," they'd say, or "Little cooler today," to show they weren't downright opposed to speech; but that was the end of it—even as they spoke their eyes drifted leftward in their milky slits, then right again, slowly, as if reading the horizon—and then back they sank into their sullen, raging silence. They were born furious, the people of southern Illinois. You could see it in the babies at the hospital. Beef-eaters, hyperglycemics. Red, round faces, as round as the bone-white electric clock that stared inhumanely from the white wall behind them, the clockface dazzling, the white wall dazzling, designed to blind them or anyway to teach them to observe the world asquint, and squint they did, squint they would, from the cradle to the grave. Sternly, gingerly, the nurses held them up like blanketed dolls that might have bombs inside them, which in fact they did, hearts tick-tick-ticking toward the hour appointed, hardly seconds away as astronomers count time—held them up to the wide, glinting window—he'd been there with a client just a week ago—and red-faced, rolling-eyed, the newborns shook their fists and showed the hell-pit blackness inside their wailing mouths, Southern Baptists already: *Time is Misery.*

Tully took the twenty and looked down once more, scowling, still chewing, though as always he had nothing in his mouth but the taste of the injustice of things. He opened the desk drawer, took out change, put in the twenty-dollar bill, paused, slowly and carefully making sure he'd done everything right—Craine could see him as a schoolboy, rechecking his columns of addition in panic—then counted one more time, pulling at each bill, and at last gave the doctor his change and the gray, scribbled sales slip. Craine laid the book on Sanskrit on Tully's desk and put a dollar on top of it. Tully took the dollar, opened the book to hunt nearsightedly for the price—50¢ in red—wrote the sales slip, furiously chewing, and reopened the cash drawer.

"It has fascinating implications, this new split-lobe psychology," Dr.

Tummelty murmured confidentially. "You know what I mean, the left lobe governing one set of faculties—reason, logic, mathematics, language—the right lobe governing a different set—emotion, our feeling for melody and color, all that's 'feminine,' so to speak—"

"Yes, right," Craine said quickly, almost gruffly, edging toward the door, pocketing his sales slip and change. The vague sense of dread had flared up in him, much stronger. He could feel the eyes on him, some angry young woman, he'd swear to it, though there was no young woman in sight. Something flashed in his mind, white as snow, too brief to catch. Dr. Tummelty came after him, part of his attention on dusting the dictionary with his hand-kerchief—the magnifying glass was in his pocket now—then folding the hankie, dust in, to keep his suit coat clean. The suit coat was elegant, silvery gray, as soft and thick as a rabbit's coat. He must have gotten it up in St. Louis or, more likely, Chicago. There were no such suits for sale here in Carbondale, much less Murphysboro; checks and plaids were what the crocodiles wore, though maybe at Sohn's you could find a suit fit for a student.

Beyond Dr. Tummelty, in the dimness of floor-to-ceiling stacks, the young man who'd just come in stood poking his head out, watching Craine. He wasn't the one who'd been spying on him, such was Craine's opinion. Electricity was different. The moment Craine's eyes met his, the boy looked down and, like a groundhog, drew his head back. Two-heads Carnac was nowhere to be seen, though Craine seemed to sense him everywhere, as if he'd turned himself into the ceiling, the floor, the walls.

"You're familiar with the idea of complementarity in physics?" Dr. Tummelty was asking. Gently, he touched Craine's arm to draw his attention back. Craine squinted, waiting. If it weren't for the slight alcoholic haze, he'd have noticed long ago that there was something peculiar in the way Dr. Tummelty had latched onto him, clinging like a burr. Someone else, of course, would have dismissed it at once as an old man's loneliness. (That, as Craine often remarked, was why Craine was the detective, not someone else.) "It's not a concept I fully understand," Dr. Tummelty said, "but I gather it suggests that the physical universe may be constructed in completely different ways, so that it shows itself to us in one way or another depending on how we look at it. Ask questions that assume light travels in waves, and the universe obliges us by answering in waves. Ask questions that assume light flows in particles, and the universe answers you in particles.

There's no resolving the conflict—no 'wavicles,' as some scientific wag once expressed it. The universe is this, but also that—that's complementarity, if I haven't got it wrong. It's a fascinating business. Look at it one way in isospin space . . . isospin space . . . and an object's a proton; look at it another, and it's a neutron. Science, religion . . . rationality, intuition . . ."

Craine glanced at him, then down again, half eager to move on, half arrested, his scalp prickling; the sensation that someone was observing him was increasing by leaps and bounds. (Without his knowing it, his hand drew his pipe toward his mouth. His teeth caught the bit and his hand reached into his coat to look for matches among the paper scraps.) The only time he'd heard the bell above the door, he was almost certain, was when the boy in the oversized red sweater came in. Was the girl still there, then? the young woman in the long black cloak? Was she police?—was that it? But if so, why him? He squinted, chilled. Why not, after all? It was the oldest trick in the handbook: pin it on some drunk. His head gave a little involuntary jerk and his mouth fell open. Never! They knew him! Never in a million years! But the flushing in his chest told him otherwise. He strained to clear his wits, get cold sober for an instant—just one clear-headed instant was all he'd need—but all he could get, strain as he might, was a surge of witless fear that made him jerk his right hand toward the bottle. He stopped himself by such ferocious force of will that his hand hung there shaking like a machine.

"Suppose the two lobes see whole different universes, *both of which are there,*" Dr. Tummelty said, still touching Craine's arm, searching his eyes as if with feigned innocence—as if someone had hired him to check Craine out, or maybe delay him while a trap was set—"one universe superimposed on the other, so to speak. Or interdigitated. On the one hand, the universe Carnac sees; on the other hand . . ." He studied Craine as if to make out what he thought. Waving his left hand, dismissing innumerable objections, he hurried on: "Suppose in addition to physical particles—quarks and anti-quarks, neutrinos, muons—there are spiritual particles—prayerons, say." He smiled, looking over Craine's head, not quite joking. "Suppose that in that accident Two-heads had, some curious rewiring of his brain resulted, something analogous to the operation formerly done in Tibet, we're told—the opening of the mystic . . . so to speak . . . third eye. I don't say I believe all that, mind you, but one of the things we've been learning lately—"

"Mmm," Craine said. "Here, let me get that door for you." Like a man stepping over a crevasse, Craine threw one foot forward.

As his stretched hand went for the doorknob an explosion of barking went off behind him. Craine jumped, violently and awkwardly, throwing one arm out but nearly falling even so, and swung his long sharp nose around in the same motion, just in time to see a gray paper airplane come to rest in the shadowy space between his feet and Tully's desk. Tully stared at him, his caved-in mouth wide open, black as a pit. The airplane had been made from the page of some old book. The dog, half up on his feet, barked once, twice more, then stopped, embarrassed, looking around over his shoulder at Wilbur Tully.

"*Hyah!*" Tully yelled, throwing all the force of his fury, all his rage at the universe, at the dog. Craine shrank, cringed as the dog did, averting his gaze. His eye landed on the airplane. On one wing, in pencil, Carnac—or someone—had drawn a picture of a large, staring eye with enormous lashes.

"Goddamn you!" Tully was bellowing. "Goddamn you sons of bitches!" The yell came out distinctly, nothing ever clearer, but his mouth was, all the while, tight shut.

"You all right, Detective?" Dr. Tummelty asked, catching Craine's arm.

"Fine," Craine said, and jerked his arm back, harder than he meant to. His weak eyes searched wildly, trying to make sure it was Carnac who'd done this, but he couldn't make out even the back of the store. "Never better!" he said, and gave a quick, fierce cackle. He lunged forward, snatched the door open, and stepped out into the light.

Two

The day was blindingly bright and clear, the sky and the sunlit walls of buildings charged with that yellow-white, tropical brilliance of sunlight unexpectedly encountered after hours in a movie theater, except worse, more like the darkness of Mammoth Cave or the center of the earth. Pain shot in through his eye sockets. Coming out into the daylight had been a mistake, he saw; but after all that business he could hardly go back. He shaded his eyes with the book on Sanskrit, then, gradually adjusting to the dazzle in every atom on the sunstruck street, groped forward, lowering the book, reaching out vaguely, like a swimmer, his shoes stumbling close to obstructions in his path, then away again, his right elbow now clamped tightly on the book. His eyes adjusted more and, leaning close, touching things, he began to get his bearings. The grainy configurations in telephone poles, the finely sifted dust on car and truck fenders, the humps and jagged cracks in the sidewalk—grass pushing up through them, insects thriving on them, ants and wood ticks, ladybugs, mosquitoes—took on at last, even for Craine's thick-spectacled eyes, their proper definition, that and somewhat more, the unnatural sharpness of objects observed through the lens of slight drunkenness—a sharpness less unnatural to Craine than to most people, and one he accepted with pleasure now, anchoring his mind by it as he straightened from his inspection of the cracks at his feet and unsteadily turned left, heading downtown in the direction of his office. He paused once, feeling those eyes on him, and glanced back over his shoulder at Tully's, just in time to see Carnac come flying out onto the sidewalk as if thrown. A moment later, in great distress, the old doctor emerged, his arms extended, one reaching back toward Tully's door, the other (the one that held the book) toward Carnac. He resolved his dilemma in favor of Carnac, hurrying to him, chasing the hat for him, then helping him to his feet. Two small black children stopped to look and one of them bent over, picked up something from the sidewalk—a feather—and held it toward the doctor. The doctor took it from her, bowing and smiling, and held it toward Carnac, who stood furiously slapping at the seat of his choir robe, his narrow shoulders hunched. That was as much as Craine saw of the event; people on the sidewalk came flowing around them, hiding them from view. Craine set off again toward his office.

The street—"the strip," as they called it these days—was crowded with life, as always—students in old Volkswagens, on motorcycles and bicycles, standing by store windows, holding hands, looking in; farmers in their pickups poking along toward the depot or Dillengers' feed store; town and university people bustling through their errands; cats in upstairs apartment windows or preening on the painted-brick hems of porches; cardinals and blue jays, nuthatches, sparrows in the bushes and trees or up on tarpaper roofs; and everywhere—sleeping in doorways, tied by their leashes to parking meters, sniffing at the gutters, the coats of passing strangers—particolored, brown, gray, black, and pepper-speckled dogs. He passed Low's Jewelry, where the clock in the window ran backwards, the clockface reversed, and like a man who has bitten into a lemon, he screwed his mouth up tight and squeezed his eyes shut, offended by the obstreperous clutter of things, toying with the idea of going back to his hotel room to bed. When he opened his eyes, it was of course all still there, slightly left of where he'd thought it would be, a universe stuffed like an old spinster's hope chest with junk . . . "Junk!" he said aloud, angrily, clenching his fist, though he was conscious of no emotion.

"Morning, Craine," Denham said, nodding from the door of his old tobacco shop. "Fine weather."

Craine nodded, touched the brim of his hat, returned his hand to the neck of the bottle in his overcoat pocket, and hurried on. The sense of being watched was still with him, still strong. It gave solidity to his step, determination. He walked cocked forward, as if pushing against wind—wind, small planets, meteors, imploded stars—his lips sucked in, his eyes slightly bulging behind the thick, tinted glasses, and from time to time he would glance over his shoulder, as if hearing again Carnac's warning. No wonder, of course, reinforced as the warning was by the doctor's opinion, however tentative and mysterious, on the possible trustworthiness of Two-heads' miswired mind. All very well to mutter, "Maniac, maniac!"; the fact remained, he could feel those hostile eyes on him. He glanced nervously at his watch. A door opened to his left, whispering *"Sh!"*—so much like a human warning that he jumped and, for an instant, stopped muttering. He studied the man now emerging from the aqueous dimness inside, an old, bearded Negro, then turned and looked carefully back in the direction from which he'd come. No sign, or anyway none he could make out. Beyond twenty-five feet, the world, to Craine, was like the floor of a clean, bright ocean. His hand, unbeknownst to him, reached up to his mouth with two fingers. His shadow on the sidewalk, stooped and hatted, lay patiently waiting for him to move again.

Abruptly he darted forward and turned left down the alley beside the dimestore. At the office, they'd wonder what on earth had become of him, but no matter; it was high time he settled this. If he was smart, of course, he'd go straight to the office and get help; this business of being tailed was no joke, Lord knew—maybe tailed by the cops, hoping to set him up, maybe by some lunatic who got his kicks, or hers, out of rolling old drunks, maybe pouring gas on 'em and lighting 'em. "Better play it smart," Craine whispered, pausing, narrowing his eyes. He whispered it again, then again, then again, varying the delivery and intonation, getting it just right. But even as he spoke he forgot the point of it, that he should go back to the office and get help. He clamped the book on Sanskrit more tightly under his arm and walked bent farther forward, almost running. The echoes of his footsteps whispered on the dark brick walls and grumbled among garbage cans. He looked behind him—no one there, or no one he could see in the alley's dim light, large blocks of shadow. When he emerged he turned right into what once had been the A&P parking lot, now half grown up in weeds, then left at the street, then left again at the corner, doubling back toward Tully's. The eyes still seemed to be following him, if ever they had been. Yet the streets were busy; no way to be sure. He intensified his effort, cranked up his cunning. Once, turning suddenly, he spotted Two-heads Carnac at the back of an old building, sorting through large cardboard boxes. Craine flattened himself more against the wall, then crept away. Carnac sorted on, holding first one box, then another, up to the sun. "Hoo! Ha! Nah bad! Sum-bitch!" He smiled like a man sorting paintings.

So Craine continued for another twenty minutes. Turning corners, moving through the town's decayed center, he would step off quickly in the new direction, then stop, hidden by the brick or wood of the building on the corner he'd just rounded, and would light his pipe, squinting, waiting, his right hand wandering with a mind of its own toward the whiskey bottle. Once or twice, drawing out the bottle, sack and all, he took a quick restorative. So far as he could tell, no one who came around the corner was the one he was waiting for. He saw old women with shopping bags, their eyes forlorn; fat businessmen angrily gesturing and talking or simplemindedly beaming, dreaming of profits—makers of instruments of torture, for all he knew (America was the number one manufacturer of instruments of torture, he'd read); students on fire escapes or skipping across streets, some with long hair, some with Afros; a minister with whom he'd done business once; doctors, college professors, most of them young, full of twitches and fierce opinions, their faces as innocent as the faces of children; heavy-booted asparagus- and hog-farmers, bespectacled, scholarly, awkward down off their tractor seats, all with that look of slight confusion, as if they suspected that somehow they'd been tricked. Craine knew the whole dreary catalogue of their troubles, past, present, future—the troubles peculiar to each of them, from the old women to the farmers. Mortal tribulation was his stock in trade. But their troubles were not what he was thinking about now. People noticed him, some of them, but hardly registered the fact, hurrying on; and after a moment he would hurry on behind them, moving more or less in a spiral that would lead to his office.

He glanced at his watch. It had stopped at a quarter to eleven, or so he thought. (At the bookstore, he'd fixed one fifteen in his mind. It was now his settled conviction that it must be two or so.) His secretary, Hannah, would be fit to be tied, wondering where he was; but no matter. He was his own boss, and he had nothing to do that couldn't wait. He hadn't been involved in what he'd call a real case—or would have called a case in his Chicago days—in years. He scowled, carefully not thinking about the past, stepping on the squares of the sidewalks, not the cracks, and abruptly, surprising himself, he stopped and, throwing one arm out for balance, spun around. The student he'd seen in the bookstore, in the oversized red sweater, was crossing the street diagonally, pretending not to know Craine was there. He was hurrying—loping, in fact, arms economically swinging like a jogger's. Given the distance and the weakness of Craine's eyes, that was as much as Craine could tell, but it would do. He knew about coincidence, probability. Heart thudding violently, he ran out into the street—a screech of tires, the bright yellow hood of a car bobbing downward with the suddenness of its stop—and Craine shouted, *"You!"*

The boy turned, jumping like a rabbit, looked at Craine, and ran. Craine ran after him. *"You!"* he yelled again. He lifted his long feet high to keep from tripping.

"Help!" the boy yelled. "Murder! Police!"

"Easy now!" someone said, and seized Craine's arm. The man's grip was firm as iron, official, planted right square on the crazybone. Craine, lifted half off his shoes, swung his head around and squawked.

"Some kind of trouble, Mr. Craine?" the man said. He was a tall, professorial person of about fifty—Craine had a feeling he'd seen him before. High, pink dome, horn-rimmed glasses, dark flat trapezoid smile with crooked little teeth behind it. Though he meant it to be genial, the smile had a hint of ferocity, flashing like a knife.

"That's a criminal there," Craine yelled, pointing toward where the boy had disappeared. He tried to pull his arm free.

"That why he's calling for the police?" the man said, and smiled again. The heavy, dark shadows of buildings and trees, sprawled along the street, gave a shudder of disgust or laughter, then lay quiet again.

Craine had placed the man by now: Detective Inspector McClaren, professor of crime and correction at the university, lately made part-time criminal investigator with the Carbondale P.D. It came to Craine the same moment that it was *not* the boy who'd been spying on him, but someone else, he'd settled that long since. Some young woman. Yet how odd, he thought, suddenly putting his hand over his mouth, that McClaren should be planted just here, just now, perfectly set to intercept him.

Craine's face, unbeknownst to him, put on its cunning look. "He's been tailing me," Craine said. "Follows me everyplace."

"That so?" Detective Inspector McClaren said, brown shaggy eyebrows lifting. He studied Craine, looking down from high above him, then slightly loosened his grip on Craine's elbow. "Well, never mind, Gerald," he said. "We'll see to it. I'll have someone look into it." If the use of Craine's given name was intended to intimidate, the obscene trick worked. It made McClaren seem securely, ominously adult. One could imagine him signing important papers, giving firm, polite orders, shooting his cuffs for increased efficiency, sitting serious-minded and metaphysically alone at his orderly desk, head and shoulders thrown back, a certified, no-nonsense, horn-rimmed intellectual, beloved and feared by his inferiors.

Craine glared at him, angry as a goat, still trying to jerk free. "How the hell do you intend to look into it? You don't even know him, and you've let him get away!"

"Oh, I wouldn't say that," Inspector McClaren said, blushing again, red as a beet, but smiling. He kept an eye on the people passing by on the sidewalk, careful of his dignity. "You know how it is in a town this size. With a little quite simple technology—" Though his eyes remained dead, smoky blue, ice cold, he stretched his mouth into a still wider version of the trapezoid grin, chin thrown forward—the expression of a professor being patient and studiously unvindictive with an irritating student who no longer has a prayer. He drew his left hand from his sport coat pocket—brown coat, leather patches, a gift from his new, young wife, no doubt (Craine had heard about that; sooner or later he got all the filth)—raised his thin, freckled wrist for a glance at his watch, then looked back at Craine. Soberly, he said, "See here, Gerald, do you by any chance have time for a cup of coffee?"

"Dime?" Craine said.

"Time," the inspector said, slowly and distinctly, as if speaking to a dull-witted foreigner.

"Oh, time!" Craine hesitated, pondering, thinking about the bottle in his pocket, imagining himself at the diner pouring Scotch into his coffee-with-cream, keeping the bottle steady by holding it with both hands. It was painfully tempting: McClaren would take the check. But suppose it was true that they were setting him up as the Lady Killer, planning to let him make them heroes? Head lowered, lips sucked inward, he slid his eyes toward McClaren, sizing him up. He was a man it might be useful to have a fix on, in point of fact, now that McClaren was working with the police. For a private eye, especially a tiresome old bum like himself (Craine had no illusions; that was the one decent card he had left), there was no such thing as good relations with the police, not in a place like Carbondale; but it was nice to know the enemy. McClaren felt the same, of course. It was the reason for his kind invitation. McClaren stood waiting, bald head tilted, mechanically smiling, as if someone had turned off his power switch.

"Don't mind if I do," Craine said at last. "Matter of fact, I haven't had time to get lunch yet."

"Fine! Jim Dandy!" the inspector said, looking at him oddly. With his right hand clamped on Craine's crazybone, he turned Craine around like a peeping Tom taken into custody and marched him back into traffic. He raised his left arm to stop oncoming cars (Craine snatched his hat off, not to be outdone, and waved it furiously, leaning out past the inspector's paunch), the inspector murmuring in his just-slightly-backcountry, reedy voice, "Glad I ran into you! Splendid piece of luck!" Craine racked his brains to place the accent. Northern South, he decided; east of Kentucky and West Virginia. Baltimore, maybe, where they murdered poor Edgar Allan Poe.

"I've been meaning to get over to see you, Gerald," the inspector said, helping him up onto the curb as if Craine were a cripple. Two dogs drew back from them in alarm and a woman raised her hands. Craine waved his Stetson at her, then mashed it back onto his head.

The inspector was saying, "But you know how it is, *mutatis mutandis* and all that." He smiled and gestured grandly with his free left hand to show Craine that, though a gentleman and scholar, he wore his learning lightly. They turned toward the Chinese restaurant, McClaren steering. (Craine hated Chinese restaurants.) Abruptly, as if just now remembering something, McClaren bent forward. His face showed concern. "I understand you've been ill," he said. "You're better now, I trust?" As if guiltily, he released Craine's arm.

Craine smiled inwardly, registering that flicker of guilt in McClaren, and tightened his grip on the book. They were a wonder, these people: wanted to find a scapegoat with a terminal disease. No question about it, the world was in good hands! Craine clamped his lips. He would volunteer nothing. Let the bastard pull teeth. "I'm fine," he snapped, and gave his head a little nodding jerk.

"You had"—McClaren tilted his dome, looking down at him at an angle—"you had some kind of operation, I understand?"

"That's right," Craine said. The inward smile widened, and a crackling like burning pine boughs began inside his head. The noise distracted him but also put him more determinedly on guard; it was something he'd experienced before, he couldn't say when.

"Nothing fatal, I hope?" the inspector asked, then blushed.

"Everything's fatal in the end," Craine said, and gave a cackle. He turned to aim his nose at the inspector. "So you've joined the P.D.!"

"Yes," McClaren said. "—Yes and no." He hesitated. He seemed to cling for an instant to his hope of getting more on Craine's illness, then relinquished it, looking down. He interlaced his fingers, thumbs upward, on his paunch. On two of the fingers he had heavy gold rings, one of them a wedding band, the other one the setting for a large red stone, perhaps a ruby. "Yes, I thought I'd get my hands 'down into the dirt a bit,' as Juvenal says. It's no good being too theoretical." By the lift of his eyebrows and the tilt of his head he gave Craine to understand that no one in the universe was his match when it came to pure theory. Craine had, as usual, his suspicions. He wondered, among other things, whether Juvenal had ever said anything of the kind. McClaren's smile sharked out again. "Criminology," he said, "is the science and *practice* of crime control."

They'd arrived at the restaurant, and McClaren stopped, sweeping his bejewelled left arm out to open the door, pleased with the way he'd expressed himself and insisting, having won the advantage, that Craine enter first.

"Me before you?" Craine said. "You think there may be hit men inside?"

McClaren seemed not quite to hear him, and stared blankly at his grin. *"Après vous,"* he said, smiling, tipped forward and sideways so that his bald head slanted toward the door.

Craine hesitated for just a moment longer, leering, inspecting their two reflections in the blacked-out restaurant window to the right of them—his own pitched forward, debauched and stooped, a shabby old stuffed-with-rags clown of a creature, prowler of the sewers, his wide hat brim level with his thickly glassed-in eyes—Detective Inspector McClaren's form larger, more distinguished—he might have been the last of a noble line of owls, or a member of the Scottish country gentry, stuffed for posterity—tilted at the waist, the legs long spindles below the beer paunch. Beneath his trousers—brown corduroys—McClaren's legs would be as white as boiled eggs, Craine thought, though maybe that was wrong: under his sport coat he wore a black cotton T-shirt, the kind boating men wear. Perhaps he had a Chris Craft, out at the marina on Crab Orchard. His legs would be dark brown, then, with bleached-out hairs. On the boat he'd wear a captain's hat, drink martinis with people who sold real estate. (Craine smiled. "Most dangerous animals Nature's ever known," he'd told his neighbor Ira Katz. "Never mind the butler! Keep yer eye on the man in checked pants!") On his wrist, the inspector had a sportsman's watch, a two-hundred-dollar gold Seiko.

Craine stepped in through the door McClaren held and paused a moment to let his eyes adjust. It was a place he'd never been, so high, cool, and still it gave a feeling of murky temple ruins, possibly an old-fashioned roller-skating rink. A smell of must, maybe bones and hides, fell over him, and a darkness that had nothing to do with photons or the energy of the sun. McClaren came in behind him, closing the door softly, like an undertaker closing a coffin lid, and began to wipe his feet on the entryway mat. He took a long time at it, head bowed devoutly, making sure he did it right. Craine looked up at the ceiling. It was cluttered with objects; he couldn't make out what. Blocky things, feathery projections. It was like being trapped inside a crystal.

"This is where I always come," McClaren said heartily, his ritual ended. Craine looked at him. "I see."

There were mirrors on all the walls. Craine looked instinctively from one to another of them, hunting for some sign of whoever it was that had been spying on him, but there was no one, not even a shadow. His uneasiness increased. The room seemed to Craine to grow larger, more empty, by the moment. Again McClaren seized Craine's crazybone, to guide him to a table near the enormous, black-lacquered bar. They were alone—no waiters, no bartender, nothing but dead objects from a dead civilization—so Craine put it to himself. The red, mirrored walls were a chaos of masks, old weapons, fake scrolls, queer musical instruments, lanterns, unidentifiable carved things as dusty as spiderwebs, and rising above the rest an immense, brightly painted papier-mâché lady, Indian, not Chinese.

"I like the company," McClaren said. In the dimness his face was lead-gray.

As Craine seated himself, the inspector went over to the bar and, with the flat of his hand, came down hard on the service bell. Then, pleased with himself, pulling with both hands at the tail of his sport coat, making it fall neatly, he came over, inspected the table—red-lacquered plywood—pulled out his chair, inspected the chair seat, and sat down. From the way he lowered himself—the smoothness of the thing—Craine got a momentary alcoholic vision, quite alarming for an instant, of a spider descending, tiny legs flying, huge dome floating like a sinking balloon or a large, bright stone falling slowly to the bottom of a pool. As soon as he was seated a waiter appeared, a long-torsoed Chinese Craine was certain he'd seen before somewhere (as it happened, he thought that of all Chinese), a high-school-aged boy with hair slicked so flat it seemed painted to his skull. He hurried to their table and, grinning, speaking in near whispers, took their order: whiskey for the inspector; for Craine, coffee with cream. The boy bowed and fled.

"Whiskey gives you cancer, you aware of that?" Craine said, then after an instant realized he hadn't really said it, clearly as he'd heard himself; had only thought it.

"So!" the inspector said, and threw back his head and shoulders, smiling grandly.

Craine nodded, hunched like an invalid, peering nearsightedly around the room. He could relax here, there was no way anyone could observe him; yet he remained as tense as ever. His left hand picked at the book on the table in front of him, his right hand fiddled with the neck of the bottle in his coat pocket. Somewhere in the room a cat moved. Craine jumped.

"This is indeed an unexpected pleasure," the inspector said. "An occasion, as they say. I'm acquainted with your exploits in Chicago, needless to remark." His "remark" was protracted, an elegant southern drawl that seemed to slip from just one side of the pitch-black, trapezoidal smile. He fixed Craine firmly with his smoky eyes, though his smile was intended to be disarming. "What ever induced you to bring your practice to a place like Carbondale?"

Craine drew his pipe out, spilling scraps of paper without noticing, and toyed with it, smiling absently, staring at the center of the table, sharp-eyed, part of his mind trying to remember. "I forget."

"You forget!" McClaren said, and laughed, slightly wincing. For an instant an anxious look came into his eyes, his bald head reddening to a blush again; then he swung forward and put his elbows on the table. "It's none of my business, that's true, I concede." A gold tooth glinted as his smile flashed. "I just wondered. Natural curiosity."

It was at this point, drunkard that he was, that Craine made his mistake.

"It's a fact, actually," he said, just a touch irritably, his voice ironed flatter than before. "I never remember anything, except sometimes when

I read." He got out his tobacco and penknife and opened the red Prince Albert package. When he looked up, McClaren was studying him, trying to make out whether his leg was being pulled. Craine's blood chilled. If it was true that they were seeing if he'd do as a scapegoat, then what a piece of luck—this discovery that Craine had no memory! Craine winced, squinting. It was as if he were setting up the whole thing himself. He tensed all his muscles, straining to clear his head, make himself fit to take care of himself; but he knew it was useless, he'd do what his drunkenness pleased; no doubt feel proud of it.

"You actually don't remember why you moved?" McClaren said.

"I never remember much of anything," Craine said bleakly, stuffing his pipe, poking with his finger. "Anyway, nothing about my"—his face went wry—"personal life."

"That's very strange," McClaren said. A kind of stillness had come over him, a hovering, as in zero gravity, the wide-awake stillness of a hunting dog who's picked up a scent. It was so subtle that only a fellow detective would have noticed it, but it was there all right, unmistakable, and not unexpected. Everybody's got one twisted spot, one knot in the wiring where the heat builds up; that was axiomatic in Craine's profession. And McClaren, with the instinct that made him what he was—unconsciously scanning, Dr. Tummelty would say—was aware that he'd stumbled onto Craine's. Craine sighed. The inspector spoke lightheartedly, chattily, nosing closer. "You never remember anything about your personal life! Good heavens!" He gave a laugh. He pushed his head forward, chin first, white and gold grin flashing. "You're speaking figuratively, I take it?" He grinned on.

On the curtain that led to the restaurant's innards, across the room, something white appeared—an animal, possibly a rat, Craine thought at first, heart leaping—but it resolved itself at once into the Chinese boy's hand, drawing the curtain back, bringing in—centered like a jewel on a round, black tray—Craine's coffee. The boy stopped at the bar and fixed whiskey for the inspector, then hurried to their table.

"Thank you, my good man," Inspector McClaren said. He sat erect, his right hand closed on the front of his sport coat just below the lapel. Picture of a dandy. A Baltimore lawyer at home among magnolias and row houses, sunny of disposition, elegant. He should be wearing a vest, a Phi Beta Kappa key. *Beware of him,* Craine thought wearily. *Small silver knife.*

"Will that be all?" the Chinese boy asked.

Craine lit his pipe, thinking, as he always did, lighting his pipe, of lip cancer, lung cancer, heart attack, the shadow inside him.

Inspector McClaren surveyed the table, then raised his head abruptly, eyebrows lifting, his black mouth distorting to a trapezium. "My colleague here," he said, "wanted coffee *with cream.*"

The waiter bowed and, as if in self-parody, put his fingertips together, then hurried off.

McClaren leaned forward again, interlaced his fingers above his whiskey glass, and said, "You were saying you have trouble with your memory."

"I wasn't saying it's trouble. It's no trouble at all," Craine snapped. "People are always deciding what's trouble for other people. It's an interesting quirk." He caught himself and smiled, not quite genial, and took a suck at his pipe. "Trouble for *you,* maybe." He smiled harder and let out smoke. "That's what we usually mean when we talk about other people's trouble."

McClaren looked at him oddly, thought of saying something, then thought better of it. The gears were working. Click, spin, click. He raised his whiskey glass. "Cheers," he said, and drank. Craine set his pipe down, drew the bottle of whiskey from his pocket—spilling more paper scraps—uncapped the bottle, still inside the sack, and, with slightly trembling hands, carefully poured a little Scotch into his coffee. He set down the bottle and picked up the cup. "Bung-o!"

"Still," McClaren said, setting down his glass, eyebrows lowering in an irritable but lightly conversational frown, "how do you do your work if you forget things?"

"Oh, I remember *that* kind of thing, for the most part." He capped the bottle, wrung the dirty paper sack closed again, and with a hand not too noticeably wobbling set it to his left, beside the soy sauce. Then once more he closed both hands around the cup, preparing to lift it. Why he continued, getting himself in deeper, he couldn't have said—the crackling of electrons in the back of his head had grown louder—but he did, and in fact it gave him pleasure. Joy of coming clean, he thought. Beauty is Truth. "I remember pretty much everything, when I'm working on a case. But when it's over, that's it."

"Odd," McClaren said.

"Yes, that's true," Craine said, "I'll admit it. But you know how it is with a private detective—Sam Spade, Lew Archer—" He shrugged, smiling crookedly—a smile he'd practiced at his mirror as a child—and he reminded himself again to be careful. "It's much more a matter of style, with us. Columbo, for example. You've seen Columbo on TV?"

"I've watched it, yes," McClaren said, watching Craine. He whispered something that Craine didn't catch. Again he raised his glass to drink. As he set it down again he said, "I don't believe Columbo's 'private,' actually. And in any case, you know as well as I do, those are fairy tales. Actual police work, when compared to its fictional representation on TV—" He cleared his throat, prepared to launch a lecture.

"True!" Craine said, "but more true for you than for me, that's my point. In *my* line—private as opposed to public—we have to keep in mind what our clients expect. 'Image,' that's the name of the game with us." He leered. "We have to be *characters*. You think I like this getup?" He pointed to his ragged cuffs, the large brown stain on his overcoat sleeve. He sat back, cocked his head. "You, Inspector. You've got a wife, children from a previous marriage . . ." How he knew McClaren had children he couldn't say; instinct maybe; contact with "the bioplasmic universe," as Dr. Tummelty had said. He must think about that, remember to write himself a note about it; something fake in the way Tummelty had said it, maybe—but for now he must hurry on, step lightly, beware of getting tangled in his shoelaces. "You think I like making these sacrifices?" he asked. He leaned forward and raised the coffee cup with two hands, sipped the Scotch-coffee loudly, then set down the cup again. "But there are forms, you know. We have to accept that. Right ways and wrong ways of doing things, you know. Not true forms, mind you. Not *Platonic* forms." Craine's voice, unbeknownst to him, was sorrowful. "Social prejudices, expectations, that's what we're discussing." He leered again, his sagging eyes morose. "How do I know you're a professor?" he asked, slightly nasty. "Because you behave like a professor, you dress like a professor, you occasionally throw in a little French." He let out what he meant for a smile, squinting, and raised his cup again. When he'd sucked in, loudly, intending to offend, he hurried on, lowering the cup, picking up the pipe, relighting it. "So it is with us. Form is function, as the physicists say—and vice-a-versa. What does the American private detective do? Lew Archer, say? J. T. Malone? He drinks Scotch! Every time he turns around, every scene he walks into, more Scotch! It's hard on the system, but you see how it is, we have no choice. Just like the Avon lady can't be too fat. And when he's shadowing people he reads newspapers, magazines, books. Thass less harmful, probly—" He felt the slur coming into his speech and took hold of himself. "Depends on what you read." He pointed with his pipe stem at the old book on Sanskrit beside his cup.

McClaren looked at it, shook his head, the glass hovering in his still hand halfway to his mouth. "I believe this is the strangest conversation I ever got into," he said.

"Yes, that's part of it too! I'm glad you noticed! Sam Spade pretended to be dishonest, remember? You've seen *The Maltese Falcon,* I imagine. Yes of course. Everybody has. *Yer going over for it, baby. I'm not gonna play the sap fer you.* Humphrey Bogart. Me now, I play crazy." He cackled, the sound so crazy in the great, dark, empty restaurant that for an instant he was frightened.

"Now wait a minute," Inspector McClaren said, scowling, prepared to smile if it should prove that Craine was joking.

"It's the number one problem of existence," Craine said, "finding the adequate function for your form, or coming to understanding of the form behind your function, in common parlance *value* or *motive,* criminal or otherwise." He showed his teeth. "Now the determinists maintain—"

"Listen," Inspector McClaren broke in. He touched the corner of his horn-rims with his thumb and first finger. "Let me see if I understand this." He pointed at Craine's coffee cup, then frowned, raised his eyebrows, and looked over at the curtain where the waiter had disappeared. He forgot his question—one could see the gears shudder and stop like huge old mill-wheel gears when the mill's foundation breaks, giving way to the flood. A blush of fury rose up in him and he pushed back his chair, got up, went over to the service bell on the bar, and clanged it. When nothing happened, he clanged it again, stared at the curtain for a moment, then came back to the table. "This 'character' you put on, this strange manner of behaving—"

He saw by Craine's face that the waiter had appeared, and he swung his head around. "Waiter, what happened to that cream?"

"Ah!" the boy said, throwing both hands up, laughing. He went back out through the curtain. McClaren pursed his lips, still angry, then after a moment checked the chair seat and carefully sat down again.

"That now," Craine said, leaping with both feet into the hole in the conversation, meaning to kick it in yet another direction—he pointed toward where the waiter had been, and leaned forward to speak more confidentially—"that's a typical case!"

"Case?" McClaren said.

"Brute substance," Craine said. "Here we are having an intelligent conversation, a meeting of minds, as one might say, and what happens? A zenseless—" He checked himself. "Senseless accident! We don't think of events as brute substance, but they are! Of course they are!" He hit the table. "In the war of mind and matter we have to keep these things clear. Nothing's static, that's the great lesson we've learned. Process, the meaningless spinning of wheels—click, spin, click—that's materiality! So how do you work?"

"Pardon?" Inspector McClaren said and blinked.

"How do you work?" Craine pushed his hat back, thinking of Sam Spade, and waited, showing his rat smile, deeply interested.

"How do I work?" Inspector McClaren said. He looked at Craine over the tops of his glasses. He had the expression of a man on the verge of becoming airsick.

"Technique," Craine said. "M.O."

The Chinese boy came through the curtain with the cream, glided to the table, and set it down. "Everything aw-right?" he said.

"Fine," Craine said. "Wonderful." He winked at him.

McClaren glanced from Craine to the waiter, then back into his glass. The waiter left. Craine poured cream into his coffee and Scotch. He smiled and waited.

"Let me ask you this, Gerald," Inspector McClaren said at last, as if forgetting Craine's question, or maybe thinking himself clever to have managed to avoid it so easily. "Do you remember nothing whatsoever of your personal past?"

"Nothing," Craine said.

"Your parents? Your schooldays? University?" His head slowly tilted, and his right hand moved up to take his glasses partway off.

"Nothing."

Inspector McClaren pushed the horn-rims back on, then raised his whiskey glass and swirled the yellow liquid. The ice had all melted. He was frowning ferociously. "How about things that happened, say, two weeks ago?"

He was zeroing in now in earnest, Craine saw. Figuring out how much of the decline in the quality of American life they could pin on him.

"I sometimes remember some of that," Craine said. "It comes back to me when I need it, more often than not. I have what you might call 'practical memory.' I could tell you my father's name, if you give me time to think."

"Incredible," McClaren said. He worked on it some more. "Perhaps you drink too much?"

Craine leered and raised his cup.

"Even so," McClaren said, blushing, "to have forgotten your parents, your *affaires de coeur*—if you don't mind my saying so, it would seem to indicate—" Again he shot Craine a furtive, scrutinizing look. "You're teasing me," he said, and abruptly smiled. "It's part of that *act* you spoke of."

"Well, think what you please," Craine said. If he was smart, he knew, he'd claim that, yes, it was indeed an act. His chest was full of panic: it was like playing with dynamite, fooling with a creature like McClaren. But some madness was in him, some craziness finally metaphysical, or chemical; same thing. No doubt to McClaren it was Craine who seemed the enemy of mankind, outrage against decency and reason. No doubt to Mc-Claren it was Craine who seemed the alien, the terrible beast from deep space, the spider. Oh yes, yes, one could easily understand these things, take the larger view. Suddenly, Craine felt defensive, annoyed. Though perhaps it was just his drunkenness, it seemed to him now that it was a serious matter, this door he'd closed on his past, closed on all of it, and sealed up tight, so that hardly a shred of light broke through. How many people in the history of the world had ever done such a thing, freely, for no reason, for the pure existential élan of it? or if not that (for no doubt he was exaggerating now, it had not been entirely voluntary), if not that, then how many people, having found themselves forgetting things, had confirmed and approved the unsettling process, voluntarily shaped it as a sculptor confirms and shapes the design in marble? He was a walking proof of the physicist's proposition that everything that can happen in the universe does happen. Once in the history of the universe, it could be said from now on, a man locked himself outside Time. A petty-minded fool would say, "Why? What caused it?" The man of heroic vision would say, "Behold what has been caused!"

Craine found himself whining. "It's the truth, actually. Most people don't like that kind of thing. If *they* don't do it—in this case, forget things—then it shouldn't be done. That's the universal law. 'Herd law,' I call it, as in cattle, not ears."

"Ah yes, Nietzsche," the inspector said.

Craine nodded, grimacing. "Perhaps. But I ask you, why *should* a man remember things? I grant you, there are various opinions about Time. There's the popular, simpleminded one—no, let me finish, let me explain!" Craine raised his hand.

McClaren leaned back in his chair, letting him hang himself.

"There's the popular notion, Time as an onward rushing stream, a river—a notion that brings with it the corollary assumption of a moving present moment, the little bubble of *now*. But obviously the meaning of *past* and *future* must be determined not merely at the surface, that is, the psychological level—you can see that yourself—but also at a deeper, ontological level. All around and in between the *no more* and the *not yet come* lies the eternally present and at the same time eternally absent time zone called *now*. Correct? Absent in the same sense that if Time is the whole created universe from Big Bang to Fizzle, then we're not it, we're a hole in it, or rather we're the mice in the hole in it." He laughed. "But neither of these times, psychological or ontological, gets mentioned at all in the mathematician's or the physicist's description of Time, or rather Space-time." Again he raised his hand. "No wait, I'm not finished!" He took a sip from his cup, spilling a little down his chin in his haste. His whine became, even in his own ears, more petulant. "In the physicist's description of the universe, there's no provision whatever for a flowing time or, by implication, a moving *now*."

"That may be so," McClaren began.

"It's all a trick, you see," Craine explained, leaning forward still more, both hands clinging to the cup as if without it he'd be dragged—like Atlantis, like Rome and the British Empire—into the darkness below the table. "These notions of time and space we have, it all comes of thinking too much about objects—including ourselves, you see, the 'subjects' embedded in the general clutter of objectivity. Now I, for one, have refused to be deluded! What I cannot endorse, I take no part in."

"But you *are here,* sitting at this *table,*" McClaren said uncertainly.

"Only for practical purposes," Craine said.

McClaren frowned, slowly shaking his head. He feigned professorial patience, a decent man's willingness to hear all points of view—leaning back comfortably, glass in hand—but his eyes were smoldering, as if he suspected his intelligence was being trifled with. "You've got all this from that book?" he asked, nodding toward Craine's book.

"No, a different one," Craine said. *"The Avengers.* It's a comic book. You'd be surprised what a man can learn from comic books." He cackled and threw McClaren a wink, then raised his cup two-handed and drank.

"Crazy stupid shit," Inspector McClaren said; or perhaps Craine only imagined it. "I see," McClaren said. He considered the matter from all angles. "What I don't quite follow," he said, "is why this makes you forget things." For all his studied dignity—the professorial jacket, the carefully cultivated look of one who has encountered this question a time or two before—he looked vulnerable as a chicken, as if he feared that his question might have given him away, might have revealed that, contrary to the impression he'd so diligently labored to create, that huge pink dome was empty.

"Ah, that!" Craine said. "Why do I forget things? Yes, that's the question we must grapple with."

Slowly, as if Craine had drained off some of his vital energy, Inspector McClaren leaned forward again and settled his weight, more heavily than before, on his elbows. "You actually have no memory of your past whatsoever?"

Dogged *son of a bitch,* Craine thought. But he thought it almost fondly. His glimpse of the man's vulnerability had put him off his guard. He'd be sorry, he suspected, but he nodded soberly, solemnly, and sipped his Scotch-coffee.

McClaren turned his glass, empty now, between the palms of his hands. "Ordinarily," he said, like a professor reaching deep into his treasury of information, "when we forget things it's for one of two reasons, as Sigmund Freud observed."

"That's right! Exactly! Sigmund Freud!" Craine said, but McClaren kept coming, like a bulldozer.

"Either because we're repressing them—refusing to look at them—or because we're looking with all our attention at something else."

"That's it!" Craine said. "That's Freud all right!" He pointed at McClaren's glass. "You want more whiskey?"

"The second explanation might well be the correct one in your case," McClaren said. "You're familiar with the theories of Sigmund Freud, I presume?"

Craine rolled his eyes up, clear out of sight, but McClaren, looking straight at him like a slightly baffled dog—a boxer—seemed not to notice.

"By reputation, at least, you're an excellent detective, or were at one time"—he blushed, quickly smiled—". . . no doubt still are. Yet this failure of memory is so *extreme*, as you describe it . . ." Mysteriously, his shoulders and dome began to rise. Craine stared. The odd phenomenon continued. The large man rose from the table as if levitating, unaware of it himself, or so it seemed, all his faculties engrossed, and, still talking, he drifted toward the bar like a somnambulist, stretching his arm out through the murky room, groping. "It's hard to believe that what blocks out your past is an intense preoccupation with the present, the details of your work, and so on. Surely the cases you encounter in a place like Carbondale . . . And also, of course, there's the matter of your drinking. Ordinarily that wouldn't seem to indicate . . ." His hand rose over the service bell, moving as if independent of his will, and came down hard, clanging it. Even though Craine had been waiting for the noise, he jumped. McClaren seemed not to hear it. His hand came down again on the bell, clanging it a second time; then he came drifting back toward Craine, still, it seemed, thinking out loud. "You're a complicated person. I'm told you won a number of medals, up in Chicago. That's very good, admirable—so it is!—and yet I always distrust such things. 'Why was he so desperate to prove himself?' I ask. Pessimistic, I admit, though it's a fault you share, I suspect." He smiled, conspiratorial, lowering himself like a descending spider into his chair. "We wouldn't last a minute in this business if we weren't a bit distrustful, eh?"

"Now you've got it!" Craine said, cackling, and slapped the table. His voice rang loudly in the hollow, gloomy room.

But McClaren was onto him. "I admire you, Gerald. The energy it must have taken! You've never been to a psychiatrist, I suppose. Never been hospitalized, nothing like that—"

"No, nothing like that," Craine said, laughing, "no."

"Well if it works, *do* it, as the philosopher William James would say—brother to the novelist." He gave Craine a little look. "Most people don't know they were brothers, I find."

"Brothers?" Craine exclaimed.

The inspector looked uneasy and hurried back to his subject. "You have no idea what it is you're suppressing?" he asked, "—what it is you feel guilty about?"

"None," Craine said wearily, and smiled.

The waiter appeared at the curtain.

"Whiskey here," McClaren said. He glanced at Craine's cup. "And more coffee—with cream. A little Scotch in it." He leaned toward Craine. "This is on me, Gerald. You keep what's in the bottle." He smiled like a mother, head tipped.

"Thank you," Craine said. "Thank you very much!"

The waiter disappeared.

"I imagine you saw the movie *The Seven Percent Solution*?" McClaren said. "Excellent movie. Very good acting in it."

"Yes I did," Craine said. He hadn't, in fact. For that matter, he'd never seen Columbo on TV. "It was excellent. I thought the acting was very very good." Instantly he saw he'd again gone too far. McClaren was smiling, far back in his chair, his smoky blue eyes murderous. The darkness of his blush was alarming.

"You take us all for fools, don't you, Craine," he said. "The police, I mean. Perhaps because few of us read books about Sanskrit."

Few of us, Craine thought. McClaren too had put wonderful energy into becoming what he'd become. Guilt flooded through him, the kind of guilt he felt, at times, with Carnac. (He glanced at his watch and saw that it had started again, though it was still, of course, behind.) Mock all he liked—and mockery was Craine's nature; a serious fault, he admitted it—the inspector had a good deal invested in that ludicrous image of his, the genteel, all-knowing professor who almost without thinking could talk like *The Decline and Fall of the Roman Empire.* Who was he, Craine, to make light of it? All the while Craine was thinking this, something else was happening, and now, suddenly, he came awake to it. Inspector McClaren was whispering, his lips slightly parted, not visibly moving, *I'll get you, you cocky little son of a bitch. You'll make your mistake, taking us for fools, you'll steal somebody's money, or you'll kill some poor bastard, and I'll be down on your little white ass like a duck on a daisy!* Craine jerked so badly that the coffee remaining in his cup splashed all over him. McClaren jerked too, first forward, as if instinctively defending himself, then back, almost knocking his chair over, getting out of the way.

"Shit!" Craine exclaimed. He hit the table with the flat of his hand.

"Jesus, Craine," Inspector McClaren said, trembling.

The waiter appeared, wide-eyed, hurrying toward the table with the coffee.

"They told me you were crazy," the inspector said, "but I must say, you out*do* yourself!"

"It's the liquor," Craine said. "Bane of my existence!"

"I can see that. You should check into a hospital!" He was wiping his lapels with both hands. Craine glanced at his watch.

Now the waiter was mopping up the table with a cloth from the bar. "It's all right," he said, laughing. "Everybody spill things." When he finished he went to the bar for the inspector's whiskey.

"Actually," Craine said, "I haven't read the book on Sanskrit myself. I just got it."

McClaren, still wiping his lapels, looked at him as if it was the craziest thing he'd said yet.

"I did read a page or two, at the bookstore, before I bought it." The image of Two-heads Carnac rose up in his mind, then the airplane with the eye on it, and he shuddered.

McClaren studied him, his left hand mechanically going out to take the whiskey from the waiter. Graceful as a dancer's, the hand brought the glass directly to the inspector's mouth. The mouth opened and drank. The waiter poured Scotch into Craine's coffee, then backed away and, in a moment, was gone.

"It's an Aryan language," Craine said soberly. Absentmindedly he reached out to open the sack, uncap his own Scotch, and pour in more. "The Vedic priests did an interesting thing. They analyzed the sounds in Sanskrit with a kind of mechanical contraption, a little brass plate with grains of sand on it. They discovered that each sound made a different kind of pattern in the sand—an *o* makes a circle, for instance—and they revised the sounds until the patterns corresponded, or so they believed, to the fundamental forces in the universe. This was in 58 B.C."

McClaren stared at him.

"How they knew the fundamental forces, I'm not sure. But in any case—" It occurred to him that McClaren was right; he was crazy as a loon. It wasn't news, but it made him uneasy. He noticed he had the cap of the Scotch bottle in his hand—he couldn't remember how it had gotten there—and carefully, trying not to shake too badly, he reached to the bottle and, after a moment, got the cap back on. He twisted the sack shut, his chest full of guilt for no conceivable reason, as if he'd mocked and scorned not just McClaren, but others more important somehow, perhaps the person who'd stood watching him from the stacks at Tully's bookstore (only the skin on the back of Craine's neck remembered it with absolute clarity). "As for the trouble I have with my memory, it's an interesting question," he said, "you're right. I've wondered about it myself, to tell the truth."

As he spoke, a strange thing happened. Neck hairs a-tingle, he got a flash image of his aunt Harriet in her coffin. A single frame—maybe two or three—as the people who make movies say. (He'd read articles on the subject.) She looked serene, a wax figure. Beneath the closed lids, he knew, the pale blue eyes were staring. The memory stirred no particular emotion, or none beyond his surprise and alarm at remembering. He had a feeling that if he concentrated, he might remember something more. His fingers shrank inward, making fists.

McClaren was uneasy, restless. He was watching himself in the mirror beside their table, image of himself a split second ago, removed from him forever, locked behind the glass. (Craine thought of mentioning it, then decided he'd better not.) "Language is an interesting thing," Craine said. "There are some who maintain that we're imprisoned inside it. I have a neighbor, a poet, who's very troubled by that idea."

"You remember him, then?" McClaren asked.

"Dimly." Craine smiled and opened his hands as if to show he was un-armed. He must remember to think about why McClaren was so angry.

McClaren drank, glanced down at his watch.

"Time Lost Can Ne'er Be Recaptured," Craine said and smiled again.

And now for a second time (so far as Craine was aware) a brief memory flamed up in him, so powerful it made his hands shake. He was a child in his room at his aunt Harriet's house, looking up at a picture on the wall, an engraving of the sphinx. It stared out horribly—such was his impression—at miles and miles of desert. Did it follow that Eternity lost could ne'r be recaptured? He reached into his inside coat pocket for his pencil and a scrap of paper, laid the paper on the table—there was something written on it already—and jotted down his question on the edge of it.

"Something's occurred to you?" McClaren said, distant.

Craine raised the paper and pretended to read it. "Remember to pick up laundry." He folded the paper and put it, with the pencil stub, back into his pocket.

For a full minute they sat in silence, Craine listening to the stillness, thinking nothing whatsoever, as far as he was aware, the inspector staring into his glass. At last, thoughtful, the inspector looked up. "That boy you were chasing on the street. You say he was tailing you?"

"Actually," Craine said, "I believe he was a sexual molester."

"Ah?"

"There's no lower form of life," Craine said. His hands began to shake again as he got into it. "Vermin!" he said. "Filth! Hanging's too good for them!"

"Nobody hangs people in Illinois," McClaren said. "At least not legally."

"They're fiends incarnate," Craine said, and showed his teeth. "They follow some girl into some dim, dark alley, or they lurk in department store dressing rooms—"

McClaren tipped his dome, writing invisible letters with one finger on the tabletop. "Does it ever occur to you," he asked softly, thoughtfully, "that this lunatic act you do might get out of hand?"

"Detective, I kiss you on the lips," Craine said.

Detective Inspector McClaren blushed deeply, and once again, for an instant, his eyes showed rage. That moment, the front door of the restaurant opened, throwing light along the floor. A figure came in, closed the door, and stood adjusting itself to the darkness. McClaren turned in his seat to see who it was. "Sergeant Eggers," he called. "You looking for me?"

"Ah, there you are!" the man called back, waving both arms in a broad, slow gesture like flying. He groped his way toward them, taking off the police cap as he came. Craine hunted through his pockets for a matchbook, carefully not spilling any papers this time, then, when at last he'd found his matches, poked down the dottle in his pipe with one finger and lit it.

"Have a seat," McClaren said. "You want coffee? Hit the bell." He pointed toward the service bell on the bar.

"No, thanks," Eggers said, "just got through with a cup. H'lo there, Craine." He took a chair from the table across from them and drew it up.

"Afternoon, Sergeant," Craine said. He looked for an ashtray for the match, then laid it neatly on the table, lined up with his book.

"You feeling all right these days?" Eggers asked. He seated himself and laid his hands, pointing inward, on the fat of his upper legs. "I heard you were away at some cancer clinic."

"Cancer?" McClaren said, reproving, as if Craine had held out on him.

"Well, there's some rottenness in all of us," Craine said.

"Amen," Eggers said, his tone so serious that Inspector McClaren glanced at him.

"Sergeant Eggers is a born-again Christian," Craine explained. He blew out smoke.

Eggers smiled, lowering his eyelids modestly. He had a button chin, bright cheeks, ears that stuck out like sugar bowl handles. "Well—" he said.

Now McClaren was watching Craine again. "This cancer," he said, "what kind was it?"

"Colon," Craine said. "Pain in the ass, believe me." He cackled. The others didn't smile.

"They got it all out?"

For no reason, Craine cackled again, playing madman. "Clean as a whistle," he said. "It makes a feller think, though, I'll tell you that!"

McClaren studied him. "I imagine so." After a moment, he drew the horn-rimmed glasses partway off. "You must think I'm a pretty insensitive person, getting over you that way, at a time when . . . I assure you, I had no idea."

"On the contrary," Craine said, waving it off. "You'd be surprised how seldom you get a chance to work ontological time into the conversation."

McClaren laughed politely, eyes snapping. Eggers looked at him, hoping to be let in.

Craine's cup was empty. He put down the pipe and poured in Scotch from his bottle.

"That stuff good for you?" Eggers said.

"Drives away the horrors," Craine said, and winked. He pushed the whiskey sack toward Eggers. "Have some?"

Eggers shook his head, distressed.

McClaren was thinking again. "That boy you say was following you," he said.

"The pervert."

McClaren let it pass. "Has he been following you long?"

"You think it's paranoia?" Craine said, wobbling the cup two-handed toward his lips. He drank, then set the cup down, almost empty.

"Somebody's been following you?" Eggers said, eyes widening.

"Everywhere I go," Craine said. He made his face mock-cunning, playing crazy again; he knew himself that he was overdoing it, tipping his hand.

Foolishly, drunkenly, kicking himself as he did it, he pushed on. "Every-where!" he said, throwing his hands up, crazier than Two-heads Carnac. "Above me, below me, behind me," he raved. "Eyes on me! Watching me!" That instant, he felt those hostile, sullen eyes again, as he had in the book-store and on the street. He was shocked and for some reason filled with shame, as if he'd betrayed someone, horribly and crudely. So the eyes main-tained. In fact they said something . . . He tried to think clearly, stepping back from the part of him that raved. Suddenly, conjured up from God knew where, he saw again—more clearly than before—the small, round, female face with the clipped, Egyptian-looking beard. The eyes, just percep-tibly slanted, were large and dark, soulful as a doe's, yet baffling; dangerous.

"It's the Lord," Eggers said, simply, directly, with such authority that, though he knew the idea was ridiculous, Craine jumped. He found himself leaning forward as if eagerly—McClaren watching him—Craine's eyes hungrily searching the sergeant's plump face. "I had that, before I was saved," Eggers said. He brought his lips together, slightly trembling, then looked down, embarrassed.

"I doubt that Gerald will believe that's his problem," Inspector Mc-Claren said. "He doesn't strike me as a religious type."

"Ah, but I am!" Craine said, "—that is, I was once." Vividly, he saw himself in the choir at his aunt Harriet's church. A touch of nausea swept through him. Something quite incredible was happening to his mind: in a rapid succession of vivid images—as if the walls were cracking, letting in light, or some healer had lifted the scales from his eyes—he saw himself going through museums with his aunt, saw himself riding in a bus of some kind—he was very young, dressed in dark blue short pants, a stack of books on his knees. "Gerald?" his aunt said, right behind his chair.

"Excuse me, where's the rest room?" Craine said, pitching forward.

McClaren looked around the room in alarm, at the same time reaching out, touching Craine's shoulder. "Through there, I think." He pointed to-ward the curtain.

Craine got up quickly, unsteadily, clenching against the force in his un-predictable bowels, and hurried toward the curtain. He found himself in a grimy hallway, the kitchen at the far end of it. The rest rooms sign was halfway down the hall. He got his pants down and his seat over the toilet just in time. An explosion, a ringing in his chest like sorrow, a brief, sharp pain behind the star-shaped red gouge where his colostomy bag had hung, and he was better. He sat forward over his knees, straining, his head pounding furiously, then reached for the toilet paper. The image or vision, whatever it had been, was gone now, vanished from every cranny and closet of his mind. His past was gone too, as if fallen to the center of the earth.

When he returned to the table, Sergeant Eggers and Detective Inspector McClaren were standing, getting ready to leave. They were talking about a poker game, apparently one not yet played, for which McClaren had high hopes. He broke off when he saw that Craine was listening. "Everything all right, Gerald?" McClaren asked.

"Wonderful," Craine said. He picked up his pipe from the table and put it into his pocket.

"If you wanted to come to . . . one of our prayer meetings . . ." Sergeant Eggers aimed his eyes above Craine's hat.

"Thank you very much," Craine said. "Thank you."

McClaren was looking at his watch again. He'd put money on the table, though the waiter had brought no check. "It's been a pleasure getting to know you," he said. "Can I drop you off someplace?"

"No, I'm heading for my office," Craine said, and reached across the table for the whiskey sack. It occurred to him that he'd forgotten to get lunch. McClaren came toward him. Too late, Craine realized that the hand was coming for his crazybone again.

"Well, take care of yourself," McClaren said, and grinned. He gave the crazybone a squeeze, then drew his hand back.

"I'll do that. Thank you very much." He moved with them toward the door. Somehow he bumped a table, and the soy sauce went over the edge and thumped on the rug. Eggers stopped quickly to pick it up, looking sheepish as if he'd knocked it off himself. "It jumped me," Craine explained, pointing to the table with his whiskey sack. "You have to keep watching every minute."

They smiled politely.

"Most people don't realize how much things move in this world," Craine said. "They don't mean to make trouble, I recognize that. But you know how it is, things get boring for them."

Now McClaren had the door open. Eggers put on his cap, one hand in front, one in back, getting it just right.

"You think it's the Lord, eh?" Craine said, "—hounding me for my sins?"

Eggers smiled vaguely, slightly hurt.

It occurred to Craine that he couldn't go out there, not yet. Where the sun hit the chrome on the cars along the street, it was like looking at the light of a welding torch. And there was, of course, that other problem. Whoever it was would be waiting—standing on the sidewalk opposite, perhaps, reading a book, waiting as if all eternity were not too long. *Book!* he thought, and looked down. He had the whiskey sack in one hand; the other hand was empty. "I forgot my book," he cried. "It's back there on the table."

"Well—" Eggers said.

McClaren tipped his dome and half-smiled, solemn. "I'm glad I ran into you," he said. He raised his hand to touch the side of his glasses. "Drop by the office sometime. We'll do this again."

"Yes, good," Craine said. "Thank you very much." He willed them out the door, and at last, when the door swung shut behind them, he turned quickly, furtively, and went back for his book.

"Worried?" someone said. He started violently, raising his hands in self-defense. In the chair opposite the book, where McClaren had been sitting, sat a large gray cat, one paw extended toward the table. "Worried?" the cat said again, pretending to yawn, watching him ironically.

Cautiously, Craine reached for his book and slid it across the table toward his belly. "Of course not," he hissed. "Don't be ridiculous!"

But the cat was onto him.

Three

In his dingy, grim-walled hotel room that evening, Craine sat motionless, breathing shallowly, like an invalid trying to make out whether he's better or worse. He'd come to that familiar part of the day when healthy, happy men pause for a moment, relax with a beer, and look out over their lawns, their children's bicycles, the new Toyota wagon, taking stock; a time men like Craine spend carefully not thinking, drinking whiskey and smoking strong tobacco without a flicker of thought about cancer or heart attack, since they've been drinking and smoking for six, seven hours now, and if they're going to stop—as perhaps they will, who knows what will happen from one day to the next?—they can stop tomorrow, first thing in the morning, which is still a long way off. Despite the day's unsettling events—not that much worse than any other day's, he could see now, putting it all in perspective—his situation was not yet critical. What one had to bear in mind, he thought, gesturing with his pipe stem as if to an audience in the street below, was that (McClaren was right) when the mind plays tricks, it has reasons. His face began to twist like the face of a State's Attorney conducting a difficult trial. In the end, of course, there could be only one reason—not drink, overwork, even loss of conviction; all those were mere evasions of the bottom line: psychological pain. Craine nodded, a movement so slight that only the sharpest eye could have caught it in the mottled dusk. So the question was, he thought, his face twisting more, what was he doing, unbeknownst to himself—what was he doing that he hadn't been doing for the past twenty years—that was causing psychological pain? Craine pursed his lips to a sudden small O and stared blankly, eyes slightly widened, as if some fool, some irrumpent stranger, had broken in on his thoughts to raise the question. He frowned, trembling, pretending to consider, then cleared his throat, relit his pipe, and looked down at his book.

As he sat at his window, reading the old tome on Sanskrit by the failing light outside, the shadows on the street grew longer and sharper, eerily alive, it seemed to Craine—jumping up like panthers when a truck cut through them, or fluttering like starlings in a sudden gust of wind—until once, when he looked out, he saw that their blocks and lines had vanished, or rather had spread everywhere, consuming the street. He heard sharply clicking footsteps, a young woman running. Distress stirred in him, but of course it was nothing, just night again. Voices came up to him, children playing football in the empty dirt lot of the railroad depot across from where he sat. The depot was old, once grand as a palace, chimneys all over it like headstones on a hill, black as coal, their corbeling ornate and clean-cut against the gray, still starless sky. He thought for an instant of the view from his window in Johns Hopkins Hospital—Osler dome and the streets of Baltimore—then concentrated, resisting memory, on the depot. The building had been padlocked and boarded up for years, and like everything else faintly tinged with nobility in Little Egypt (nobody could say there was much along that line), the depot was said to be haunted. Craine had no patience for country superstitions, but it was easy to believe that if any-thing anywhere was haunted, the Carbondale depot was the place. The ghosts would not be of the dangerous kind: weary black men pushing bag-gage carts, lean old conductors implacably chewing the insides of their cheeks, countrified young men dressed up to travel . . . striped cardboard suitcases, haircuts shaped by bowls . . . Craine focused on the book, resisting a minute rise of sadness. "Ghosts," he muttered. He closed out, just in time, an image of children around a fireplace in a cabin at the edge of a dark mountain lake. "Not likely," he said aloud. Nothing in the depot but heavy old boards half rotted out, crumbling concrete, rusty iron; pigeonshit and rats.

The children in the shadow of the depot had been playing for hours now, he was dimly aware, or clearly aware with one small part of his brain—playing as if they'd begun just a moment ago, as if time had been suspended—as it was for Craine, at least so long as he could escape into dozing, as he managed to do from time to time, or could engross himself in his Sanskrit book. Their faces were surprised and indignant when the father of one of them called, poking his head out the window of his old black panel truck—the truck just visible in the rising flood of darkness—"Stephen! Stephen!" and then, a moment later, when the boy had walked over to him—the man still shouting, so that the rest of the players would be sure to hear—"It's getting dark out, boy! You got your mothah worried sick!" Craine gazed out guiltily, as if it were he who'd stayed out too long. Beyond the makeshift playing field, the railroad tracks gleamed dully, more dully every minute, gradually disappearing.

His sense of being watched was not as strong as before, nowhere near so. If he could be sure that someone had actually been watching him, he would have to say now that they'd quit for the day, gone home. Yet something of the weird discomfort was still there, a ghostly residue like the dread a man feels the morning after. That was why he sat by the window to read, the window shade up, the room growing steadily darker around him, his bottle dull amber in the windowsill, his pipe between his teeth, Scotch glass in his gray left hand. He was presenting himself for his enemy's inspection, if the observer was his enemy (his sense of the whole thing was more and more unsure), stating by the act of sitting there that he had nothing he knew of to be ashamed of, nothing, and was not in the least afraid, not at all, not "worried," as the restaurant cat had claimed, not even anxious; nothing of the kind. By his presence at the window he made plain to all the world that if the stranger would come up and knock on his door, like a civilized being, Gerald Craine would be happy to talk, make an effort to explain, put forward his defense.

His calm was an illusion, of course. When for a moment it seemed to him that the stranger had really done it, had climbed the narrow, dimly lit stairs and stood quietly knocking at his door even now, Craine started violently, bursting from the depths of his absorption like a rabbit, such terror in his chest that he thought he was having a heart attack. His hand jerked, splashing whiskey from his knee to his chin; then he sat silent and jittering, holding his breath, mouth wide open, waiting for the knock to come again. It didn't. Slowly, his heart still painfully beating, he put the book down on the floor beside his shoe, put the glass on the windowsill to the right of him, put the pipe in his pocket, rose silently from the armchair, and, carefully avoiding the floorboards that creaked, crossed to stand listening at the door. Except for the scramblings of mice in the wall and the sea roar in his ears, there was nothing. At last, with his right hand on the handle of the gun in his shoulder holster, he reached out with his trembling skinny left hand, turned the knob, and jerked the door open. Across the hall, in front of his neighbor's door, a shabby person in a suit was bending over, trying to poke a pamphlet through the door crack. At Craine's feet lay a similar pamphlet. He stooped to pick it up. *What Does God Require of Me?* he read. When Craine looked up from the pamphlet, the shabby person was smiling at him and nodding. Craine glared, his emotions in a turmoil, feeling at the same time both encroached upon and curious, even eager to find out what the pamphlet said. That too was the whiskey, he understood. If he thought about what he thought, he didn't give a hoot in hell what God required of him.

Without returning the stranger's nod, he closed the door, crumpled the pamphlet in his fist and threw it in the direction of the wastepaper basket beside his bed. He thought, with a brief little tingle of alarm, of the incident at Tully's, the paper airplane. He stood bent forward in the nearly dark room, scratching his bewhiskered Adam's apple, then moved back toward his chair and book. As he stood at his window, fingertips on his glass, he said aloud, crossly, "Ought to turn the lights on." But he stared at the street, unconsciously looking for the watcher's eyes, and, hardly aware that he was doing it, poured whiskey into his glass. His hands were relatively steady again, as they almost always were late in the day. *Late in the day,* he thought, and smiled grimly. He sipped the warm whiskey and ran his tongue around his lips, lost in thought.

He sat down and picked up the book again.

All languages, the Vedic priests believed, were descended from one original divine language, now corrupted and lost. The concept will be familiar to Western readers through the legend of Babel and the mystic tradition of the kabala. Especially in the 19th century . . .

The street outside his window was almost deserted. Farther down, in the direction of the university campus, there was a faint roar of talk and music along the strip; the evening was beginning at Zack's, Bonapart's, the Zombie's, Merlin's. *Damn fools,* he thought, looking back at his book. He wiped sweat from his forehead. Fever? he wondered. In his mind he saw the crowd of college students, a few of them dressed like elegant savages, the rest of them got up, with careful vanity, to look like junk collectors, sandhogs, farmers, pharmacists time-warped from some other thoroughly insignificant moment—1912, 1932, 1957. (His eyes moved steadily, line after line, four inches from the book, his right hand automatically picking at page corners, turning pages.) As if morosely, they nodded with the music,

hands mechanically raising beer mugs to their mouths, or marijuana cigarettes, eyes gazing dully, hungrily at the girl in the wrinkled dark green
blouse or at the boy in the tank top, mechanically snapping his fingers. Out
on the highway toward Murphysboro, the big, stainless-steel Massage Parlor
on Wheels would be rolling toward the Mississippi River, glinting in the
darkness like a pistol barrel, a movie on the screen in the room behind the
driver, on the bed a young Arab with his hands behind his head, grinning
eagerly, sheepishly, at the girl rubbing oil on his chest and belly, then down
along his loins, professionally teasing toward his towering, crooked member, softly whispering as her face came nearer, "Tickle?" Mournfully, Craine
lowered the book into his lap, thinking he was thinking about the sentence
he'd just read, his dim eyes groping along the bookshelves to the old Zenith
television set he'd never used, then to the dresser, the rickety table and chair
near his bed, the apartment fridge, the imperfectly closed bathroom door
beyond which he could make out the gleam of what he knew to be the
bathroom sink. Pitiful objects—they'd all been living here when Craine
moved in—each with its miserable little history, forgotten.

The legend of the grandfather's clock came back to him, *Time
Lost . . .* and quickly, refusing to think again of the person in the stacks,
he got up to cross the room and turn the light on. When he flicked the
switch, everything around him was changed for an instant: the rug showed
its faded and threadbare solidity—atoms to be counted on, its immense
charge discrete and self-contained, no threat; Craine's paperback books,
hardbacks, and magazines waiting patient and dependable in their sagging
shelves or strewn along the baseboard; his suit coat on the chair back fast
asleep. But then, the next instant, nothing was changed; his confusion and
distress were everywhere, wide awake, rocketing through the room. From
somewhere nearby—Ira Katz's room, perhaps—came a food smell, toast
and coffee.

He'd eaten nothing all day, it occurred to him. He'd forgotten lunch,
and when he'd finally gotten to his office—both Meakins and Royce were
gone by then, and Hannah was putting on her coat to leave—he'd been
too busy keeping his condition from Hannah (she waited, taking off her
coat again, while he glanced through the mail she'd slit open for him) to
think of anything so practical as supper. It was an outrage, having his comings and goings observed and judged, subtly ruled, in fact, by a fat, middle-aged black secretary. If he'd meant to be a slave he'd have gotten married

and had children, like Meakins. (In his mind he saw the second of his agents, Emmit Royce, hips slung forward, hands in his pockets, no doubt playing with himself, grinning lopsidedly at some college girl maybe half his age, his steel tooth glinting like his murderous eyes, big dimple flashing, the handle of his gun poking out, suggestive, from the pocket of his old leather jacket. By midnight he'd have her under him. By two a.m. he'd have forgotten her, maybe found another.) When Craine had glanced through the last of them, he stacked his letters more or less neatly at the side of his desk. He wasn't drinking, though the bottle in its sack was in his overcoat pocket and God knew he was thinking about it. "Deal with them tomorrow," he'd said, nodding at the letters.

"You all right, Craine?" Hannah said, eyes screwed up tight.

"Wonderful," he said. He stood up, carefully, supporting himself with both hands on the edge of the desk.

She put her coat on again. "Wonderful," she mimicked. She'd raised boys; she knew pretty well where he was coming from; but she decided to smile. "Lan-a-Goshen," she said, and patted her forehead with a tissue. "You wanna lock up?"

"I'm coming now," he said. He'd done it to torment himself, or so he would have claimed, not that he'd thought about it; had done it to make himself be with her a little longer without revealing the extent of his condition. Or partly that. It was a complicated business, of course, like everything. The quirks of human motivation, his stock in trade, spiralled down and down. She was a test of his ability to cope, partly; but also, he had a right to do whatever he pleased, and, leaving with her, maybe falling down the stairs—who knew? who cared?—he would show her his lordly indifference to whatever she might think. Also, of course, he was afraid to be alone; she had a beautiful voice, and a heart as immense as her bosom. Possibly she'd ask him some question, and he could spill it all out. *I've gone crazy, Hannah.* He would laugh as he spoke, reserving certain rights. *You think I was crazy before, but listen!*

As soon as they'd come out on the sidewalk, there was that feeling again. Eyes nailing him like headlight beams. He got an image of Eggers' meek face, then McClaren's—nostrils twitching, pale eyes snapping.

The smell of food was stronger now, and it came to him that what he chiefly desired in this world was a talk with his neighbor Ira Katz. Impossible, of course. He would be busy grading papers or writing poetry or whatever it was he did nights. Listening to his clocks. Or he'd have some young woman with him, yes. Embarrassing all round.

A queer tingling came over him and he looked up. His right hand knuckles and wrist ached. Too much smoking, no doubt. Thickening the blood, pushing the pressure up, loading the system with carbon monoxide. Incredible what the old corpse would tolerate! With the tip of his tongue he touched the sandpaper roof of his mouth just behind the front teeth. His gums were painfully sensitive, as always; advanced case of stomatosis, he'd been told. It wouldn't become cancer—Craine's opinion, not the dentist's—he'd be saved by the law of parsimony; his weak spot had already been found. He hadn't bothered to mention his theory to the dentist, naturally, lest the dentist convince him that the theory was, as Craine knew, nonsense. Craine frowned, glanced crossly at the door. It was a strange business, how a man rushed tail over tin cup toward the grave, kicking and swinging at every guardian angel that stupidly rose up, batting its wings and blocking his path, yelling, "Halt, maniac! Turn aside!"

When they'd diagnosed him—"colon carcinoma"—in the hospital just across the parking lot from the Baptist building where his offices were, he hadn't felt the slightest trace of fear or shock; he'd simply been interested; perhaps—strange to say—almost pleased. He'd been sick for weeks: diarrhea, cramps; he couldn't say how long ago it had started. They'd rammed in the old sigmoidoscope, casual and fierce as veterinarians, and that was that. So it's cancer, he'd thought. He'd assumed from the start it meant curtains. He'd never known anyone who'd been told he had cancer and not died of it. With cancer of the colon it wasn't necessarily that bad, people told him. Tom Meakins had an uncle who'd lived forty-one years after a cancer-of-the-colon operation. But the doctors at Johns Hopkins, where the doctors at Carbondale had immediately shipped him, had spoken guardedly, neither holding out nor withholding hope, so he'd gone on figuring he was done for. Better than a twenty-minute death by angina pectoris, which was what he'd been expecting, he'd thought—better than bouncing around, slamming against walls, screaming his head off with pain, nothing anyone could do. And of course he *was* done for. They could take out the growth, get all of it out, as apparently they'd done, but he still had cancer, a shadow inside him for life, the same drab shadow that lay over the world. *Well, well!* was all he'd thought, *so Craine is to go to his reward!* His indifference had gone deep. Even here, far from home, in Baltimore, he hadn't had a

hint of a nightmare. When friends, or rather acquaintances, had stopped
in to visit him, happening by plane or train toward Washington, even coming on purpose—true foul-weather friends—and had delicately skirted the
subject of death, piously mentioning prayer and God, bringing him amulets,
miraculous diets, a cut-glass-windowed silver case which contained what
appeared to be a very small part of the tooth of a saint, Mother Seton by
name (tell him no more about modern enlightenment: someone had sawed
that poor woman to bits and laid her aside like money in the bank in the
hope that, in spite of the odds, she might one day be canonized), he'd nodded
as politely as patience would allow, had hurried them over the difficult parts,
and soothed them with Styrofoam cups of the Teachers' Scotch he kept hidden in his nightstand.

It should have been one of the most significant periods of his life, he
would have said. When a man thinks he's dying, that's when you'd think
he'd take stock in earnest, face up to things. Take stock of what, though?
The meaning of life? There he'd take his stand with that fellow Céline, best
writer in the world, in Craine's opinion: *"Shut your eyes, that's all that's necessary. There you have life seen from the other side."* Dying did not change what
he knew to be the case, that one way of life was as good as another. Farmer,
priest, murderer . . . Ah, when you were young, watching the colorful,
noisy parade, one set of bandsmen took your fancy above all others—perhaps it was the one with the silver trombones, or the one where the drum-
mers threw their sticks in the air, or perhaps it was the one where the drum
majorettes were young gentlemen in drag—no matter, you made your
choice, threw in your lot with them, chose their company as if all other
companies were ludicrous, contemptible; you fell in behind them, hopping
to get in step, sucked in your belly, prettily lifted your chest and chin, threw
your elbows out left and right like corn knives, and by diligent apprentice-
ship you became, by God, what you became. Very good; congratulations!
And so the world paraded, overwhelmed with itself, until dusk, when the
music petered out and the marching stopped, and, standing in a light, smoky
rain, all the bandsmen—band on band from horizon to horizon—stood trying to keep their cigarettes lit, grumbling about wages, waiting for the char-
tered bus. It was all proud, childish foolishness. Third Reich, Mother Russia,
China, driving permit, merit badges . . . shit clouds collapsing into planets,
proud boulders in space . . . That had been Gerald Craine's opinion before,
and it was his opinion now that he was dying. Bankers against bank robbers;

indignant, trembling teachers against proud or distressed ignoramuses; priests superstitiously kissing their crosses against bug-eyed, whimpering atheists pissing on altars. Righteousness, patriotism, "good manners" on one side, crouching in fear and brave comradery beside the cannons that cautiously peeked out, small dark O's of alarm, above the battlements; on the other side, in the woods beyond the moat, Flint's bedraggled cult, ready to die like heroes—nay, martyrs—for General Fornication; Anarchists United —outrageous idea—willing and eager to die for freedom from the accidental chains of geography and geometry, the rivers, mountain ranges, invisible dotted lines that invest one set of hills with unholy majesty far beyond that of all other green tumescences and can send you to prison if you fail to see the glow; and somewhere, sulking behind the worshippers of flesh and the anarchists, the unwashed and uncivil—tanned, half-naked bums huddled on the heat vents of the sidewalks of Washington, D.C., in the middle of winter, kings of disgust to whom style, even *thank you* and *please,* is more loath than Treblinka . . .

He, for one, had nothing against any of them. Perhaps, when he was young he'd imagined that he was working for Law & Order, but he'd been disabused of such foolishness long since. In the mindless game Winning-or-Losing-One's-Case, he served whoever got him when the teams chose up. In that, he was no different from any other, in his opinion. Take a perfectly good, decent Republican young man from the pastures of Ohio, put him in a large university—in English, sociology, or political science—his conscience would drive him to the Democratic Party within the year. Send him to BankAmerica as a responsible executive, and reason—common decency—would turn him Republican within the month. Make him a policeman, within a week he'd start memorizing football scores. One must talk, after all; share interests with the people one's surrounded by. What kind of humbug, in a city of rapists, holds out for the dignity of womanhood? No crime; no shame. Reality! So the life force rose up sometimes as an elephant, sometimes as a tree. No harm; Craine had no objection—no serious objection. Nevertheless, having noticed that the whole game was rigged, one had to concentrate, make small adjustments, to keep on playing.

Ironically, Craine had been the darling of his doctors, a marvel of good attitude. He healed as if magically, seemed hardly to notice the pain or confinement. The first cut in his abdomen had infected—no fault of Craine's;

the intestines are known to be a filthy place—and so he'd lain for weeks
with gray packing in the wound, which nurses came to change every three,
then four hours, and doctors would come, every three or four days, to pick
at a little with their knives. Craine read, slept, read. "It must make you
want to scream, just lying here like this," his surgeon, a woman, had said
to him once, not looking at him, running her eyes over his chart. She was
lean as a sapling; hard-boned, sharp-eyed. Her blond hair was cut like pillow
feathers. Her chin was like an Indian's stone knife. "Well, no," Craine had
said. Sometimes, troubled by intestinal cramps (this was later, after his second operation, when he'd begun to be mobile), he'd considered screaming.
It was the worst pain he'd ever experienced, and where pain was concerned,
Craine was no novice. He'd been shot, wrecked in cars, beaten, et cetera,
the usual fol-de-rol of his witless occupation. But the idea of screaming
was tiresome and depressing, especially the idea of screaming over a thing
so unheroic, even bestial, as intestinal cramps. Screaming, even if the cause
was Justice or Truth or earthquakes in Chile, seemed to Craine a little baby-
ish, a foolish exaggeration of one's importance in the world—though groaning was all right, a little honest groaning could be a blessed thing, like
healthy defecation. Inhale: silence; exhale: groan. Like the rhythm of the
womb. It was not, like screaming, an appeal for pity or even interest. A
noise, simply; a temporary annoyance of one's neighbors, like traffic sounds
or bells of a clock tower out of tune, a noise that, making no demands,
could be endured, tuned out. He'd clenched his teeth and hobbled up and
down the hospital corridors—the usual cure for intestinal cramps—inching
along like a ninety-year-old man, gripping in his right hand, half-leaning
against it, the aluminum tree from which his tubes and bottles hung.

Friends—acquaintances—came by, sent cards, wakened him with phone
calls, sent flowers. It was astonishing that he, testy, cold blooded old bastard
that he was, should be so rich in friends or anyway acquaintances. Showed
what a remarkable capacity people had for self-delusion. Yet there he was
lying a little, of course. It was standard practice, in Craine's profession, to
give the client every possible benefit of the doubt; standard practice to lay
yourself out for every asshole that hired you. Snarl as he might, it was Gerald Craine's nature to assume that even the most despicable of mortals had
something to be said for him, at any rate as much as could be said for the
miserable bastards who rose up against him. He defended the indefensible,
blanched at nothing, mothered the monstrous; and this was his reward, a

roomful of friends whose names for the most part escaped him. If anyone had pushed him, he'd have admitted more: that he was glad to see them. Sometimes when one of them came grinning through the door, Craine's eyes, to his shame and indignation, would well up with tears. He was tempted to say to himself, "Life means more than you thought, you old fart. Look how many people, as the saying goes, 'care.' " He imagined an army—Craine's people against the world. A woman he'd helped with her divorce years ago came, packed like a pigeon, in a tweedy suit, and gave him a "friendship ring." Her lips were shiny as wax, like the lips of a cadaver in state. A young man, formerly of Carbondale, now fisherman on a boat on the Chesapeake Bay, told Craine how Craine had changed his life. Craine accepted it, smiled grimly, listening—all with the same sublime indifference, or anyway the same metaphysical indifference, that made him heal more quickly than the doctors had had reason to expect. Better people than Craine howled and fought against death, rang their bells for the nurses, asked their doctors for more detail, more detail. Craine visited them—travelling to ward off more cramps—meaninglessly passing his time. To one of them, a pretty young woman without a hope in the world, he gave his Mother Seton tooth. Temporarily, she improved.

He'd had three operations: the exploratory, from which he emerged with the abdominal infection; the extraction of the cancerous section of his colon, which left him with the colostomy bag and cramps; and the colostomy takedown. Coming out of anesthesia for the third time, after the third operation, he came to the realization that each of the three times, just before waking, he'd heard the same queer sentence, a series of syllables in what might have been Finnish, a pronouncement he somehow understood. He hadn't thought about it, the first and second times, had simply registered, after he'd opened his eyes, its hollowly resonating gibberish—he could not now recall the words, if they were words—and had mused briefly, until present reality took precedence, on the eerie sensation of rising from one plane of existence to another, not as one rises from a dream to waking life, it seemed to him, but in a fashion quite different, something not even he, adept at fancy language and rant, could express. This, perhaps: like being drawn abruptly to human consciousness from the consciousness of a fish. (There was a sound, like the noise on a television set after "The Star-Spangled Banner"; it was through this noise that the other came.) He couldn't remember, afterward, who had been there with him in the recovery room—possibly one or two nurses, possibly his doctor. He'd had an impression, after each of his awakenings, that after the sentence of, perhaps, gibberish, what he'd next heard was a man's voice, some intelligible sentence in English, perhaps "Wake up!" or "Mr. Craine, open your eyes!" Perhaps a nurse had joined in the command. But he'd had, the third time, a distinct impression that what the doctor said was not at all what the voice of the drug had said; and, more important, he'd had the impression—it amounted to a chilling certainty—that the sentence in gibberish was exactly the sentence he'd heard both times before. In fact this third time he'd known almost certainly, hearing the strange sentence, that in an instant he'd be awake, and then he was. It was not hard to think of physiological explanations; nevertheless, it was a queer effect. He must have remained awake, if it could be called that, only for a moment before dropping back into sleep, a different sleep now, familiar and comforting, morphine luminous but otherwise no different from an ordinary sleep, or such was his impression. He couldn't quite remember that either, afterward; in fact, though after the second operation he'd spent three days in the recovery room, he'd found when he was back in his own room—a bright, large private room, with a print by Matisse, on the seventh floor of the Nelson Building—he could remember almost nothing about the recovery room, nothing but the fact that the walls were gray—exactly the shiny, snake-belly gray of the basement walls of the grade school he'd attended fifty years ago, forgotten until now—and that down there in the bowels of the hospital, where the work of life and death was done, the cloth screens set up at the foot of his bed were gray-green, like the garb of those who worked there and the sheets on his metal-railed bed.

One end of his room was now a hedge of flowers and potted plants. Half hidden by the plants, a window ran from one wall to the other, looking out on the old Johns Hopkins tower, Osler dome, reared against the skyline of Baltimore, a dark brick dome cut by arches and blocked-in windows, below it high chimneys ornately corbeled, their flues sealed off half a century ago—stiff, plugged throats around a colossal, brooding dove.

Not that his view of the city displeased him, the sleepy miles of soft gray buildings, copper steeples, stone towers—among them one tower crudely Florentine, with a lighted clock that had letters instead of numbers: B R O M O S E L T Z E R—and not that the symbols he registered without interest reflected any deep unhappiness or distress on his part, much less fear. At night the sky above the city was soy-red beyond the blackness of the dome, and the streets stretching westward were hung with colored lights. When he awakened in the morning, just before dawn, when orderlies came in to take blood from his arm, the sky was dark blue, sprinkled with stars, and the drab, unlit buildings were a misty gray, as if the ocean a little to the east of where he lay had crept nearer when no one was looking. He saw nothing ominous in this or in anything. Life went on, and he was part of it, but not partisan. He thought of Lazarus, tyrannized back, jerking up onto one elbow, opening one eye, then the other, suddenly interrupted in some thought. The voice he'd heard just before awakening, it occurred to him, had been asking him some question, or making some demand; the voice, perhaps, of a German officer.

By day his hospital room was wonderfully pleasant, full of Naples-yellow light, crammed with cards, plants, flowers, sometimes visitors: Tom Meakins and his wife; a Carbondale lawyer for whom Craine had done odd jobs, now visiting Baltimore relatives; old friends from Chicago who'd come to Washington on business; a young man whom Craine had once gotten out of prison; people Craine had helped out, they said, in the six-ties—gone bail for or gotten lawyers for, he no longer remembered—now solid citizens, working for NPR or building nuclear power plants, storage tanks for nerve gas (leaky, like all the rest), making car payments, house payments, worried about The Schools . . .

At night the nurses left the door open, and the light that came in made him feel as he'd felt in his forgotten childhood, alone in the dark but safe. He lay on his back, the only position available to him, listening to the com-fortable clicks and hums of the sleeping building breathing and dreaming like an animal around him, the occasional swish of a door, the suggestion of footsteps, now and then a distant voice—perhaps some guard, or doctor or nurse, or for all he knew, some patient's TV. He slept, then wakened again as (as if in a dream) the heavy, Virginia-hills night nurse named Au-drey came and changed his dressing, emptied his urine can, freshened up the water and ice in his blue plastic pitcher. "Forty years," she said, and winked at him. "Would you believe it?" He had no idea what she meant at first, but he liked her country face and pretended to be astonished. "Forty years!" she said again, and shook her head as if even she could make no sense of it. She patted his hand as she would a child's. "Get some sleep now, Mr. Craine." She snapped the light off. Before her square shape was out the door, he was asleep. Then it was day again—blood samples, breakfast, bustling activity, as if everyone who came here to Nelson had come for pure pleasure.

Visiting his neighbors up and down the hall, he walked in a bubble of time exactly like childhood time: in the morning it never occurred to him that it would soon be noon, then afternoon, then evening. His neighbor to the left was an elderly Jew, formerly of New York, who'd once been America's chief manufacturer of Panama hats, or so he said, and it was probably the truth. During World War II, the old man explained, hats went out of fashion. He had theories as to why. He'd become America's chief historian of the Popular Song. He'd published several books. He had them there with him in the hospital room, in case anyone should care to look. Craine did. Bicycle-song period, baseball-song period, circus-song period. Changing styles in the political song, the nostalgia song, the love song. There were numerous illustrations—engravings of musicians and public figures, covers of sheet music. The scholarly comment was learned and tirelessly wry. The old wife sat smiling, proud beyond words of the brilliant, crotchety old man in the bed. The books had been published, she mentioned from time to time, by the Ohio University Press. "He never even started this history business till he was sixty-two years old," she said. "Everybody said he was crazy. Some crazy!" "Mama," the old man said, "you already told him." The old man had two sons, one an engineer for Bell Telephone, the other a professor at Hofstra. Both of them came to visit, day after day, the engineer small and hearty, elegantly dressed, the professor large and sullen, nearsighted, shabby, both argumentative, impatient, and inconvenienced, but there at his bedside nevertheless, having flown in at once as if nothing were more natural in the world. Sometimes young women came, perhaps the old man's daughters; also children. When no one else was there, the old woman sat long-nosed and hunchbacked, sleeping in the vinyl chair beside the bed, or worrying and fussing, complaining to the nurses, between times reading the old man jokes from magazines. Once, when something went wrong with the old man, so that he had to be placed in an oxygen tent and no one could be with him but his special nurse, the old woman went striding up and down the corridor, mile after mile, staring straight ahead, eyes like the eagle eyes of Moses. Craine, moving carefully with his aluminum tree, had been afraid to say a word to her. He saw, that day or another day just like it, a picture in a magazine, Jews in a concentration camp, behind barbed wire so messy and tangled it looked as if crows had built it. All the Jews in the picture were now dead. One of them was a girl of about twenty, beautiful. He was sexually aroused, and he looked up from the picture in distress, repelled by all existence, though when he thought about it he understood, of course, why he was aroused, why there was no more reason to be disgusted by that than by bedpans, say, or projectile vomiting, or the woman with her feet cut off. Nature's way.

Everything he saw, in short, had confirmed him in his opinion that life was interesting, if one chose to see it that way, but not important, by no means a matter for joyful celebration. He was an excellent patient, uncomplaining, steadily healing. The only real unpleasantness in his hospital life, aside from the occasional shaking that came over him, was the food. Each time he lifted the cover off the tray—a yellow plastic cover dripping with condensation—the smell that wafted up was like ensilage, or mulch, old hay in a barn. Sometimes for days in a row he ate nothing but the Jell-O. Then the simple expedient occurred to him of putting on his clothes and walking out (he was unhooked from the tree by now). He knew the hospital routine like the back of his hand, and it was an easy matter to slip down the hall to the stainless steel back elevator, descend to the first floor, and walk past the guards there—no one looked up—cross to the front-door public telephone and call himself a taxi. He began going out to restaurants while he was still on the colostomy bag; an awkward business. Emptying the bag in the toilet was easy (every time he ate he had to empty the bag almost immediately, especially if he drank wine), but rinsing out the bag was tricky: he had to bare his gauzed and bandaged belly, hold the plastic to the faucet to get the rinse water in, worst of all empty small bits of feces in the sink, one eye on the knob of the rest room door, since if someone came in . . . but never mind, he managed; he was quick and as cunning as a weasel; he was almost never caught. After the takedown it was trickier yet: he had no more idea than a day-old baby when his bowels would move. Very well, he had accidents. But he managed. After one had lived in a hospital for a time, one pretty much lost all sense of shame. Vomiting, elimination, even one's old-man dangling nakedness came to be as public as politics, less one's own business than the business of one's blond young nurse. It was a lesson in philosophy, another proud illusion blown rearward and flushed, as if cleaned from his system by an enema.

So Craine continued, day after day, visiting fellow patients, reading, more or less enjoying himself; and then the time came for his release. Tom Meakins arrived again, pink-cheeked, bulging in his too small checked brown suit. The nurses found boxes, which they loaded to the lids with Craine's plants and gifts, his huge paper sacks of tape, gauze, pads, medicines, and bottles of saline solution, then stacked in two wheelchairs to carry to the taxi down below. Craine, leaning on Meakins' arm, started down the corridor, waving his good-byes. He did not say good-bye to the music historian who'd been his neighbor; the old man had died two days ago and had been removed without anyone's knowing—not a sound, not so much as a whisper, so far as Craine knew—in the middle of the night. "Good-bye," Craine called to the woman who'd had both feet removed; "good-bye" to the huge, gray freak of a man sprawled like a mountain in his special chair, brought in for an operation meant to save him, whatever his opinions in the matter, from being buried alive in fat. The man stared back, too gloomy to show anger or disgust. Tom Meakins chattered, talking about the weather—it had snowed last night, maybe half an inch, a significant snowfall for Baltimore in March. Meakins' voice was high and thin, filled with emotion. He placed his small, glossy shoes with care, taking short, timid steps, as if Craine might go crashing to the marble floor at any moment, only Meakins' sharp watchfulness could save him. "You lost a lot of weight, old man," Meakins said, and smiled, then turned away his face and wiped his forehead.

It was not until Craine was in the plane for Chicago—from there they'd fly down to Carbondale—that the truth burst over him and he began to weep. He was going to live. The plane groaned and shuddered, then quieted, taking off. Never in his life had Craine experienced such emptiness, such revulsion and despair. Meakins, in the seat beside him, turned to look at him, wide-eyed, then reared forward in acute distress, reaching to touch Craine's arm with both plump, young-womanish hands. "Jerry!" he cried softly. Never before had Meakins called him "Jerry." Meakins wet his lips, baffled and embarrassed, blushing, then brought out, "Does something hurt?" Now he too had tears in his eyes, as if he'd guessed what the trouble was.

Craine shook his head. He couldn't speak a word for fear of bursting into whooping sobs, part sorrow, part childish rage. He covered his face, pouring the tears into his hands.

"What's the matter?" Meakins said. "Can I get you something?"

There was no way, of course, that Craine could say what was the matter.

Time was the matter; the fact that people lived and died for nothing, and horribly at that. Meakins' daughters, once pretty, now grotesquely fat. Craine's parents, dead when he was too young to remember; the poor old-maid aunt who'd raised him, Aunt Harriet, her silly existence vanished from the face of the earth like a puff of her Evening in Paris face powder. His friends, all those people who, incredibly, had come to visit him—faster than the airplane was rumbling toward Chicago, they were flying to their graves, all for nothing, all part of the vast, unspeakable foolishness. Women he'd loved, should perhaps have married—he no longer knew even where any of them lived—all, all were shooting like greased lightning toward the grave, or were perhaps there already.

He pulled off his thick-lensed glasses to wipe his eyes, but the tears came pouring more profusely than ever, and a whimpering, uncontrollable, began to push up from his throat. All his defenses had abandoned him at once, even that comic, ironic detachment that had until now gotten him past the worst life could dump. He saw himself as the people now craning their necks must be seeing him, a hawk-nosed old derelict with deep-sunken, red, weeping eyes; an old limp suit grown three sizes too large; long, crooked fingers, stained fingernails. He could conjure up neither amusement or disgust, only sorrow at the waste, one more poor unlovable orphan wailing its heart out to no one in particular, for no good reason.

"Listen, let me get us a drink," Meakins said. He reached up and pushed the stewardess button. "It's emotional exhaustion, that's all," he said. "It's a natural reaction." He loosened his tie. "You've been holding it all in, that's all. It's natural."

Now the stewardess was coming. When she reached their row she pushed the button that turned the little light off, then leaned over to look at Craine, then, in haste, at Meakins. She was blinking rapidly, probably wearing new contacts.

"My friend here would like a martini," Meakins said, "—double; straight up, two olives. I'll take the same."

"Brothers and sisters, let us drown our woes in gin," Craine said, and tried to laugh. At once he was sobbing again. There was a movie he'd seen once, German propaganda—he'd seen it in connection with a case up in Chicago. Thousands of childlike men and women in rows—braids, trim crew cuts—doing click, spin, click calisthenics . . . something about "Christ the Athlete" . . . movie lighting that made the field where they exercised seem the pastures of heaven, terrible new Eden, mind of God with prefrontal lobotomy . . .

The stewardess looked at him, stopped blinking for an instant, then nodded to Meakins and backed away, turning and stretching out one arm, trailing it like a dancer, as she went.

The mood had eventually passed, of course. That was one thing you could say, things eventually passed. Perhaps it *had* been a significant period of his life, all things considered. For all his stubbornness, not even Craine could claim he was the same man he'd been before his brush with death. His beliefs had been secure, his patterns and emotions as solid as frozen ruts in a country lane. He'd known who he was, where he stood, what mattered in the world—almost nothing: good Scotch, healthy defecations (they were mutually exclusive, of course), a minimum of inconvenience, especially the inconvenience of dealing with people who had opinions, knew slogans, found significance in things. None of that had changed except—what? The way his heart leaped, blind to good sense, when he read the words *What Does God Require of Me?* It was as if the high fortress walls he'd built with the best of materials, the finest of plans, had for no earthly reason begun to open up seams so wide they let in rain and daylight, both radioactive. Sometimes, for no reason—but more and more frequently, these past three, four days—flashes of the closed-off past came back to him: an image of his aunt in her classroom, talking with her head tilted. She wore a blue dress—high collared—and small, light blue earrings. In his mind he heard the music that went with her: classical. She always played classical. In the long maple music bench she sat on when she played—it was glossy and smelled of lemon, he remembered—she had faded yellow books of Chopin, Schubert, Bach, Czerny, and one red book that said *The John Thompson Method.* He must have stared at it often as a child of six or seven, maybe older. He could see it plain as day. Craine squeezed his eyes shut tight, then opened them.

All languages, the Vedic priests believed . . .

When he looked over from his book, he saw, as he'd known he would, a mouse under the bed, crouching motionless, as if aware that Craine was watching him. Craine thought of the cat at the restaurant and looked down at his book. Outside, he was aware without looking, it was now completely dark. His hands were trembling. A police siren wailed in the distance and passed perhaps a block or two away, speeding toward the edge of town, still greater darkness. He remembered the Scotch on the carpet beside his foot and reached down for it, but with the tips of his fingers on the rim he for some reason hesitated, listening again. His neighbor was playing music on the record-player, something classical: orchestral; German. He raised the glass and drank, then, setting down the glass again, drawing the book up to his eyes where he could read it, felt for his matches. With a part of his mind he was aware of a second mouse moving in stops and starts toward the first.

The reason he knew it was a young woman following him, he realized all at once, was that he'd seen her. Her face was soft and obscurely Oriental, possibly Semitic, like the faces on the walls of Egyptian tombs. In the momentary vision she was beautiful: dark hair, dark frightened eyes, large and slanted—curiously shaped, in any case, like the eyes on old statues from Cyprus. It was only for an instant that their eyes had met; he could not now remember where or even when: a day or two ago, perhaps. Quickly, he'd looked away, but not before he'd glimpsed something disquieting, even shocking, in the look she gave him: some ravenous appeal or legitimate demand, some claim she had on him, mystic and outrageous, nothing common nature could explain. There were words, in fact: *Mr. Craine, you're supposed to save my life—and look at you!* Her lips had not moved. His heart had floundered, but then instantly his senses had come back to him and he'd known it was nothing, his drunken imagination playing tricks again. She was young, maybe twenty. They'd never met in their lives. *Pretty girl,* he'd thought, pursing his lips and frowning, turning his head slowly and casually to look again. She was gone. (Craine's eyes moved left and right, left and right. His lips puckered tightly, sucking at the pipe. Smoke clouds billowed above him.) His hands trembled badly. He drank again. If his neighbor was listening to music, it occurred to him—now Craine was squinting, looking up over the book, crafty—then he couldn't be writing poetry; too distracting. On the other hand, of course, if he was grading papers, or if some young woman was rolling around on the rug with him . . .

There was something important he'd been thinking about, or had meant to think about. He cast back, groping, but he'd lost it.

It was increasingly hard to keep his mind on the book. He'd slept, off and on, when he'd first come home, but he was drowsy again; no doubt the whiskey. Also the print grew increasingly blurry. Why he forced himself to read he could hardly have said, but he did, or rather tried to—drunkard's discipline, yes—lipreading, insisting that his mind pay attention. His mind slipped around him, closing his eyes without his noticing, offering him a different, more surprising book. He read with increasing interest, increasing astonishment, until the whiskey glass slipped in his hand, waking him. He righted the glass, then on second thought set it on the floor beside his shoe, unaware that, of course, he was tricking himself again, making it easier to fall asleep. He pressed his rear end back farther in the chair, put his burnt-out pipe in his shirt pocket, and bent forward over the book, lipreading again, following the print with one finger. He read with fierce attention, but again he fooled himself, for though his eyes moved dutifully, focusing on the print, he was running over images in his mind.

Linguistic proliferation, the Vedic priests believed . . .

Craine had paused, a block from his office, Hannah Johnson standing ample and sweaty at his side. He'd turned around abruptly, but there was no one, or, rather, only those people he might have expected to see—shoppers, high-school students, people leaving work. He kept his panic hidden, eyes darting left and right, finding nothing. Almost without his knowing it, his eyes continued searching, waiting to pounce on some movement in a doorway, some shadow where there ought not to be one. Yellow leaves and old newspapers blew across the street, caught in the gutters, lifted over, and hurried on, like businessmen running with their heads bent. The air had the heavy tornado-weather smell that would be normal back in August, a month ago. He glanced at the sky—wide blue, slashed by jet streams and smudged, down lower, by yellow-white clouds from the smokestack at the edge of the university campus. They were running on crushed and oxygen-blasted sulfur coal; an experiment. "Whole country buried chin-deep in shit," he muttered, less to Hannah than to the whole sinful nation. His bleary eyes aimed at the smoking horizon, out beyond the last of the city's low buildings, southward. In the sky, high above the smoke, two hawks hung floating like kites. Craine's head shook slightly, as if with palsy. He stood with his elbows clamped tightly to the sides of his chest, the left one supporting the Sanskrit book, his right fist, just above his overcoat pocket, closed around the top of the sack that held his whiskey. Through the smoke, he could make out traces of the gouged yellow hills, once thick with oaks and pines and, on the lower slopes, orchards. To the north, once corn land—beyond the range of his vision—lay five-mile-long strip mines, co-balt-blue, blood-red, and rust-colored pools where nothing was astir but invisible insects and the tongues of lizards.

Hannah Johnson bent forward and touched his forearm. "Don't think about it, Craine," she said sadly. "You'll give yourself a heart attack." To a passing stranger it would have seemed that she was giving him a quarter. Hannah was well kept, matronly, dressed too warmly for the autumn day. She wore a light, purple coat.

She turned her head, following the direction of his angry stare, and pursed her lips unhappily. "I remember when up there was the prettiest scenery in the world," she said. The corner of her mouth tucked in—a trace of a long-suffering smile. She had the voice of a singer. She stood with her weight on her left leg, her right leg thrown jauntily forward. Her shoes were red. She said, "There was an old Baptist church out on Boskydell Road where my family used to go every Sunday in George Elroy's pickup, all us children in the back." She laughed and lightly slapped the air with her hand, remembering. "George Elroy would always sweep it out and put applecrates in for us to sit on, and down the road we'd go in our Sunday good dresses, all hooting and hollerin and wavin at the people . . . oh yes! The church was in the hollow—pretty white church just up among the trees from the railroad tracks where the granary set, before the fire. You wasn't here when they still had the granary." She glanced at him, her expression grieved, checking. "No, you was still in Chicago then, that's right. It was a regular little village, Boskydell. Big old granary and apple barn, filling station, houses . . . That ole fire pretty much took all of it. The church is still there, though; mostly white folks now. That's the way it is, y'know." She tipped him a little smile and a shy look, as if slapping her knee. "You just get the neighborhood cleaned up nice and doggone it, in comes the white folks!" Craine grimaced back, not real anger, just whiskey, as Hannah no doubt knew. "Don't think about it, Craine," she said again, suddenly heavyhearted, and patted his forearm. "Everything gonna be all right. We got the Lord's own promise."

"We'll see," Craine muttered, looking angrily to the left. Hannah's talk of God was no better for his temper than whiskey. The whole world's dying of leukemia, he could have told her. We got twelve thousand tons of TNT for every living person on earth, if you call that living, and more every day, by the trainload, as fast as we can make it. But he said nothing, merely crunched his teeth together. His childish rage was more disgusting to Craine than all the rest.

He shook his arm free, not quite roughly, muttered his farewell and, turning with hardly a nod, walked on. She stood where he'd left her, queenly, surrounded by autumn gold, shaking her silvered head, looking after him. In his mind he watched her, though he walked in the opposite direction. She lived northeast, the Negro section, in a small, crowded house with tin-patched linoleum floors, purple carpeting, red and purple flowers in the windows—geraniums and purple statice. Craine lived downtown. She couldn't help him, heaven knew. No one, as she must know, could help him. Not that Craine wanted or needed help (Craine set his jaw, sliding his eyes from left to right), staggering through his days, his drunkenness almost unnoticeable except to the canniest eye, he told himself—though perhaps he'd gone a little far there, today; crossed the line there with Mc-Claren and the talking cat.

Craine hurried on toward his hotel room. If someone were to tell him the fates had set him down to be shot dead tomorrow (so Craine mused with the part of his mind not reading), he'd never bat an eye. He had no relatives, no friends, no possessions he cared about; he had no future, no past—a creature moving comfortably outside Time, as he'd tried to explain to McClaren.

His mind toyed briefly (his eyes moving over the page, left to right and downward, steadily) with the thought of Hannah Johnson's sharp memories. He'd seen it many times, how she dipped into her past as if the whole thing were running like a movie in her head, Greer Garson and Alan Ladd—her husband T.J., just home from the war, grinning like a fool in his uniform; the birth of her children, their baptism days; the big house they lived in on Sycamore, up among the whites, before T.J. got in trouble. She spent half her time harking back or casting forward. A curious way to live, it seemed to Craine. He glanced over his shoulder; someone slipped into a doorway. Craine remembered, abruptly, something from his navy years—he'd served on a submarine in World War II. A few frozen images: his commanding officer with wrinkles around his eyes and his hand on his chin; a sunrise on the Pacific like a cheap picture postcard. And he remembered, less dimly, though dimly enough, some three, maybe four of the books he'd read then; it was there that he'd picked up his reading habit. *The 42nd Parallel;* a biography of Lincoln; a book on the formation of the universe—the slow collapse of dust clouds into solid, hot masses: creation as the closing of a fist. Try as he might, he could bring back nothing of the cabin, not even the bunk he read on or the color of the blankets. He could remember warm light, soft and yellow, as in a house, but he couldn't remember the source. Casting back farther, back into his childhood, he could call back, except for an image of Aunt Harriet at the piano—nothing whatsoever. Now he was imagining—or rather dreaming, nodding over the book—that he was in dispute with someone about memory. He sat at a huge iron desk, trembling and defensive. "Why should I?" he snapped, cantankerous, full of business. He was both himself and the other man, it seemed. "Nothing?" he asked mildly—or the observer asked; the identification was not so clear now. "Nothing at all," Craine answered with a touch of defiance, whimpering in his dream. The observer, bearded and bespectacled, was on guard; he knew himself at the edge of some old unpleasantness. "Nothing!" Craine said firmly, angrily, in the darkness.

He waved his hands, explaining, and even as he did so he remembered traces of what it was that he could not remember. He was fishing from the bank on his uncle's farm with his trim-bearded father, who was somehow a woman, his father aloof, his cuffs cocked high above his citified socks, his pose as patient and serene as the sunlight in the snakegrass around them. All this Craine saw, though staring down in intense fascination and half-mystical alarm at the slow-moving, clay-yellow water, thick gumbo, from which the deadmen would rise. He knew what was down there, or some of it: snapping turtles, gars, enormous slick frogs, and at the bottom, where the wood and flesh of the deadmen turned slowly to earth— bewhiskered catfish. When the line went taut Craine's heart leaped, terrified, seeing already what would happen in an instant—the fish wildly fluttering above the water, like his heart, spinning in the light like a large silver coin, then thumping to the grass, where it would flop and suck for breath, already dying, laboring against air. His father's neat hands were like a doctor's, touching it. His glasses blinked light. Little Craine stared, wide-eyed, and held his breath. So it went again and again, each time less frightening. After a while one got used to these things, death and life touching, like his father's pale fingers on the fish. The threat drew back a ways, retreated into the shadows of the nettles, then farther, into the trees. He sat in warm sunlight, the world grew increasingly rational; his father cleaned his glasses. Though Craine's heart beat rapidly, perhaps he had already begun to forget. Soon nothing would remain, of this or of anything else from his childhood, except at night. At night, years later (so he told the icy observer, hurriedly whispering), he would dream of murderous black catfish, slow-moving as zeppelins, prowling among the stars.

"That's your explanation?" The interrogator sneered, though—raising his hand—he tried to hide it. Craine's language had been maudlin, a fault the stranger could not abide.

"It is, sir. That's my explanation. Yes, sir."

Speaking aloud, Craine wakened himself. He stared around the room.

The book had closed itself, sinking between his legs. The room seemed more miserable and drab than before, paltry in comparison to wherever it was that he'd been in his dream—he could remember none of it, not an image, not a word; he had only a vague sense of the dream's intensity, whether joyful or ominous he could hardly say, but emphatically alive, more alive than anything in this world was.

The music was still playing in his neighbor's room, and again he experienced an intense, drunken wish—totally out of character, he would have said—to talk with someone; that is, talk with Ira Katz. The image of the young man came clearly into his mind, the dark, ragged beard, strangely gentle eyes that reminded him of . . . He searched his wits. When it came to him, he laughed aloud, two sharp barks. Reminded him of Christ Our Lord! Craine got up from his chair and dropped the book in the seat, still laughing, but soundlessly now, bent half double as if borne down by the irony of things. Abruptly, he stopped laughing and frowned, deep in thought. It was interesting, after all, that he should feel as apparently he did about the Jesus of his childhood. He wiped sweat from his forehead, then pulled at the tip of his nose with two fingers, as if shaping it like clay, trying to make it still longer, all the while seeing in his mind's eye the picture on the wall of the Sunday school room, *Jesus in the Garden.* Stupid, sentimental. Light beaming down out of heaven like a spotlight in a theater. All the same, there was something there, however buried in foolishness. The man had a kindly face—acquainted with sorrow, as the saying went. (Ira Katz, Craine had a feeling, would not like the idea of being identified with Christ Our Lord. Craine smiled, showing his rat teeth. Never mind; it was interesting.) He stood looking around the room, trying to think of some excuse, some errand that would justify a visit to his neighbor. On the table across from the bed stood his hot plate, salt and pepper, half-filled sugar bowl. Craine nodded as if at some suggestion from the walls, the mice. He took a cup—a cracked white one, the only one he had—from the top of the refrigerator, dusted out the inside with his fingers, and started toward the door. He paused, reconsidering, then went back for his suit coat and whiskey bottle, put on the suit coat, put the bottle in the right hand pocket, picked up the cup, and started for the door again. Again he paused, looking around, hunting through his pockets with his left hand, then, shifting the cup to the left hand, hunting with his right. He found papers and empty match folders, but no matches. In the top dresser drawer, among more slips of paper, rolled socks, and his second pistol, he found a matchbook, nearly full, that said Ace Hardware. He dropped it in the pocket of his shirt, beside his pipe, shifted the cup to his right hand again, ran back to the chair for his tobacco pouch, then hurried out.

At his neighbor's door, as soon as his hand touched the handle, a kind of nightmare came over him. He seemed to be standing not in the dim, shabby hallway but somewhere outside, under trees. Someone was coming toward him, hands raised as if to catch him. Though it was dark, he could almost see the face. Then he was standing in the hallway again, frightened and for some reason sick with guilt. He stood for a long time, listening, head bowed and cocked to one side. Nothing came to him; whatever it was had fallen away, back into darkness. He raised his hand from the doorknob and, softly, knocked. After a moment he knocked again. Inside, someone turned down the stereo.

"Coming," Ira Katz called. "Just a minute."

Four

"I wonder, Mr. Katz," Craine said, twisting his face to an obsequious smile, holding the cup in both hands by the fingertips, his shoes toeing inward, "if you could spare me a cup of sugar?"

Ira Katz looked from Craine's face to the strap of his shoulder holster and down to his cup, then back at his face, not suspicious, exactly, but thinking, grinning nervously, his mind half there, half somewhere else, dark brown eyes gazing out at Craine like those of some Talmudist roused for a moment to reflection on the present. He was always like that for a minute or two when Craine dropped in on one errand or another. Craine smiled on, waiting for it to pass. The room smelled thickly of chicken—or possibly fish—and cooked cabbage, also coffee, a suggestion of burnt toast. Craine's hunger died away. "I seem to have run out of sugar," he said.

The young man's eyes were dark and heavy-lidded, not in the sleepy-looking or secretly cunning or bedroomy way but in another more complex and troublesome to Craine, as if Ira Katz had seen to the heart of things, had suffered and forgiven all the evils of humanity for maybe thousands of years and was doomed to continue in the same way down through the centuries for thousands more, perhaps—weary, full of personal and impersonal griefs, faintly grinning with alarm, no less innocent or compassionate than the day he began, but bereft of all hope for himself or his fellow man. It was an illusion, no doubt—or largely that—an accidental effect of the structure of his bones, his eyebrows, the flecked brown pupils of his eyes; but from earliest childhood, Craine surmised (his face momentarily shrewd, almost cunning), Ira Katz had imposed that illusion without knowing it, so that people had trusted him, confided in him, poured out their fears and woes as Gerald Craine would do now, given half a chance,

not that Craine greatly admired himself for it. In the course of time—
or so Craine imagined, and he was usually correct about these things—Ira
Katz had become, if he wasn't from the beginning, what his face made him
seem, a man put on earth to bear the sorrows of the whole human race.
Craine pushed the cup out toward him, half-smiling, half-grimacing again.
Abruptly, as if Craine's ludicrous request had only now broken through,
Craine's neighbor smiled more openly, a large, boyish smile full of gleaming
teeth, on all sides of it a fury of black moustache and beard.

"I don't know," he said, "let me see." He took the cup from Craine's
hands and, preparing to turn away, gave Craine's face one more quick look.
"Come in?" he asked. He held the door open wider. Craine glanced left,
down the hallway in the direction of the bare lightbulb dangling in front
of his own door, then looked at Ira Katz's doorway again and, after an instant, hurried through. He felt a brief afterflash of the nightmare or vision,
the man coming after him in the dark; then it was gone. He was suddenly
aware of the ticking, clicking, and knocking of his neighbor's clocks. There
was no sound from the stereo. The record had ended; the turntable arm
was at rest in its gray metal cradle, the red light glowing like a ruby on
the amplifier.

Ira Katz, in stocking feet, went through the kitchen door, opposite the
door to the hallway, and switched on the light. "I don't even know if I
have any or not," he said. "I hardly ever use it." He put the cup on the
counter and stood with his fists on his hips, looking around as if the kitchen
were someone else's. He wore a blue work shirt, the sleeves rolled up past
the biceps—the muscles were large and tanned, like a laborer's—black suspenders, black slacks pulled up tight by the suspenders, and below the cuff-
less pant legs, black stretch socks of the kind old men wear. The cat called
Rooster came silently into view, an enormous tiger-stripe with Chinese
eyes, walking and stretching at the same time, as if wakened from a snooze.
He stood looking up at Ira Katz for a moment, then with great dignity
rubbed his head against Ira's leg. Ira ignored it, reaching up and opening
a cupboard. "Ah!" he said.

Craine looked away and tried to put his hands in the pockets of his
suit coat. The left one went in easily; the right one bumped against the bottle
and kept poking, witless, Craine's mind too far away to help. In the livingroom, laid out to the right of where Craine stood, swaybacked pine and
used-brick bookshelves covered all the walls, right up to the window look-

ing out on the street and up to the sides of the door to the bedroom and bathroom, opening off the end of the livingroom to the left. On the tops of the bookshelves, on the narrow table that held the stereo, on the stereo speakers, on ornate old wall shelves and on the rickety tables at each side of his overstuffed chairs—grungy and misshapen, as old as Craine—Ira Katz had his antique timepieces—clocks, fancy watches, here and there an hourglass. Except for the hourglasses, most of them were running; none was in complete agreement with any other about the time. Craine moved unsteadily, hardly knowing he was doing it, toward the farther of the chairs. Propped among the clocks and silver watches on the table beside it stood two photographs, one of them a picture of a straw-yellow-blond-headed smiling young woman, the other a snapshot of two solemn dark children holding a kite, one—the elder—a boy, the other one a girl. Craine bent over to look more closely. The pictures were new, or at any rate Craine had never noticed them before. They glinted in the light from the wooden floor lamp behind the chair. As Ira Katz came back into the room with the sugar, Craine straightened up and pointed. "Yours?" he asked, and smiled one-sidedly, accidentally ironic.

The young man glanced in the direction of the photograph and snapshot, his expression clouding for an instant, then smiled and, just perceptibly, nodded. "You're in luck," he said, and held the sugar toward Craine. "It's not quite a cup, but you're welcome to what there is."

Reluctantly, grimacing, Craine approached to take the cup from him. "Thank you," he said. "Thank you very much." He glanced toward the door but remained where he was. His neighbor stood waiting, watching him. "You're right," Craine said, and gave a sharp little laugh, "sugar's poison. You're smart to stay clear of it." He leaned toward his neighbor, explaining quickly, confidentially, almost losing his balance, steadying himself with a hand on the wall, "Pancreas can't handle it except if vitamins come with it, the way they do when you eat fruit. Take sugar without vitamins—sugar with your coffee, you know, or sugar in a candy bar—the pancreas has to steal vitamins from elsewhere. Robs you of nutrients—thief in the night! I'm a detective, that's why I'm informed about these things."

His neighbor smiled. It wasn't clear that he got the joke.

"The worst of it," Craine said, touching his neighbor's arm with the sugar cup and leaning in closer, "is that the sugar turns to fat—fat on your heart among other things. It's a murderer, in the end. First a little harmless pilfering, you know, a little vitamin snatching when nobody's on the look-out, but then one thing leads to another, as we know—" He chuckled and winked. The young man looked at him strangely.

The cat came in from the kitchen and rubbed against Ira's leg. As before, Ira seemed not to notice. "I don't really have any theories about it," he said, slightly smiling, apologetic. "I've got friends who are health nuts, macrobiotics . . . But personally—" He shrugged. "I had a girlfriend who used to use honey for everything." An obscene image came into Craine's mind. He doubted that Katz had intended it. "I got hooked on it," Katz said. He leaned down to touch the cat's large head with two fingertips. The cat pushed up against him.

Craine took a sideways step toward the door, then paused, eyes furtively darting around. "Must be hard to know what time it is, with all these clocks," he said.

Ira Katz smiled and nodded, glancing at the clocks, then straightened up again. After a long moment he said, "Can I offer you a glass of wine?"

"Oh, no, no, thank you very much," Craine said, and took another quick step toward the door. Again he stopped, grinning, unconsciously closing his hand on the neck of the bottle in his pocket. "Wine and I don't get along, Mr. Katz. I had an operation on my colon, five, six months ago—I think I may have told you—and ever since, one little glass of wine and *whoosh!—where's the rest room?*"

"Rest room?" Ira Katz raised his eyebrows.

"Whenever I drink wine," Craine explained. "Also coffee, but less so." He made his face look as if a thought had just occurred to him. "But I'll tell you what. I've got a little Scotch here!" He drew out the Scotch and, too eagerly, held it toward his neighbor. "Scotch and beer go through the kidneys."

Katz looked sadly at the bottle—resigning himself to the waste of a perfectly good evening, perhaps—then up at Craine's face. "It wasn't serious, I hope—the operation."

"Cancer of the colon," Craine said. He opened the front of his suit coat as if showing off his wounds. "But they got it all out, they say. Clean as a whistle."

"I'm glad to hear it." He turned toward the kitchen, reaching out and touching the door frame. "I'll stick with wine, I think. You want water and ice?"

"No, thank you," Craine said, "wrecks the color." He grinned. As Ira Katz went back into the kitchen, Craine strode, slightly staggering, to the middle of the livingroom and stood looking around, bent forward, as if taking possession. In the kitchen behind him the cat said something Craine didn't catch, some irritable question, and Ira Katz said something back to him. Above the ticking of the clocks Craine heard a growling sound, something like "Ow, ow, ow!"—an electric can opener, it came to him—then the sound of a spoon hitting the side of the plastic cat dish, and his neighbor's voice, talking softly. The cat said nothing. Craine set his cup of sugar on the nearest of the bookshelves, between two tall clocks, and bent close to read the top row of titles. A long stretch of them—French paperbacks—were called *Situations*. At last Ira Katz came in with a fat Almadén bottle, a wineglass, and an empty glass for Craine.

"Have a seat," he said, and gestured vaguely, letting Craine choose his chair.

Craine, as usual, chose the chair that seemed less likely to be his neighbor's favorite, the one farthest from the photograph and snapshot, took the glass his neighbor held out to him, and carefully—steadying the bottle against the rim of the glass—splashed in Scotch. His neighbor, standing by the other chair, pouring wine for himself, smiled with just his mouth, like a man lost in thought, then finally seated himself—his head under the lamp so that the black hair shone brown in a ring exactly like a halo around his head—put the bottle on the carpet to the right of his feet, raised his glass as if to say "cheers," and took a small sip. Craine took a slightly larger sip, then set the wobbly glass down. For a long, awkward moment, they sat listening to the clocks. The cat came wandering in from the kitchen, his wide head tipped, eyes grumpy, to see what they were doing. At last he went over to lie down with his head against Ira Katz's shoeless left foot. As if by magic, the instant the cat closed his eyes all the clocks began chiming, first one, then another. Ten o'clock.

"Ten o'clock!" Craine said, surprised.

His host half-smiled and nodded. The cat lay quiet as a doorstop, pretending to be asleep.

Craine got his pipe out, loaded it, and lit it, all the while frantically trying to think what he might say.

Ira Katz leaned forward, resting his forearms on his knees. After a moment he asked, "Is something wrong, Craine?"

Craine jumped at the terrible simplicity of the thing and, to cover himself, reached for the Scotch glass on the table beside his chair. "I've been thinking about what we talked about the last time we talked," he said. He shot a look at Ira, but the poet's eyes showed nothing. Craine put the pipe down in his lap to hold the glass with both hands and keep it steady. He drank, then leaned forward. The lines and colors of the books in the lamplight behind Ira's head were slightly sharper and brighter than they ought to be, intensified by the whiskey. Ira Katz waited, slightly smiling, his eyes sad and distant.

"We were talking about novels, you remember, and detectives and exi—" He paused, stopped cold by a memory lapse, struggling in vain after the word, though he knew it as he knew his own name.

"Existentialists?"

"That's it!" He took another gulp, then put the glass down and picked up his pipe. "Existentialists, yes!" He paused, feeling awkward about leaping so abruptly into serious conversation. Katz looked bored, as if the word *existentialists* annoyed him. No doubt it did. He'd know, as a university man, the stupidity of all those big words, all that talk, talk, talk. Craine listened to the clocks—a patternless, frantic clicking like a random beating of electrons—then in spite of himself, in spite of Katz's displeasure and his own sure knowledge of the uselessness of it all, pressed on: "We were talking about how the existentialists feel about detective novels. It was interesting, and the more I got to thinking about it, the more interesting it got. You don't like them, I think—these existentialists—but I believe that's what I am myself—what we have to be, us detectives."

Ira waited. His shadow lay perfectly still, draped over the cat and reaching halfway to Craine. Another shadow, fainter, stretched up the wall behind him and to the right of him, cast by the dim light coming from the bedroom.

"The world's neither one thing nor the other, that's what we believe," Craine said. " 'Complementarity,' as the physicists say."

"That's not exactly—" Ira began, then stopped.

"We're simply here, that's the thing," Craine explained, hurrying, sensing that he'd made some mistake. "We don't know what happened before we came onto the case, who did what or why, nothing, and we don't give a damn; not really." He squinted, playing crafty detective. "We're not committed one way or the other, that's our profession. Dispassionate."

Ira straightened up—the shadow leaped back with him—and looked at his glass. "I suppose that's true," he said. He seemed now a little like a detective himself, trying to see around behind the conversation.

Craine laughed, trying to make light of it. "A detective cares no more for the victim than he does for the murderer," he said. "His heart's cold as ice. He's a man without a past, you might say. No past and, for all practical purposes, no future." He laughed again, then, trembling, put his pipe between his teeth and relit it. Ira Katz watched him, lips pursed, waiting just a touch impatiently, glancing at the bedroom door. "It's a terrible thing, of course," Craine said, "a man with no earthly connections, suspicious as a rat; but, you see, that's how it is." He gave another little laugh.

"Yes, I suppose," Ira said.

Craine had a feeling he still wasn't following, and no wonder; he was half lost himself. "Put it this way," he said. "It wasn't *us* that made the laws—we don't *care* about the laws—we just make up a theory about who did what to who, and that's it, that's reality, or as much of it as counts, one tiny bubble in the"—he paused, then gestured impatiently—"the foam."

Ira nodded and smiled, making light blink in his hair. Judging from his face, he was as baffled as ever. "But sometimes the theory's true and sometimes not—you'd agree with that?" he asked.

"Maybe so, but you can never be sure," Craine said. "And what's the difference?"

Ira thought about it, tapping the rim of his glass with one finger. "Interesting," he said. It was not quite ingenuous, Craine could see. He'd thought it all through before, though he pretended otherwise. He still seemed reluctant to pursue the conversation—no doubt old stuff to him, junk food for freshmen—but after a moment the hint of a smile came back and his eyes met Craine's. "Tell me this," he said. "Suppose you should decide to take that gun out of its holster and shoot me, right here and now, and suppose in half an hour you should fall into a river, gun and all"—he gave Craine a quick, apologetic glance, maybe just a touch of hostility in it—"and no one in the world could prove that it was you that killed me. Wouldn't it be true just the same that it was you who did it?"

Craine narrowed his eyes, thinking hard, on the look-out for traps. "No, not for practical purposes," he said.

"No, not for practical purposes, I suppose." Ira tapped the glass, slightly grinning. "All the same, it would be true in God's eyes." His face showed no apology for the mention of God.

"I suppose so. Yes."

Ira Katz smiled broadly, delighted, as if that was that, now Craine could go home. Craine sipped his whiskey. At last he set the glass down and leaned forward again. "But practical purposes is all we've actually got," he said. "What God knows is one thing. If you can't make God spill the beans, then detectives are what's left."

"You having trouble with a case?" Ira Katz asked, eyebrows lifting.

Craine laughed sharply and waved it away. "I don't get cases like that. I haven't had a murder case in fifteen years, and even that one we all knew who did it from before the beginning. Lady ran over the garbage man, tried to grind up the evidence in the truck. Whole neighborhood saw it. We're talking theoretically."

"I see," Ira said. It was not clear that he did see.

"The point is," Craine said, pointing with his pipe stem at the middle of Ira Katz's forehead, "the detective makes up a theory, the best one he can think of, and if worse comes to worst he stakes his stupid miserable life on it. That's what we do in this world. That's reality."

"Maybe so," Ira said, "but I don't think so."

"You've got no *choice*," Craine said, and jabbed at the air with his pipe stem, suddenly fierce. "That's how the *world* is."

Ira Katz smiled and held his hands out, elbows on the chair arms, the right hand holding the glass in it. "Take it easy," he said. "You said yourself we're talking theoretically."

Quickly, blood prickling in his neck, Craine calmed himself. For no reason, except perhaps the whiskey, he was close to tears. It wasn't that the idea was so terribly important: it was the shortness of the time a man had to get things right. He must leave soon, let Katz get back to his poetry or whatever. His glass, he found, was empty. Guiltily ("why guiltily?" he wondered, "what's the difference?"), he reached down for the bottle at his feet and refilled, spilling a little on his pant leg in his haste, hardly noticing. "Excuse me, Mr. Katz. I guess I got a little excited there." He laughed, a brief cackle. "The point is—" He set down the bottle again. "The world is like a mystery, exactly as you've said—a detective novel that we're locked up inside of, the same way we're locked inside our language, as you pointed out yourself—an interesting idea, as I told you at the time."

"I said *some*thing like that," Ira Katz said, not quite interrupting.

"Whatever," Craine said, brushing it aside almost angrily. "But you follow what I mean. The writer that wrote the novel may know the story from end to end—he might or he might not, I wouldn't know about that—but the characters, what do *they* know? They come in at, say, page a hundred, maybe page two thousand. Before that they didn't exist. Not a trace of them. What are they to do?"

Ira Katz smiled patiently. His glass was still nearly as full as when he started.

"I'll tell you what they do if they're smart, Mr. Katz." He leaned forward, intense and emotional; he hardly knew why himself. In a minute he'd be crying. "They don't eat the cake till someone else has tried it and not died of it. They don't make friends, they don't make enemies. They don't go up on rooftops or wander around in the shrubbery or down in cellars. They keep their mouths shut and pay very close attention."

"It's a hard way to live," Ira Katz said, again not quite following, or so it seemed.

"That's the truth," Craine said, and shuddered, tears leaping into his eyes, then drank. The thread of his argument had slipped from him. The click of the clocks had a hollow echo. He was drinking much too fast. He stared hard at the cat as if for help. The cat slept on.

Ira Katz said playfully, carefully not making it too clear that he was playing—indeed, there was a chance that he was serious after all, "Some of us have to be the victims, though, and some of us have to be the people left over at the end, the suspects who didn't do it."

Craine nodded, petulant, still looking for the thread. *Everybody did it,* he thought, but that made no sense. He drank again, furiously wishing he'd stayed sober. Then it came to him. He reached out sharply toward Ira Katz, gesturing with his glass, spilling whiskey. "That's just bad luck, though, that's the thing—the ones that get killed and the ones that happen not to, the poor dumb bastards that die or have children and never think. It's the *detective* we have to watch. *He's* the one to think about. The others can be as passionate as they want to—good luck to 'em! But the detective, he's got to be objective, scientific. No commitments. He's like a man from outside Time. That's his secret. Maybe he's a foreigner, like Hercule Poirot. Maybe he gets stoned on cocaine, like Sherlock Holmes."

Ira Katz was studying him from deep in his chair, for all the world like Holmes making cunning deductions. "Craine," he said suddenly, "what are you driving at?" Again he glanced toward the bedroom door.

"Sherlock Holmes," Craine said, and waved his glass. "Hercule Poirot!"

"I know," Ira Katz said. "That part I'm hearing."

Craine sat perfectly still for a moment, his insides overtaken by a curious trembling. Again, for an instant, he'd gotten a flash of the beautiful young woman who was following him. "We're talking about the man who solves the mystery," he said. A tear escaped onto his cheek, and quickly, furtively, he wiped it away. "We're talking about the solitary hunter, cold-blooded as the moon!"

Ira Katz studied him. "Is that what you want to be?" he asked. He spoke too gently, like a psychiatrist.

"As I told you," Craine said crossly, with dignity, "I never get murder cases. We're talking theoretically."

The young man nodded. For a long moment he stared at something just above and behind Craine's head. At last he dropped his gaze to meet Craine's and cleared his throat. "I'll tell you how it seems to me," he said, and colored slightly. It seemed for an instant that the clocks ticked more softly. Ira Katz looked above Craine's head again. "It seems to me that the man who's a lover is more likely to make a good detective than the man who's not. That's my impression, anyway, or my impression at this moment." His smile was, again, apologetic. "We all know the disadvantages. He gets overinvolved, he's not objective, he runs a risk of missing things—those are the arguments. But I don't know. I'm not sure. The detective who's involved—not just with the woman, if it's a woman that's in danger, as in the usual plot, but with everyone, everything—I think that's the man I'd put my money on. If I were to make up a new kind of detective—a new and different kind of Ellery Queen or Dr. Fell or Perry Mason—I'd use—I don't know—maybe an Indian guru, some man like Swami Muktinanda—you've heard of him? I'd choose a man half crazy with empathetic love for all the universe. Someone who needs an assistant to keep him from walking into freight trains or falling down in trances—some merry-hearted lunatic who understands the language of goats and trees." He looked at Craine and grinned. "My novels wouldn't have much suspense, I admit. The minute the detective meets the killer, that's that, no more mystery. 'Ah!' he'd say, 'so it's you!' Big smile from both parties. And my novels might not have much in the way of emotional catharsis, either. My detective would never turn the murderer in, he'd simply cure him by a beatific look, or maybe confirm his existence for what it was, as he would a cobra's, and send him on his way. But then—" He gestured vaguely, smiling, letting it go. After a moment his expression clouded and, glancing down at his glass, he said, "Or then again I might choose just the opposite, some rolling-eyed, half-crazy paranoid. They too have their in-volvement—involvement of a kind, anyway. They can be wonderfully shrewd." Craine's mind flashed an image of Dr. Tummelty talking of the woman who walks down the street unconsciously scanning. Craine leaned forward, raising his glass to object, but Ira Katz, looking over his head again, seemed not to notice.

"I'll tell you the problem with existentialists," he said seriously. His voice became teacherish, as if he'd said this many times and had a good deal invested in it. "They begin with the assumption that we're free—'existence precedes essence' and all that. The trouble is, it's not true. You remember Jean-Paul Sartre's image, the man who stands on a cliff looking down. He feels dizzy, a little nausea. That's the experience of freedom, Sartre claims—the man's sense that he could throw himself into the abyss if he chose to. The trouble is, most people don't—they step back. If we were really free, about fifty percent of us would jump."

"But surely that's just fear, Mr. Katz," Craine broke in. "If they dared to face up to their freedom and act—" His voice came out unexpectedly loud. It wasn't so much the whiskey outrunning him as the speed with which Ira Katz hurried from thought to thought, dropping names, queer images —the man on the cliff—as if Craine should have heard of them a hundred times, which perhaps he had; he was too foggy to remember. "The mere fact that we don't jump, even if we're miserable," Craine began.

"But we don't, you see. That's the point." He spoke patiently, as to a child. "Being mammals, and sentient, we're aware that it might hurt, land-ing on those big jagged rocks down below. We obey the age-old law of mammals, the law that precedes our particular existence: *Try not to get hurt.* It seems to me that our proper business should be to try to figure out what the secret laws are for sentient mammals—what hurts us and what doesn't, physically, psychologically, spiritually." He flashed a smile, too quick and neat, a smile he'd used in lectures. "We should work at discovering what values are built into us. Learn to survive—learn what makes us *fit.* The exis-tentialists point us in the opposite direction, that's what's wrong with them.

They encourage us to think we can make up values, like Midas deciding, on insufficient evidence, that what people really need is a world made of gold, or like Nietzsche deciding, on insufficient evidence, that the future belongs to 'the sons of the Prussian officers.' "

"But what if it does?" Craine burst out, flustered. "By your law of mere fitness, what if he was right? Take people's hatred of the Jews." He looked away from Ira's face, then resolutely back, straight into his eyes. "You think it was beaten when Hitler lost the war—if he *did* lose the war?" He was aware, too late, that it came out like a snarl, as if Craine were the chief and most deadly of anti-Semites.

Ira Katz shrugged as if the matter were of no great importance to him, but his eyes lowered, and his voice became more serious, studiously reasonable and offhand. "If Nietzsche was right, then his position will win. Survival of the fittest. Millions upon millions of gentle, well-meaning creatures have been wiped out by the centuries."

There was a silence, as if both of them, in their embarrassment, had lost the thread. Craine's eyes settled on the snapshot of Ira Katz's children. The photograph beside it was of their mother—not Jewish, it came to him. He quickly looked away and busied himself relighting his pipe, then refilling his glass. It was late, he must be going. An increasing sense of urgency churned in him. Whatever it was that he'd come to find out, they hadn't gotten near it, or rather, one moment they'd be edging in on it, the next they'd be light-years off. He was like a man who'd stayed late at a tedious party, hoping against hope, and now the others were leaving, the talk of the few who remained was turning insidious, his hopes were growing slimmer by the moment. He raised his glass with a quick jerk and drank. Like a train in the station, starting up before you realize it's done so, the room began to move.

There was a trace of a quaver in Ira Katz's voice when he spoke again, as if Craine's accidental attack had stirred memories. "Whatever is true is true," he said. "We have to live with that." He shrugged as if trying to submit to his own rule. His eyes, looking down at the carpet between Craine and himself, were solemn. "We were talking about detective novels. About getting at the truth. There's something I tell my students . . ." He took a deep breath, as if he couldn't get air enough. Craine noticed only now that the room was hot. Sweat ran down his neck. Ira was saying, "We have only two ways of finding out what's true, what will work. By history's blind groping, one damn thing after another, as they say"—he took another deep breath—"or by rigorous imagination, which in the end means by poems and novels." He flicked his eyes up at Craine. "Get everything exactly right, and maybe you save people the pain of history gone wrong."

"Ha!" Craine barked, not in scorn but only to stop the talk for a moment, make the room stop moving, give himself time to think—though scorn was what it sounded like, Craine knew.

Ira Katz shrugged and leaned back in his chair, abandoning him. The room now moved steadily to the left. Ira Katz remembered his wineglass on the table and took a sip, then put the glass down gently and glanced at the clock just beside it. Quarter to eleven. Again he took one of those deep, pained breaths, and his glance went briefly to the bedroom door. This time Craine registered it. Was it possible that the man had a girl in there? If so, she was as quiet as a corpse. For an instant he imagined it clearly: a lead-gray dead girl, some college student with long blond hair, naked on Ira Katz's bed. Craine shuddered and drank. No, not possible, he thought, and briefly understood with perfect clarity what Ira Katz was saying about imagination testing truth. At once Craine lost it. "Nonsense, nonsense, nonsense," the clocks said everywhere around him, heavily sibilant but clear as day. He was imagining it, of course, he told himself; but in fact, he saw the next instant, he was not. The word was unmistakable. They'd been saying it all night, it came to him. He sat still as a boulder, stunned by the discovery. The Vedic priests were right: sounds corresponded to natural forces in the universe. Everything was language, the very atoms maniacally whirling in the chair where he sat. *Word of God,* he thought, half ironic, half crazily gleeful, and for an instant closed his eyes. He fell through space, plummeting, and at once snapped his eyes open and was stabilized.

For all that was happening—Time off its rhythm, as if rushing out past the edge of the universe—Ira Katz was saying calmly, reasonably, "You may be right that it's impossible for human beings to know the truth, but whatever the real history of the world is, we're part of it, made of the same material. The minute we step outside it—or allow some son of a bitch to push us outside it—we're done for. That's what survival of the fittest means, being made of the same thing the universe is, and able to move when the universe moves. In that sense all novels are detective novels, or ought to be. People hunting for connections." Incredibly—since usually, drunk or sober, Craine was like lightning at catching such things—Craine realized only now that Ira Katz was in some way talking about himself. He, Ira Katz, was the man not fit to survive, or so he thought—not "connected." Was that what it was about, then, the poetry writing?—the endless, passionate turning over of trivia—autumn days, the eyes of chickens? Strange that Craine should be surprised by it. He'd known for years that it was hardly for himself alone that the jig was up.

Before he knew he would do it, Craine heard himself saying, "I've been having some queer experiences lately." He glanced past his shoulder, then leaned forward again. "I keep feeling someone watching me. Crazy, eh? Ha ha!" His free hand slapped the chair arm.

Ira Katz nodded, eyebrows lifted, and tentatively smiled, alerted.

"I've got a friend who maintains it's the Lord watching me. I laugh. I don't believe in such things, naturally. But I'll tell you, it gives me the jeebies!" He had an odd sensation—not quite frightening, but curious—of sinking chair and all into the floor.

"I should think so," Ira said and again just perceptibly nodded. He raised his wineglass and sipped. His eyes had gone vague.

Craine desperately focused his attention on Ira, keeping the chair from sinking further. "I don't believe in connections—especially metaphysical connections," Craine said. He laughed, alarmed, as if his words tempted devils, then hurried on, focusing still harder on Ira Katz. In his drunkenness he believed he was zeroing in on the heart of the matter—he would not think so tomorrow, perhaps, but his feeling that he was getting at the truth at last was intense. In a burst, struggling with his thickening tongue, he told Ira Katz how Carnac kept pursuing him, hounding him, and how even as he fled he felt mysteriously bound to the man, doomed to some terrible brotherhood with him. He spoke of the bookstore and how Tummelty had strangely latched onto him, hooked in like a burr, pretending it was Carnac's mind, not his own, that interested him. Craine laughed, three sharp yelps, as he spoke of how Tummelty had tried to fool him. The feeling that he was onto something grew by leaps and bounds. As he was about to speak of the woman who stood watching from the stacks, unseen—a woman with cat's eyes, black as coal—there came a terrible whirring and, out of sync, the clocks all struck eleven. Craine stopped short, mouth wide open, listening.

To Craine's drunken ears, the whirring, pinging, and bonging of the clocks was monstrously mechanical, at the same time mocking and despairing. He strained to hear the words, but if any were there they eluded him. It seemed to him that he knew where the wild noise came from, the pitch-dark hole at the center of the universe, aclutter with dead things—old planets, *prima materia,* a cosmic Sargasso sea from which came now only the sound he'd heard as he came back to consciousness after his operations. His eyes leaped toward Ira Katz. Ira, he saw to his amazement, had heard something totally different, innocent. Craine felt himself quietly slipping under again, drowning toward the whisper.

Ira Katz had set his wineglass on the table beside his chair, the glass still almost full. He sat—or blurrily hovered—with his fingertips together, like a priest. He looked up and ran one hand through his hair.

"Yes, it's interesting," he said, "the work Dr. Tummelty's been doing." Craine had to concentrate, tensing so hard his cheeks twitched, to make the words make sense. Ira was saying, "I got a copy of his book—*The Shattered Mind,* I think it's called. I only read a little of it. You know him well?"

By Ira's tone Craine understood for the first time—dimly, as he understood everything just now—that Dr. Tummelty was in some way famous. Perhaps he'd heard that before, in fact. No use hunting; his mind was like a dead man's. With his right hand he was gripping the chair arm, with his left the glass of whiskey, still struggling against the horror of that chiming from the depths. "I've talked with him once or twice, that's all," Craine managed to bring out. His speech was badly slurred, beyond all control now. He could feel the long tumble of the room through space. Struggling for sobriety, he tried to think what Dr. Tummelty had said, but his mind had quit as if forever.

"He works with people who've had head injuries," Ira said. His voice came out hollow, the words dirge-slow; a dream voice. "People who've severed certain nerves or something. They can write, for instance, but they can't read—not even what they've written. Neurophysiology. It's a scary business. You introduced him to Carnac?"

"No," Craine said, "something . . ." He could call back none of it, or nothing but one phrase, *the bioplasmic universe.* Then that too slid away from him. He felt his eyelids sinking and struggled to stay awake.

Ira Katz was increasingly impatient to see him gone; he could barely hide it, Craine saw. But the door was far across the room. If he stood up and tried he couldn't make it, not a chance. As if he'd actually gotten up, he saw himself staggering, falling against bookshelves, knocking down clocks. Again, he jerked his eyes open. "Psychics," he said.

Ira Katz looked at him. "Pardon?" he said.

"Tummelty's in'rested in psychics," Craine said. It took all his energy to keep his eyelids partway open. He saw himself as Ira Katz must be seeing him, a newly dead corpse, two narrow chinks through which his icy blue, unfocussed eyes peered out with hushed malevolence.

Then, like a collision of clocks thrown together, maybe sliding from a dump truck, there came from behind him the deafening jangle of Ira Katz's phone in the bedroom. Ira started as if in fear, then, controlling himself, rose to his feet. *"So that's it,"* Craine thought, and would have cackled if he could have—one last feeble burst of demonic intelligence—*he's been ex-pecting a phone call from his wife!* Craine's eyes narrowed more, murderous as the cat's, and he strained all his powers toward the difficult business of eavesdropping, but before the phone could ring twice, he was fast asleep.

He slept for forty minutes, or forty-five, perhaps fifty—the clocks were in rough agreement on ten to twelve. It took him a long time to remember where he was and even longer to realize that it was his neighbor in there, still on the phone, speaking angrily and loudly, confident that Craine was asleep, or else indifferent to his hearing. "I didn't say that," he was shouting. "Listen, we need to *talk*—"

Craine's arms and legs were leaden, his head strangely clear and indiffer-ent, remote. The room around him was like a sharply focused old photo-graph, blurry at the edges. He listened, unsurprised, to the crackle of rage in his neighbor's voice in the bedroom. It was nothing unusual, in Craine's profession, this murderous enmity of separated husbands and wives. Chances were they'd be together again in six months, or amicably parted, sending birthday cards. He smiled, cold as ice, then slowly turned his head. The red light on the stereo was off now. The cat stood by the door to the bedroom, watching him.

"Kill them!" his neighbor shouted. "That's a wonderful idea! Jesus Christ, that's terrific! Listen, I got a better idea. Kill them and pin the thing on me!"

Craine thought, for no reason, of drawing out his pistol and shooting himself. He smiled again. His arms lay flat on the chair arm, heavy as deadmen at the bottom of a pond. He saw himself sitting here in Ira Katz's chair with his head half blown away, blood and hair on the wall behind him. His arms remained perfectly still, as if he'd done it already.

"Nonsense, nonsense, nonsense," the clocks said.

It was curiously interesting, the thought of being dead. Like a midnight swim in one's childhood, or a journey by train.

Craine's eyes again fell shut and, like a stone, he slept.

When he awakened the second time, Ira Katz was at the window, staring down into the street, one hand flat on his beard. There was an afghan over Craine's chest and legs. According to the clocks, it was quarter after twelve. The cat, in the chair where Ira had been sitting, had his eyes fixed on Craine. Craine looked away, as he would from the stare of some stoned young bore at a bus station. It no longer mattered that someone was following him, spying on him. It was all the same, the connected universe he'd dropped out on. Maggots. After a minute Craine's hand rose unbidden to his forehead, as if seeing if it was there.

"Headache?" Ira Katz said, turning slowly. His mind, for all his solicitude, was far away.

"Not yet," Craine said.

Ira Katz studied him, eyelids puffy, as if he'd been crying, then turned his face back to the window. "I know what it's like," he said. He stroked his beard. It seemed that he would say no more, but then, surprisingly, as if speaking to the darkness outside the room, he said, "I used to do it all the time—knock myself unconscious with martinis. It's a very inefficient way to kill yourself. You want some aspirin?"

"If you've got some handy," Craine said.

Ira nodded, thought about it, then crossed to the door to the bedroom and bathroom, hardly glancing at Craine as he passed. He switched the bathroom light on—a ribbon of white shot up the wall across from Craine—then ran water. When he'd turned the tap off, he said—still in the bathroom, standing there looking into the mirror, perhaps—"I knew a woman once managed to kill herself on whiskey. Hemorrhage of the esophagus. Managed to rear up, spouting blood like a geyser, and make a few last interesting remarks." He switched off the bathroom light, blew his nose, and after a moment emerged with a glass of water and three aspirin.

"You were there, I take it," Craine said, not looking at him, leaving him free to ignore it if he pleased. To Craine it hardly mattered. He was not floating now. He'd sunk to the center of things, the ultimate idea of stone.

"Intimate part of the conversation," Ira said. He held out the aspirin and glass of water.

Craine took them from him, clumsily, put the pills in his mouth, and drank. "Thank you," he said, and rolled his eyes up. "Thank you very much." He handed back the glass.

Ira turned away, looked at the cat in the chair, the photographs, then set down the glass on the bookshelf behind Craine. With a part of his mind, Craine registered a noise, perhaps the door opening at the foot of the stairs. He listened more carefully, listless, not even interested—alert in spite of himself, he would have said, like some criminal who'd lost all taste for life yet finds himself paying attention to every strange footfall. There was nothing now, only the ticking of the clocks, the absolute stillness of mounded white sand in the hourglass on the table beside him. Ira went over to the window to stand with his hands in his suspenders, looking down again.

"Personally," Craine said, "I put such things out of my mind. Gone like smoke." He leaned his head back and looked at the ceiling.

"I know," Ira said.

There was another sound, someone on the stairs. He strained to separate out the sound of the clocks. Even now he felt no interest, only a morbid curiosity. The miraculous does not come to those out looking for it. Beauty, high adventure . . . He closed his eyes.

The man was muttering something, standing there angrily muttering at the window. *Stupid bastard, stupid fucking bastard . . .*

Indignation leaped up in him, but he forgot the next instant. He saw the doorknob turning, the door slowly opening, a leather-gloved hand reaching in, groping toward the lightswitch.

"What?" Craine said, snapping his eyes open.

Ira Katz looked at him, far away. "Maybe that's your trouble, Craine," he said.

"What?" Craine said again, heart racing.

"This feeling you have of someone following you, spying on you. Maybe it's Time's revenge." He studied Craine a moment, then shifted his gaze away, out the window, down into the street. "I have a theory," he said. "We have an idea of ourselves, when we're kids: noble-hearted, honorable, unselfish. It's a beautiful image, and in fact it's true—it's the truth about us—but we betray it, or the nature of the world betrays it. We betray it again and again, one way or another. We can't do what's decent. Our commitments prevent it, or it's beyond our means. There are only so many causes you can die for, only so many good women you can love with all your heart, and even the best twist you downward, limit possibilities, limit your potential. So we lose touch with ourselves, turn our backs on the image, believe ourselves to be the ugly thing we've by now half-proved we are. The image is still there, the shadow we cast into the future when we were young. It's still there haunting us, beckoning us toward it; only now there's that second shadow, the shadow, behind us, of all those acts unworthy of us." He put his hand on his beard. At last he said, "I heard a story. There was this girl, a student of one of our graduate students. It seems she saw a rape—or a murder, I forget—and she was afraid to report it. It was years ago, I think. Anyway, all this time she's been brooding on it, trapped in the past. Snagged on it, that unfulfilled moment. Everywhere she goes, everyone she meets, out pours the story. It's the most important thing in the world to her. People hide behind trees when they see her coming. You see what I'm saying. Maybe in your case—"

Something astonishing was happening in Craine's mind—a blinding flash of white, as if all matter had exploded, then blackness, then everything as it was. She was there, out in the hallway, her small ear pressed against the door, dark eyes rolled up. He could hear her breathing.

Ira Katz was looking at him, eyebrows lowered. Craine sat forward. "It's late," he said, and shuddered—shuddered from head to foot, like a man just come in from icy wind and deep snow. "I lost track of the time," he said, and laughed. He rose unsteadily to his feet, three fingers on the chair arm for balance. His legs were like wood.

"It *is* late," Ira said.

Craine's eyes fell again on the snow-white sand mounded up in the bottom of the hourglass, absolutely still.

"I'll just use your bathroom," he said, and moved very carefully, like an old, old man, toward the bedroom door. When he was seated in the dark—he'd been unable to find the bathroom lightswitch—his sense that she was listening in the hallway outside became a certainty. He heard her purse snap open, saw her hand slip in. He tried to hurry, full of life again, but his bowel track refused to be rushed, shooting miserable dribbles and insisting with pressure like a wail that he wait a minute longer. Pain tugged at the red gouge five inches below his nipple, another pain lower, where the remains of his anus had been sewn to the remains of his tubing. He strained with all his might, then gave up—he'd take his chances—wiped himself, pulled up his trousers, and flushed the toilet. His heart pounded fiercely, the rest of him sodden and heavy as new concrete. Then the knock came, exactly when he'd known it was coming. Quickly, one hand on the bathroom doorknob, he drew the pistol from its holster. When he heard Ira Katz walk over in his stocking feet and open the hallway door, Craine stepped out of the bathroom and crossed to the door to the livingroom, then, after an instant, stepped out suddenly—smiling like a storm trooper—to greet her.

At once he saw that the woman staring at him was not the one. She was tall, middle-aged, all skin and bones, most of her straggly brown hair up in a bun. Her dress was vaguely Indian; over it, she wore a pale purple cardigan sweater and green beads. Her face went white—all except the birthmark like a coin on her cheek—and the hand that held the purse dropped lower. Ira Katz, too, was staring at Craine's pistol. He drew the woman back toward himself.

"Craine," he said at last, eyes wide, "this is April. She's a friend." He pulled at the side of his collar with two fingers, letting in air, still looking at the pistol—now aimed at the floor. He stood carefully balanced, like a man on a tightrope thousands of feet up. He said, "April, this is my neighbor from down the hall, Detective Craine."

She just stared.

Craine smiled crazily, bending forward over the gun. "I just came to borrow some sugar," he said. He glanced at the cup on the bookshelf, then down at his pistol. He put it away hastily, fingers shaking. "I thought you were here to steal my sugar," he explained, and gave a laugh.

They looked at him.

"It's late," he said, soberly nodding, then laughed again. He went to get the cup from the bookshelf. "I lost track of the time," he said, hurrying toward the door. He made his face so sober that, unbeknownst to himself, he looked furious. Tears ran down his cheeks. "Thank you very much," he said. "Sorry I had to trouble you. Thank you very much."

Five

It was not that he felt guilty; he'd drunk too much to be vulnerable to guilt. Nor was it exactly that his mind was churning. He seemed to be thinking nothing, lying there flat on his back like a corpse patiently awaiting resurrection. He lay in his underwear on top of the covers, head cocked forward by the pillows, his arms at his sides, bare feet splayed outward. He was strongly conscious of the room around him, the faded gray wallpaper splotched and cracked, bulging here and there, like an old bum's forehead; the padless, once wine-red, threadbare carpet lumped up into ropes, like the veins on the backs of his hands. It was his story, this room, this miraculous decay—the books that spelled out his consciousness wedged into bookshelves of cheap, stained pine, strewn along the baseboards, stacked up in corners; on the bedpost above him his pistol precariously tilted in its shoulder holster; on his dresser, in its dusty old Bible-black case, the pitted, once-silver cornet that he hadn't touched in years. A streetlight made the night smoke-gray outside his window, lighting up telephone and electric lines and throwing a negative shadow along the floor toward his closet. The closet door hung open, too warped to close; it had a broken spool for a doorknob. The interior of the closet, just visible from Craine's bed, was crowded with dark forms. He thought, without emotion, how some murderer might crouch there, waiting for him to sleep. At once he found himself thinking of the women who'd been killed. He imagined their terror as the dark shape detached itself from the other dark shapes and came forward, signalling for silence, reaching out to snatch them. Abruptly, Craine sat upright, threw his feet over the side of the bed, and got up.

For fifteen minutes he stood at his dresser, wearing only his underwear—he had the lights on now, the shades not pulled—sorting through paper scraps from his pockets and the dresser drawers, laying them out like puzzle pieces, lifting them one after another and squinting, trying to read them, but to no avail; his eyes refused to focus. He worked in increasing desperation, growing angry or frightened, he could hardly say which. All at once he found himself listening to something. Perhaps he'd been listening for a long time. It was a creaking sound, rhythmical and urgent—some machine, he thought at first, something to do with torture. Then the truth broke through: Ira Katz's bedsprings. He reached out, automatically, and turned out the lights. In the darkness that leaped up around him the sound seemed much louder. He groped his way back to the bed and lay down as before. The sound went on and on. They were still at it, banging away like demons, when Craine's stiff muscles relaxed and he sank into sleep.

He slept quietly for a time, though the creaking continued and the walls were full of scraping and gnawings, the scamperings of mice. One poked his head out from the hole in the corner, a hole too small for notice, almost hidden by books, then came cautiously into the room, stopped in the light from the window, and stood listening. Soon the second one came, sister to the first, this one from the closet, darted out onto the carpet and paused, nose tipped upward, whiskers atremble, watching Craine's bed. Craine slept on, and the mice moved quickly to his trench coat and squirmed into the left-side pocket, where there were crumbs. Now Craine's eyes began to move under the lids. "Turn under!" he shouted, and the mice in the trench coat froze, hearts slamming, heads down, ears cocked. His voice diminished to a mutter, and they returned to their business, hurrying, still listening for danger.

In an unknown language which Craine was for some reason able to understand, Carnac was explaining, with brightly glowing eyes, that the room where they were locked with the five dead women—their throats had been slit—was a mystery novel; all the walls were words. There were paths across the floor in a pattern like Parcheesi, and above them, out of reach, was a hanged man, slowly turning. Emmit Royce, Craine's assistant, wearing only his leather jacket, was crawling slowly, on all fours, from one to another of the dead women, spreading the legs of each in turn, then raising them by the hips and inserting himself. He moved mechanically, sweating, as if someone were forcing him. Craine, though the whole thing annoyed him, distracting him from his problems, did nothing to interfere. All reality, Carnac was urgently explaining—looking past his shoulder in terrible fear—was a cliché; that was why they must speak new languages. Someone was watching from the shadows in the corner of the room. "There," Craine said, and pointed.

Suddenly he was awake. The night was quiet, though he'd almost have sworn that a second ago, before he was awake, he'd heard something—perhaps the door at the foot of the stairs outside his room, possibly a voice. Garbage men? he wondered. There were brown plastic garbage bags at the foot of the stairs. But it was still pitch-dark, and the garbage men never came in for them anyway; they waited for the bags to be moved out onto the sidewalk on the proper days—Mondays and Thursdays. He tried to think what day it was now, but his mind was a blank. He stared at the ceiling, fragments of the dream coming back to him again—so vivid he was tempted to look at his hands to see if he had blood on them. For an instant it seemed to him that he could smell the blood, but then, the next instant, he was uncertain. A car started up on the street below—right in front of the hotel, it seemed to him—and he thought of going to the window to look out. But his legs and arms were heavy, and the car was now far down the block. He let it go. At last he closed his eyes again and, after a time, went back to sleep. Again he lay perfectly still for a while, before his eyes began to move below the lids.

He dreamed he was a child of three, preaching aboard a Mississippi riverboat—a grand old sidewheeler of white and gold, with a Negro orchestra and staterooms of glowing black and crimson. His father and mother stood encouraging him and laughing, his mother's curls shiny, his father a trim, scientific-looking man, neatly bearded like a pharaoh, the whole crowd admiring their plump child's stern, slightly pouted lower lip, the ferocious pokes of his finger. "Praise the Lord!" cried a huge old man in gray, with a tie clasp of rapidly changing numbers. He had a huge, loose jowl and heavy eye bags. His laughter seemed malicious. There were streamers, champagne bottles, a peculiar scent in the air that he couldn't quite place.

Craine was preaching in the way he'd seen his grandfather do—a worldly, vain man, as ministers go, but a showman, and learned; he could read both Greek and Hebrew. In the dream Craine saw himself exploding golden curls; he was looking across the room into a mirror, perhaps. His heart skipped, delighted and baffled at receiving such attention. Why the harmless dream had the effect of a nightmare was not yet clear—the images had nothing to do with the emotion, or so it seemed—but Craine whimpered in his sleep, snatching out frantically at the sheets. In the dream his parents and the rest of the passengers were laughing like children and raising their glasses. A drunkard appeared in the doorway, holding out a very old letter with earth and stains on it, but no one noticed. A woman stood half in shadow behind him. Now the orchestra began to play, some noble old hymn or patriotic piece, and a few of the passengers began singing. More and more joined in, music sweeping around as the lights from the slowly turning mirror-globe swept across the walls of the ballroom—image of the universe from the still, dead center (so he reflected, studying the dream as he dreamed it). His mother wore black. Hastily, by some woman with a face that appeared to be a skull, blue-white as mist, he was whisked away to bed.

Craine awoke early, as usual, his eyelids heavy, his body lead-gray—only his hands, neck, and face were red—as tired as he'd been when he went to bed last night. He was filled with a sense that something of the greatest importance had happened, as if he'd made some terrible discovery and then forgotten. He rose irritably, full of inexplicable dread, and reached out, shaking, to the bedpost, the chair back, the wall, then the door frame as he moved into the bathroom, where he poured a little Scotch into his glass and checked the mirror to see if his skin had a yellow tinge—if it was there, he couldn't see it—then sat for half an hour on his cracked wooden toilet seat. On his bony knees he held his thick, discolored book, *The Mystery of Sanskrit*. "Tomes," he muttered, "—tombs," and grimaced as if someone else had said it. He sucked at his teeth. All around him in the bathroom lay stacks of old hardbacks, paperbacks, magazines. He had no girly magazines. Fifty-some years of existence had taught him, so he often claimed, that on inspection no woman holds up. Show him Cleopatra, show him Helen of Troy, he'd see through her. He'd discern around her mouth a faint hint of crabbyness or weakness, stubbornness, sullenness, or vanity; a certain tenseness around the eyes that showed a slight inclination to take notice of pain and make intolerable small demands; he'd make out that her hands, too quick and strong, suggested a habit of impatience. He understood that his complaint was against humanness itself, even life itself. He knew the antique identification of womanhood and the World, Mother Eve and the Apple, symbol of our bruised, thin-skinned planet. Though he watched fearfully for that tinge of yellow, Craine had lost his taste for the planet.

He read on, sucking at the dryness of his mouth, wincing at the book, muttering as if the page had not only the gift of language but also ears. He remembered his grandfather, for no reason, he believed—for no better reason than that the book spoke of Hebrew. He saw the man standing in his natty robe, arms outstretched behind the pulpit—moustached, slightly plump, his spectacles blanked out by light. He was Presbyterian, Craine remembered; pastor to a well-off congregation in St. Louis. "So that's it," Craine muttered, and winced again. It had come to him why at times, when drunk, he flew into complicated, passionate lectures and quoted Scripture, his mind on automatic pilot. He was, at such times, like a man possessed. Facts fell to hand like fruit in Eden; logic revealed itself like a goddess undressing. Afterward, everything he'd said, every wham of his fist, would be gone like smoke.

Suppose glossolalia were a real thing, he'd thought. Suppose Carnac was, in some sense, sane. Suppose glossolalia was what Craine had heard, anesthetized on the table, and the man in the dark, the girl he imagined to be following him, somehow crying out to him, friend or foe . . .

He got up from the toilet, flushed it, put down the book and picked up a paperback, easier to carry, and prepared to confront another day. In the underwear he'd slept in he brushed his teeth, then shaved and touched up his hair dye, black. Outside his window it was another clear autumn morning, almost no one out yet, two or three cars, a Bunny Bread truck, Ned Bugrum's mule-drawn junk wagon coming across the tracks, not making a sound.

Craine squinted and sucked again at his loose, dry mouth, thinking about his grandfather as he put on the socks he'd left hanging to air out on the doorknob, then his shirt, trousers, shoes, and shoulder holster, then his sagging brown jacket or rather suit coat, once part of a suit. Some taint of the nightmare emotion remained with him, coloring the miserable gray room around him, decayed and alive as the duff on the floor of a forest—he couldn't say why; perhaps the discovery that he was haunted. Though his past had been dead for a long time, buried as if under grass and huge stones, it was now clear to him that, somewhere down there, some part of it still wriggled, alive. For an instant, incredibly, he remembered his father, then forgot. He glanced past his shoulder at the window. He couldn't explain the crotchety feeling, subtle as the look of death in the sheen of a cancer victim's skin. Scowling, slightly squinting, he poured more Scotch into his glass, drank it, then cracked his revolver, making sure it was loaded, though it always was. He stared at the bullets in their chambers for a moment, vaguely reminded of the brasswork on a ship; then he closed the pistol, slipped it into its holster and, taking the whiskey with him, left his room. At the head of the stairwell his neighbor's cat sat warming itself in a trapezoid of sunlight, its one open eye on Craine. He moved toward it, then, with a startled look, turned back to his door. He bent over the lock, managed to get the key in, locked it, carefully tried the doorknob twice, and glanced around furtively at the cat. The hallway was full of some strange, strong smell. At last, stepping cautiously, groping like a blind man, making hardly a sound, he descended the long stairway, his right hand on the bannister, in his left the bottle of Scotch in its brown paper sack. The thought of memory rising from the dead had made him think of grave robbers, mysterious incantations, King Tut's curse. Someone with a beard and a wide-brimmed hat was at the window in the door at the foot of the stairs, looking up at him. Craine paused, gripping the bannister more tightly. The person stepped away. The same instant it seemed to Craine that some animal stirred among the garbage bags. His heart gave a jump and he leaned down to look. His mind went blinding white, then blank.

Two-heads Carnac sat motionless among the brown plastic bags as if someone had hastily and indifferently dumped him there, one more piece of trash for the garbage truck. Craine ground his fists into his eyes, then looked again. It was no mistake. Craine stood staring, his hands out for balance, then hastily dropped to his knees to see if Carnac was alive. He reached toward Carnac's one good eye, the right one, with the intention of opening it and peering in, but three inches away his hand stopped as if of its own accord and jerked back. Caked blood lay on Carnac's cheek and forehead, blood from a scalp wound, Craine thought at first, but then he found that that was wrong: though Carnac was sitting upright, the blood was from his nose. He'd lain somewhere head upside down at least long enough for the blood to dry, then someone had picked him up and moved him. There was more caked blood on the chest and right shoulder of his robe. It wasn't likely, then, that he'd been hit by a car, knocked into a ditch, and then later picked up and brought here. He'd been upright when the bleeding started, then later he'd lain upside down, then still later he'd been moved. All this Craine took in in an instant, by second nature, no longer than it took for his hand to jerk back then move forward again without a pause, and open the eyelid. It was too dim in the hallway for Craine to be sure of anything; he pressed his ear to Carnac's chest. He got the heartbeat at once, steady as the rumble of train wheels.

Only now did emotion leap up in him—panic, rage, whatever—so that he jerked back, twisting his head around, yelling, "Help! A man has been injured!" And then: "Ira! Help me!" No sound came from above, though he'd shouted with all his might, and he scrambled as if drunkenly to his feet and leaped to the door onto the street, pushed it open, and yelled, "Help! A man has been injured!" On the sidewalk people jerked and looked at him, hesitated an instant, then moved toward him. Now there was a thundering on the stairway behind him as Ira Katz came rushing down crazy-haired, wearing just a bathrobe, crying, "What's the matter? Jesus, Craine!" Then he stopped, seeing Carnac, and his eyes went comically wide.

"Call the police," Craine yelled, "call an ambulance!"

Bug-eyed, as if in slow motion, Ira Katz turned and began to climb two steps at a time back toward his room. Now three of the people from the sidewalk were with Craine in the entryway, standing like rabbits, their hands in front of them, looking at Carnac and waiting to be told what to do.

"Don't touch him," Craine said, "a call has been put in for an ambulance and the police."

One of them, a man Craine knew from somewhere, said, "What's happened? What's going on?" The door had closed behind the three who'd come in. Outside, others stood peering through the window, crowding to get a look. None of them made a motion to open the door. The three inside had a trapped look, as if suddenly they'd realized they should have moved more slowly.

"He's been injured," Craine said. "I was coming down the stairs to go to work . . ." He explained how he'd found him, just sitting there like that; apparently someone had beaten him up again. Craine had a queer, familiar sense of floating above himself, watching himself chatter. He thought of the curious expression he'd used: *Help! A man has been injured!*—and felt the faintest flicker of an impulse to laugh; but all the while he mused on the absurdity, he was talking, chattering away like a citizen, telling his audience how he'd seen Carnac sitting there and couldn't believe it, would have thought he was a drunken bum just sleeping it off except the blood—the smell of it—had stopped him right away. He couldn't believe it. One of the three, an apartment-house owner by the name of Ayers—Craine had had dealings with him, off and on—stepped partway out, holding the door open, to tell the crocodiles on the street what had happened. The crocodiles began to argue, God knew why. Ira Katz was coming down the stairs again, gray-faced; he'd pulled on black pants and slippers. "The police will be right over," he said.

"You called the ambulance?" Craine said.

Katz nodded. He was looking down at Carnac. "Shouldn't we do something?" he asked. "Wash off the blood or something?" Then, quickly, as if interrupting himself, "Jesus, what do you think happened?"

"Offhand," Craine said, "I'd say somebody pounded the shit out of him."

He would have thought it was obvious—in fact he'd said it before—but all of them jerked up their heads at him at once, as if thinking they too might have the shit pounded out of them. "Listen," Craine said suddenly, pointing at Ira Katz, "did you hear anything? A car? Something that might've been a scuffle?"

Katz thought, then shook his head. Half a mile away, a siren began to wail. The people who'd been looking in from outside began to leave, two by two, three by three.

One of the men who'd come in—a short, splotchy man with frizzled gray hair—said, "How long you think he's been laying here?" He glanced at the door as he spoke, thinking of getting out.

"No telling," Craine said.

The man nodded soberly, pulling the front of his coat together, struggling painfully over whether or not it would be morally acceptable to leave.

Craine leaned toward him, sly. "Listen," he said, "if I were you I'd make a run for it."

The man stared and blinked, then laughed. "No," he said, blushing, "it's all right. I have an appointment, that's all I was thinking. It's all right." He blushed more and pushed his hands into his pockets.

The police car pulled up, and, a few minutes later, the ambulance.

The patrolman was Jimmy Throop, fat and officious. The cloth of his pant legs, when he bent down on one knee to look at Carnac, was as tight as skin. He peeled his gloves off, then put one hand gently on the underside of Carnac's chin—no nurse at Johns Hopkins could have done it more gently. With the other hand he lifted the eyelid. "Mareezus, Craine," he said.

Craine scowled and said nothing.

Throop laughed, boyish, as if afraid he'd offended. His dimple showed. "If you're gonna have these wild parties, you should warn us in advance!"

"Next time for sure," Craine said.

Throop had bright straw-yellow hair and freckles. He was big as a horse, maybe two hundred seventy pounds, mostly fat; farmboy from Makanda. Craine knew him well. When Throop was a rookie, the first job he'd been sent on was a female drunk and disorderly. She'd refused to be arrested and had hit him in the jaw, though she was only a third his size. Believing it was wrong to hit a lady, he'd called home for help. He'd never live it down, but as a matter of fact he wouldn't willingly hit a lady even now. The part he liked best in policework, he said, was speaking on bicycle safety in the schools.

"It's something, this town," Throop said, sliding his hat off. "Months of quiet, and now suddenly two in one night—first the woman, now Carnac!"

"Woman?" Craine said.

"Woman with some kind of funny name, like—April?"

Craine glanced up the stairway. "Dead?" he asked.

"Gone to glory," Throop said. He gave his head a little shake, not smiling now, embarrassed.

"Where'd you find her? What happened?"

"She was sitting in somebody's van, no clothes on. It wasn't in the van that she was killed though. Mud and leaves on her."

Craine breathed softly, his right hand automatically going for the whiskey. "That's all you know?"

"That's all we know."

Katz was coming down the stairs now. For some reason, Craine kept his mouth shut. Behind them on the street, the ambulance siren started growling.

Over breakfast, at the diner where he always ate, crowded at this hour with working people and thick with cigarette smoke and the smell of fresh coffee, Craine skimmed his paperback, his ears shut tight against the talk all around him. The book spoke of how the pit viper can see waves of light we cannot see, namely infrared, and so lives happily in dark places. Craine didn't necessarily believe what he read; he had his own opinions. But his cheek muscles twitched and he sucked at his teeth, interested. He closed his book and for a long time stared blankly. People spoke to him, asking him things, passing behind him to reach the stools still empty, farther down; he did not hear them. At the window, a bearded, stooped figure stood watching, then fled. Craine did not notice.

"Coffee, Mr. Craine?" asked the woman behind the counter.

He jumped, both hands flying, then glared at her, shaking, covering his embarrassment with anger. "Coffee," he snapped at her, stalling while he thought. "Coffee, yes. Don't I always have coffee?" He glanced at the Scotch in its sack, as if not quite sure.

She wearily shook her head, threw a look at the man to the left of him, and poured.

Craine smiled in sudden panic and gave his neighbor a wink. He was himself again, he thought; hard as iron; no ambitions, no regrets. He watched the sway of the woman's seat as she moved away again, then, catching himself, frowned. It seemed to him now, though perhaps it was in his mind (he was certain of what he saw, yet it was queerly like a dream and he was assailed by doubt), that the shabby man on the stool to the left of him—a miner perhaps, bearded, uncombed, with milky blue eyes—leaned close to him and whispered, spraying toast from his lips, " 'Shall the body be raised from the dead?' That's what Our Savior asked the Pharisees and Sadducees. Some said one thing and some said another—the texts were indefinite, there were conflicting traditions. Said Our Savior, 'You are quite mistaken!' "

Craine looked at the man, almost certain it was the same one who'd come to him last night with the pamphlet. The man stared back mildly, his narrow lips trembling with emotion. Craine drank the coffee down scalding hot and called to the waitress for another. "I didn't sleep much," he explained to the bearded man beside him. "As a Christian, I'm sure you'll understand my predicament. I can't seem to wake myself up." Craine laughed, slightly spitting.

Another man, the man on his right, asked furtively, "You hear about the murder, Craine?" He glanced around, making sure no one had heard him.

"I can't answer that," Craine said, "don't crowd me!" Then he whispered, "He's right here in this room!"

"Really?" the man asked, stiffening.

"Shit, how do *I* know?" Craine snapped, strangely angry. He remembered his dream of preaching, those golden curls. "What the hell do you people expect of me?" he whispered.

The man on the right, then the man on the left, drew back a little. With both hands, trembling, Craine raised his coffee cup and drank.

BOOK TWO

Editor's Note

Hereafter, the narrative loops. In several variants, the first line of what follows is the first line of the book. There is a definite break between the capture of Elaine Glass—with its assault on Emmit Royce—and the unit thereafter where Craine first talks with the girl. The chairman of the English department, Professor Davies—an early name for Detective Inspector McClaren—seems, to this reader at least, constructed in haste. But a novel so concerned with time and perceived causality can incorporate a glitch or two in its program; the elements here introduced are, clearly, part of the plot.

One

Craine's work was a bore. His associates were bores, his clients were bores, the people he spied on were pitiful bores whose secrets, when he finally nosed them out, were boring beyond all description. "If I were you, Craine," some observer might have said to him, perceiving Craine to be too old, too decrepit, for the kind of work he did—and discerning, behind that whiskey-fog, a mind still keen enough for nobler occupation—"If I were you, Craine, I'd seek employment more suitable." "Good point," Craine would have snapped. He had knots in his shoestrings. His fingers shook so badly, till noon or so, that he had to use two hands to elevate his glass. (He'd been an all-day drinker for fifteen years.) Often when he visited old friends in Chicago, former business associates, he was mistaken for a bum. He had wrinkled clothes, dim, bloodshot eyes behind thick, tinted glasses, and in his facial cracks, drab gray whiskers.

"But what would you have me become?" Craine would have added, drawing his pipe out and speaking acidly from the side of his mouth. "A master criminal? A philosopher?" And he'd have laughed, nasty, like a man always one step ahead of you, and he'd have pushed the pipe back in and splashed himself more Scotch.

He was right, of course. We've slipped past the age of exciting adventure, no question about it, though the fact may fill young people's hearts with dismay and drive fools to malevolent fictions and secret societies. Craine had read about such things. Waiting in his office for the phone to ring—hunched forward at his desk (red skin, sharp bones), shoulder holster dangling from the back of his chair—or waiting for people he was shadowing to come through the doorways, he'd skimmed through innumerable books and magazines. He consumed the written word ferociously, indiffer-

ently, like a library fire. Never reading deeply, never with full attention—one ear always cocked toward the business of the moment—even
when he slept, one ear tipped cautiously toward the ominous potential of
the universe. But he read; he thought things over; he caught on. A puzzle
solver from way back. His trade.

He'd read of West Coast fertility cults—even met a fellow once who
had claimed to be a demon, the one time Craine had made a trip to San
Francisco. Craine had perked up. "Demon?" he'd said, supposing it must
be a slip of the tongue but straining to make out, with his watery eyes,
some oddity in the eyes of the stranger. "In ancient times," his aunt Harriet
had told him solemnly, when Craine was about six, "demons were supposed
to be all around us, even in us. Our Lord once chased a great flock of them
into some pigs and made them run off a cliff." His aunt had been a dabbler
in things antiquarian, going through old bookshops, visiting museums. She'd
placed in his bedroom (it had given him nightmares) a greenish black statue
of the Horus bird. His aunt had been odd in a number of ways. She'd been
a sleepwalker. Sometimes in the middle of the night she would drift down-
stairs and sit in darkness staring out the window.

The San Francisco demon had proved, of course, a disappointment.
Plump-faced boy of twenty-one, slanted eyes, pink sunglasses. Craine had
sighed, half-sneered, and turned away. It was everywhere, of course, that
hunger to get free of the facts, float high above the patched and ragged
earth as the plane he'd been on then—bound for San Francisco—floated
high above the tinkle and pachinko of Nevada. Ah, spirituality! Alpha
waves, Do-in, Silva Mind Control! Better Carnac's tarot, his dowsing for
telluric centers of the ancient gods' power. That was sanity, in a man who'd
had his head smashed. Yet the child in Craine hoped on, of course, like
the rest of poor hopeful humanity; hoped on, scorning hope. Craine
scowled, shook his head, and lit his pipe again, thinking of cancer. Hannah
glanced in, moving past his door, but did not stop. The mail hadn't come
yet; they had nothing to do.

Craine understood how it was with the world. Zeus-cult revivals in
Boston and New York, and here in the old, plain-brained Midwest, secret
organizations of loyal Americans, disloyal Americans, people who hated
Jews, people who hated gasoline, people who hated banks or universities
or churches, women who hated men—the whole tiresome range of deranged
human spirits whose personal and professional disappointments they'd

nursed into cosmic monsters, foul, dark beasts as dreary as any to be seen late at night on the snowy TV of some run-down motel outside, say, Decatur—but monsters that in fact had the power to kill, given their bulk and mindlessness. Mesopotamian bulls, animation by Disney. Malevolence and stupidity huddle all around us, cowering in chrome-furnished bedrooms with their *Playboy* magazines, or gliding down the aisles of the A&P with a vengeful raised consciousness not even the Muzak can disarm. All empty. That was the miserable fact, the fact that remained. Gerald B. Craine would give you his word as a specialist in these matters, a man who'd been studying—or anyway outfoxing—the abnormal psyche for a quarter of a century: there were, at least among particular persons, no cat-women, she-devils, goddesses come back; there were only bores, fools, and lunatics—also some good people, though he could think of none—and there were therefore no openings for your old-time True Adventurer.

That was general knowledge in the world these days, though fools might struggle infernally to deny it, wearing charms, smoking pot, buying lottery tickets. Disillusionment was king, except with morons. It used to be, even here in southern Illinois, that a boy could aspire to be a lion tamer. Now if he was lucky he got a job as attendant for the kiddie-kar rides at the Murdale Plaza; or he saved up his money and rented an office like Craine's, above the Baptist Book Store, with a view of the flower-lined hospital parking lot, sparrows on the window ledge, and got himself a pistol and a ball-point pen and a sign on the cracked, frosted glass of the door, GERALD B. CRAINE DETECTIVE AGENCY.

No business for a person in Craine's condition. His bowels were the least of it.

His agency covered, in theory, the usual: civil and criminal investigating, guarding, patrolling, confidential and undercover, missing persons, industrial, personal injury. . . . He had a large staff, for a town like Carbondale: three, or, counting himself, four. He'd had sixteen people in his Chicago agency, but in a place like Carbondale, sixteen would be an army. When need arose, which it rarely did, he could expand his staff by stepping down the hall to the Hannon Agency, or Curtis, across the street, or by signing on a few university students or calling in various down-and-outs worse off than Craine himself, old business acquaintances—the usual practice, cheap labor. Put 'em in a uniform and prop 'em up in a conspicuous place and, if nothing else, they tended to discourage vandalism. He'd seen many a night when, discounting the police—which it was wise to discount in any case (sitting in the station, hardly answering the phone, watching TV in the cell-block with the prisoners)—the town had been placed in the sole guardian-ship of addicts and flat-out alcoholics. You could walk from the ABC Liquor Store, downtown, to that field with the cinder-block building on it, which the Carbondale Council called its industrial park, and you'd never encounter but two night watchmen with their peepers open—and those two, for all you could tell, dead.

But mostly the four of them were all the Gerald Craine Agency re-quired—himself; his secretary, Hannah Johnson, who occasionally stepped in as a female operative, though she'd never been licensed; his man Tom Meakins; and that pushy, irascible little banty Emmit Royce, ex-Marine, big chin with a dimple in it—a man Craine ought never to have brought down from the city, but it was too late now. Fire Royce and the son of a bitch would shoot you. It was possible. Royce got meaner every year, like an old German shepherd. Forty pushups a day, despite his emphysema. Played with his gun like some hopped-up kid, had it always within reach and, in a joking way, would pull it on people, especially big, tough blacks from the Northeast, the Negro section. He'd do it anywhere—gas station, whorehouse, hardware store, some stinking, grimy public lavatory. "Gotchoo, you bastard!" Royce would cry, eyes glittering with excitement, icy as a dog's eyes, and he'd push the gun tight into the black man's jaw and with his free hand reach into the black man's coat and relieve him of his heat. The black man would roll up his eyes in mock terror, playing, always, playing, though deadly for all that; then both of them would laugh and Royce would toss the gun back, with a fierce, sharp-toothed grin, say-ing, "Watch yourself, that's all, you dumb black bastard!" Royce meant nothing by it, nothing whatsoever, merely keeping his hand in, but eventu-ally someone was going to kill him—if not some irate black then some irate husband—it was a foregone conclusion. Yet time went by and nobody did it—Royce must be pushing forty-five by now—and Craine, when he recalled that it hadn't yet happened, would be surprised, but only slightly. Detectives know better than most people do what incredible stupidity and inconvenience human beings will put up with.

So the work was a bore. They'd called Craine an artist, in his Chicago days, and they were right; that was his problem. He knew all the tricks and had practiced them for years with weary mastery until, bored to drink (he remembered no details), he'd thrown it all away and come down here to Carbondale, to semiretirement, where diligence and thought were unnecessary. "Maybe do some reading," Craine had said. A joke of sorts. He'd been known even then for his insatiable consumption of the word. "Maybe take a course or two. College town," he'd said. But here it was even worse, he'd discovered. Craine himself, though head of the agency, had done more than his share of sitting all night in an old pickup truck inconspicuous as a stump, with a bottle beside him, his pipe in his hand, trying to read by the moonlight through the window and waiting for some housewife—her husband off throwing their money at the ponies—to come sneaking down the back-porch steps and away through the bushes to her cabdriver lover. He'd done more than his share of skimming through old papers at the *Southern Illinoisian* or scrawled official records at the Murphysboro Courthouse, figuring out who was the cunninger liar, his client's enemy, his client's enemy's lawyer, or his client; and more than his share of questioning some poor bastard about people the man knew no more about than he knew about the night of his conception. It had made Craine testy, cranky-philosophical. "I've had it," he said aloud. He got an image of himself, walking bent over, the skirt of his overcoat nearly dragging on the ground. He'd had it, no question. He talked to himself pretty constantly, often about what some would call extraordinary things. "All that can happen in the universe does happen. Primary law of physics. Ha!"

Odd as an ostrich, no question about it—as Detective Inspector McClaren was aware. What a windfall for him: a direct connection between Craine and the latest of the victims! Craine's mind shied back.

They all knew he was harmless. The people of Carbondale were tolerant of oddity, excused him more quickly than he excused himself. If he got seriously drunk in some bar and lashed out at astrologers and witches, quoting Scripture, bewailing the experience of Samson, they said, "Amen, brother," and bought him more whiskey. (People would sometimes tell him later what he'd done.) If he leaped in horror at nothing, they patted him and calmed him. He did no harm, old Craine. Everybody knew it. His checks were good, he'd never been known to womanize, like Royce (Two-heads Carnac was, at times, a flasher). Despite his line of business it was acknowledged on every hand that, except if he were pushed to an extraordinary degree, old Craine would never hurt a fly. They watched him cross the street, teetering like an acrobat, clutching the paper sack in which he carried his Scotch, or they watched him stop abruptly and ask questions of a door, and they smiled and shook their heads. "Poor crazy Craine," they said. (He knew what they said.) They told the story of his shoot-out, twenty years ago now, with the psycho on the Marshall Field roof. He was nothing to worry about, except maybe to Hannah.

She stared daggers whenever he poured Scotch into his glass, and made remarks under her breath. Sometimes, after he'd left the office, she'd get up from her desk and grab her purse and follow him, staying out of sight. Usually Craine was aware of her behind him, spying on him, hounding him. She was big as a courthouse and black as coal, hard for even an old drunkard to miss. He would grin wickedly and make cunning little feints, circling like a fox until he'd lost her, and then—at Sohn's, for instance—he'd watch from behind a clothes rack as she went up to the girl at the register and said, "Honey, you seen Mr. Craine?"

One morning when she was tailing him—he hadn't been aware of it that time, as it happened—some fool had jostled him as he was about to cross the street and he'd slammed down flat on his back. As he'd lain there swearing, slightly dazed among crumpled cigarette packs and gum wrappers, Hannah had run up and set her fat, clay-dark legs like the columns of some squat Ethiopian temple, had reached down her arms as if Craine were her child, huge tears in her eyes—he'd stared in amazement—and she'd said, "Oh Mistah *Craine!*" Later, on his back in his foul gray bed in his foul gray hotel room that looked out on the tracks, Craine had scowled at the window as if in fierce disagreement with it—he couldn't see the tracks, only the gleaming wires leading off toward nowhere—and later still, sitting on the toilet with his pipe in his mouth and his trousers around his shoes, a book in his lap and his glass of Scotch on the linoleum beside him, he'd suddenly looked up from his reading—*Tarzan and the Ant Men*—and snapped his fingers and said, "Bingo!" If he'd meant something by it, he'd forgotten what he meant that same instant.

No doubt of it; his work—or his solitary ways, or his "drinking habit," as Hannah called it—had unhinged him. It worried him a little, but not much. (Did it? He thought about it, frowning. It did not.) Certainly it never made him doubt the morality of the work he did, never made him feel, like Tom Meakins, theologically uneasy.

"It's a shame, this work we do," Meakins had once told him. Or words to that effect. When Craine slid his eyes up from his magazine, Meakins was shaking his big, pink, baggy-eyed baby's head and sadly looking down past his pink and blue suspenders at a surveillance report he'd just now typed—likely some wife who'd been fucking the mailman, and Meakins didn't blame her, or some faithless husband whose better half was snaggle-toothed and stupid. He was a large man, Tom Meakins—red-headed when Craine had first hired him, years ago. Now Meakins was balding, the hair around his ears turning yellowish white. Sweated perpetually; fatter than a mule. It was a wonder Tom Meakins had never had, so far, a heart attack. He was a family man—five daughters, all fatter than he was and two of them prostitutes, not even call girls: Calumet City. Meakins had once mentioned it, speaking louder than he meant to, sitting in the flickering darkness of the Cypress, watching cowboys running and shooting each other on the screen above the bartender's head. He spoke of his daughters' prostitution with sorrow and a touch of distaste but no definite condemnation. They still visited him in fact, every two, three years, dyed blond and painted, wide as church doors, smelling up the world like smoldering incense or a roomful of flowers at a funeral parlor. That easy forgiveness of his daughters was nothing exceptional, for Meakins. If a dog came up and bit him on his own front walk, Meakins would work it out that he'd had it coming. He could be hard when absolutely necessary, of course, capable even of squeezing off a shot if his life depended on it—though there was no way on earth he could work up the cocksure, pure lunatic meanness of that damn fool Royce, heart black as bile, black as cobra's blood, living for the day when his next chance came to kill somebody.

Meakins, poor devil, had no such clarity of purpose. Existed in a condition of sorrowful bafflement, loving father and husband, self-sacrificing heart, a man obsessively aware that there are always two sides. Craine gave him, for the most part, legwork, paperwork; and though his squeamishness was, to Craine, a source of irritation, he made no attempt to reform him. They'd grown old together, "worn out in the service," as Meakins said. From the lugubrious tone (his voice, however, was high, like a boy's), you'd have thought he had in mind some kind of church service. But Craine more or less understood Tom Meakins; had a good deal in common with the man, in fact. Meakins too had been drinking too much since God knew when. His belly and hind end were as soft as Bunny Bread; his huge, rumpled trousers hung limply from his suspenders like some poor woman's wash from a clothesline. On his right hand, his gun hand, he was missing two fingers, and you couldn't help but think, from the looks of him, that he'd lost them by pure carelessness, maybe just misplaced them in the junk on his desk. He was, like Royce, a doomed man. Self-destructive tendency, indifference to disaster.

"Don't fool yourself, Meakins," Craine had said that morning, looking at him over his spectacles, severe, or mock-severe. (Craine himself could hardly have said which—in fact he no longer remembered exactly what he'd said, if anything; he had a tendency, in these reveries, to make things up—but his voice had been, or would have been, intense, as if someone had done him a disservice.) "Society needs us. We redress grievances."

Though it might have been sarcasm and then again might not, Meakins took it simply. He lifted his eyebrows, feeble and inoffensive. "Not often," he said. "At least that's *my* opinion. Mostly, seems to me, we just snoop into other people's business." He turned away, pivoted toward his office like an elderly, fat dancer or a slow-brustling whale, ready to dismiss it. But not Craine, not today.

"That's true *too,*" Craine barked, and his voice went taut as harpoon line, holding him. "But we're professional snoops. Imagine what the world would be like out there if all those crazies did their *own* snooping." Boredom and irritation lured him further, toward rhetoric. High-falutin language was one of his talents, a gift he'd inherited from his grandfather, perhaps. "We're objective, dispassionate. Bring me your suspicions, your free-floating guilt, your grudges, your fears, your dark secret hungers and unmentionable willies; I'll defuse 'em, lay yer ghosts in triplicate, guaranteed! It's a fact, Meakins. To them—" He pointed out angrily at the street. "—to them it's a matter of life or death: revenge, safety after dark, reputation. To us it's statistics. So many credit skips, so many divorces, so many cases of dogs fed glass. We're the pressure valve, Meakins! We dry up their fury to courtroom talk!"

Hannah Johnson was bent forward at her desk, looking in through the door at him, eyes yellow-white against her midnight skin, her halo of steel-wool hair.

"All I meant," Meakins said, staring at Craine's glass.

Craine glanced down suddenly to the writing in reverse, like Arabic or Hebrew, on his desk blotter. "I wonder," he said, "what happens to all that emotion we defuse?"

"Beg your pardon?" said Meakins.

"Nothing," Craine said, and with eyes gone suddenly petulant he shot out a look at the man, more annoyed at the stupidity of his own muttered question than at Meakins' having half overheard it. "Talking to myself."

"Sorry," said Meakins, and tentatively bowed. He moved away toward his own, smaller office, at the far end of the suite.

"Damn right," Craine said, his hand slowly coiling around the whiskey. Something stirred behind him, and he turned his head slowly, glancing—heart racing—past his shoulder.

"Meakins!" he said, and carefully raised his glass.

"Sir?"

It seemed to Craine that there was something odd about the way Meakins stood, as if it were not really Meakins but someone else, an ingenious impostor, master of disguise. He thought, God knew why, of the article he'd read over breakfast that morning, or some other morning, black holes spiralling out through space, grinding up all that came near them, even light, even dreams, Tom Meakins' fourth and middle fingers, and—the opposite of black holes—white holes in space, energy fountains inexplicably spewing out brand-new creation—soybean hamburgers, pyramids for sharpening old razor blades—and between those murderous black holes and strangely fecund white holes, million-mile chasms crazed with time warps, gloomy with intelligence, aclutter with vast, unearthly bodies drifting phlegmatically through patches of antimatter, leavings of some older universe, perhaps, like dark, archaic ships sailing mine-filled seas. He felt a queer trembling coming over him and saw an image of a towering ship, ablaze with lights, all around it blackness.

Meakins stood waiting with his hand on the doorknob, his mouth slightly open, eye bags sagging down his dull, freckled face. If he were not Tom Meakins, father of prostitutes, he would be, perhaps, some god of the rain forests gazing morosely through the veil of illusion, weighty with ruinous knowledge and unlikely to speak.

"Never mind," Craine said at last, and waved him away. Again Meakins bowed, distant, perhaps wounded, and something flashed through Craine's mind—a faintness. When that too passed, Craine's world, though normal, felt odd, endangered, as he felt when alone after dark in some faraway place like Moline, where there were whores on prowl, laughing, circling outward from the darkest streets, dimmed-out rubies, practically invisible; yet he felt, at the same time, back in command: he'd found the thread of conversation again. Detectives were objective, dispassionate. Yes. (He thought of Inspector McClaren and suppressed quick alarm.) Did their work without personal involvement: bored professionals.

"Hired killers do the same," some observer might have told him, gaze moving off toward the corner of the room.

"Good point," Craine muttered, loud enough to hear, then slyly glanced around to see if anyone, anything, was listening.

So Craine's mind ran, half remembering, half dreaming, making up his life out of bits and pieces, some real, some not, as if Gerald Craine were indeed fictitious—Craine almost wholly unaware that he was doing it, sipping his whiskey from time to time, some of the time half asleep. The mail came, Royce just behind it, chewing gum. Hannah slit open the envelopes and skimmed their contents, fat, pink Tom Meakins at her elbow. "What the devil!" she said suddenly. Royce looked over at them, red-eyed and grouchy; he'd been up all night—so he told them all—in pursuit of a young woman who in the end had cried and vomited. Tom Meakins leaned closer to read.

"What you got?" Craine called.

Hannah came over with the letter.

The minute Craine's hand touched the paper the letter was written on, he was filled with a sharp sensation like anguish. He was not yet ready to admit it to himself, and later, when he was ready, he would have forgotten the event. Nevertheless, the letter came up through his fingers like a shock of electricity. If you'd asked him, he could not have told you that he knew who the letter was from; nevertheless, he knew. The first time he'd seen her—a passing glance—he'd registered her face more deeply than he'd registered anything in years. Who knows why? Perhaps Goethe's *Die Wahlverwandtschaften,* some powerful chemical affinity only a poet would risk belief in. Or perhaps, "scanning," as Dr. Tummelty would say, he'd unconsciously locked on to something his consciousness could never have guessed. He'd thought her quite beautiful, as he would again think her, by the time he remembered (an objective observer would have said she was not)—though also he'd thought her dangerous, alien. From that moment on, each time she watched him he'd been dimly aware of it, though his drunkenness confused him. He'd been walking down a corridor, the second time, and, glancing past his shoulder, he'd seen her behind him. She'd been wearing a

poncho, gray and black, and her hair was as black as coal, he'd thought—
mistakenly. She had about her an alarming intensity, as if she were a creature
from a collapsing planet, every pound of her body like a thousand pounds
on earth, though she walked without a sound, light as air. He'd nodded,
embarrassed. She'd nodded back, eyes widening. It had of course not yet
occurred to Craine that she was following him, watching his every move.

In any event, he could now see that his sense of being watched, shadowed as if by spirits, was perhaps no more than this, an eerie combination
of his whiskey-blur and the fact that he was, indeed, being shadowed, if
the letter told the truth. (Why it made him furious he couldn't make out.
He was shaky with rage.) Hannah loomed silent and large beside his
desk—one hand on her hip, the other on his desk top, small-fingered and
elegant as the blue jade hand of some Oriental figure in the *National Geo-
graphic*—watching him read through the letter and waiting for his comment. He was aware of her as he read—faintly, neither pleasantly nor
unpleasantly distracted; fractionally drawn from the immediate to the timeless, from the mortal nuisance of the daily mail to the age-old comfort of
beings with whom one feels at home, more or less unjudged. Hannah had
no doubt been beautiful in her time. Tall, high-domed, queenly, full of confidence in herself. She had even now a sanguine, handsome face, eyes just
noticeably slanted, nose like an Indian's. She had beautiful daughters, handsome sons, all the color of her husband, coffee with cream, none of much
account. T.J. was locked up in Menard Prison. He'd been there six years
and on numerous occasions. If he ever got out, he'd be back within a month.
Prison had become his philosophy of life. It was what he was best at, "a
man's world," as Hannah had once said cheerfully. He knew how to duck
the risks, draw maximum benefit.

Craine's fingers tightened on the edge of the letter; his cheek muscles
tensed. The sender's handwriting was like a pinched, self-pitying female
yawp. He could see her, not at all as he'd dreamed her—big, soft mouth
slightly trembling, murderous wet eyes.

Tom Meakins gazed down at the hospital parking lot, undecided as to
just what expression he should wear. His wife, Margaret, wrote fierce, illit-
erate, and God-filled letters to the *Southern Illinoisian* about Women's Liberation. It led, she claimed, to promiscuity. "Could be," Meakins had said
when Craine had asked him what he thought. As for Royce, he sat in his
chair, big-jawed, big-shouldered, clowning with his gun as usual, waiting

for the coffee in the yellow percolator on the table by Hannah's door, and waiting for Craine to give him his day's assignment. Though it was hot in here—hot and dry, full of hisses and sudden sharp clunks (the office was steam heated)—Royce had his heavy leather jacket on. The front was unzipped and his work shirt was open to show off his iron medallion—some kind of religious medal—and curly, silver hair.

Craine reached over for his Scotch glass, then paused, lowered his eyebrows, and changed his mind, rereading. "In the Yellow Pages you're the only detection agency in Carbondale that advertises male and female operatives," the letter said, "and for this reason I've chosen your organization. I might mention that after personally shadowing your agency's activities for several weeks, I'd like to know just where you keep your alleged female operatives."

Craine sucked at his teeth and glanced up at Hannah.

"Go on," she said. She was interested, pleased with the oddity of the thing, watching him with slightly narrowed eyes.

He read: "Someone is trying to murder me, as they murdered the lady across the street from our house in Evanston. I enclose a clipping that will tell you the story. It was a man, some stranger I never saw before." Something tingled in Craine's mind—déjà vu—but he couldn't get hold of it. "I saw him running away, and he must know this, because he's now here in Carbondale. He's the psychopathic murderer of those women, I have reason to believe. I've seen him, in fact—same jacket, same crew-cut hair. Possibly those murders are intended to obscure the one he's really concerned about—myself. So I desperately need your female operative's help. I say *female* operative because, besides the known superiority of female intelligence, the murderer was a male, and studies have shown that male detectives are sympathetic to male criminals, especially in sex-related crimes. Although I would like to employ a female operative, I know better, however, than to come to your office in person and be sold a bill of goods about how a male operative is what I really need. I know your kind, believe me! Rather than be subjugated to such undignified treatment—all too common in this world (notice how the media have virtually suppressed the very *fact* of these horrible murders!)—I suggest the following. If you agree to my conditions and will not go against my human rights and will issue me a female operative (if in fact you *have* one!), no questions asked, then walk to your window and nod. I'll be watching, though of course you won't see me. If you do *not* agree, please return my check in the enclosed self-addressed envelope. I also enclose a retainer, which I hope is enough." The letter was signed, "Sincerely, E. Glass."

Again Craine looked up, and Hannah placed on the desk before him a newspaper clipping and a cashier's check, drawn by an Elaine Glass on the Carbondale First National Bank, for five hundred dollars. No self-addressed envelope, Hannah said, had been enclosed.

"Jesus' Peter," Craine muttered.

"The check's legitimate," Hannah said. "I talked to Mr. Renfro. Tried to get a description of the woman's brought it, but the teller that sold it to her didn't come in today. Sick with the 'flu." From the way she said *flu*, eyes wide and skeptical, it seemed that she suspected the teller of malingering, or suspected some more wicked, more ancient evil, of which Charles Renfro at the bank had dared not speak. "I got his phone number at home," she said. Craine looked at her blankly. She stood with her head tipped, ready to pick up the receiver on the phone, and the present clicked back.

Craine dramatically waved his pipe and ducked his head, dismissing the suggestion. He was in a calm panic, like the eye of a tornado. He was feeling . . . He winced as if trying to get it clear and ran one wrinkled, leathery hand through his flat, dead, dyed-black hair. Far wearier than usual, he concluded.

"What do you think?" Hannah asked.

Meakins was still looking mournfully out at the parking lot, probably trying to locate those spying eyes. Royce, with his left hand tightly closed on his right wrist, was aiming his pistol at some speck on the gray-green wall. Craine closed his eyes for a moment, sighed, then drew the clipping toward him, sliding it in across the desk blotter, and bent forward to read it. The print was slightly blurry, but even for Craine's weak eyes manageable. The usual tale: old woman living alone opens door to killer; neighbors chatter, say nothing. There was, of course, no mention of Ms. Elaine Glass. He looked at the check again. It told him nothing. Dated three days ago, drearily official. So the urgency was fake. He'd assumed it was, of course. Yet how odd, he thought—how Goddamned tiresomely incompetent—to claim there was someone hunting you like a rabbit and back up the claim with a five-hundred-dollar check, and then, lured on by irrepressible hatred, blow the whole story with this news of having tailed him, this palpitating red neon sign of raw she-wolf rage.

But laugh as he might—though he felt crowded, too, no denying it—the check was real: she was in earnest. What could she be after, except, at very least, to humble him a little? For advertising female operatives, maybe, and hiring only men. Probably worse. It was a lot of money. Here in Little Egypt you could hire a man murdered for forty-five dollars. Craine had read what women had to say about men these days—stories, novels about lecherous uncles, malevolent employers. However ridiculous the thing she held against him—her father, her brother, Uncle Fred in the garage—and whatever her stupidity and incompetence, she might just get lucky and shoot a hole in him. Unless, on the other hand, the rant against males was a clever trick and it was the "female operative" she had some reason to be down on. *She?* he thought, frowning—denying, for an instant, everything he knew. He looked more carefully at the handwriting on the letter. Surely it was a woman's. Black ball-point, fine tip. (A sentimentalist, no extravert; touch of the legalist, maybe mannish as well, otherwise the ink would be blue or green.) Slanted writing, small but loopy, with meticulous little flourishes and oversized caps. (A careful writer, secretive, but an egoist, slyly flashy; capable of acting like a crazy; impulsive.) He got a nightmare image—just a flicker—of huge, pale breasts, filed teeth, a scent of blood. He pushed the letter and the clipping away.

"See anything, Meakins?" he asked without turning, opening his pipe knife and attacking the stone-hard dottle in his pipe.

"Nothing suspicious," Meakins said. "It would be easy to watch us from one of the hospital windows, behind the blinds, or from somewhere down the street, with binoculars."

Craine banged his pipe on the ashtray cork and poked the knife in again, hands meaninglessly shaking. He was dehydrated, as always; so dry that if he spit he'd spit dust. "She's not that smart," he said. "She'd screw it up."

"Fuck 'er," Royce said. "Cash the fucking check and the fuck with 'er."

Craine gave him a look. Royce shrugged.

"It's illogical," Meakins said. Voice like a detective. "Somebody's trying to kill her, so she goes out on the streets and starts tailing somebody. You'd think she'd stay in bed, or maybe under it. It's—" He paused, hunting for the word. "Fishy." He narrowed his eyes, thinking hard.

"That's true, Craine," Hannah said.

Craine rolled his eyes up, clear behind the lids, a gesture that, though overdone, meant, "Lord send us patience." He was unaware that he'd done that act for them many, many times.

"You got it solved then?" Meakins said. He stood waiting, fingers interlocked to hold his belly up.

"Not solved," Craine said. "But you know yourself there's only a few possibilities, case like this." They were all waiting now. Even Royce was watching with the corner of his lip raised in something remotely like interest. There was a time, Craine thought, when he'd have savored that, would have rubbed his hands, metaphorically speaking, and grinned at the wall— the cheaply framed licenses, the framed apparition of himself at twenty-four in his police uniform, eager young man wearing crew cut and dimples; a time he would have gloated and inkled them slyly toward the obvious. But his ability to see to the end of things—his talent, drunk or sober, for catching by logic or a flash of intuition what would be mysterious for days to a lesser private eye—no longer gave Craine pleasure. There are no new stories (he was thinking of Ira Katz), that was the dusty, gray bone of the matter—no startling discoveries to be made about the character of man. Age on age, dead civilization on dead civilization, from now till the witlessly spiralling universe vanished in thin air, there was only plodding labor, dull problem solving, the profession (not even a duty, to Craine) of determining which story it was this time.

He opened his pouch and with a cracked, dry finger began scraping tobacco into the bowl of his pipe. He said—sourly, since they'd come to it themselves if you gave them two, three weeks to think—"We know we're dealing with some woman, or else some peculiar young man, who's a liar—a person who may and then again may not have anything to do with that clipping they sent—whole thing may be a plot—and for that matter may and then again may not be watching for a sign from this window. They don't need to, after all. It's no matter for suspense. I've got the check." He shook his head. "I'm in the business."

Meakins moved nearer, bent forward, and touched Craine's desk with his fingertips. "You think it might be a *man,* Craine?" His eyes were wide, indignant.

"Mere possibility. Anyone can put on a wig and go buy a cashier's check."

"That's true," Hannah said. Her chin drew inward and her eyebrows rose.

Meakins said, snatching up Craine's line of thought, "Maybe it's two people working in cahoots."

"Maybe it's a whole invasion force of intergalactic aliens," Craine said, and leered.

Royce grinned, showing his teeth. Hannah and Meakins were offended.

When Craine said no more—trying to get hold of some thought that had escaped him, had flared and vanished, some alarming recognition—Meakins asked, "So what are we gonna do, Craine? Put Hannah on it?"

Craine considered the question, or pretended to. Something was at work on him, quiet as a shark, down below the floor of his drunkenness—a fearful and attractive, maybe lurid emotion of the sort he'd sometimes felt when he was forced to pass a night in some decaying, gray-balustered old hotel on the river—no, more specific: down in Cairo it was, where he'd done guarding and patrolling at the time of the troubles. He tried to sink deeper into the feeling, get hold of it. The wide Mississippi lay glinting, brown, placid on the surface, no sound but the whippoorwills now, at dusk—day and night inextricable as the water and mud of the marsh from which the gloomy, antique city rose. It was the hour of the wolf, as astrologers say; the hour Gerald Craine had been born in.

The image was strong, as firm in his mind as a photograph; the swollen river—floodtime was approaching—dark leafless trees on the farther bank, the river hurrying, an unspeakable power, greater than a cyclone yet making no more sound in the deepening twilight than a swift-moving snake. He stood waiting, cold sober. He could hear tinkling music; some dive farther in. Black girls in hotpants. Wind briefly touched the hotel like a footstep; a wooden door banged, as if slammed in anger. Then nothing. He looked out across the water. It seemed the earth, not the water, that was moving. He was a grown man; he'd played with death many times, both the slow kind and the quick. Why was he afraid?

Craine drained his glass, carefully set it down, carefully lifted the bottle and splashed in more Scotch.

When he picked up the letter to study it again, one phrase leaped out at him: *the known superiority of female intelligence.* He knew, all at once—as he'd known the first moment he'd glanced at it—what kind of person had written the letter. (Again he saw the river. It was like a code beamed down at him, some foreign mind laboring, terrible and serene, to get through.) And it seemed to him now that he'd known from the beginning what it was that he intended. "What I'm *not* gonna do," he said suddenly, drily, "is nod out that window."

Dreams, illusions—they should've known better than to play with him! He was Lazarus come back from the dead, not amused. If God were in the room—a metaphor, a metaphor—Craine would have shot him between the eyes.

The pipe in his hands came cleanly into focus, the dirt in the cracks of his fingers, the crooked, gray nails. The room was suddenly full of the smell of perked coffee.

"Royce," he said, and sat forward, preparing to get up, "we're going hunting, you and me." He rose from his desk, steadying himself with his left hand, drained the Scotch in the glass and set the glass down harder than he'd meant to. "Meakins, check out this Elaine Glass. If that's really her name, she's probably university, probably a student, undergraduate."

Hannah broke in, "What makes you think—"

"Glass. Jewish. Has to be university." He added quickly, nastily, "Whole thing's too bold for those faculty people, and for a graduate student, too expensive. Undergraduates have daddies." He hurried on, pointing his pipe stems at Meakins. "Also, check out this clipping." He groped for, found, and jimmied himself into his shoulder holster, clumsily, as if he'd never before done it, and shoved in the .357 magnum. Hannah looked alarmed, and no wonder, no wonder; something had gotten into him. Though his hands were shaking badly, he felt unnaturally calm. He glanced at Royce, who was pouring himself coffee. And now back again came the frightening, ungraspable memory. The room flashed white and it seemed to him that blood came out of Royce's mouth. He struggled to think clearly, get control of himself, and immediately everything was perfectly normal, except distant, as if seen through clear, high-quality tinted glass. Meakins was supporting him, looking at him oddly, with his mouth open, but helping him into his old brown suit coat and, after that, into his limp gray overcoat.

Meakins said, "You mean you want us to—"

Craine nodded. "That's what I mean. Exactly."

Hannah, over by the window, cried out suddenly, "Craine, there's somebody watching us!"

Craine turned, in fact jumped, and looked out in pure terror. Despite the weakness of his eyes, he spotted immediately a frail, dwarfish creature with a ratty brown beard and a rounded back, lumpy shoes that toed inward. He was standing in plain view in the parking lot—Craine had seen him before, though he couldn't think where. His hands were crammed down into the pockets of a beltless, uneven trench coat—now one hand came up to touch his beard—and he stood bent forward, looking up as if myopically, like a rabbi, at Craine's window. He had on the back of his head a wide-brimmed gray hat that might have come from an old-time gangster movie. Craine's heart hammered.

Royce, who had sharp eyes, gave a laugh like an explosion. "It's *her,*" he said. "She's put on a Goddamn phony beard."

"You gotta be kidding," Hannah said. She leaned closer to the window and her faced moved toward righteous indignation. "Damn if you ain't right," she said. She looked at Craine.

Craine showed no surprise. The truth clicked in his mind as if he'd known it from the start.

Royce laughed again, harder this time. "Jesus Christ if that don't beat hell!" he said, and slapped his knee. With the coffee cup in one hand, he towed Meakins toward the window with the other. "Lookee that," he said. He doubled up with laughter, balancing the cup, never spilling a drop, so that the whole performance looked fraudulent, ugly. Meakins merely looked, troubled and sorrowful, then glanced at Royce with distaste, then over at Craine, who was watching Royce's antics with the look of a man from a distant planet. Not even Hannah smiled. Royce wound himself down, still pretending it was funny. He was aware by now that his amusement wasn't catching. He went back to his chair, still shaking his head, laughing as if just beginning to get control, balancing the coffee, then sat against the wall, whipped out his pistol, left-handed, and raised it to his temple as if to shoot himself.

Strange, strange man, Craine mused, cold of eye as a surgeon. Somehow it made him think of something he'd read about, a word—in some African language—that meant only itself, no outside referent. *I must remember to think about that,* Craine thought. He knew he would never remember.

At last Craine said, "I'll tell you what I've got in mind, Emmit." He paused, startled by a new idea, an idea that brightened in his mind slowly, tantalizing. He squinted again, unconsciously touching the gun at his armpit. The three of them were watching him as if they believed he'd gone crazier—which he had, he understood.

Falsely casual, smoothing down his dyed-black hair, Craine crossed to the door of the coat closet and took, from the shelf above where the coats hung, a curious black object. He held it up, smiling, for them to see. It was a gift from some friend, some practical joker. He could remember the face, piglike; the name was gone.

What Craine held up for his associates' inspection was a single-piece moustache, beard, and wig. It was a ridiculous, outrageous object, the fur of some animal, perhaps a black bear, and when you put it against your face it scraped like hell's torment, dry as blowing sand. He pulled it on and, with some difficulty, fastened the metal catch on the black elastic strap.

"I'll tell you what I have in mind," he said in an artificial voice, high, almost womanish, turning his head from side to side like a creature on the late late late show. Hannah laughed, uneasy.

Craine put the back of his hand to his mouth, or rather to his fur, remembering the bottle of Scotch on his desk, and after a moment's reflection he went over to it, screwed on the bottlecap, and screwed the bottle down into his overcoat pocket. It passed through the pocket and went on down into the lining and bumped against his leg. He let it be; it would ride.

Royce, still seated, stared at him over the rim of his cup. He said, "What the fuck you doin, Craine?"

Craine smiled behind the false moustache and beard. He pulled on his hat and tipped the brim down.

Royce and Meakins looked at Hannah. She wrinkled her face up, thoughtful. "That poor girl," she said. She picked up the letter from the top of his desk and held it out to him, shaking it a little. "What if it's all true, what she wrote in here? Craine, I don't b'lieve you ought to *do* this."

But Craine's mind was not available for debate. He jerked his head toward the door. Royce pursed his lips, thoughtful, then got up and crossed to it.

Two

This was Craine's plan:

Disguised, but not unrecognizably so—at least not to anyone who'd seen before that miserable slouch, that trailing, mud-spattered, buttonless overcoat—Craine would slink out into the street, by the Baptist Book Store entrance, carrying in his arm an immense black Bible. He couldn't say himself what the Bible was for—he hadn't been to church in forty years, though as a child in the care of his maiden aunt Harriet he'd sung in the Methodist church choir and had been, indeed, more religious than he now remembered—but something would come to him: the Bible would somehow or another prove handy; all master craftsmanship is partly a matter of setting up favorable conditions for fortunate accident. Anyway a ponderous, preacherly Bible suited Craine's present disposition, his fury at this latest crude injury of a world inexcusably unworthy of man's noblest efforts, a flatulent wind in the face of a brave boy's willingness to think hard, take risks. The proverbial camel's back was broken, and the straw that had broken it was the witless duplicity of E. Glass's letter, the TV vulgarity of her five-hundred-dollar check, the bottomless injustice of her wish to do him harm, to say nothing of the wanton irreverence of that damned false beard. ("You want an adventure, Ms. Glass?" said Craine. "You've come to the right wolf's door!") Therefore Craine, dispassionate professional no longer, mere shadow no more, an avenging angel with the fire of Jehovah in his bloodshot, bleary eyes, would step forth with terrible choler onto Main Street, Sodom-gonorrhea—he smiled like a dragon—and Royce would watch as he crossed to the post office, went in, perhaps, came out again, turned right toward the half-abandoned railroad depot with its domes and porches and old-fashioned signs—the only half-dignified signs left in town—CARBONDALE (*O dread sound of doom!* thought Craine—DALE OF CAR-BON, COAL VALLEY, HELL'S PIT!)—Craine would walk along, and as soon as their bearded lady began to follow, Royce would fall in behind, at a distance, and Craine would slink on, singing to himself, muttering to strangers like an old drunken lunatic going on his senseless diurnal rounds—the Ben Franklin Store, the Singer Store, Denham's Tobacco Shop, wherever whim or heaven's sweet influence took him to spread the fear of God, so to speak. When they'd played with her a while, given her a taste of the pleasures of the hunt, Royce and Craine would sandwich the lady and be done with it.

The woman at the counter, someone even prissier than the regular people, stood horribly wincing—at the whiskey stink, presumably, or perhaps at the curious stream of Craine's muttering—but she accepted the money Craine's jittering hand held out to her; and though her soft red mouth opened, she made no objection as Craine drew the Bible from the counter, one covered in gilt and limp white plastic, with the words *Holy Bible* squared off, literally, by gilded lilies—the only large Bible the clerk had in stock. The gilt and white cover had a queer effect on him, as if he'd seen it before, perhaps done all of this before. The Muzak was going, toothless and soulless, not religious music—"unless maybe," Craine muttered, staring gimlet-eyed at the woman behind the counter, "the music fat farting old Satan listens to, sitting buck naked with his feet wide apart on his desk at Hell Incorporated, heh heh." The woman's eyebrows lifted. "God bless you," Craine said, emphatically malicious, profoundly bowing, and with the tip of his pipe he scratched under the beard, revealing that the beard was fake. The woman only stared, horribly wincing, perspiration on her bucked-out upper lip, as Craine backed away, carefully turned left, supporting himself on the flimsy display rack of lumpy religious cards, and made for the door. "Hypocrite! Moron!" Craine snarled past his shoulder. The woman slightly jumped. Craine opened the door—with such difficulty that Royce was on the point of coming forward to assist him with it—and stepped down onto the sidewalk, the whiskey bottle banging against his knee. A cold gust of wind made his face sting.

"Praise the Lord," Craine said loudly, belligerently, reeling; but somehow—indeed, it was a miracle—he did not fall.

He made his way across to the Post Office, went carefully up the steps and inside. To kill time he went to the window, set the Bible on the counter, and asked for postage stamps.

"Is that you, Craine?" the small, lean black man at the window said. He smiled, clean of eye as a scout master. He was an orderly person. His rubber stamps were ranked like lead soldiers on the ink pad. He was a good man as well, Craine cunningly deduced, and a loyal citizen; at any rate, like Craine, like Socrates, he was not among the Wanted.

Craine glanced mysteriously behind him and raised one finger to the fur near where his mouth was.

The man leaned forward, lips pursed as if to kiss him, eyes rolling. "What's happening?" he whispered. He had, it seemed, one small imperfection. The thought of murder, arson, regimental rape was exciting to his soul.

Craine lowered his glasses, winked portentously, and again raised the skinny, crooked finger to his mouth. The man looked past him, blinking rapidly. Except for Craine, the man at the window, and someone in back throwing boulders into a truck, there was no one at all in the post office. Craine paid for the stamps, picked up the Bible, turned carefully—the floor was marble—and made his way back to the door, shakily trying to put the stamps in his wallet, the Bible clamped so tightly under his right elbow that his shoulder stood up sharply, like the shoulder of a hawk. When he pulled at the pitted brass handle on the door—relic of a former, nobler age, an age in which letters still had human significance (comfort for the prisoner, relief for the destitute, perhaps some thundering, heartfelt rebuke for the capricious politician)—it seemed to him at first that the door had somehow gotten locked since he'd come in. But then he pushed, and it swung open so easily, for all its imperatorial height, that if he hadn't been clinging to the handle he would certainly have fallen. He made it down the steps to the sidewalk, started toward the corner, then stopped, turned, and boldly—one might have thought angrily—looked back. The girl in the beard, the thick, round glasses, ducked quickly behind a parked Volkswagen just down from the plate-glass front window of Carter's store. Her reflection stood hunched like a scrawny pheasant, head erect, rear end out, beak tipped. Royce, leaning against an electric pole not ten feet away from her, shook his head and grinned. Light flashed from Royce's hands, and Craine made out that he was paring his nails with a jackknife.

. . .

At the Ben Franklin Store, thick with the smell of ammonia and cheapness and the deafening chatter of unclean birds, Craine set down the Bible, scratched under the beard, and pretended to study brooms. "They don't make 'em like they use to," Craine told the salesgirl.

"I just sell 'em, mister," she said. She was square and blond, large-bosomed, regally bored. When she was old her chin and nose would meet.

A woman with a shopping cart went cautiously past Craine. There was an animal, a huge black-eyed woodchuck, that made a strange clicking noise on the cart's lower shelf. Craine started violently, so that the bottle in the lining of his coat banged hard against his ankle, and again he almost fell; but nothing happened, the cart and woodchuck moved on calmly down the aisle, out of sight behind the remarkable kelly-green pant legs of the woman's slacks, legs like two shocking-green elephant's legs, or two trees wading into a sewage lagoon.

Craine glanced suspiciously at the salesgirl. She stared back at him, straight through him, as if she thought he might be handing out *Watchtowers*. She had a mouth like an infant's. "You, young lady," Craine told the salesgirl, suddenly jerking the pipe from his lips and stabbing the bit in the direction of her face, "you, you scarlet woman, are the sole reason the world's in the miserable condition it's in to*day*." He leaned toward her slightly, a trifle unsteadily, studying her mammoth, fallen breasts. "Cow," he said. "Prick teaser."

"You want me to call the manager?" she said.

Near the front of the store, Elaine Glass was pretending to look at paperback novels. Royce stood right beside her. As Craine was watching her (the store was now moving, steadily, evenly, like a merchant ship, and the identity of the girl in the beard had momentarily slipped Craine's mind), she turned and squinted down the aisle at him, and then, belatedly, jerked away her face and snatched out, quick as a cat, and caught hold of a book.

Behind his false beard, Craine smiled at the salesgirl. "You natives here in Little Egypt," he said thoughtfully, "have a curious way of speaking. You just set your mouth in one position and talk."

Now for the first time the salesgirl looked at him. "How come you got on that false beard?" she said.

"False?" Craine barked. He leaned still nearer, threateningly, and she drew back from the stink. "I keep up with the times, you she-devil, you foul reprobate, you scandalous little crotch!" he snarled. "The *times* are false. Look at these brooms!"

She tried to pretend he'd gone away. She unwrapped a stick of gum. Her eyes flicked up at him. "Mister," she said, "go fuck yerself."

Craine smiled his murderous, yellow-toothed smile, started away from her, then cautiously went back, touching the brim of his hat with two fingers. "I almost forgot the Good Book," he said and pointed, then bowed, smiled timidly, and gathered it in his arms.

At the front door he stood for a long time trying to remember why he'd come. Abruptly he went out onto the sidewalk, turned right, and started walking. He stopped again.

Standing with the whiskey bottle weighing down his coat, his eyebrows arched, eyes screwed small, smells all around him from the hippie soap-and-candle shop, Craine thought suddenly of his aunt Harriet, experiencing for no clear reason, and to his great surprise, a burst of memory. Two sets of images came: first an image of his aunt at her dressing table, carefully putting on rouge, then powdering over it. Her hair was copper-colored, shiny as shellac, tightly finger-waved; her slip was blue, as blue as her prints of Maxfield Parrish—small-breasted, naked girls, blue mountains. She had a long nose. Perhaps she was going to a Bible-study meeting—she was fervidly religious, though she no more spoke of it than she spoke of her rabbit's foot or her aversion to nuns and black cats—or perhaps she was going with her friend Arline, a fellow teacher at the high school, to some lecture. His aunt taught French and Latin. Her room smelled of bath salts, powder, and perfume—artificial lilac, light blue, pink, and ivory-yellow bottles—a scent he had never encountered in connection with a human being since, except once on a younger woman who was nothing like his aunt—a terrible, revolting encounter he had long since blotted out, or virtually blotted out. Her name was Alice; she'd nearly pinned a rape charge on him, though it was she who'd invited him to her prissy little room—town outside Chicago—and she who . . . memory failed him; he'd been drunk. He could remember almost nothing more about Aunt Harriet; nothing but the fact that her eyes were a startling blue, the eyelids and lashes like a rabbit's. He hadn't seen a photograph of his aunt in years and had nothing to jog his memory, but his impression was that, except to the small boy he'd been at the time, she was not pretty. She had yellow-white combs and brushes with pale pink flowers on them, roses. These he remembered with absolute clarity. He had no memory of his parents and did not think of them now, merely studied, for the moment the memory burned, his aunt's expression: pursed lips, narrowed eyes. He saw her face in the mirror, and his own, behind hers, and saw her little jump of alarm as she realized he was there, at the open door. The memory was intense and painful; he was not sure why. No doubt soon after the moment he remembered, some neighbor had come in to look after him while Aunt Harriet went out, perhaps some neighbor he disliked. His aunt's hind end, on the dressing-table bench, was to his child eye, in some inexpressible way, mysterious. Even now, in the memory, the lines of her hind end were as mysterious as some blurred old legend or inexplicable ruin. He'd been looking at that part of her the instant before he met her eyes. "Gerald!" she'd cried, startled, then had blushed at having jumped, and had laughed her feathery little laugh. What charged the memory, needless to say, was not the slightly blurry recollection of his aunt, but his own long-forgotten anguish—love and shame. "I'm sorry, I didn't mean—" he'd said, or something of the sort, and she'd said, smiling eagerly, as if in terrible panic, "Of course not, dear!" and then, in quite a different tone, "Hmm," and she'd studied him narrowly.

Craine shook his head, whether to make the picture clearer or to drive it away he could hardly have said. They had not been close, though she'd made cookies for him—they'd be waiting in the yellow and white cookie crock when he got home, two hours before she did, from school—and whenever they went downtown she'd taken him to tea rooms, where he sat, among blue-haired old ladies and ate cucumber and watercress sandwiches. "Isn't this fun, Gerald?" his aunt would say (she'd been slightly buck-toothed, it came to him now) and her shy, affected-sounding laugh would float lightly above the table. His aunt had had no idea what to do with him, this knee-splitting, sneaker-wrecking legacy from her younger sister. When his grades were bad—and they were always bad, though she knew he wasn't stupid, or so she'd told him—she could only say, "Gerald, what are we to *do* with you, dear?" When he'd quit school and joined the navy she had cried half the night out of guilt and relief. In her letters she implored him to please not do anything dangerous. The letters were full of clippings about people from his high school, usually people he'd never met. "Evelyn Kelley has asked to be remembered to you," she'd write. He could remember no one named Kelley.

The second set of images that came into his mind began with his aunt at the polished mahogany table, staring down as if at her reflection, her hand, white and thin, around her forehead. He couldn't recall what it was that had drained all color from behind the rouge, though he remembered clearly, or perhaps supplied now by some mental trick, the dry lace curtains on the window behind her, the parakeets in their cage, the silver-gray flowers on the wallpaper, the blue china cup. He was older in this memory, eleven or twelve, and this time the charge of the memory was guilt and dread. Whether or not there was any real connection, he remembered she'd fired the maid, because he, little Gerald, had told on her. The maid was sixteen, a girl named Delores, from the orphanage. He could recall her face only dimly. She'd been more than just a maid, more like an all-round hand-maiden. She'd taken him to movies, washed dishes while he dried, and told him—shyly, both of them blushing, avoiding each other's eyes—her erotic dreams. Once unfortunately she'd told him something that had not been a dream, or so she'd claimed. She had a boyfriend named Frank, some years older than she was, a brakeman on the Illinois Central. He'd persuaded her to let him put his thing inside her, because they wanted to be married and it would be wrong if the two of them didn't fit. The revelation had distressed Craine immensely, for some reason, and though he'd known it was a secret, the darkest in the world, he'd told his aunt. He had no idea now how he'd managed to bring it up, though certainly he'd known it was treachery. His aunt, ashen-faced, trembling in her fury and cold as winter, had fired the girl at once. "After all I've done for you!" she'd whispered. She had the tone of an outraged conspirator. "Unspeakable!" she hissed, "unspeakable!" The girl had backed away from her, her close-together eyes welling tears like a child's (Craine had seen it all through the crack in the warped bedroom door.) Her door stood wide open when he looked the next morning—the room where she'd taught him to kiss, one night. A cunning business. She'd told him stories about boys who'd lost girlfriends by not knowing the right way to kiss—"and things like that." She'd taught him in the dark. She'd be embarrassed, she said, to teach someone to kiss with the lights on. What kind of girl did he think she was? He'd gotten stiff as a tree, and when she'd accidentally touched him—touched his trousers, that is—she hadn't realized and had let her hand linger there a moment. She kissed him harder, making her mouth more wet and soft, and then suddenly his aunt was home, calling up the stairs. They'd both of them nearly had heart attacks.

Afterward, Delores would never let him kiss her, always teasing him, sliding her eyes at him, letting out, shyly, the details of what she did, or more often almost did, with Frank. Gerald had stolen a pair of her panties and had hidden them in his bed, between the slats and the mattress. So now, the day after he'd told on her, her door stood open, the room full of dust-specked light, stark and empty as a crypt. And so in this later *now* of Gerald Craine, in the image that had triggered these embarrassing recollections, his aunt sat, drained, at the table; and like the gloomy vaults in the museums where they sometimes went on Saturday or Sunday afternoons, the room was full of serpent coils and wings. "The Babylonians," his aunt had said on one of those excursions, "worshipped wicked, filthy things." "What things?" he'd asked. "You'll learn when you're older," his aunt had said. "Like snakes?" he'd said. "Well—" she'd said, "well, yes. Like snakes." Intuition had leaped in him, and he'd looked at her, cunning. "Horrible dark caves?" She glanced at him, then looked casually over at the guard. "I don't know if the Babylonians had caves or not," she'd said.

For all its galaxy of associations, the image of his aunt at the table flashed only for a moment in Craine's mind, then receded, taking all it had brought with it—sank away to darkness. Its passing, as if it were the passing of his life, left him numb. The world was pink now, as if he were seeing it through a sickly ruby. He felt alarm. Something had gotten into him. It made his stomach convulse, and for an instant he believed he would vomit. But the sidewalk he stared at eased back toward focus—at the edges of his vision small animals scurrying: rats, perhaps, yet not so definite as rats. Whatever they were, they were suddenly gone; the jagged lines of the sidewalk had closed like steel jaws, and his stomach quieted. He remembered, with a start, why he was here. Royce, up the street, was looking at him oddly; and no wonder, no wonder—old Craine planted on the sidewalk like an oak, three fingers on his beard, staring into dazzles of nothing like an old-time prophet out too long in the sun. Had he spoken? he wondered, glancing around in embarrassment. He was speaking now. *I'm speaking now,* he was saying.

He snapped his mouth shut and started walking.

. . .

It was in front of the Varsity Theater that Elaine Glass first became definitely aware that Royce was tailing her. It came about because Craine abruptly stopped, struck by a perfectly terrifying thought—a vision, rather—a great electric flash like an explosion of blinding white snow across his mind, a sudden, awful silence as if all the Muzak in the world had been ended by the indifferent flick of some stellular switch. The wide intersection into which Craine had been preparing to lower his left foot was shoetop deep, from curb to curb, in blood. Staggered by the sight, gaunt and trembling, as gray as a terminal cancer case, Craine turned on his heel (carefully, carefully) and started back in the direction from which he'd come, that is, walked straight toward bearded, stooped Elaine Glass. She stopped, open-mouthed, looking horror-stricken, awkwardly bent forward like an upright ant, then quickly pretended to be studying the glassed-in Coming Attractions. She looked to be maybe eighteen or nineteen, twenty at most. (Her type could fool you though.) She had a sickly, sulfur-yellow doughy complexion, hands so long-fingered you'd have thought she could fly with them. So far as you could tell, considering the baggy, shapeless coat, she was skinnier even than Gerald Craine. Royce nearly bumped into her, coming right behind her when she suddenly stopped dead; and when she turned toward the theater posters, Royce also turned and brazenly pretended he too was interested in the Coming Attractions. She seemed not to know him. If she'd been spying on the agency, as she'd claimed, she was a very bad spy. Craine looked, full of apprehension, above their heads.

It was a theater from the thirties. Over the marquee and on the walls around the entrance there were comets, stars, planets, also large Egyptian-looking symbols, probably meaningless. Great, mindless red lines flowed out from a tombstonelike central wedge, then plunged toward the sidewalk like the copper-wire groundings of a lightning rod. The girl was clearly frightened—though not, like Craine, of the theater's strange symbols. She could think of no escape, merely stood there, bent toward the picture of a man who held a rifle with a telescopic sight and a woman in a partly torn-away red gown, her hands covering her breasts. Craine walked by, quiet as the moon, watching like a man in grave peril, listening behind him without turning his head. As if absentmindedly, but making it obvious, Royce slowly drew out his pistol enough to expose the barrel. Then, as if encouraged, he drew it all the way out from the left-side pocket of his scruffy leather jacket and shifted it to the right. Elaine Glass, adjusting her beard, froze, then turned her head, mouth gaping, and stared at him, then swiftly turned back to look at Craine. The lenses of her glasses, especially the right one, were extremely thick. Royce smiled. His silver tooth was like stainless steel.

Craine shuddered, unthinkingly checked to see that his gun was still there and his headpiece straight, then hurried on.

Earl Denham, standing at the door of his tobacco shop, said, "Morning, Craine." Craine paused and turned, touching the black beard and looking up at the man from the shadow of his hat. Denham was a large man of English stock, a tasteful moustache, a Yorkshire vest. Inside his store, full of tobaccos and teas, it was the nineteenth century. Except for an occasional whimsical pipe, he sold no novelties, no gewgaws, no trifles, but a customer could get from him curlicued signs like the one hanging over his cash register: DUE AND REGULAR CONDUCT.

"Good morning," Craine said. He shifted the Bible around in front of him, to hold it in both arms.

"I see you've got the Word this morning," Denham said, and grinned. He fit the pipe back in between his gold-framed teeth.

"So I have," Craine said thoughtfully, as if with perfect seriousness, and decided, on sudden inspiration, to go in. He gave Royce the signal for the sandwich.

The capture went, an observer might have said, as smoothly as a person in Craine's condition could reasonably expect. He stood at the antique, greenish glass counter looking down at the pipes, both hands and elbows still closed on the Bible. Denham went around behind the counter, the soul of dignity and duty, thoughtfully smoking, bent forward just slightly in the gesture of a storekeeper pleased to be of use, though perhaps, for all that, ill at ease. When his wife came in from the stockroom in back—a small, pretty woman, lightly moustached—Denham said at once, with a careful nobility that made Craine smile, "It's all right, you won't be needed, Margie." She pursed her lips, looked startled, then instantly withdrew. Elaine Glass was at the window, full of panic, staring in. Royce was not in sight.

Craine bent down as if to look more carefully at one of Denham's pipes. "D'you mind if I use your back exit?" he said, and reached up and tipped his hat.

"Do I mind—" Denham said, straightening a little. He was in a momentary quandary. Craine's request—Craine's very existence, in fact—was by no means due and regular. But Denham's habitual good manners resolved the question. "Be my guest," he said. His smile was, under the circumstances, hearty. He seemed, even now, only mildly surprised and, though helpless in the face of this affront to regularity, not alarmed. For all his gentility, for all the comfortable dimness of his shop—the dark glowing wood of pipes and shelves, the civilized smell of Virginia, Turkish, and Latakia, the quiet so deep you could hear Denham's wife humming "You Wore a Tulip" in the stockroom, Denham was not out of touch with the world. He'd seen movies; he read the papers. He perhaps even had, in his shaded, high-gabled house on Springer, a television set.

There was still no sign of Royce. Craine made his way to the door of the back room, looked past his shoulder one more time, then stepped through into the gloom of carefully stacked boxes, tobacco canisters, shelves of tea. Mrs. Denham was nowhere to be seen, at first; but when he'd gotten further in, he saw that she stood over by the workbench, under the hanging light, wielding tin snips. Neatly stacked around her on the floor she had wired-up parcels, their latest shipment. "Can I help you?" she said. Her eyebrows lifted. Craine silently raised his finger to his mouth and she pursed her lips, puffed her cheeks out, and said no more. He lurched awkwardly between the floor-to-ceiling storage shelves that darkened the right-hand side of the room—blocks of shadow in which stood faintly glowing tobacco cans—and stumbled around behind the last of the stacks out of sight. A window loomed behind him, high on the wall, and Craine had a sharp, unsettling impression that under the window, among carefully stacked cans and packing crates, stood a large black bird. Fighting down fear, he bent to look more closely. It vanished, became a stain on the wall. Craine pursed his lips and tapped the white plastic Bible cover.

When half a minute had passed, the girl in the beard and loose, beltless trench coat came blundering through the door, head craned forward, eyes rolled back to make certain Mr. Denham hadn't seen her. She groped six feet into the room as if blind, then saw Mrs. Denham and gave a yelp. "Excuse me," she said. Mrs. Denham said, "What on *earth!*" and looked over at Craine. "What next!" she said. Now she seemed alarmed. Craine stepped out of hiding, and Elaine Glass, hands flying to her mouth, turned to run out, but there stood Royce, obscenely grinning, his legs far apart and hips thrown forward, the pistol in his right hand, braced on his heavy left forearm.

Mrs. Denham jumped back, lifted willy-nilly off her feet like a puppet, and Elaine Glass screamed and came leaping, more agile than a gibbon, toward Craine, reaching for him wildly, like a woman who runs after a baby carriage, and Craine, before she hit, had a fleeting impression of her beard swinging sideways, her trench coat flaring, her bra-less boobs like two buoys rising slowly, then falling again, first one, then the other when the tide comes rolling in on the California coast. When she hit him, straight on, exactly like a truck for all the slightness of her frame, he had an impression of her mouth as a bottomless chasm smelling thickly of chocolate malt, and then the room fell upward, or rather Craine crashed floorward, slammed down by speed and intransigeant bone, landing so solidly on the bottle in the coat that it was amazing, as he later told Meakins, that he didn't break his ass.

The wind was knocked out of him and her hair was in his face. The muscles of his stomach automatically tightened, locked around his belly and chest like a cramp, and however he might labor, eyes bulging, fingers clawing, feet jerking, he could suck in no air. From all around him, as it seemed to Craine, came the shrieks of the girl and a clatter of falling boxes and some secondary confusion that he gradually identified as the shouts of Mr. and Mrs. Denham. Royce was bending over Elaine Glass, struggling to pick her up off Craine, pulling her toward him as if mounting from behind, his square hands closed around her bosom. She twisted her head around, wild with terror, and screamed still louder. Royce roared back. At last, quite suddenly, Craine got his breath. It rushed in like a stinging wind, a nearly blinding flood of light. Mrs. Denham, lips pursed, held a heavy glass canister of tobacco in both hands, high above her head, and in the doorway Earl Denham stood shaking a mop, bellowing like a bull, with his pipe between his teeth. At each side of Denham stood Hannah Johnson and Tom Meakins, wide-eyed, jittering, banging their knees like a dance team. "No!" Hannah screamed, and her hands flew wildly. "No, Craine!"

Incredibly, Craine had his pistol out and was pointing it at Royce's head.

He could not remember, later, getting back to the office. He remembered standing there, heart beating wildly, in the Denhams' store, then sitting, at Mrs. Denham's insistence—she came to him with a chair, telling him, "Sit down now, just sit down, Mr. Craine"—and Meakins taking over, face patchy red, loose skin trembling, more upset than Craine had ever seen him before, an anguished mother, woebegone fat widow, and Royce meek as a lamb in the corner, like a middle-class citizen arrested for indecent exposure—a terrible momentary ruin of himself, humanity stripped naked of its jokes. —All this, of course, Craine thought only later. At the time he thought nothing, merely sat patting himself, one pocket, then another, like a lunatic seeing if he was there. Hannah ran in, ran out, ran in, talking with the Denhams, with Royce, with the girl. "You just cry, honey. Do you good. I be with you in a minute."

Then, somehow, they were back at the agency, and Craine had his overcoat and suit coat off. Like a man with a concussion, he kept looking around, trying to find the Bible.

"Craine," Hannah said, "I'm 'onna tell you somethin. You're lucky as hell and don't forget it!" She seated him at his desk and poured whiskey in his glass. She was so angry she was wheezing and blowing; he'd never seen her so angry. She was sweating, sour as a raccoon. "Crazy Royce, he don't know you was fixing to shoot him dead, least he don't know for sure, since he's all the time clowning with that pistol of his, so maybe you was too. That's *one* reason you lucky." She struck the air with a raised index finger, like a great black female judge.

He was having trouble with his glass, his hands so wobbly he couldn't lift it. She scrutinized him, heavy lips pursed, then reached over, squinting, put one hand around his two, and helped him bring the whiskey to his mouth. He took a gulp and she helped him set it down again.

"And as far as a outsider would be able to say, it's the girl was in the wrong, what with the beard and all. That's reason number *two.*" She struck the air with two fingers. She could see, he knew, that he was hoping she'd help him again, but she drew back her hand, with a blistering look, closed the hand to a plump, tight first, and buttressed her hip with it. She tilted her head, chin lifted. In the next room Meakins was talking softly to the girl. Royce wasn't there. "Get outta here," Hannah had said when she'd finally gotten to Royce. "Emmit, go take a vacation." The sun was overhead now, no shadows in the parking lot. "And reason number *three* is"—she shook three fingers—"the Denhams never called the police, thanks to me and Tom Meakins."

Three

The experience was not an unusual one for Craine; detectives develop a kind of sense. He opened his eyes slowly, squinting at the gray metal dashboard for an instant before he rolled his eyes left, toward daylight and the sidewalk opposite, and saw her. She saw him the same second, and it was as if someone had struck her on the head from behind. She stood spraddle-legged, face thrown forward, mouth open, immobilized by panic—or so it seemed to Craine—too terrified to scream. Behind her, on the shaggy lawn bright with autumn leaves and long-shadowed sunlight, three students, two boys and a girl, were throwing a Day-Glo orange Frisbee. Craine winced, though he was hardly hung over at all this morning. He had an odd sensation in his ears, as if his mind were uncrinkling; otherwise he was fine. Carefully, he opened his eyes again. The day was clear and plain, not a hint of a shadow or apparition. Half a block away a small group of students in jeans and long hair moved, talking and laughing, toward the campus. Farther away other groups drifted in the same direction. It was eight, perhaps nine, o'clock. Craine had no time for a glance at his watch.

Hurriedly he rolled down the window and leaned his head out. The weather surprised him, gone suddenly warm. It would bring rain. "Everything all right, Miss Glass?" he called. He heard an unintended hint of nastiness in his tone. With a touch of surprise, as if he hadn't listened to his own voice in years, he recognized the tone as habitual. The girl said nothing, staring as she'd have stared at a scorpion. He called again, more gently, he hoped, though he too was in a panic, one hand fumbling for the whiskey in the seat to the right of him, making sure the bottle was still upside up. "Everything all right?"

She bobbed her head up and down, turned to crane her head in the direction of the university as if for rescue, then jerked it back, looking at him again.

"Off to class?" he called. He got his pipe out, fumblingly, stuck it between his teeth and patted his pockets for matches. Partly the pipe was meant to put her at ease; partly he needed it because at the notch of his collarbone his heartbeat was a white-hot pain. He had no idea what Hannah and Meakins had told her. He was betting they'd put the whole burden on Ms. Glass, protecting the agency; betting they'd telephoned her parents and made them squirm. Again she was bobbing her head, this time with a panicky smile. Her long-fingered hands were moving, beside the pockets of her coat. It was camel's hair. She had knee socks—heavy, like a soccer player's—and shoes like a Puritan's, with large, square buckles. On her head she had a navy blue beret. He understood more now, seeing her dressed in her normal attire. Her mother was pretty, probably dyed her hair slightly red, probably had gold tiles leading down the hallway to the bathroom. Her father was timid and intellectual, tendency to snap. Not a handsome man. She took after her father. Craine called out, "You forgot your books."

"I have to get breakfast first," she called back, then looked frightened again, knowing what was coming.

"Hop in then. I'll treat you." Craine grinned.

It seemed certain she would flee, but after a moment's hesitation—to Craine's mild astonishment—she looked left and right, head thrown forward myopically, checking for traffic, then came hurrying across the street and, watching him to see that he didn't run over her, edged around the front of the truck. He leaned over, reaching past the whiskey, and pushed open the door. She poked her head in, wide-eyed. Her mouth was large and full and as plain as a bagel.

"You don't know what it's like," she said—speaking in a burst above the restaurant noise, shoveling her egg in, chewing with her mouth open, sometimes jerking back from her plate, stopping suddenly, eyebrows jerking upward, eyes slightly bulging, her long hand poking at her breakfast with her fork as if she thought for a moment she'd discovered a hair in it—possibly a spider—but finding nothing and popping the bite into her mouth, chewing again very carefully with her mouth open, eyes cast over toward the corner of the restaurant as if analyzing the texture of the egg for the hair she'd missed. "Boy! You don't know! They come driving from Chicago—my parents never fly—my mother loves flying but my father's scared shitless, so everywhere they go they take the car or the train. So they come driving from Chicago and we all go to the Gardens, it's the only restaurant in *Gourmet* magazine—they do everything in style, if you know what I mean, and they *tell* you about it—you know what I mean?"

Craine nodded, carefully spreading jelly on his toast. The restaurant was crowded—students, telephone men, bakery-truck drivers with yellow writing on their coats. Craine had to lean in to hear. The brick and glass walls sent back a primal roar, the deep pythonic rumble of silverware and talk, and in the kitchen and at the pass-through, plates slammed, bacon hissed, busboys and waitresses cried out sharply to the two black cooks.

"It makes me naushus when we eat in fancy restaurants," Elaine said. "When I was little I used to throw up. Sometimes I still do. You know what I mean?"

"It's all right," Craine said, trying to calm her.

"All right? Are you crazy?"

At first he misheard her in all the noise, but then he got it. "I mean you don't need to be nervous. It's all right." He had his whiskey in the booth seat beside him. He'd decided it was better not to leave it in the truck. He resisted the temptation now to pour himself a shot, concentrating instead on finishing off his toast. He was not a big breakfast man. Even the toast went down heavy as remorse.

Tentatively the girl poked hashbrowns into her mouth. "So we sit there with these fountains all around us, the place is practically dark, and these waiters in black standing over us like buzzards, listening to every word we say but not showing it, faces just like wax, you know?—and every time my mother gets a cigarette out, or my father—they both smoke like maniacs, trying to kill themselves, it's the truth, they really are—there's the waiter's silver lighter."

Fork upside down, she trapped the last of the hashbrowns and raised them to her mouth. Her eyes were large now, and not only because of the magnification of her lenses.

" 'Elaine, we just don't understand,' my mother says. As if right from the beginning it was all in my head. It was *their* idea I should hire a detective. 'We're not so poor we can't afford a little safety,' says my mother. 'To your father and I there is nothing in this world more important than your welfare.' She calls up Uncle Phil, he's not really my uncle, he's a lawyer, she thinks he knows everything. He's a member of my father's camera club and sometimes he and his wife and my mother and father play bridge. He asks around, these people he knows there, detectives or something, and he tells my mother, 'There's a man down in Carbondale named Gerald Craine. I'm told he's the best.' I was suspicious right away. I mean, people talk, and you're sort of a local character, you know what I mean? But what am I supposed to do? Who am I gonna ask? You don't know how hard it is for a person to make friends in a place like this. The people in my classes, well—I'm Jewish, for one thing. It gives you an unfair intellectual advantage, and they hate you, it's a well-known fact. They hardly even look at you, the kids in my classes, and if you raise your hand and answer a question they look disgusted. I do it anyway, because you have to get an education or you're a victim all your life, especially if you're a woman." She looked down, frowning as if she'd glimpsed the image leaping up in Craine's mind, not that she possibly could, he supposed—an image of Elaine Glass sullenly leaving the classroom, notebook and textbooks clamped to her chest, head thrown forward, chin lifted, eyes lowered, avoiding whatever looks her classmates gave her, whether mocking, friendly, or utterly oblivious, poor sad alien child darkly wrapped to the eyes in defensive righteousness. She wrung her hands. "I forgot what I was saying," she said.

He closed his fingers around the bottle but again changed his mind. "You were suspicious when your family's friend suggested me," he prompted. He tried to catch their waitress's eye to ask for coffee. She saw him but coolly looked away.

Elaine Glass nodded, less embarrassed now. "Right. That's right. So I went and got the cashier's check—" She glanced up at him. "It's not true that I spied on your agency for weeks, but it is true that after I'd mailed you the check—"

Craine smiled, touched by her earnestness. "I know. It's all right. Go on."

She nodded her head up and down like an eager student, running her fork around and around the plate though there was nothing left but grease and maybe two bits of egg the size of rice gains. "I was scared, that's all. I was afraid you'd—I don't know. You hear stories, especially a woman living all alone the way I do." She said *woman* as if she'd learned to call herself that only recently.

"So anyway," Craine said, helping her again, "Hannah called your parents and they came down."

She nodded again, guilty. "And they took me to the Gardens, like it was my birthday or something. 'Your father is very concerned about you,' my mother says. There he sits, cutting his meat in little pieces—he has trouble with his teeth—and every r.ow and then he takes a peek at his watch. He has to get back, can't even wait till morning. Big contract in the works. My mother's gonna have to drive so he can sleep; they have the Cadillac. But he's very concerned, right? Right." Quickly she forced herself to soften the tone, but only for a moment, her anger too much for her. "I don't know, maybe he is. Anyway this is *her* business, not his. The woman is the homemaker, husband's supposed to take care of the prayers and credit cards. 'Your father is very very concerned, Elaine. Look at him, he hasn't been able to eat since he heard.' He's been eyeing my wine all night just in case I don't drink it all. All the waiters stand around listening, and the people at the tables around us keep glancing over, you know, annoyed at us. They all have blue eyes. It really makes me physically ill. 'Listen, Elaine,' my mother says—she puts on this expression, making sure I won't shriek at her—'your father and I believe you should find yourself a good analyst down here, someone you can see on a more regular basis. Maybe Dr. Metzger can recommend someone.' He's my shrink at home. 'It's a university,' says my mother. 'They must have good analysts. Are there Jews on the faculty?' I want to scream, I'm so embarrassed. 'Ma,' I want to say, 'I'm not crazy.' What I really want to do is get *out* of there, make them bring me home. Home to Evanston, I mean, the place where we lived before we moved, the place I told you about, where I saw—" She broke off abruptly and glanced at Craine, then away, nervously running her tongue around her lips.

"The place where you witnessed the murder?" Craine asked.

She nodded, swallowing. "Not the murder itself, actually. But I did see the murderer running away. He had on these satiny blue and white gym clothes, and short, brown hair, a sort of crew cut. The way he jumped the hedge, he was like a hurdler."

Her hand was trembling. Craine studied it, then glanced at his own, trembling too, presumably not for the same reason. He got out his pipe and tobacco. "You told the police that?"

"I phoned in an anonymous tip. I was afraid, you know what I mean?"

"You did the right thing. It's all right." He patted his pockets for matches. "You saw his face?"

She shook her head, looking down.

"But the person you see following you now is the same one, that much you're sure of."

Elaine Glass nodded, but hesitantly. Perhaps only now had she begun to have doubts. When she raised her head there were tears in her eyes. Craine started, thought of touching her hand, then thought better of it. The waitress came hurrying toward their booth, carrying a tray, and he raised his hand, beckoning, but she ignored him. He was secretly glad. He found his matches, struck one, lit his pipe, and took a puff or two. Casually he drew his bottle from the paper sack on the seat beside him and poured two, three fingers of it into his emptied water glass. He saluted Elaine—she was looking away, trying to see the clock, or trying to hide from him the fact that her long, agile fingers, quick as bird's wings, were brushing away tears—and taking advantage of her distraction, he drained the glass. Then, gently, giving her no excuse for anger, Craine asked, "You have boyfriends, Elaine?" At once he added, to mislead her, "Someone you could call if—"

"No," she said. Again her eyes filled and she turned away sharply, pawing at the tears with the back of one wrist.

Craine threw a scrutinizing look at her, then poured himself another splash of Scotch. He registered—and hurriedly forgot—the thought that he was drinking too fast. It was a thought too complex to lead to action anyway. He wanted to keep his mind sharp, wanted not to rouse her doubts and fears, but also the curious excitement he was feeling was making him jittery, and if he had to keep consciously remembering not to drink . . .

"Men are not exactly the meaning of every woman's existence," she said. She spoke mainly to the farther wall, the clock. When he said nothing she continued, turning back to him, "Are you aware that before this present civilization, women ruled the world for centuries?"

"I hadn't heard that," Craine said. At last the waitress acknowledged his eye. When she was near enough to hear him, he said, "Two coffees." Then, to Elaine, not looking at her directly: "You'll have coffee?"

She shrugged irritably. "I guess." This time she dabbed at her tears openly and sniffed.

"Two coffees?" the waitress said, mainly to Elaine. Craine nodded. The waitress hesitated a moment longer, then left.

"It's true," Elaine said. She took a breath, getting control of herself. "When Caesar fought in Gaul, most of the generals who fought against him were women. Society was matriarchal. You know what I mean? For thousands of years it was the Mother Goddess that ruled everything. Look at Stonehenge. It's a circle, right? And those tumps in Ireland and Wales, or wherever." She looked up at him. "You know what tumps are?"

"Not offhand." Craine sipped his Scotch, eyes lowered.

"They're very ancient." Her voice became teacherish. "We studied them in anthropology. They're these man-made hills, they have a door facing east, at least some of them do." She remembered her paper napkin and used that on her tears. She had herself in hand now. She wadded the paper napkin, then changed her mind, smoothed it out, and folded it. "At dawn on the day of the winter solstice," she said, "the sun's first light goes in through the door and down this long shaft and hits a sort of target that's carved in the rock, a sort of spiral, you know what I mean?" With the index finger of her right hand she showed a flow of light into the palm of her left. He was increasingly surprised by the length and quickness of her fingers.

"Hmm," Craine said and nodded, still looking at her hands.

"Other places in the tumps there are these ledges with bones on them, human skeletons. They're burial places. There are spirals there too. Anthropologists think they have something to do with rivers. Eddies rippling out, something like that." With her fingers she made eddies.

"I see," Craine said.

"Personally, I think they're mistaken, they've missed the *whole point.*" She shook her hands indignantly, palms toward her face, then, as if her gesture had startled her, looked at her fingertips.

The waitress came bringing the coffee. Elaine sniffed, then leaned left, talking around the waitress.

"One of the tumps is a model of a huge, you know—" She thought a moment. Her hands shaped an upended bowl. "Womb. Made of different kinds of sand? It's at Salisbury, I think. So that proves it, they were worshippers of the Mother Goddess. The pyramids were probably the same—that's what I think—only geometrical, which means modified by the male principle—the left lobe, things like that. The tumps were much earlier. I think the spirals represented, you know—the female."

Craine nodded, cheeks tensed by his effort to let none of it slip past him, since she was speaking very fast.

"Can I tell you something else?" she asked, clasping her hands. She flashed panic.

Craine hesitated for an instant, put his hand around his glass, then nodded. He remembered his coffee and decided to measure in sugar, then Scotch. She seemed to have forgotten hers completely.

"For some of the tumps, and for the rings—like Stonehenge—they dragged the stones overland for hundreds of miles. According to this one book, by someone named Thom or something, all the stone rings are built to the same measure, which means they were all built by this one civilization, from the Arctic Circle clear down to the Gaza Strip. There was once a ring of stones there called the Giant Bed of Og. It's in the Bible. So their civilization—this one huge civilization—lasted hundreds and hundreds of years, and they must have had practically no wars, you know what I mean? Otherwise they couldn't have done it."

"Interesting," Craine said again. He pushed the sugar across to her. She gave a little jump, as if the sugar bowl might bite, then recognized what it was and hurriedly spooned sugar into her coffee, then poured in cream, talking:

"Hundreds and hundreds of years without war, and then all of a sudden you get the Father God, gods like Zeus and Jehovah—" She glanced suspiciously at the cream.

"I don't know," Craine said.

"What?" she said, startled, jumping as if he'd spit.

He pursed his lips, brazenly filled his whole glass with Scotch. It was strange, all right—not even Craine could deny it—sitting here arguing antiquities with a client, a female client at that, in fact a child, and a slightly crazy one. The unusual midmorning heaviness had come to his eyelids, though it was not yet midmorning, and he was beginning to feel the usual pleasant relaxation of mental faculties. Sounds around him—talk, the clank of dishes, the tractor trailer going by outside the window—were beginning to take on the usual faintly electronic ring. "Slow down, my friend," he told himself, but raised his glass and, in cheerful self-defiance, drank. As if drunkenness had come on him in one sudden chop, his eyes narrowed, his smile became superior and snaky. He was beginning to act. "Maybe your Mother Goddess did her work too well."

"What?" she said.

"Pressure of population. Isn't that what brought on wars?" He saluted with his glass, took a sip, set it down. "I don't know about tumps—that one's slipped by me. But I know about spirals." He moved his hand over to the Scotch-coffee and raised it for a sip, looking over the rim of the cup at her. "You know how it is in the detection business. You try to stay on top of things. You never know what piece of out-of-the-way information will come in handy." He wasn't so drunk as not to know that the lie was ludicrous, but he enjoyed it. "Spiral's pretty often a snake symbol. India, Sumeria—" He glanced away. Sumer? "Coiled snake," he said. "Think about it."

She was looking at her watch, where her eyes had fled from his glass and cup. Her eyebrows rose. No doubt she'd missed her class. But she said, "What do you mean?"

"Snake's a male symbol," Craine explained, as superior in his knowledge as the girl had been, earlier. "Probably as much the way he moves as his shape." He leaned toward her. "But coiled, he makes a circle. That's a female symbol. And then there's the matter of the light ray that penetrates the shaft—the shaft in the tump."

Her eyes widened more. "Are you crazy?" she said.

"What's so crazy?" he said. He rolled his palms out, Jewish. "You think female can exist without male?"

"Jesus," she said, looking at her watch again. "I've missed my class."

"I'm sorry," Craine said, flustered. He drained his cup, then looked around for the waitress to get the check.

Elaine was staring at him, her face—her whole head—grown smaller. "How come you know all this?"

"I had an aunt," he said. He raised his hand to catch the waitress's attention. "Also I read books. I'll tell you something else about spirals—" The waitress chose to see him and nodded, queenly. "The universe is a spiral. The ancient Indians knew it."

"It's not!" she said, indignant. "What do you mean? How come?"

He knew for sure now how Elaine was in class. He could see her in third grade, nodding eagerly, shooting her hand up, flashing her furious, black-eyed glances at fools who thought six threes were twelve.

"Shoot a beam of light from anywhere," Craine said, "it will curve around with space and come back to where it started—right?" She nodded, but guardedly. He jerked forward. "Wrong! Because the universe is expanding!"

"Hey!" she said. He saw her making speed-of-light connections: sex, funeral tumps, sperm-light, Stonehenge as observatory, the spiralling universe. "Hey!" she said, half out of her seat.

Craine laughed—in fact cackled—and glanced around to see who'd noticed. Ice went up his back and made his neck hair rise. At the cash register, carefully not looking at them, stood a handsome, clean-shaven, sullen young man in a satiny blue and white runner's jacket.

"Hannah," he said, bent forward, shielding the telephone mouthpiece with his hand, "get me a trace on this license. Belongs to an old red Volkswagen—college boy, looks like. Maybe graduate assistant, otherwise a sneak; he's got a faculty sticker on his windshield. Get me everything you can on him." He gave her the number.

When she'd read it back, double-checking, she said, "Craine?"

"No time for chitchat, Hannah."

The world had come alive, alive past all denying, this time—exactly as if a cadaver had suddenly opened its eyes, slightly startled, then grinned. He understood, of course, that it was only himself that had come alive; nothing had changed in the smooth, rich blacktop of the parking lot, the car rear ends lined up gleaming across from the window where Craine stood peering out. He understood too that it was what he would call, in another mood, illusion: the girl had switched on his denial-of-death machine—maybe had switched it on days ago; maybe that was why suddenly he was remembering things, his grandfather, Aunt Harriet, his childhood pleasure in prowling after dark. It was not, he sensed, an idea he'd be wise to pursue—such questions as: What was it about her, a girl not much more than a third his age, that had snapped Craine out of whatever he'd been in, headlong dive toward oblivion, withdrawal toward divinity and death. No need to ask; he knew the answers in advance. The twists of the miserable human psyche were his business. Anyway, such sober-minded questions were irrelevant, like the discouraging facts of aerodynamics to a bumblebee. It was stupid, no denying it, this excitement he'd finally quit fighting, allowed to take him over: Tarzan arm-wrestling elephants for Jane. Worse, in fact, if you looked at the thing cold-bloodedly: a sick, maybe dying alcoholic detective living in a town where a mass murderer was loose, the detective in possession of information that might possibly throw light on the murders but taking no time to get word to the police, throwing himself wholeheart-

edly into the fantasy of a half-crazy girl, betting all he had on her . . . Well,
no news. When was the denial-of-death machine not shameless?

"Craine, don't hang up," Hannah said. "Did McClaren get hold of you
yet?"

Elaine Glass was coming from the cash register now, where she'd collected his change. She looked no less flustered, no less panic-stricken, than
when he'd given her the check and the money, telling her he had to go,
call of nature. "Mr. Craine!" she'd cried out; but he'd had no time to take
pity on her; had to see where that kind in the runner's jacket went, what
car he drove, if any. Now Elaine was looking to left and right, perhaps
afraid Craine had skipped out on her. He said into the mouthpiece, speaking
more quickly now, turning his back to Elaine, "Put Meakins on it, Hannah.
I wanna know how many times a day that boy pisses."

"Did you hear what I said, Craine?" Hannah asked. "McClaren's been
burning up the telephone. He says to tell you it's urgent."

"Of course I heard you."

There was a brief hesitation. "You drunk again, Craine?"

"Not *me,* sister!" He grinned. On reflection he saw that he was, yes,
drearily drunk again already, but sober enough to be annoyed by it—he
could be downright furious, if he let himself—and annoyed by his own
theatrics. "Tell you when I get in," he said. "Any word on Carnac?"

"He's come to," Hannah said. "McClaren mentioned it."

"Does he know who beat him up?"

"He says St. Cyril."

"Jesus." Craine slightly turned, peeking past his shoulder, making sure
Elaine Glass was still there.

"You know the man?" Hannah asked.

"Died a long time ago," Craine said, brusque. "Martyred some Egyptian
witch, if I'm not mistaken—alchemist, mathematician; I forget."

"You think it means anything?"

"Not likely. Listen, why don't you see if you can talk to him. Maybe
with you—"

"You think we should get involved, Craine? McClaren said—"

"We *are* involved, or anyway I am. They dumped him on my door-
step."

"*Dumped* him?"

"Tell you about it later," he said. Then: "Hannah?" He glanced in

Elaine's direction. She'd seen him now and was coming toward the phone booth, her face slightly puzzled, maybe hurt. "Hannah," Craine said, "what happened to that Bible I had? White one—you know the one I mean?" As he spoke of the Bible a kind of tingle went through him, premonition of the terrible white flash. DT's, yes, he knew that; but what did it mean? A sober man—a doctor, an analyst—could explain the thing till hell froze over. Thanatos-fixated; unresolved conflict of blood in the toilet bowl and his aunt's sweet face singing hymns. Yes, true, all true. Nevertheless, maybe he was onto something—that was how it felt—one foot in an alien universe, territory of devils, old, sleeping gods.

When his mind came back, Hannah was saying, "It's here. I brought it from Denhams'. What you want with it?" He strained to pay attention. He could see her squinting at the phone, perplexed.

" 'Fraid I lost it, that's all. Wanna know how it comes out. Listen." He glanced at Elaine again. Another tingle, premonition, whiff of blood. She stood turned away from him, hands in her coat pockets, waiting. His mind raced, lost, then dug in. "Hannah, see if you can find me a book about tumps."

"Tumps, Craine?"

He spelled it for her.

"Why in the world—"

"Never mind, just see if you can find one. Royce all right this morning?"

"He didn't come in. Craine, what's got *into* you, askin about Royce? Where you phonin from?"

"Tell him to take the day off if he comes in. Tell him I'm raising his salary."

"You *are* drunk. Listen, you see Royce you stay clear of him, hear me?" When he said nothing she insisted, "Craine? You hear me what I'm telling you?"

"Gotta go," he said. Excitement leaped in him—no reason he could think of. "Keep an eye out for sin."

Outside the phone booth, as Elaine Glass turned to him, he said loudly, heartily, "Sorry. I remembered I'd better call my office."

She nodded, breaking in at once with how much everything had cost, how much she'd tipped, how much change she'd been given, as if scared to death she might have gotten something wrong or he might think she'd embezzled; then at last she counted the change out carefully into his hand. "That's good," he said. "That's fine! Take it easy!" He checked automatically to see that he had his pipe, tobacco, whiskey.

When they were seated in the cab of the truck she said, "Funny-looking sky." She hunched forward to look up under the visor.

Craine hunched in the same way, starting up the engine. The clouds were high and fast, the sky a sickly yellow, almost green. "Storm on its way," he said, and nodded. He backed out carefully, both hands on the wheel, shifted, and drove to the exit and out onto the street. He felt the tingle coming, and concentrated. It faded back.

"I hate storms," she said. She was sitting with her shoulders against the plastic of the seat back. She pursed her lips as if thinking deeply. "I'm scared to death of them."

"Oh, no need to worry about storms," he said. The air had gotten still warmer, hot as a cow's breath.

She turned her head sharply to look at him, eyes wide with indignation. "Are you kidding? If a tornado hits your house, that's *it!*"

"It won't," he said. "I've been living here—"

"They say one hit Murphysboro and blew half the town away." She reached out to the dashboard with her right hand as if to brace herself.

"That was years ago," Craine said.

She turned her face forward, still bracing herself, thinking about it. "Jesus," she said, and then: "I feel naushus." Her face was gray.

Ahead of him, the railroad gate went down and he slowed, then, thirty feet back from the gate, eased the brake on. It was odd how carefully her presence made him drive. Normally, give him a whiskey or two and it was every dog and cat for himself. As the switch engine slid into view he said, "Elaine, how many people did you tell about the man in the blue and white runner's clothes?"

Again she turned sharply. "Nobody," she said, then frowned and turned her face forward once more. "I wrote a paper about it in advanced composition. I guess the teacher read it in class."

"You guess?"

"He did, I mean." She nodded. Abruptly, her mouth fell open and she jerked her face around to stare. "You believe me! You saw him! That's why you called your office!"

"I didn't say that," he said. A semi pulled up behind them, brakes hissing.

She wasn't fooled for a moment—no dolt, this girl, he was beginning to see. But then, Gerald Craine was no dolt either, no beginner, he told himself, sitting with a wry smile, watching the switch engine slide back out of sight. He hung weightless an instant, waiting for the tiny electric tingle. He saw he must somehow get his mind much clearer and, with an effort, did so, like an optometrist snapping on a lens that brings the eye chart to focus. "It must be a terrible thing," he said—an ironic drawl—"to live your whole life in a state of wild panic." He didn't need to glance at her to know that the gentle attack had distracted her. "Afraid of tornadoes a month after the season for 'em, afraid of restaurants, afraid of phantoms wearing blue and white clothes any fool can get from Sears if he's got twenty-four dollars. Afraid of detectives, afraid of men . . ." The gate went up. He eased carefully forward, crossed the tracks, and turned left onto University, heading for Church, then Ash. "You ever try living with a man, Elaine?"

When she said nothing he glanced at her and saw that she was angry and alarmed; rightly enough. A thought of the bottle in his pocket came briefly into his mind. "I didn't mean to offend you with that question," he said. "Part of my business is figuring psychological angles, you know what I mean? But you're the client, it's your money. You don't like the way I work—" Still she said nothing, and Craine sucked the insides of his cheeks, thinking fast. "It's a hard thing, working for a client that doesn't trust you—client that thinks you don't respect her human rights." He kept the irony—a mere hint. "I've noticed how you've been. I don't blame you, understand." He glanced over. She was listening. He reached inside his suit coat pocket and drew out his pipe. They were coming up on Ash, and though he drove more slowly than a farmer between fields, he knew he'd never bring her around before she was out of the truck and free of him. Hurried though he was, he fitted his pipe between his teeth and got out matches, then looked at her. The lines of her face were too sharp; another trick of the Scotch. "I can let you off and wait for you, if you like, and then drive you to class."

"I missed class," she said. She looked straight ahead. "I haven't got another one for an hour."

"Well, in that case—"

They'd come to the house. Craine eased over to the curb and parked.

He left the motor running. The girl's lips were pursed, and Craine thought without a trace of intent of kissing her.

She put her hand on the door handle, then said, staring forward, "You say you've noticed how I've been. How have I?"

He lit his pipe, taking his time, then shut off the engine. On the porch of the house where she had her apartment, three students sat talking, looking without interest at the truck.

"Well," Craine said, "talkative. Eager to give no offense." He rolled down the window to let the smoke out. Warmth rushed in. "Desperate, you might say. Scared half to death because you think I'm a crazy old drunk."

She nodded.

"Which I am, of course. Though it seems to me I'm the best hope you've got."

To his surprise, she nodded again, brow furrowed, eyes still gazing straight ahead. He risked closing the fingers of his left hand around the neck of the bottle in his pocket.

"You don't believe he means to kill me," she said.

"No."

"But you believe he exists."

"I'm not sure about that yet." The pipe had gone out and the matchbook was empty. He reached in front of her—she pressed back against the seat—to open the glove compartment and get out more matches.

"You think it's someone who heard that paper of mine."

Craine lit his pipe. "It could be that."

She continued to sit with her hand on the door handle, gazing forward. "Is it really too late for tornadoes?"

"They're not likely, anyway, this time of year. I suppose it's possible."

She considered it, or considered something else. He had no choice but to smoke and wait. Suddenly something flew straight at the windshield then shot up and right. He started, but inwardly. Elaine, he saw, had missed it. He tightened his grip on the matchbook. She said, "Why did you ask me that . . . question about men?"

"Just groping," he said. He blew smoke out the window, masking his alarm. There was that tingle. Something stirred behind him, or perhaps stirred in the truck's side mirror—flash of steel, sudden light—and he froze.

But the street was empty—an old Pontiac down the block, moseying home like an old woman who's been to market; nothing more.

The girl said, "I'm not really as bad as I sounded in that letter. Once a teacher of mine, an older man—"

The flash came, ghostly, too brief to register except as an afterimage. "I don't need to know," Craine said. "It's all right."

"He was married."

"Don't tell me. I shouldn't have asked." He pocketed the matches, put the pipe on the dashboard. Out of the corner of his eye he saw that the girl's hand on the door handle was trembling, all wrinkled and spotted, not a young girl's hand but a palsied old woman's. He turned to look straight at it and it resumed its former shape.

"Look, if there's something I can tell you that will help," she was saying.

"I'm a detective," Craine said. "Just a detective."

She turned her head to look at him, her eyes brimming tears, and then, with sudden violence, she pushed down the door handle and opened the door.

"Wait!" he said, and grabbed her arm. His mind snapped clear. He was as surprised by what he'd done as she was, and said quietly, "I'm sorry."

They sat for an instant like statues, both of them painfully embarrassed. He should let go of her arm, he was thinking. He should check into a mad-house. If an objective observer should see him now . . .

"Mr. Craine, I really have to go," she said.

He nodded. "One more minute." And now, thinking about it, he did let go. She made no move to get out, sat motionless a moment longer, then turned her face away. "Listen," Craine said, "you don't have to be afraid of me. I'm your friend, or anyway I'm trying to be. That's the truth."

She said nothing. He wanted to touch her arm again, fatherly. The softness of it was still in his fingertips. Instead, he put the pipe on the dashboard with his right hand and with his left drew out his whiskey. He unscrewed the cap and took three swallows. She said nothing.

" 'Why do you always have to drink, Mr. Craine?' That's what you're thinking." She slid her eyes in his direction, then away. He put the cap back on. " 'What is it *you're* afraid of?' That's what you'd like to know." He smiled.

"I really do have to go," she said. She shifted a little as if to do so. "I believe you about wanting to be my friend."

"Well, I'll tell you one thing," he said, "it's not death I'm afraid of. I've thought about it, I've watched myself. It's something, all right, but not that."

She nodded, and Craine felt a lunatic urge to ask her what it was, this unholy dread in him. He said, "I've been shot at, I've been in car wrecks—more wrecks than you've had years in your life, Miss Glass. It doesn't faze me—maybe speeds up my pulse, that's all. I could tell you about fear."

She sat miserably listening, head bowed, enduring. Her right hand was still on the door handle. With her left she was bunching up then smoothing then bunching up then smoothing her coat. He couldn't make out, at the moment, what was wrong with her, though he was certain he'd understood a minute ago.

He said, "The first time people were afraid in this world was the minute they killed something and ate it. So they made up bear gods and grain gods and so on . . ." She threw him a look, but he continued. "The second time was the minute somebody killed a human being, or else when somebody made himself king over all the other people, and forced them to do what was good for them, or so he thought. So they made up gods to blame the rules on, that is—" He paused. "They *saw* that there were . . ." He looked at her. "You follow what I'm saying?"

"Mr. Craine," she began.

"The third time's the one I can't figure." He studied the bottle, then thoughtfully uncapped it, preparing to take another swig. "It's the time a man realizes—or a woman, same thing—" He remembered all at once why she was upset: because he'd told her he was just a detective, she could ask no more of him. And even now, now that he'd tried to fix it . . . He was nobody's friend, if he told himself the truth. Her damned Jewish neuroses, her self-absorbed daddy, her stifling mother, her sex-death fantasy of a blue-and-white pursuer—what were they to him? She was right. It was true. Suppose he reached out and took Elaine Glass's hand. Suppose he said, "Don't worry, I'll be watching night and day! I'm your guardian angel!" A terrible weariness came over Craine, a numbness like a sleep of the soul. He looked at her, frowning, not a studied frown, for once—not even knowing he was frowning—and abruptly cleared his throat. Once the case was finished, he'd forget her in a week, or anyway forget how he'd felt for a minute a few minutes ago. *You're on your own, kid,* he thought, *like all of us.* He got an image of his aunt in her casket, primly dead, her head propped too far forward, uncomfortable; it was amazing that she didn't wake up.

Elaine sat sniffling, her ear poking out through the stringy black hair, and it came to him that one of the things he'd thought, a few minutes ago, was that she was prettier than he'd thought in the beginning. Strange, he thought, how vision changes from second to second. So for an instant, it seemed, he'd been in love with her; no doubt an effect of her having spoken of having had an affair with an older man. A man of twenty-six was what she'd meant, no doubt, or maybe thirty, and here was Craine pushing sixty, with a liver of maybe eighty. He looked at the bottle, took the swig he'd been planning, and put the cap back on.

"Never mind," he said, "you're right. You should go in."

"No," she said, "go on."

"Go on?" Craine struggled to remember what he'd been saying.

She was looking at him, waiting. A motorcycle went past them, sound like a vacuum cleaner, two doll-like figures in gold helmets. "Go on with what you were saying, about the third kind of fear."

He struggled to remember what he'd been thinking. At last it came. "The third time is when a man or woman realizes he's—or she's—gotten separated from himself. Or herself. Gotten split off from his feelings."

"And some kind of god takes care of that, too?"

He shook his head. "I don't know yet."

"But it does make them feel afraid."

"I think so. I'm not sure."

Elaine Glass turned away, took off her glasses, wiped her eyes, then wiped her glasses and put them on again. "It's interesting," she said.

Strange girl, he thought: looking even now into his curious idea merely because it *was,* for the moment, an idea. Studying her nose, her slightly protruding eyes, he corrected himself: Strange tribe. Against the day's eerie light her skin was brownish golden, and again, for an instant, he thought her beautiful. She swivelled her knees around, preparing to get out, carefully bracing herself with her left hand on the dashboard.

"Thanks for the ride, Mr. Craine," she said, "and thanks for breakfast."

"My pleasure," he said. He watched her walk with long strides up the sidewalk to the house, up the steps, and into the darkness. Briefly, the students on the porch stopped talking as she passed.

· · ·

Where the snake came from he did not see. The sky flashed white, and the snake was there, a foot across, maybe thirty feet long, greenish-golden. Hatchet head raised, tongue flicking, it moved with the assurance of a familiar visitor up the sidewalk toward the steps. Without thinking, Craine threw down the bottle, pushed open the door on his side, half-jumped, half-fell from the truck, and ran around the front. It was gone—gone inside—and he ran after it, drawing his gun. The hallway was dark as pitch, but even before his eyes adjusted he was aware of a great crowd standing all around him, looking out through doorways, some in beards and black hats, some in babushkas, neither helping nor hindering, mournfully looking on. *Let me be lucky!* he thought, his mind as clear and sharp as broken crystal. It was all very well to lay plans, he thought—his mind had never been clearer in his life—and all very well to count on friends' concern (the tragic crowd of Jews looked on solemnly, without a word)—but in a universe where anything could happen at any moment, where an enormous snake could appear out of nowhere . . . A door stood ahead of him. He crashed through it, stepped into space, and the next instant was banging down head over heels into a darkness more dank and deep than the darkness in the hallway. The stairs seemed endless, slamming now against his head, now his shoulders, now his back, now his knees, now his head—leaden blows without sting, familiar surprises; he'd fallen in this drunken way many times before—and now, with shocking suddenness, he was perfectly still. He realized the gun was no longer in his hand and, with an effort, raised his head. Lights came on; voices came down at him, shouts at first, then mumbles.

When the mumbles became clear and Craine's vision adjusted, Craine was lying on a lumpy couch, Elaine not far from him, Tom Meakins standing next to her, on her right. At the foot of the couch and elsewhere in the room there were other people, college students Craine didn't know.

Meakins came forward. "You awake, Craine? You all right?" His voice was crabby, his face dark red, and stern.

Craine nodded, then ruefully shook his head. "Must've missed the top step," he said. Someone laughed.

"I'd say you missed most of them," Meakins said. "With your feet, anyway. Think you can sit up?"

He made an attempt. Pain shot up his elbows. "What time is it? We gotta get Miss Glass here to her class."

"I'll see to it," Meakins said. He came forward and bent down to pull

Craine up into sitting position. "I'm taking over for you. Hannah's orders. How in hell you manage to get so plastered so early in the morning?"

"It wasn't that," Craine said. "If you'd seen what I—" He thought about it, then nodded. "Must've gotten carried away," he said. He squinted at Elaine, wondering if she knew the extent of his insanity. Her face wouldn't focus, and when he reached up he found that his glasses were missing.

"It's all right, I've got 'em," Meakins said and drew them from his pocket.

Craine continued to pat himself—pants pockets, coat pockets. "You find my gun?" he said.

"Hannah says you're not to have it," Meakins said. "Think you can walk?" Again he reached for Craine's armpits.

"I'm all right," Craine said, testy, though he was glad to have the help. When he was standing he could feel all the places he'd hit, lump on his head—when he touched it he found it was large and broken open—pain in his elbows, back, and legs. The first step he took, his left leg buckled. Meakins caught him. "Sorry," Craine said. He did not sound it.

"Come on, we'll get you home first," Meakins said. He took Craine's left arm. Elaine came around on the other side. "Lean on me," she said. They helped him out onto the porch and down the steps toward Meakins' Chevy.

Craine pulled back. "Can't leave the truck," he said.

Meakins pulled him forward. "The hell you can't."

"Nobody'll bother it, I think," Elaine said. She let go of his arm and stepped ahead to open the car door. In the front seat lay the plastic-covered Bible. Slowly and carefully, favoring his bruised parts, Craine got in. "Tom," he said, "Hannah find anything about tumps?"

Meakins came around to the driver's side before answering. "She says they're not even in the dictionary." He held the door open so Elaine could get in back.

"Anything about—" Craine hesitated—"that license?"

"You're on vacation, Craine," Meakins said. Though his voice was boyish, it was fierce, closing the subject. "Sit back and close your eyes, or read your Bible."

Obediently, Craine closed his eyes.

"Do you hurt a lot, Mr. Craine?" Elaine asked.

"I'll make it."

The car swung out onto the street. Meakins switched on the radio so he wouldn't have to talk. Craine, head back on the seat, opened his eyes just enough to look at him. They were taking over for him, it was plain to see—Meakins and Hannah. No harm, point of fact. No business for a person in Craine's condition. If someone had said to him, "Craine, if I were you I'd seek out employment more suitable," he would have said, "You're right. I will."

Meakins said, "Craine, what made you suddenly run in there like that?"

Craine sighed. Never mind that his brain was a shambles. If they were going to take over they'd have to smarten up. What if the answer he'd had to give, there in front of the girl, was "I thought I saw the murderer." He thought of telling the truth, pretending it was a joke, then at once thought better of it. He closed his eyes. "I had to pee," he said. Then, with his eyes still closed: "Royce all right, after yesterday?"

"I'd stay clear of him, if I was you," Meakins said.

Craine looked at him. Tom Meakins' face was dark again, his mouth firmly set, distressed.

"You've heard from him then?" Craine smiled and let his eyes fall shut. "So he says he's gonna get me."

Meakins was stubbornly silent. They came to Craine's hotel.

"Get some sleep, Craine," Meakins said as Craine climbed out.

Elaine Glass leaned forward in the back seat, eyes wide. "Don't do *that,*" she said, "it's the worst thing you can do! When I was knocked down one time on my bicycle—"

Craine closed the car door, ducked his head to smile and wave at her, climbed the narrow stairs to his room and went to bed.

Four

He slept like a log for hours. Then dreams came. He dreamed he was visiting a House of Horrors with a woman of uncertain identity—sometimes she seemed to be his long-dead aunt Harriet, sometimes for a moment she seemed to be Elaine. At times both his aunt and Elaine took over as narrator of the dream, as if all that was happening was a movie or book. He was excited, reaching up to pay for his ticket, which cost seven cents. He could not make out who was selling the tickets, but the hand that reached down to him was white with age and palsied. All around him, people in black hats or black shawls waited patiently for a small dark green door to open, then went in, three or four at a time. Inside, where they could not turn back, a sign said, PROCEED AT YOUR OWN RISK. They made their way carefully over a long narrow plank, black and slippery with oil, that spanned a pit containing rattlesnakes and people who had fallen. Occasionally people screamed, or a sudden mechanical shriek came, accompanied by the brief illumination of a green, dead face, a descending axe, a huge winged bull that came charging on steel tracks, a striking serpent head four feet wide. The deaths were real—gushing blood, rolling eyes—but most of the visitors moved safely past each horror. Sometimes the woman who was with him would cling to him in terror, but neither of them spoke. He found himself comforting a young man who had died and come to life again. "It was like another world," he said. "It was white with clouds and beautiful trees . . . a beautiful, sunny day." An old woman said, "I know what he means. I've had it too. I was floating in air toward a wide-open door with light all around Jesus. Behind Him was a long staircase with angels lined up the stairs." Someone said—a doctor, perhaps; he was holding a stethoscope to a severed head—"About twenty-one percent of the people I've interviewed have had these experiences. The Florida team had eleven out of fifty, which is very close to my results." They were standing on a sparkling white linoleum floor, all around them a great silent crowd wearing black. From the ceiling above them, and above the many balconies crowded with people, rising ring after ring, came a booming noise. No one seemed to hear it, so carefully were they listening to the doctor. "My reaction was initially one of skepticism," the doctor said, "but now I'm totally convinced that these experiences are real." The booming became louder, and a voice began shouting, "Craine! Craine!"

He jerked his head, awakening, and realized that the booming was coming from his door, and the voice was that of Emmit Royce. He sat up, put his legs over the side, and called, "Just a minute! I hear you!" He started for the door, automatically feeling for his shoulder holster, then stopped, his mind momentarily gone blank. He remembered then that Meakins had taken his gun. He started once more toward where Royce waited for him to open up, then again stopped short, and with an expression of bafflement looked around the room—the glass-knobbed deal dresser, three handles missing; the rumpled bed; the desk, trunk, television, disordered piles of books.

"Craine?" Royce bellowed again.

"Coming. Just getting my pants on," Craine called back. His expression was cunning now, like an animal's, and like an animal—a wolf—he stepped without a sound to the dresser and opened the top drawer. He drew out his second pistol, felt under the socks and underwear for the bullet box, and loaded the gun. He pushed it down into his belt, where if he made a mistake he'd blow his cock off, then quickly stepped back to the bed for his suit coat, pulled it on, and buttoned it. Hurriedly, noisily, he went to the door, turned the night latch, and opened it. Royce stood a little crooked in the hallway, soaked by rain, his right hand clamped around a beer can, a cigarette in his left.

"I thought you was dead for a while there," Royce said. He let out the beginning of a grin, then changed his mind, slightly squinting, and raised the cigarette for a pull.

"Damn near," Craine said. He stepped back from the door, holding it open, and Royce came in.

"Jesus," Royce said. "Stinks in here."

Craine nodded. "Pipe smoke, whiskey, old age."

"Smells more like socks and piss."

"Them too."

Royce stood square in the middle of the room now, where he could see into the bathroom and everywhere else. He stood with his cap on, his fists on his hips, one of them holding the cigarette like a pencil, his black boots solid on the floor as a farmer's. "First thing I'd do," he said, "I'd burn all these books."

"Might set fire to the window shades," Craine said.

Royce tipped up the beer and drained it, his back still to Craine, crumpled the can in his fist—no big deal, though it was meant to be ominous; the can was aluminum—then at last turned around to look at him. He had his shoulder holster on. He looked at Craine for a long time, the way a black would do, over in his own territory, backed up by friends. Craine made no scene about meeting the man's eyes, merely looked out the window at the telephone lines, the gray rain, the day hardly brighter than the gray of the room, then casually went over to the lightswitch and flicked on the bulb.

"You got anything in this hellhole to drink?" Royce said.

Craine smiled. "Emmit, you drink too much."

Royce laughed, a snort, and for an instant his eyes flashed anger. "I got a hundred dollars here says you got Scotch."

"As it happens, I do have a little Scotch whiskey," Craine allowed, still smiling and went over to the dresser, opened the middle drawer, and drew a new bottle out. He held it up against the light, pretending to admire the color, stalling to break down Royce's resolve.

Royce went over to the john to throw his cigarette in the toilet. "You got glasses here somewheres?"

"On the sink," Craine called.

Royce got the glass and started back out into the room, then changed his mind and, without closing the door, stayed to piss. Over the noise he called, *The Building Blocks of the Universe.* You read this shit?"

"Just the pictures," Craine called.

"What?" Royce called back.

"Never mind," Craine said. The sound of Royce's pissing went on and on, then the toilet flushed and Royce came back into the room, lighting another cigarette as he came. That was new, it struck Craine now. Royce hadn't smoked since they'd told him about his emphysema. He came straight toward Craine—it looked as if he'd gotten his anger back—but the thud of the boots was unsure, as if the man were even now of two minds. He held his glass out. Craine put away the first aid box, then uncapped the bottle and filled it. Royce sipped, sloshed the whiskey around in his mouth, and wet his lips, frowning. "Listen, Craine," he said.

Craine inclined his head as if interested, moving past him toward the bed to get the dirty glass standing on the floor there. As he picked it up and filled it, Royce sipped again, pushed his cap back. "You want the chair?" Craine said, and waved his glass in the direction of the only chair he had, the lumpy old platform rocker by the window.

"I'm all right," Royce said.

Craine shrugged, stooped again for the ashtray near where the glass had been, straightened up again—or straightened as much as he ever did—and walked with the whiskey and ashtray to the chair Royce had refused. When he sat down, Royce settled on the windowsill a few feet away from him, gray rain behind him, the sky off-color, the breeze coming in through the window unnaturally warm. "Could turn into tornado weather yet," Craine said.

Royce glanced past his shoulder, annoyed, then looked back at his glass. He seemed to struggle over something—whether to take another sip of whiskey or a puff at his cigarette—then abruptly raised the cigarette to his lips and sucked in hard. His collar was open, flattened by the holster belt, and it came to Craine that what Royce wore on his hairy chest was not a religious medallion but some kind of war trophy, a piece of shrapnel, or what was left of a bullet. He smiled, then noticed Royce's eyes on him.

"What you grinning about?" Royce said.

Craine tipped his head back and pretended to close his eyes, still smiling. "You're a damn good man, Royce. God only knows what I'd do without you."

"Bullshit," Royce said, a small explosion, not loud but fierce.

"You *are* a good man." He opened his eyes again, innocent, and leaned forward.

"That's not what I mean." He launched his hand out at Craine, the cigarette dangling between two fingers. "I was thinking of coming here and blowing your head off. Whattiya think of that?"

Craine made his face incredulous.

"You're a foxy bastard." He shook the outstretched hand in warning.

"Shit only knows what goes on in that fucked-up head of yours. But I've had it. I'm telling you."

Royce was squinting, talking like a killer on TV. Craine made his face not just incredulous but scared, and suddenly Royce lost his nerve, or got confused, drew his hand back and took a gulp from his drink. Behind him, the rain fell harder, the sky had gone darker. "That stunt you pulled yesterday. Shit." He shook his head.

"Yesterday?" Craine said. He patted his pockets to find his pipe and, exaggerating clumsiness, drew it out.

"Jesus *Christ*, Craine!" Royce said. It was almost a wail.

"Oh, that!" Craine said. He sat forward as if alarmed and with the back of the hand that held the pipe momentarily covered his eyes. At last he lowered his hand, eyes closed, and took in a deep, slow breath.

"You know something?" Royce said. When Craine looked at him, guilty, Royce was holding his empty glass out, eyes remote. "I don't believe one fucking word of this. Everything you're doing, I'd bet you a hundred dollars it's a fucking act."

Craine shook his head and, with a start, as if he'd just noticed, reached down for the bottle by his shoes and held it out to fill Royce's glass. "Hard bet to prove either way," he said sadly.

"Lie detector?" Royce said.

Craine shook his head and drew the bottle back. "I'm not a betting man. Matter of principle. But I acted pretty crazy, I won't deny it. Whole thing had me spooked."

Royce drank. "Bullshit," he said when he'd swallowed.

"You think I wasn't spooked?" Now he put on a keen look.

"Whatever you were, count me out from now on. I quit."

"You *quit?*" He got out his tobacco and poked his pipe in to stuff it, hands trembling. He pretended he was thinking, trying to understand it. He was, of course, thinking. He should thank his lucky stars Emmit Royce was quitting, yet here he was fighting it—fighting it, it seemed to him, for Royce's sake. Nobody'd take a man like Royce up in Chicago, and he'd never get an agency moving on his own. Garbage man? Job with the fire department? Yet it wasn't entirely for Royce's sake, of course. It wasn't Royce's fault, what happened yesterday. He felt something near him, crouching, and glanced past his shoulder. Craine lit his pipe and took quick little puffs, then lowered it and raised his hand unsteadily to drink. In a minute he'd be flat on his ass again, yet it seemed to him his mind was quick and clear.

"I'll tell you what you're missing, Royce," he said. He leaned toward him, dead serious. "You think there were three of us yesterday—you, me, the girl. But there were four of us. That's what you're missing."

Royce glanced at him. "Bullshit."

"Call Hannah," he said. "Ask her."

"You crazy bastard! I got a hundred dollars says—"

"Call her," Craine said.

Royce stared at him, then down at the cigarette. "You telling me that murderer she thinks she saw in Chicago—"

"I don't say it was the same man," Craine said carefully. "I'm only saying there was somebody, and he was there again this morning when I took the girl to breakfast, and if you'll just move your ass to that phone and call Hannah—"

Royce thought about it, taking slow drags on the cigarette, then pursed his lips, ground the cigarette out, and looked over at the phone on the desk. "You're trying to make me believe," he said, "that when we put her in the sandwich who you thought I was was—"

Craine said nothing, crazy with glee, heart racing.

At last Royce stood up and went over to the phone. He stared at the dial as if he'd never really looked at one before, then lifted the receiver, jutted out one finger and dialed.

Craine drank while Royce talked, laughing inwardly, like a witch. When Royce was finished he came back and stood in front of Craine with his hands on his hips. "They got him down there now," he said. "Meakins brought him in this afternoon. Havin a little talk with him."

"No foolin," Craine said.

Royce nodded to himself. "Some graduate student, Hannah says. Girl had a class with him."

"Hot dog!" Craine said. "We should get in on it."

Royce was still shaking his head, grinning now. His right hand came up to scratch the hair on his chest. "You foxy old shit," he said. For an instant, his face clouded. "All the same you could've blown my damn head off."

"I know that," Craine said, but he couldn't stop grinning. "You got your car down there?"

Royce nodded, scratching on. "I still don't believe you," he said. "I don't believe one fucking word of it."

Carefully, Craine eased himself up out of the chair, capping the bottle, pushing it down into his suit coat pocket, then poking his pipe into the pocket inside. "It's right of them to bring him in for talk," he said. "We're only human. We make mistakes." He chuckled.

Royce waited at the window, looking out at the gusty storm, dark as night now and gathering more force, while Craine put on his overcoat and, at the last minute, picked up the heavy white Bible from the bed, looked at it a moment, and decided to carry it along.

Royce said, coming over to leave with him, "You taking that with you?"

Craine said, "I take it with me everywhere. For luck. Belonged to a world-famous gambler, you know that?"

"Bullshit," Royce said, "I saw you buy it."

Craine frowned. "That's true," he said. "Well, we all make mistakes. We're only human." He held the door open and Royce went out, just a little unsteady. Craine followed, switching off the light as he went, and closed the door behind them. "You should think about it, Emmit," he said, "—what it means to be human. I remember when I was young, in the navy, I used to stand at the rail of the ship, and I'd look out at the endless, starlit sea—"

Royce glanced at him, missed a step, caught the bannister, and swore under his breath.

On the street, gusts of rainy wind made signs turn and creak. The street lamps went out for a moment, then back on. A car went by hissing, and Craine—mistaking what it was—at first jumped. When they were seated in the car, he said, "We're vulnerable, Emmit." He waved in the general direction of the buildings, the darkened sky. "Everything's vulnerable." He noticed that the edges of the pages of the Bible were wet. Carefully, like a man on a precipice, he set the Bible in his lap, unbuttoned his overcoat, suit coat, and shirt, then lifted the Bible, fitted it in next to the skin of his chest, stretched the shirt over it and fastened the buttons, then buttoned the suit coat and overcoat. Royce drove hunched over, having difficulty seeing through the rain.

Five

Halfway to the university he was jumped again—suddenly, without warning, as usual—by his colon. "I don't believe it!" he whispered. He strained
against the pressure with all his might, about to explode, nothing in the
world he could do but pray, not that Gerald Craine was a praying
man—pain shooting up through his intestines to the gouge from his colostomy bag, far worse than usual—no question about it, Craine was *in* for
it!—and floored the accelerator, then at once let up again, alarmed by the
jouncing as the truck sped up, jiggling his abdomen, and like a glider pilot
when the wind drops from under him, he sat balanced, weightless, his expression frozen, until abruptly, soundlessly, the damage was done. Shocked,
on fire with righteous indignation, Craine slammed the brakes on, violently
swearing and spinning the steering wheel, slid the truck around one-eighty
degrees, half tipped over like a Western-movie stagecoach—by accident
striking no curbside trees, parked cars, or pedestrians—and roared, blue ex-
haust clouding thickly behind him, for home, the bathtub, and new clothes.
Still furious, several swigs drunker, by no means philosophical, he started
out again.

He parked in the library parking lot, asked directions twice, and cut
through the woods in the direction pointed out to him. The skirt of his
overcoat kept snagging on branches sticking out into the path, and once,
drunkenly missing a turn, he almost stepped on lovers. He tipped his hat,
backing off. "Excuse me."

The English Department was a lavish suite of offices on the third floor
of Faner, the huge new building of poured concrete at the edge of the
woods, a structure like a larger-than-life-sized battleship, concrete wedges
and wings flying out at peculiar angles—ramps, high patios and bridges,

huge light globes—in its shadow a bazaar of vegetable and fruit carts (nubbly and worm-holed, strictly organic), stalls of ceramics, paintings, blown glass, and loomwork. It would make a fine setting for a Hollywood thriller, he thought, pausing, looking up at free-standing balconies, vast sweeps of window, trying to get his bearings. At the far end of Faner he could make out the Planet X towers of the Student Union and, far beyond those, the walkways and blast chimneys of the chemistry building. To his left lay the "old campus," castlelike buildings with battlements and towers, formal gardens, huge trees, brick walkways and fountains, the wide sweep of lawn where Old Main had once stood before somebody, at the time of the troubles, had burned it to the ground. Beyond the library, back through the woods behind him, there were places even better for a murder film—the radio, TV, and theater building, the plywood and Fuller-dome slum thrown up by the Design Department, the campus lake, smooth as glass in the dappled shade of trees.

He started up the ramp, surprisingly steep, helping himself along with the aluminum railing. The students, no doubt some of them graduate students, looked to Craine like young children, junior-high-schoolers, maybe. One out of ten, maybe twenty, was in a wheelchair; another one out of ten was blind. He passed them in silence, eyes straight ahead, like a man who profoundly disapproved.

Peeking through the glass into the English Department, he had a brief attack of nerves. The place was very classy, like a dean's office—carpet on the floor, three desks for receptionists or secretaries, whatever, near one of them a complicated telephone switchboard—and just inside the door soft, leatherlike chairs, coffee tables, ashtrays, heavy wooden bookcases in pleasant disarray: fat, hardbound books, old magazines. Student workers moved in and out, talking for a minute with the secretaries, carrying away papers, fat envelopes. Sometimes one of the doors behind the secretaries' desks would pop open and a man would poke his head out—the chairman, perhaps, or some other official—and one of the secretaries would jump up to run some errand for him, or would reach for her phone. Craine frowned, his eyebrows ramming toward his nose. Three secretaries, thirty thousand dollars at least; four student workers, say two hundred a month, and God only knew how many more of them in the woodwork—say forty-five thousand dollars in office help, conservative estimate; all for what?—to get grants, play politics, save and increase the Scotch-tape, rubber-band, and paper-clip budget! He heard himself letting out a growl and clamped his mouth shut.

The young secretary in the silver wig was looking out at him, smiling and nodding encouragement. He jerked forward—the glass door stood open—went up to the front of her desk, and snatched his hat off. "Good morning," he said, slightly bowing.

She studied him, wonderfully polite but noticing the whiskey stink. "Can I help you?"

"I'm looking for one of your employees," Craine said. "Man named Ira Katz." He smiled, head tipped. He held the hat in both hands.

Still smiling, she gave him a calculating look, seeing if he was putting her on. The secretary at another desk called over, "Ira didn't come in today."

"Didn't come in?" Craine said, as if offended.

"I'm sorry," the one in the wig said, and smiled more widely.

Craine jerked his hands out sideways, as if astonished, playing crazy. "He just 'didn't come in'? Didn't call in with an excuse or anything? Just *didn't come in?*"

"It must not have been one of his teaching days," she said.

He already had his mouth set to start up his mad scene—offended taxpayer, *What kind of bidness you running here?*, etc.—when he was stopped by the pictures on the walls. He covered his mouth with his hand and squinted at the one over her desk, then swung around and looked at the others, one by one. They were interesting; that was what was strange about them. Not all interesting in the same way, like the pictures in the office of an art museum. They were pictures of utterly different kinds, in fact—a photograph of barns and a tree; a lithograph of ruins; a theater poster; some kind of modern-art print even Craine, for all his reading, had never seen before; a small assembly of *New Yorker* cartoons; a blown-up picture from some popular magazine—a bald man reading a book.

"Who did the art?" he said.

They looked at him—all three of the secretaries and the student worker who was passing through, a boy in suspenders—then the secretary in the wig began to laugh.

"What's so funny?" he said.

"Nothing. I'm sorry!" she said and covered her mouth. She was pretty, it struck him. All three of them were pretty; so was the boy in a faggoty way. Bunch of movie stars.

"It's not often you see interesting pictures in an office," Craine said, moving in on her. "Very good PR. I take my hat off to whoever's responsible." He tapped the side of his head. "Parent comes in, sees the pictures on the walls, right off he says, 'Cultured, very cultured' around here! This is the place for my Deirdre.'"

Now the other two secretaries were smiling, watching him like something from the zoo. He began to catch on. His eyes opened wider. "Nobody did it, it just happened," he said. "You all put up whatever you felt like, and this is the result!" He saw that it was true. "Interesting!" he said. He clasped his hands behind his back and went over to look more closely at the lithograph of ruins. "Interesting," he said again. He took a slip of paper from his pocket and a pencil from the nearest of the desks, discovered that he'd forgotten what he meant to write down, drew a face, folded the paper, and put the pencil back. He returned to the desk of the secretary in the wig, hunted for the license in his suit coat pocket, found it, and held it out to her. "Pictures on office walls are usually pretty phony," he said. "Nobody really notices, they wash over you like Muzak, but they always have a message. You know—these lousy crap paintings in a doctor's office; travel-bureau posters, pictures of ducks and fish in the dentist's office, photographs of government buildings at City Hall. —You're sure Ira Katz isn't in today? It's pretty important, actually."

She looked up from the license to his face. "I could give you his number at home, if you like."

"Yes, good. Good idea. Maybe I could borrow your phone for a minute."

She flipped through a file, reached for a slip of paper, and wrote down Ira's number. "Here," she said, "I'll dial, if you like." She lifted the receiver and, without listening for the dial tone, began to dial. When she was finished she handed the phone to Craine. "I hope it's not trouble," she said.

He gave her a vague headshake and listened. The phone rang and rang. Nothing. "Anyplace else he might be?" Craine asked.

The secretary at the desk nearest the door said, "You might try the computer center."

The girl in the wig, Janet, nodded thoughtfully, pressed down the receiver button, and began to dial again. Behind and to the left of her an office door opened and a white-haired man looked out, concerned. He gave Craine a little nod, at the same time sliding off his glasses. Craine returned

the nod, then looked down at the secretary's dialing finger, carefully showing no expression, struggling to get his mind crystal clear. Had the man
been listening? Was Ira in trouble with the department? He cleared his
throat.

The secretary held up the receiver. "It's ringing," she said.

As soon as he had it at his ear, a voice said, "Computer center."

"Hello," Craine said. "Tell me, is Professor Ira Katz there, by any
chance?"

There was a pause. "One moment please." Half a minute later she was
back. He wasn't there.

Craine hung up, and glanced at the secretary. "No luck," he said. He
drew his hand back and pushed it down into his overcoat pocket. "Tell
me," he said, "what does Ira Katz have to do with computers? I thought
he was a poet." He shot a furtive look at the man with white hair.

"Excuse me," the man said, suddenly smiling, "perhaps I can be of help.
You're Detective Craine?"

"I am," Craine said. It crossed his mind that he sounded like a man in
a Victorian novel. The man in white hair would appreciate that; he might
well be one of the few people in Carbondale who would notice. Perhaps.
Craine glanced at the man's face again, then down at his belt buckle. It said,
"Colt 45." Craine sighed.

"I'm glad to meet you," the man said, coming toward him, sticking
out his huge, clean hand. "Ira's mentioned you. You're neighbors, I think?
Come in!" He had a grin like a baseball star.

Uneasy, against his will, Craine shook the man's hand. When the man
put his other hand gently on Craine's back, Craine went into the office with
him. Softly, the man closed the door.

"I'm Wendel Davies," he said, "chairman of the English Department."
He gave a laugh and waved Craine toward a chair. "Sit down," he said,
"make yourself at home!" He laughed again, perfect teeth flashing, then
went around, sat behind his desk, and put his feet up. He wore Wallabees.
"So!" he said.

Craine studied him, lips pursed, then got his pipe out. The man sat motionless, smiling, his head thrown back. Craine nodded. He knew the type.
Professor Davies was a watcher and waiter, true-born aristocrat of bureau-
crats. He could sit there warmheartedly smiling all day, playing no cards,
pretending time had stopped, waiting for the sweat to break out on his op-

ponent's forehead. Craine found his matches, lit the pipe, blew smoke out. "So you've heard of me," he said.

Davies waved his hand, dismissive, then froze again, still smiling, delighted to be alive.

"Excuse me," Craine said, and pointed the stem of his pipe at the man, "you invited me in here. If all you mean to do is just sit there grinning—"

Nothing could have prepared him for the man's look of shock—preposterous embarrassment like a child's. He blushed beet red and fell forward in his chair, his boyish face twisted to the expression of a man about to tumble from a cliff. "My gosh!" he began.

"Now wait a minute," Craine said, "I don't mean to suggest—"

The man was flailing, trying to recover himself, pushing a small stack of papers away, picking up a pencil, setting it down again. *"Crazy!"* Craine whispered to himself, squinting in astonishment. It was a judgment he was increasingly forced to, these days. Everybody, everywhere, crazy.

"Now listen," Craine said, "what's going on here?" He raised both hands. "Take it easy, take it easy!"

Now the chairman of the Department of English was laughing, one hand over his face. He was gradually regaining control.

"I startled you, is that it?" Craine asked. He leaned forward and put both hands flat on the desk. He strained his wits, studying the blush. "Ira Katz has mentioned me, you say," he said. "I see. So you're friends with him. Good! He's a good man, I'm glad to see he's friends with the boss." He snapped his fingers as the pieces fell together—the secretary's alarm when he'd showed her the license, her eagerness to help, then the chairman's stepping in. Did they know about Ira and the woman named April? No doubt they'd seen the paper, or heard a newscast, knew she was dead.

Professor Davies shook his head, smiling again, ghastly. "I'll tell you the truth," he said.

Instantly Craine's eyes hooded a little, all his wits on guard.

"I meant to sort of . . . see what you had in mind," he said. "I wouldn't want you to think . . ." He dropped it, embarrassed. "We're all very fond of Ira Katz around here. We're a close group, this English Department. That might surprise you. We're one of the largest, most powerful departments on the campus, but even so . . ."

"Sounds like good leadership," Craine said, smiling so that his teeth showed, testing.

The professor hurriedly waved it away. It was probably true, Craine mused, that Davies was good at what he did. Good-looking man, boyish for all his sixty-some years and snow-white hair. Big, easy smile, broad shoulders, eyes of a man who liked to work out in the open, as no doubt he usually did; maybe that was why he'd reacted so extremely when Craine had nailed him. Also maybe not.

Now the professor was steadily meeting Craine's eyes, his expression troubled. "You're his neighbor, more or less his friend," he said, "so I guess I may as well come out with it." The eyes moved away, gazing past Craine's ear. "I was afraid we'd find the murder of that poor young woman would have something to do with Ira." He picked up the pencil again and with both hands nervously played with it. "As you know, there's been a great deal of trouble in his life—another casualty of the marriage wars, and in the middle of all that his mother's death—" He glanced up, blushed again. "All right," he said, "I guess you caught me out. I was never a good faker. It's characteristic of people in my profession, you'll find—English professors. A certain childlike quality in all of us, or so it seems to me—never properly grew up." He gave a sharp classroom laugh, ironic, and abruptly pushed back his desk chair and swivelled to the left as if thinking of rising; but he changed his mind. He tapped on the desk top with the tip of the pencil in his right hand and continued, "I take it you weren't personally acquainted with the girl?"

"Not really," Craine said.

Now Professor Davies did rise, still playing with the pencil, and crossed to the window, where he stood looking out. He fell silent for a moment, and Craine resisted pushing him, merely glancing over the objects on Davies' desk. A few blue exam booklets—so chairmen taught courses, he reflected, surprised—an anthology of American literature, a dictionary, two or three official-looking letters, meticulously stacked, ball-point pen, small appointment calendar still on yesterday's date, October 13, every hour on it filled in up to 7 P.M., where someone had scrawled—no doubt Davies himself —*club meeting.* Odd, if his schedule was so busy, that he hadn't turned the page, Craine mused. Odd that there was no one out there waiting to get in. No doubt some days were busier than others, he thought. He glanced at his watch, then checked the clock on the wall. They agreed, half past eleven. That too seemed odd, though he couldn't think why.

"It's a shame what Ira does at the computer center," Professor Davies said. "I'm afraid he's been working on concordances. You'll say it's a terrible waste of time for a man with a talent like Ira's, and I guess I'd agree with you, but universities are peculiar places, not always enlightened. Tenure committees—" He gave a little shrug, glanced at Craine, then looked back out the window. "Ira can be difficult. I don't say I blame him, I'm just telling you the facts. He refuses to write critical articles or work on a scholarly book—those are the kinds of things tenure committees like—not that such things are beyond his capabilities; he's an excellent teacher, a really brilliant critic—at least that's the report I get. I could show you his files. But he 'prefers not to,' as Bartleby would say." He glanced at Craine. "Bartleby the Scrivener—story by Melville."

Craine waited.

Professor Davies looked down. "Never mind. As I say, he won't do what the committee wants, though he could if he would. With a little arm-twisting—on my part, mostly—he was persuaded to begin a computer concordance. That, it seems, doesn't too much interfere with the flow of his poetic spirit." He studied the pencil, which he held now by the point and the eraser, between his two index fingers. His smile was slightly rueful, perhaps apologetic, aware that he'd let a touch of irony creep in. "It's turned out very strangely, I must say. An extremely self-destructive young man. But that's not relevant just now."

Craine waved his pipe, stopping him. "What do you mean, 'strangely,' " he said.

Davies cleared his throat, sorry he'd brought it up. "Well you see," he said, "the original idea—*my* idea, that is—was relatively simple. Do a concordance, a kind of word list or index with line numbers, and so on—of the work of some relatively important modern poet—Ashbery, Ammons, Anne Sexton, or whoever—bring it out through some respectable university press . . . It might be bullshit, granted, but it's the kind of thing university committees understand. That's what I thought he was doing all this time, but it seems I was mistaken." He sighed, then again glanced at Craine and smiled. "He's been doing—or trying to do—a concordance of all 'serious' American poetry published since January 1970."

Craine thought about it. Hundreds of books and magazines? Thousands? Tentatively, he said, "That's insane."

Davies smiled, meeting his eyes. "You're telling me!" He came back to the desk, put the pencil down, and laid his hand on the back of the desk chair, as if thinking of sitting down. "But they love him over at the computer center. Not just because of the programmer time, or the absolutely incredible budget for printout. They like the *idea*. Philosophically."

Craine puffed at his pipe, trying to get it going, and waited for Davies to explain.

"You see, what they're after—Ira Katz and his mad mathematical friends—is a picture of the whole American reality, that is, mental reality. If you assume we don't live in the world but only in the world as we have words for it—"

Craine raised his pipe. "I see," he said. A tingle went through his brain.

Davies nodded. "No doubt it's a wonderful idea; I'm no philosopher. But I can tell you one thing: it will never get him tenure. Ten years—more like fifty—maybe by then he'd get something he could publish. Meanwhile, he'll be long gone from here. Don't think he doesn't know it."

Craine nodded, thoughtful. "I take it you've got some idea why he's doing it."

Davies nodded. "I think so. Partly, of course, it's because he believes it's a good idea, maybe a brilliant idea. One should never underestimate the seriousness of these young intellectuals. Tenure's the least of what they'll sacrifice in the name of their convictions. He's a poet, after all. Poets—even relatively bad ones, and Ira's not that, I think—poets have an almost frightening tenacity, not unlike hard scientists or mathematicians. They'll work days, weeks, months to get one small detail just right by their own private judgment."

"Autumn, clear as the eyes of chickens," Craine said.

Davies glanced at him, decided to let it pass. "Yes, something like that," he said. "Everything in a poem—rhymes, rhythms, line breaks, every slightest little technical trifle—aims at one single thing, saying exactly and precisely what you mean, intellectually and emotionally. Choose a slightly wrong word, let in the slightest distracting assonance, even indent a given line too far, and you change the whole meaning—disastrously! Believe me, it takes a madman—I mean in Plato's sense—to write poetry. What I'm saying may not hold for every poet—I'd say it doesn't hold for Robert Duncan, for instance—well-known poet in San Francisco—but it's true, I think, for Ira Katz and for many others like him. He gets an intuition and he follows it out; nothing on earth can stop him, all ordinary human considerations are forgotten—family considerations, anything you can name—he follows it out with the ferocious concentration of a maniac, or a cat at a mouse hole, follows it till he gets it—or it kills him."

"You admire him a good deal," Craine said.

"I envy the son of a bitch, that's the truth of it." He did not smile. "So anyway, put a mind like that on this crazy computer idea and you can predict what will happen." Now he did smile, shaking his head. "And then, of course, there's the social-psychological component."

Craine waited.

"It's a natural alliance, poet with an idea, metaphysical idea, and a group of first-rate computer mathematicians. They're already half persuaded that the world's all symbols. They encourage him, and he's flattered. You know how it is with these literary types. They're impressed by a man who can add nine and seventeen. They're a class above him, always have been. When he got C's in algebra, they got easy A's, though in every subject he was always very smart. When they talk over coffee, he's lost most of the time—yet they look up to him, they respect him. Compare what he gets in the English Department. We deal—just between you and me, Mr. Craine—with dead poets, the kind that don't ever say 'That's not what I meant!' Here Katz is, three books out and a collection of small prizes, and his fellow teachers of freshman comp and sophomore lit can't make sense of what he writes, don't even read him—don't read anybody, just Hawthorne's *Scarlet Letter* again and again, and write articles on 'Hawthorne and Alchemy,' for which they get promoted, as Katz does not. It could make a man bitter, if that were his natural inclination. Ira's not the bitter type, needless to say. But by degrees he pays less and less attention to his colleagues, occasionally lets a little slur slip out—to a student, or some friend—and it gets back, in time. These people, you understand, are the people that get to vote on his significance to the department. I don't mean to say they're mean or small-minded—not at all. We have a top-notch department, some outstanding scholars. But he makes himself an unknown quantity, if you see what I mean. Take Professor Schaffer, eighteenth-century specialist. He doesn't read Ira or any other modern poet, though he's a very good man, we were lucky to grab him. Taught at Columbia, then Princeton. Three fat books with the Oxford University Press. Kind man, beloved. Ira Katz meets Schaffer in the hall, doesn't even know he works for us! Wilbur T. Schaffer! One of the three biggest names in the field. You see the problem, Mr. Craine.

"All right. I don't mean to be criticizing Ira. I just meant to explain that there's a natural social-psychological component. Ira doesn't 'work well,' as they say, with his colleagues, and what he does—aside from his teaching, of course—is a hard thing for his colleagues to evaluate. No doubt I sound as if I'd like to see him fired. It's not true. But believe me, he's difficult. You're a realist. Think about *my* position. The job of a chairman is to some extent political. If I come out swinging for a fellow, he'd better be standing there behind me, trying to look polite! —But all right, that's my problem; not to the point.

"All right. So where were we?"

"You were saying he's self-destructive."

"Yes, good. Yes, that's the point. Did you hear about the death of his mother?"

"I don't think he mentioned it."

Davies nodded, lips pursed. After a moment he said, "Ira's mother was alcoholic; a very difficult woman. She lived with them—no doubt part of the reason for the divorce. When she died he was there at the hospital with her, sitting at her bedside. She seemed to be asleep when her esophagus burst. I suppose it must have waked her. She reared up in bed, blood pouring out of her mouth—Ira jumped up and grabbed her—and she said, 'Ira, why'd you let me *do* this to myself?' You can imagine how it is for a man like Ira to have to live with a thing like that!"

"Maybe," Craine said.

Davies shot him a look. "Maybe?"

Craine waved. "The ole lady wasn't exactly being fair, you'll admit."

"Of course she wasn't! Real 'Jewish mamma,' as Ira's wife put it."

"Ex-wife."

"Well yes, technically." He smiled, as if feeling a little trapped. "She was—is—a wonderful woman. We're all very fond of her. He had a wonderful family. Smart, good-looking kids, beautiful little house on Chautauqua—"

"The wife got the house?"

He studied the pencil, which he held now by the point and the eraser, between his two index fingers. "Jane's very social, stunningly beautiful, an excellent cook. Maybe *beautiful*'s too strong; she's just a little puffy—cortisone treatments. And of course when a man walks out on her, a woman shows the wear and tear."

"Of course."

Abruptly, Professor Davies put the pencil in his pocket and turned back toward the desk. "Well, that's about it," he said. "There's not much more I can tell you. As you can see, we're pretty worried."

"Yes I can," Craine said. He leaned forward as if to get up. "One thing," he said. "Where did he run into this other woman, this April?"

"Ah yes, April." The professor shook his head. "She was a programmer over at the center. So in a way, you see, I'm responsible."

"Yes, that's too bad," Craine said. "You know anything about her?"

"I'm not sure I ever laid eyes on her. No doubt a nice enough person. Ira's always had good taste."

"Mmm," Craine said, and now he did rise. He said, "There were others, then?"

"I can't definitely say," Professor Davies said. A coolness came over him, quite suddenly, as if with a click.

Craine looked down at his pipe and grinned a little wickedly. "Occupational hazard, I imagine," he said. "They're like rock stars, these poets. They go off and do readings, talk behind closed doors with their female students about whatever little intimacies show up in their poems . . . I imagine there must be rumors, at the very least. I imagine you'd have to be a saint to be the wife of a poet and never suffer jealousy."

"That may be so," Davies said. "But I'm afraid I can't help you."

"On the contrary," Craine said, and looked up, his smile wide open, downright friendly, "you've helped me very much!"

At the silver-wigged secretary's desk he got directions to the computer center and borrowed the phone again. As he dialed, Chairman Davies watched, on the chance that he might still be of use, then nodded, smiled, and stepped back into his office. This time he did not close the door.

"Craine," Hannah said, "where the devil are you?"

"Out in the field," he said, and grinned.

"Out in the field," she mimicked. But she knew she'd get nothing more from him and gave it up. "McClaren's still trying to reach you," she said.

"I thought he might be. I imagine I'll eventually run into him."

"I wish you luck," she said. "He's in a very bad mood. I went over and tried to talk with Carnac."

"Go on."

"Nothin. Zero."

Craine frowned. "He wouldn't talk?"

"Talked a blue streak, but not English. Funny thing was, I'd swear he was trine with all his might to get through to me."

"Scared, you think?"

"God knows. I think just plain crazy."

"OK," Craine said. "Hold the fort, I'll check in." He handed the receiver to the girl. When she'd hung it on the cradle, he asked, "You know this person, Terrance Rush? I noticed when I was writing down the name, you seemed—"

"He's one of our graduate students," she said. "I can give you his office number—it's up on the fourth floor—but he probably won't be there, he'll be over in the library, in his carrel. You'd have to get that over at the library."

He waited while she added the office number to the name and address on the slip of paper, then folded it again and tucked it into his shirt pocket, where he thought with luck he might find it. Rush, he thought. Elaine Glass's teacher. Was it possible that the thing could be that easy?

"Thank you for all your time and trouble," he said. "Thank you very much!"

"Our pleasure," she said. As he was about to turn away she gave him an earnest look, a little panicky and furtive, as if she wished the others couldn't hear what she was saying. "If there's anything I can do for, you know, the *case* . . . don't hesitate to call me. I'm Janet."

"Yes, I know." He smiled. "Thank you, Janet. Thank you very much." As he approached the door to the hallway he turned to nod good-bye one last time and caught, out of the corner of his eye, Chairman Davies' door closing, without a sound. He shot a look at Janet and saw that she too had noticed. Their eyes met firmly for an instant. Craine winked.

With magnificent self-control he passed the truck without stopping for a drink and walked on to the library. The clock over the door said 12:05. He walked faster. It was a beautiful building, or such was Gerald Craine's opinion—grand rooms, black marble columns, marble floors smooth as glass, everywhere the smell—the *presence,* as people in stereo say—of books. It seemed to him, as it always did when he came here, simply incredible that he didn't spend his life here. At the sight of students and professors lined up at the checkout computers, or copying down call numbers at the central catalogue, browsing in the seven-day new-acquisitions room, or sprawled in the carpeted lounges, reading, Craine's soul, ordinarily so indifferent to fortune, stirred toward covetousness and envy. He reminded himself, as he always did here, that maybe ninety percent of the people around him weren't interested in books, were merely faking their courses, skimming half-heartedly or reading carefully but without real interest or understanding—but he didn't believe it. Every student who passed with a great, awkward armload clamped under his chin was an affront to Craine, like a fat, smiling czar to a peasant Communist—though of course it was nonsense: he could come here whenever he pleased, if he pleased. Theoretically, at least. It was only in his mind that he was an alien here, a rat darting furtively through a room of sleeping cats.

At the checkout desk he asked a well-dressed black boy in glasses, "Where do I get the number of a person's library carrel?"

Without looking up from his work the boy pointed at the ceiling and said, "Second floor, main desk."

"Thank you very much," Craine said, bowing, and hurried to the elevator.

Two minutes later, with the number of Terrance Rush's carrel on a pink slip of paper in his hand, Craine got off the elevator at the fifth floor and hurried along the stacks, hunting for where the carrels began. Half unaware that he was doing it, he read titles as he walked. Abruptly, he stopped, staring at a dark blue book almost in front of him, at eye level: *Clairvoyance,* it said. For the first time since it had happened he remembered that something had come over him when he was standing at Ira Katz's door, a kind of dream or maybe a vision, very brief, but powerful: he—or someone—was standing in the dark, under trees, and someone was moving very quietly toward him, hands raised. Craine, remembering, put one hand over his mouth. It was that night—somewhere where there were leaves—that Ira's friend April had been murdered.

FRAGMENTS

Editor's Note

*The fragments that follow have sufficient internal coherence to justify in-
clusion—but no attempt has been made to render them sequential. Fragments number two and three are versions of the same scene but distinct
enough as presentations to demonstrate the way Gardner worked with what
he acknowledges as "borrowed material." Fragment number seven would
appear to pertain to a different story-line—and time, it's winter—entirely.
Craine has had cancer of the colon, not—as in this closing fragment—a
mental collapse.*

*Royce visits Craine's room well before Hannah's warning that he's
planning such a visit; Elaine Glass acquires a suntan in inverse proportion
to her time spent in the sun. It's as difficult for the reader as for the book's
protagonist to know the actual hour and the date.*

*Craine and his creator might have proposed a solution; we cannot.
To paraphrase Professor Weintraub's lecture on computers, there are routines and sub-routines and sub-sub-sub-routines. "How does one man, in
a single lifetime, program them all in, you ask me? The answer is, he
doesn't—and therein lies a tale."*

ACKNOWLEDGMENTS

This novel is a "construction" of sorts: The characters and plot are for the most part imaginary, but passages from numerous books have been ripped from their original contexts and inserted, slightly altered, into this story. I cannot explain in detail here—perhaps I could not explain fully, down to the last iota, even to myself—why I have not totally recast borrowed material, so that no acknowledgment is legally or morally necessary; but I can say this much: my ideal novel is a universe of voices, not a work of triumphant individual will but a human chorus, sometimes in harmony, sometimes not—an edifice modified by all who have used it, generation on generation, the way very old churches and schools have been modified, a window plugged here, a chimney added there, here and there old beams replaced by steel—a concatenation in which I, the novelist, serve mainly as moderator, keeping the various contributions more or less relevant both in the sense that they apply and in the sense that they tend to move the whole kaboodle in some direction that satisfies my intuition of where things ought to go. I don't mean to suggest that I'm indifferent to *design* (though it's true that I have no objection to "loose, baggy monsters" if they hold my attention); I mean only that, writing a novel, one is always on familiar philosophical ground. No one, not even the most ingenious writer of sci-fi, can find a wholly new domain for dramas of human personality in conflict, which is our business, mostly, or so it seems to me. And the philosophical ground of this novel, being as old, at least, as human consciousness, has been much trampled over the years and even millions of years, so that to limit one's dramatizing voice would be like stubbornly refusing to use any mathematics one has not thought up from scratch by oneself.

I have borrowed so widely that no complete list of original sources is possible. A few books I've made heavy use of are Joseph Weizenbaum's *Computer Power and Human Reason: From Judgment to Calculation,* Howard Gardner's *The Shattered Mind,* Ernest Becker's *The Denial of Death,* Robert E. Ornstein's *The Psychology of Consciousness,* and M. B. Dykshoorn's *My Passport Reads Clairvoyant.* From all of these books I take individual lines (which I make some character speak), images and symbols which may sink of their own weight to the novel's bedrock or may, on the other hand, serve as mere surface decorations, and ideas—even ideas for characters—which grope out toward everything else in the construction, helping to hold the thing together. Various other writers have influenced this work almost equally, but for them I can mention no single book. I've ranged freely, for instance, through the writings of Darwin, Freud, Jung, and Rank, and through the outpourings of both scientific and popular writers on the so-called paranormal, writers for example like Joseph Chilton Pearce *(The Crack in the Cosmic Egg* and *Exploring the Crack in the Cosmic Egg)*—writers who seem to me to range, both collectively and individually, from the profound to the unspeakably silly.

Fragment One

Nothing is stable; all systems fail. Imponderables, improbabilities . . . Not even the weary man's willing decline toward the grave is entirely to be trusted. Consider the case of Gerald Craine, detective.

Consider Craine sweating and tossing on his bed, asleep in his miserable, stinking hotel room, his mind numbed by whiskey, weighted like the dead-men in the long-forgotten swamps of his childhood—oak limbs, cotton-woods, once-towering sycamores brought down, back then, not by insects or disease or the voracious mills or by land speculation but by tornadoes and the heaviness of age. The faded gray wallpaper in Craine's one room is splotched and cracked, bulging here and there, like the old man's forehead; the padless, once-wine-red threadbare carpet lumps up into ropes, like the veins on the backs of his hands. His history lies around him, miraculously decayed. He has books everywhere, wedged into the bookshelves of cheap, stained pine, strewn along the baseboards, stacked up, dusty, in the corners of the room. On the bedpost above him his pistol hangs, precariously tilted in its shoulder holster; on his dresser, in its dusty old Bible-black case, lies the pitted, once-silver cornet he hasn't touched in years. A streetlight burns the night smoke-gray outside his window, lighting up telephone and electric lines and throwing a negative shadow along the floor toward his closet. The closet door hangs open, too warped to close. It has a broken spool for a doorknob. The interior of the closet, just visible from Craine's bed, is crowded with dark, restive forms. Old Craine cries out, as if aware of them, and his hands claw and clench. His knees jerk.

Fragment Two

He was standing now beside a long row of carrels that stretched behind and ahead of him. He looked down at the paper: number 34. He was standing almost exactly in front of it. Craine shuddered at the coincidence and moved closer. Through the narrow glass window beside the door he made out that the carrel was unoccupied, but there was clear evidence that it hadn't been and wouldn't be unoccupied long. The little room, tight and awkward as an upended coffin, was so crammed with books there was no room to stand, one would have to slip sideways through the door into the chair at the desk, hunched before an old Smith–Corona typewriter, an overflowing bright green plastic ashtray, a ragged stack of paper, more books. On the floor, half hidden by books, there was a hot plate, a coffeepot, several fat paper bags. For all practical purposes, Craine decided, this was home for Terrance Rush.

He looked around for a place to wait. Not far off there were brightly colored, plastic-covered chairs, on the wall behind them a THANK YOU FOR NOT SMOKING sign. He crossed to the nearest chair and sat down facing carrel 34, got his pipe lit, and opened the book on clairvoyance at random. There was a long passage in small print, a quotation. (It sounded vaguely familiar; perhaps he'd read the book it came from.)

By relating various incidents and circumstances in which my gift brought me specific information, I may have given the impression that it made itself evident only sporadically, whenever I concentrated on a particular person or object, or that it worked in reaction to events in my own life. But this was not the case. In fact, the crucial problem of my youth was that the psychic part of my mind was operating almost constantly, and I could not control it.

Craine skipped down a ways.

But at school I could not withdraw, and my emotional troubles began in earnest. For the first time in my life I found myself obliged to sit for hours on end in the same room with twenty or more other people.

Picture the scene: The teacher is reading a story and the class is attentive, waiting to hear the outcome. One boy, however, sits staring fixedly at the teacher's face. He already knows the outcome of the story and cannot realize the others do not. Why is the teacher reading the story when everyone knows what will happen and there is no truth in it anyway? None of it ever happened.

The boy sits in silence because he has to—but his mind is buzzing. Today as every day it whirls in confusion, filled with incomprehensible and often frightening images, sounds, smells, tastes, impressions, and sensations. He sees his classmates not only as they are now, but as they have been and as they will be in the future. And he sees their parents, friends, relatives—people he has never met—and he knows them, too.

He knows that one of his friends will fall and break his arm. The mother of another friend is very ill but does not know it . . .

Again Craine skipped, jumping past the text, moving to the next quotation.

It began with a sense of disorientation, of dizziness, almost nausea, that suddenly congealed into physical pain that took my breath away. It was like an electric shock—suddenly every joint, every muscle ached. I hunched forward, almost fell, and could not straighten up. In my mind I saw *beyond* reality. I remained aware of my surroundings—Mallee and Berbers, the modern buildings, the traffic, passersby—but I could also "see" a different town. Different streets, old buildings, unpaved, narrow, haphazard streets and lanes . . .

Then in my mind I saw a priest. Very old, bent, stooped, arthritic, crippled. He stood before us and was as real to me as Mallee and Berbers.

In his arms he held an old metal box, a chest, perhaps two-by-one-by-one-foot deep. Then he began walking away, hobbling, shuffling, limping along one of those old lanes with his crippled gait.

I followed, shuffling as he shuffled, bent and pain-wracked as he was—and ran straight into a stone wall. I stopped. The old priest disappeared. I went around the wall, and he was there, shuffling along, leading me.

Craine looked up, checking with a part of his mind to see if Rush had come to his carrel—he had not—but mainly thinking, half in a daze, about other things: Two-heads Carnac, Dr. Tummelty's interest in psychics, his own strong sense that he'd read all this before somewhere. Suppose he had not. Suppose, like the man who had written this, he simply "knew," somehow, had read the book without ever seeing it. That was nonsense, of course; he knew that, in a way. But for the moment he let himself forget what he knew. It was a fact that psychics had sometimes been helpful in discovering bodies, even reenacting killings so that the police could work out who had done them. There was one in particular, some famous Dutchman . . .

With a start, he realized that he *had* read the book. It was M. B. Dykshoorn's biography, of course. Disgust leaped up in him—an emotion too violent, he realized even as it came, to be merely disgust. Fierce disappointment, then. Yes, that was it, yes. Craine grinned, angry. Ah, the tricks of the mind, or rather heart! Poor Gerald Craine wanted to be a psychic, yes. Wanted to save Elaine Glass without the usual nuisance—not even believing she needed saving, in fact; knowing full well . . . His mind snagged, and only after a moment did he know what had snagged it. He had seen something, surely not a memory: a man standing in the dark, among trees. He could smell them now, and felt again the simultaneous terror and guilt, as if he were himself both the killer and the victim. He jerked his eyes down to the book and read:

The next morning at the town hall I found everyone in a rare state of excitement, for Mallee had come up with a remarkable discovery. On his map the day before he had charted the route I had taken on my psychic walk through the town. Because I had kept bumping into buildings and having to go around them in order to "follow" the old priest, my path bore little relation to the plan of the modern town. But when they overlaid my route on a map of the town as it had been at the time of the Iconoclasm—the year 1566—they discovered that my walk would have taken me through the streets of the town exactly as it was then—four hundred years earlier!

There were pages of comment. *Dykshoorn, like many clairvoyants of our time . . .* The next quotation from Dykshoorn read:

> . . . I am convinced that if I have a definite psychic impression that something will happen, it will happen and cannot be avoided. Neither I nor any of the people involved can intervene to prevent its occurrence. If I see that a person will have an automobile accident, for example . . .

Pages later, Craine read:

> Because of this deep emotional involvement, psychopathic murders are easier for me to work out than crimes committed in cold blood, where the killing is only incidental to the purpose of the crime. I never investigate killings by members of organized crime, for example, because . . .

He skipped again.

> Can I see my own future? The answer is yes and no, sometimes and occasionally. Whenever I *try* to find out what will happen in my own life, my gift turns out to be unreliable. I believe it is influenced by what I consciously or subconsciously *want* to happen. If I like the idea of something, or I'm looking forward to it, and I ask myself "Will it happen?" my gift always says yes, it will, and it will be just as you want it. But most of the time it doesn't happen. It's the same with my family, and sometimes with other people with whom I am very close. If I like them . . .

Craine closed the book. "Thank you very much," he whispered. He took off his glasses, folded them, and put them in his suit coat's top pocket. *Time,* he thought, and then—consciously, at least—thought nothing.

In the cloudy swirl of his mind something vaguely like this went on, not that he'd be able to use it, consciously at least: that Dykshoorn was a man who had served the police, both in Europe and America, on countless occasions. There was no real doubt that he and others like him were *on* to something, never mind what. One might doubt his assertions that he could know the future or the four-hundred-year-old past; but there was no real doubt that he could find bodies and killers, an ability at least as outrageous as knowledge of the future and distant past. Remembering Dykshoorn's book (not quite consciously), Craine remembered Dykshoorn's fury at Rhine and the statistical parapsychologists, and his annoyance at those who gave the credit to God, as if the psychics of ancient Greece, or psychics who professed themselves atheists, were not equally to be trusted, insofar as (Dykshoorn would be the first to admit) any self-proclaimed psychic should be trusted. But the interesting point, to Craine's fumbling mind, was Time. He remembered Dr. Tummelty's curious phrase, "the bioplasmic universe." Even in the depth of his daze, Craine had no real idea what it meant. But what it hinted was clear enough: that in some odd way the future has happened already, and the past is still happening.

For an instant Craine's mind switched on, shivering with anger. Most of the world would dismiss with scorn the possibilities he was secretly entertaining, even the stone-hard facts those possibilities were based on. Again and again bodies have been found, murderers have been identified, by psychic means. Matter of record. When one spoke of such matters with friends and acquaintances, their eyes glazed over, their smiles became fixed. One showed them clippings, gave the names of books. Glazed eyes. Fixed smiles. So Columbus must have felt. Galileo. Einstein. *Fools! There's a whole new world out there!*

All the same, it was exceedingly odd, no denying it—the idea that Time was a trick of perception, like the solidity of tables and floors—the idea that the future was inevitable, had happened already and could no more be changed by human will, human love, than the fall of Constantinople. How sad and silly it made all human labor!—ten thousand lives wasted moving stones for a wall that was doomed to be overthrown in half a century, surgeons working hour after hour, bent like boxers, every nerve on edge, on the heart of a man who'd been dead on the table from the beginning. If that was how God saw, the end and the beginning, then God help God! Craine clamped his eyes shut. Unhealthy way to think, he reminded himself. It was the cancer talking, maybe. A walking dead man saw the world with peculiar eyes. Young people's hopes and dreams, what were they to a man like Craine? *Fools! There's no world at all out there!*

Abruptly, Craine jerked in his chair, then glanced at his watch. He must meet Elaine Glass at one forty-five. It was nearly one now, and he had a great deal to do. Rush might never arrive. He might have gone home for his mother's funeral, he might have been hit by a train or taken sick . . .

Craine closed the book and struggled up out of the plastic chair.

At the first-floor pay phone he called his office. The book on clairvoyance was down in the lining of his coat, more or less out of sight.

"Meakins?" he said.

"Craine? Is that you, Craine?"

"I'm at the Morris Library. I want you to come down here, take over for me."

"What?"

"Don't ask questions, just listen. You got a pencil and paper?"

After a moment Meakins said, "OK . . ."

"Terrance Rush," Craine said, "fifth floor, carrel thirty-four. You got that?"

"Yes," Meakins said, distant.

"Good. Terrance Rush. He's the guy in the blue and white runner's jacket. I want—"

"What?" Meakins said.

"I said just listen, OK? I want you to come talk to him. See what it's about. He was Elaine Glass's teacher in freshman composition, or something like that. She wrote him a piece about the man in blue and white. I want you to come figure out the mystery. You got that?"

"Hey, Craine—"

"Sit and wait till he comes here. I got no time for the details, but I saw him in the jacket. He's mixed up in it somehow. He'll be no trouble—that's my opinion. But all the same—"

"You think it's serious, this 'threat' she—"

Quickly, Craine broke in: "Anything at your end?"

"Well—" There was a pause. Craine could see Meakins' blush. Meakins said lightly, "Hannah's mad as hell, you know." Too casually, he said, "Royce came in, cleaned out his desk."

Craine waited.

Meakins said, "He's really mad. You know how he gets."

Craine said, "What else?"

"I've got a note here from Hannah. She wants you to remember your checkup in Baltimore, the seventeenth."

"I remember."

"You're not supposed to eat for the whole day before. Take these enemas and pills and things. You're planning on it, right?"

"I'm aware of it."

"Hey listen, I don't mean to, but—"

"I'm planning on it."

"OK." He was silent for a moment. "Another note from Hannah. 'No news on tumps.' That mean something to you? The rest of the note says, 'Not in the dictionary.'"

"OK," Craine said. He closed his eyes for a moment, trying to think, but at once he felt dizzy and opened his eyes again. "Royce is really mad, eh?"

"Well, I'd avoid him."

Craine nodded through the phone. "Can't blame him, I guess."

"Something else," Meakins said. "McClaren keeps calling. At first he was crabby. Now he's polite."

"Sounds bad."

"That's what *we* thought."

"All right," Craine said, "I'll look him up, maybe."

"You all right, Craine?" Meakins asked.

Craine thought about it. At last he said, "Get over here as quick as you can and check on Rush. Terrance Rush. Student assistant. Check out his general feelings about Ms. Glass. Don't be too obvious, needless to say."

"Will do," Meakins said.

"OK," Craine said. "OK." Then, thoughtfully, he hung up.

Ten feet from the phone, Craine paused, put his fist to his mouth, then turned back. He checked the phone book, then called the English Department.

"Hello. Is Janet there?" he asked.

There was a pause. "Janet?"

"I'm trying to get in touch with one of the secretaries at the English Department—young woman named Janet."

"Oh. Janet Cizike."

"That's it," Craine said, not that he knew.

"One moment please," the voice said. A few seconds later he heard the voice of the girl who had offered to help.

"Janet?" he asked, making sure.

"This is Janet," the voice said.

She sounded distant, oddly unfriendly, but she was the one.

"This is Gerald B. Craine," he said. "Detective."

"Oh, hello," she said. Her voice was cooler than before. He decided to brave it out.

"You said you'd like to help Ira," he said. "As it happens, there's something you could do for me." He waited. Nothing. He said, "I think you mentioned that you have files on the department's graduate assistants."

"Yes—"

"I need to see the file on Terrance Rush."

He listened to the musical humming of the line. At last, in a changed voice, as if she were covering the receiver with her hand, she said, "Mr. Craine, our files are, you know, confidential."

"Quite rightly!" he said. "Just as they should be!" He looked behind him, then said rapidly and softly, "Listen, one minute you say you want to help him, the next you've changed your mind, or somebody's gotten to you, God knows. I try to be everywhere at once, but it's not easy. You want to help him, help him. Otherwise—"

"I'm awfully busy right now," she said. "If you wanted to call me at home, after five . . . I'm in the phone book."

"You'll have the file?"

"Why yes—at least I'll try," she said brightly.

Craine thought about it. "You're a good girl, Janet. I'll come over."

"Thank you," she said. "I hope your mother's well?"

He smiled. "She never complains," he said.

"I'm glad. Well, good-bye, then."

"For now," he said. "Thank you."

He hung up, felt in the slot to see if his dime had come back, then hurried toward the stainless steel exit doors. He showed his empty hands to the guard, remembering only that instant the book in his overcoat lining, a plainly visible lump if the guard cared to notice; but the guard nodded and at once looked down again at the paperback he was reading. "Filth," Craine said, smiling, pointing at the paperback. The guard glanced at him, half smiled back, and read on. Out in the sunlight, Craine pondered a moment, getting his bearings, then set off briskly in the direction of the computer center. The air was strangely warm, like the breath of a cow. Overhead, dark clouds scudded northward.

As soon as Craine opened the door he saw McClaren.

"Well, well," McClaren said, turning to face him squarely, his smile wide and frozen, his index fingers tucked into the pockets of his sport coat.

"Detective Inspector McClaren!" Craine said, pulling his hat off and grinning like a crazy. Two uniformed policemen stood over by the window, holding Styrofoam coffee cups, Eggers and a man named Webb, skinny and nervous; even in uniform he looked like an accountant. There were desks, secretaries, reams of pale-green and white printout. Eggers smiled and nodded.

"You finally checked in at your office?" McClaren said.

Craine put on his Mickey Mouse sheepish look. "Couldn't remember your phone number," he said.

"Ha ha," McClaren laughed grimly. "Well I'm glad to run into you. I've been trying to get in touch."

"Some kind of trouble?" Craine asked.

McClaren just looked at him, still smiling, speechless with disgust. When Craine went on staring, his expression insisting on innocence and drunkenness, McClaren, though not buying it, finally looked down. "You acquainted around here?" he said. He flicked his eyes toward one secretary, then another. "Miss Roberts, Miss Gupta"—he flicked his eyes back toward Craine, then away—"Gerald Craine, Detective." The secretaries, one pink, one dark brown, shyly nodded. McClaren nodded toward the open door of an inner office. "Come on in," he said, as if the office were his own, and moved toward it. The uniformed policemen remained where they stood. Bowing, smiling like a man caught naked, moving with the troubled advertence of a drunkard, Craine followed McClaren, who stood patiently waiting while he entered, then softly closed the door.

"Well well," McClaren said, "you do keep us guessing, Craine." He went around behind the desk and drew the chair back, preparing to sit. He studied the chair seat, his mind somewhere else, then reached down and tested it for dust with his fingertips and, after a moment, sat. He looked at Craine in surprise. "Sit down," he said.

"Thank you. Thank you very much," Craine said. When he was seated, formal as a man with his psychiatrist, hands folded carefully over his knees, he said, "So what seems to be the problem?" When McClaren merely looked at him, he added with studied stupidity, "Is this your office?"

"Hardly," McClaren said, and smiled. "It belongs to a Professor John Furth, old friend of mine—head of the computer center. He's not in today."

"I see."

The office was small and astonishingly messy, computer printouts everywhere, a typewriter, apparently not used in years, piled high with books and papers, like the desk top, the bookshelves—even the aluminum standing ashtray had books on it. There were no windows, no pictures on the battleship-gray walls. Even to Craine's half-dead nostrils the place was rank with old pipe smoke and something else, a smell like rotten oranges.

McClaren sat cocked back, his balding dome tilted, motionless, as if suspended like a balloon. *More fucking waiting game,* Craine thought, and politely smiled. He too could wait.

"So," McClaren said, flicking his eyes away again. "I suppose we may as well get right down to it. I take it you're here about April Vaught?"

"Mmm," Craine said.

"I suppose there's a natural measure of suspicion between us, I suppose," McClaren said. His fingertips drummed elegantly on one of the books on the desk top. "For my part, I'd like to cut through all that, if possible. Though each of us works in his own way, I take it we're after the same thing. Naturally, protecting your clients, as it were, there are certain things you're not eager to tell me. But if I tell you what I know, perhaps, in reciprocity, you'll tell me what *you* know."

"Mmm," Craine said again.

McClaren blushed with anger but steadily smiled. "It was in John Furth's van that her body was found. I take it by your expression that that's news to you."

"Yes it is," Craine said.

McClaren puckered his lips as if to kiss. "It's very peculiar," he said. "As if someone were interested in framing Professor Furth. We know, as no doubt you're aware, that she was murdered elsewhere."

"Mmm."

McClaren smiled, faintly admiring in spite of himself. "We've talked with all the people here," he said after a moment. "Nothing special in her life, so far as anyone knows—including her friendship with your neighbor Ira Katz." Carefully, or so it seemed to Craine, he did not look up. "She was an excellent programmer, by all reports. A food faddist, sometimes ran workshops on 'the primal scream.' No relatives, according to her file; no known former attachments. Lived in a little house in Cobden. Studied in New York, to be an actress, some years ago. Lived in Boston for a while, associated with an ashram—worked there as a cook. Beans and millet, things like that. In school she got A's in mathematics, also languages. Spent a year teaching Latin. Smart and ordinary, so it seems." Now he did look up. "What was *your* impression?"

"Smart and ordinary," Craine said.

McClaren thought about it, decided to let it go, for now. "It's a puzzle," he said.

"How was she killed?" Craine asked.

"Stab wounds," McClaren said, studying the mess on the desk top. "It's an interesting problem, as I'm sure you've noticed. They were all killed by stab wounds—but never the same knife, never the same way. You can't help but wonder if maybe we're dealing with six different murderers. It's crazy, right? Statistically impossible—six murderers in a year, in one small town. I mean, this is the hypothesis: somebody kills some girl with a knife, somebody *else* wants to kill some girl, he imitates the earlier murder as best he can, trying to make us believe it's some psychotic. Six times it happens—one original, five bad imitations. But it's queer. *Too* queer. You'd think at least two of them would kill the same way. It's like sex: how many positions can you find? Most people—*you* know—without even thinking about it, they do it the same way. You stab into the chest, or you stab into the throat . . . But six murders, no two of them the same—"

"Interesting," Craine said.

McClaren shot a look at him, for an instant believing he was innocent. "Yes, interesting," he said.

After a moment, Craine asked, "What do you know about this Professor Furth? How come he's not in today? Office like this—"

"I don't know. That's interesting too," McClaren said. "But what I was saying before—" He looked up. "It doesn't look like the work of a psychotic or a professional killer," he said. "Both of them, they'd both do the same thing every time. And I can't quite believe it was six different killers—"

"Any connection between the six different women?" Craine asked.

McClaren studied him, fingertips drumming. "Not that we can find," he said. "Nothing at all. We've had our computers working on it. You're right, of course. There's got to be one."

Craine nodded, thoughtful, then remembered to look drunk.

McClaren's head had drifted upward a little, lifting his heavy body. He pointed. "What's that in your coat?"

Startled, Craine looked down, then half rose from his chair and reached down into his bottomless pocket and drew out the book on clairvoyance. "Book I stole from the library," he said. He held it up so that McClaren could read the binding.

"Clairvoyance," McClaren said. His eyes sharpened, meeting Craine's, then he smiled. "Yes, interesting business," he said. "I imagine you're familiar with Phil Tummelty's operation?"

Craine raised his eyebrows.

"You should go check it out, if you're interested in parapsychology. He's got people over there—very strange, believe me."

Craine's heart jerked. "You're friends with Tummelty?" he asked mildly.

"Poker pals," McClaren said. He smiled.

It struck Craine now that he'd been staring for some time at the insurance company calendar, upside down from Craine, on Professor Furth's desk. Various dates on the calendar were circled and had writing around them. One was the thirteenth. *Poker,* he thought, almost in panic, hunting for the connection. McClaren and Eggers had talked of poker, it came to him, in the Chinese restaurant, the thirteenth, two days ago. That night, April Vaught had been murdered. His heart recoiled. *Wrong track.* All the same, there was some track.

"As I'm sure you know, he's a specialist on the brain," McClaren was saying. "Very famous surgeon in his younger days—author of several books. I'm afraid he's a terrible poker player." He laughed.

Craine smiled, appreciative of McClaren's implied skill.

Abruptly, the door opened and a young man poked his head in— someone Craine knew or had anyway seen before—then quickly pulled it back and closed the door again. Craine strained to remember where he'd seen him before.

"Dennis Reed," McClaren said, seeing Craine's struggle. "He works here—technician. Fixes the computers. Listen." He leaned forward, planting both elbows on the book-cluttered desk top, his elbows moving things aside as they settled in. "I've told you what I know. How about you telling me what *you* know?"

"One other question," Craine said, getting his pipe out, then patting his pockets for matches. "What's he like, this man Professor Furth? I think you mentioned he's a friend of yours."

"We've worked together a good deal, yes," McClaren said. "Over there in Crime and Correction, where I am, we frequently have use for a computer man. Believe me, Furth's the best. Experience with some of the finest computers in the world, I understand. NASA, Ma Bell, FBI, some computer in Chicago called PLATO . . ."

"Older man, I take it?"

"Oh, fifty—early fifties. I suppose you could say that's old in computers." He smiled, professorial.

"Married, I suppose?"

"No, single man. Married to his work, you might say."

Craine nodded. "Travels a lot, I take it. Some kind of computer trouble-shooter. You mentioned he's got a van."

Suddenly McClaren was uneasy, Craine sensed. His pale blue eyes bored steadily into Craine's, and his grin went dead. "That's very clever," Inspector McClaren said. It was clear that he intended to volunteer no more.

"Nothing going on between Furth and April Vaught, I suppose." Craine shook his head, saving McClaren the trouble of answering. "No, that's the first thing you'd have mentioned, if there was. So why isn't he in today?"

"I imagine it's upsetting, finding some young woman you know in your van, dead . . ." *Dead and naked,* he almost said, Craine saw, but then censored himself. He was an interesting man, this McClaren. Suppose he, McClaren, was the murderer—cracked by a profound inability to deal with the fact that we're born, as somebody put it, between urine and feces.

> *No wonder how I lost my Wits;*
> *Oh! Caelia, Caelia, Caelia shits!*

Mysterium tremendum, as somebody else said, the bottom line of creation's non-sense: to fashion radiant feminine beauty, the veritable goddesses that beautiful women are, to bring this out of nothing, out of the void, and make it shine in noonday; to take such a miracle and put miracles within it, deep in the mystery of eyes that peer out—the eyes that gave even dry Darwin a chill, to do all this, and to combine it—O horrors!—with an anus! Too much! O Christ where is Thy triumph? So McClaren, anally fixated Platonist, struck back. *("So it's you!"* the guru would say, Ira Katz had said. *Big smile from both parties . . .)*

" . . . tried him several times," McClaren was saying, "but no answer."

Craine's wandering attention returned. "You happen to check to see if the van's there?"

McClaren's eyes narrowed. "What are you thinking? That he might've made a run for it? or somebody might've grabbed him?"

"Just like to know where everything is," Craine said. "I misplace things a lot. Sometimes it takes me half the morning to find my shoes."

McClaren was watching him steadily again, so intent that he forgot to smile. What the danger was, Craine had no idea, but he understood that somehow he was in danger. "What's the date today?" McClaren asked from nowhere, as if suddenly remembering he had a dental appointment.

Craine touched the palp of his thumb against the tips of his first three fingers, one by one. "Thirteenth, fourteenth, fifteenth," he said.

"Yes, that's right," McClaren said, remembering now. "The fifteenth." He smiled. "Funny that you started with the thirteenth."

Craine smiled back, no more readable than McClaren. "Yes it is."

"So tell me," McClaren said, "how's your young friend Ira Katz?" He pressed his fingertips together, shaping a kind of cricket box over his chest.

"I haven't seen Ira since the morning we found Carnac," Craine said. "He was all right then."

"And also you saw him the night before, I think? With April Vaught?"

"Yes that's right, I did. Actually I went over quite a while before she got there, borrowed a cup of sugar and stayed a while—"

"Arguing—"

Craine glanced at him, puzzled. "No, not arguing . . . I don't think so."

"You don't remember?"

"I remember pretty well. It was late in the day, of course—"

"And you'd been drinking—"

"In moderation, yes. Since early morning." He spoke solemnly, as if humorlessly, and watched the inspector's reaction.

McClaren blushed and jerked up one side of his upper lip, baring three gold-framed teeth. *Stupid bastard,* he said, or seemed to say; the next instant Craine wasn't sure, because McClaren was saying, genial, "Put it this way, why don't you tell me what happened that night, from beginning to end?"

Craine sighed and, after he'd filled and lit his pipe, obeyed. It didn't take long. He could remember now only snippets of the conversation—which McClaren found uninteresting anyway. For no real reason, he said nothing of how the light on the stereo had gone off. When he mentioned that the phone call was from Ira's wife, McClaren perked up. "Hold on, now," he said. "You know it was from his wife?"

"I suppose I can't swear to it," Craine said. "That was my impression."

McClaren was leaning on his elbow, his head to one side, his fingers elegantly curled to support his cheek. Craine had a sudden sharp vision of him in navy whites, then, revising it, dressed him in a pea coat. There was no way on earth he could be wrong, Craine knew. Twenty, thirty years ago, McClaren had been a navy man. What it meant about his psyche Craine wasn't sure yet, but he'd get it, in due time. His left hand went into his suit coat pocket and struggled out again, dragging a paper scrap. "You got a pencil?" he said.

McClaren's eyes widened a fraction of an inch while his right hand, as if of its own accord, went for the pen in his pocket and held it toward Craine. "What's the note?" McClaren asked, one eyebrow lifted.

Craine held it up and read, " 'McClaren—former navy man.' "

"Jeesus!" McClaren hissed, then leaned in hard on both elbows. Though his blush was dark and his small, far from prominent chin slightly trembled, his voice was, though thin and nervous, even. "I've put my cards on the table. I thought you agreed in advance to do the same." (It wasn't true, and he knew it, Craine thought; but never mind.) The inspector jerked one hand out, palm up, effeminate. "What makes you think Ira's phone call was from his wife?"

"Several things—nothing that would stand up in court. His look when the phone rang, his tone of voice, the effect it had on him—only a wife can hit the weak spots with such absolute precision."

"A wife or, sometimes, a neurotic mother," McClaren said.

"True, except that Ira's mother's dead."

McClaren nodded. After a moment: "Can you remember what was said?"

That too Craine could tell quickly. He could remember only one short outburst: "Kill them! That's a wonderful idea! Kill them and pin the thing on me!"

"What?" McClaren said, looking at him harder. "You're sure he said that?"

"Don't make too much of it," Craine said.

"What do *you* make of it?"

"As an ordinary observer of humanity," Craine said, "I'd say Ira Katz and his wife were very angry, saying whatever they could think of to give pain."

"You're not making this up," McClaren said, studying him.

"Any reason I should?"

McClaren evaded it, slowly swivelling around in his chair to frown thoughtfully at the blank gray wall. "Anything else you can tell me about Katz?"

"Well," Craine said, hesitant about saying what he had in mind but interested in seeing how McClaren would react, "in the battle between Ira Katz and his wife, I'd say his wife wins hands down up at the English Department."

"Oh?" McClaren said. It seemed to come to him as news.

"I was talking with the chairman."

"Wendel Davies."

"That's him. Very fond of Katz's wife—nothing intimate, you understand. Likes her cooking, things like that. As for Katz, Professor Davies seems pretty well certain he'll never get tenure."

"Interesting," McClaren said. "No tenure, no job—no alimony, no child support . . ."

"That's true too," Craine said. "I guess they both lose."

"Funny man, Wendel Davies—as you've noticed. I occasionally see him at faculty meetings and whatnot. Independently wealthy; family's in plastics. Sometimes you get the feeling he's made of plastic himself. Great humanist, head full of poetry and fine feeling, but sometimes you get the feeling that back behind all of it . . ." He let it trail off, as if embarrassed. He cleared his throat.

"Very logical mind," Craine said.

"Yes, so it seems." McClaren glanced at his watch. "Of course I hardly know him," he added. Despite the glance at his watch he was pretending he had all day. No question about it, he was spending more time on Craine than made sense. "That reminds me," McClaren said, abruptly turning. "What about Carnac—where does he fit in? I assume you've got some theory?"

"No theory," Craine said. "I've thought about it, naturally."

"As for myself, I keep thinking of that idea of Tummelty's, that Two-heads Carnac, crazy as he seems, may in fact be an authentic psychic." He leaned forward, fingertips of both hands pressed together, as if trying out the idea on Craine. "Suppose our murderer is someone who knows Carnac well, knows he can 'see' things. That would make Carnac a threat, you'll admit."

"Carnac's about as psychic as my left foot," Craine said, and gave a laugh.

McClaren studied him, shaggy eyebrows lifted with interest. "You know that for a fact?"

"I know that every two, three weeks he gets kicked into the street because his fakery's so obvious any child can see through it. Tarot, tea leaves, that crazy mason jar—"

"Mason jar?" McClaren echoed.

"Claims it works better than a crystal ball," Craine said, and gave an angry little goat laugh. "Believe me, if he's psychic—"

"But isn't it true," McClaren broke in, "that with some people psychic ability comes and goes? I'm sure you've read of any number of cases—the Fox sisters, Eusapia Palladino, Nelya Mikhailova, for example, or better yet, the famous cousin of William James—I'm sure you've read of cases of authentic psychics who, as their powers waned, turned to trickery to keep from disappointing their disciples, or in order to stay in business, or for even more complicated reasons. Think about it a moment. Supposing that there really are people of psychic ability—and believe me, on that score Tummelty's operation leaves very little doubt—doesn't it seem natural, on the face of it, that Carnac—at least once in a while—is one of them? Think of that remarkable collection of junk in his shanty—dowsing rods, Ouija boards, canes, crank books and magazines, not to mention stuffed animals, voodoo candles, little bottles of God knows what . . ."

"Unlike you, I have never been in Mr. Carnac's shanty," Craine said.

"Be that as it may," McClaren said, "the question is, Why is he so interested in such things? If we begin with the assumption that he *has* had certain psychic experiences from time to time—disturbing experiences, more likely than not, since that's the usual case . . . I'm sure in all your reading you've run into these things . . ." Detective Inspector McClaren was rising from his chair as if having an otherworldly experience himself. He dipped his fingers into his sport coat pockets and half-turned away as if to look out a window, though there was no window there. "They're almost always unpleasant, and usually extremely unpleasant, these psychic experiences. I was reading, in a book Dr. Tummelty lent me, about the dreams people had before the Alberfan disaster in Wales, back in 1966. You probably remember it—coal slide that killed a hundred forty-four adults and children. More than two hundred people reported dreams and premonitions—all exceedingly unpleasant. One woman dreamed of children standing by a building—the school—below a great black mountain. Hundreds of black horses came thundering down the mountainside dragging hearses! Think of Abraham Lincoln's recurring dream just before his death—alone in a boat, drifting out farther and farther on a still gray sea. But dreams are the least of it. Think of the horror that must have tingled in the back of the mind of that schoolboy who said—famous case—'How can I be lying down there if I'm standing up here?' Shortly afterward he was drowned in the well. Or worse yet, think how it is with psychics who work on murder cases, like Hurkos or Croiset. I had the dubious fortune to watch such a psychic myself one time. There were four murders, each of them quite horrible. One after another the psychic went through them, experiencing the pain of each murder himself. I saw him choke—you'd swear there was a wire around his neck—it made his eyes bug out . . .

"Heaven knows why it has to be this way, but it's sorrow and pain that leaves the strongest impressions, as they say in the trade. So you can imagine how it would be for a man like Carnac—not a clever man, in fact somewhat dull-witted, so it would seem. He gets these terrifying visions—smells, tastes, sounds, not to mention things seen . . . No wonder he buys books, tarot cards, black candles, does everything he can to understand and gain control. Surely all this has occurred to you, Craine. There's no one in Carbondale closer to Two-heads Carnac than you are."

"Not true," Craine said, "or if it is true, it hasn't been *my* doing."

"Perhaps that's so," McClaren said. "My point remains the same. We have every reason to believe that Carnac may in actual fact be a psychic—and no reason, offhand, to doubt that the murderer has reached the same conclusion. If so, that would explain, of course—"

"You got this idea from Dr. Tummelty?" Craine asked.

"Not exactly. It's true that we discussed the subject. He's been interested in Carnac for some time."

Craine sucked hard at his pipe. No smoke came through. "It's strange to me how you people all know each other," he said. "University of twenty or more thousand students, must be a faculty of hundreds at least, and yet all you people"—he held out his left hand, fingers extended, and counted with the tip of his pipe stem—"you, Dr. Tummelty, Professor Davies in English, the computer-center man—what's his name, Furth—"

McClaren smiled. "All department heads, you'll notice."

"Ah! So that's it!"

Again McClaren stole a glance at his watch. When he saw that Craine had seen, he said, "Quarter after one. I'd better get a move on! By the way, I had a talk with the Denhams, this morning—Denham's Tobacco Shop."

"Yes, I go there all the time," Craine said.

"So I understand. You were drunk, I presume?"

"I suppose you could say it got a little out of hand."

"You remember what happened?"

"Very little of it."

McClaren thought about it, then nodded, grim. "It's interesting, this weakness of memory you claim. I did a little checking on your agency in Chicago, especially the last few weeks there."

"I thought you might."

"You can't really pretend you've forgotten all that."

"Only when people let me."

"That young woman, your client, the one who disappeared. What do you think happened to her?"

"I imagine she's dead."

"Hmm. Yes. I thought so. So do I." He got up off the edge of the desk and took a step toward the door. "Well, good day, Gerald. Glad you happened by."

Craine remained there, thinking nothing of importance, thinking how he was supposed to be shaken, and was, no doubt, but if so, shaken too deeply for any surface effect, so that it made no difference, at least for now, then rose at last, his knees trembling, and made his way to the door.

"Can I help you?" the Indian woman asked, looking up at him with a start.

Craine stood turning his limp hat in his hands, obsequiously smiling. "I wonder if there's someone I could ask a few questions. My name's Gerald B. Craine, Detective." He hunted from pocket to pocket for his license, but it was mysteriously gone. With a jerk, he reached out his hand and dangled it in front of her. She looked at it a moment, then reluctantly reached up her small, thin fingers, and shook hands with him. "I thought perhaps my old friend Professor Furth—"

"I'm sorry, Professor Furth isn't here today." She brightened, almost bloomed, suddenly confident, now that they had between them some common reality.

"Perhaps someone else then—"

"What kinds of questions did you have in mind?" she asked.

"Oh, things about computers, the staff here—I hardly know. You see, I'm working on a case. In fact, several cases." He smiled, once more clutching his hat, looking to the woman at the second desk for help, but the second woman had no suggestions, simply hunched her back and made a face. "Just a moment," the Indian woman said. She rolled back her chair, swung around sideways and up, and crossed to a door opposite Professor Furth's. She opened it a foot, poked her head in, and called "Dennis?"—then, "Murray . . ." She opened the door a little wider, slipped through, and partly closing it, her hand still on the edge—fingernails reddish black—talked with someone inside. After a moment she came out again, just behind her a plump, short man with curly hair and thick glasses. "Detective Craine," she began, and hesitated.

"Hello," the man said, "I'm Murray Weintraub."

"How do you do!" Craine said, eagerly bowing, almost throwing his arms out to make up for the stillness of the man who stood before him, planted on his small feet (sandals, dark blue socks), like a placid Chinese figurine. He wore a tie, slightly loosened, an Oxford-cloth shirt a little tight at the waist, a woven leather belt on which the buckle was cocked askew. "I'm a friend of Ira Katz—perhaps you know him?" Craine asked.

"I know Ira," the man said. His expression showed no change, though his use of Ira's name was as familiar as a relative's. From his balding, curly head to the soles of his sandals not a muscle moved; he was the soul of non-expression. Even when he shifted his eyes to the right, the movement was expressionless: It was as if he had simply decided to look at something and had looked. "Won't you come in?" he said, and turned, pushing the door open. When they were both inside, the door falling shut behind them, he said, standing motionless again, "What did you want to know?"

"As I was just now telling your friend out there, I'm not sure," Craine said. "Who his friends are, what he does here—what all you people do here—what you know about Miss Vaught . . ." When the man showed nothing, apparently still waiting, still assessing the situation, Craine broke in on himself. "What should I call you, 'Professor'? 'Doctor'?"

"Murray's fine, or professor—whatever you like." He slightly turned his head, the rest of him unmoving. Craine followed his gaze.

"When did you last see him?—Ira Katz, I mean," Craine asked.

"An hour ago, maybe an hour and a half," Weintraub said. He stopped walking for a moment, watching lights flick on and off, then moved forward again. "He was here when McClaren came. They had a long talk."

"I see," Craine said. His voice showed nothing of the alarm that leaped up in him. How odd that McClaren had kept it to himself! But no, not really odd. Craine sighed and pushed his hands into his pockets, slowly shaking his head. He'd do the same thing himself, in point of fact. If it moves, suspect it; also if it doesn't move. What was the saying? To a man who has nothing but a hammer, the whole world's a nail.

"What does all this do?" Craine asked, waving at the machines.

Professor Weintraub for just an instant smiled. "That's not easy to explain," he said. "Briefly, it creates reality. Cup of coffee, Mr. Craine?" Economically—hardly more than the movement of one hand—he indicated a coffee maker, Styrofoam cups, cream and sugar, black and white plastic chairs.

"Why yes, thank you," Craine said, and at once got out his pipe. Carefully, with gestures as expressionless as his face, Professor Weintraub filled two cups and, at Craine's direction, added sugar and cream. "I understand," Craine said when they were seated, "Ira Katz has a fairly ambitious program going."

"I imagine he does," Professor Weintraub said. "I'm not familiar with it, but all the programs that come through here are ambitious. It's all nonsense—practically all nonsense." His eyes moved, looking around the room, the rest of him quite still. "You're in Bedlam, Mr. Craine."

"I see," Craine said, and waited.

Professor Weintraub raised his cup and drank, then lowered the cup to his knee and sat motionless again. "You asked what we do here," he said. "It's an interesting challenge, a question like that. Let me see if I can tell you." He crossed his legs at the knee and stared at the line where the wall met the ceiling. He sipped his coffee, then—motionless again—began: "I myself came into computers through mathematics. Computers, to me, are simply large, fast calculators. They add, subtract, multiply, and so on; sort things very rapidly, by various criteria; remember things infallibly—in other words, they remember and manipulate formal symbols, figure out the values in a particular case of, say $F = ma$ or $E = mc^2$, to say nothing of equations vastly more complex; and in some cases they show you, on a viewing screen or printout, pictures of what they're doing or have done. You've seen examples—computer games, random patterns . . . You can get a computer to show you what the planet would look like if you travelled past it faster than, by the Einsteinian laws of energy and mass, it's possible to travel. We did that once at MIT. Or take a humdrum example. On my office wall I have a map I'll show you when we get there: it locates all earthquake activity since 1960. There's an interesting point to be made about that; remind me to come back to it.

"Perhaps the best way to get at what we're after is to explain what computers *can* do and what they *shouldn't* do, not that they can't (from a certain point of view), and why we're in trouble when computers are set to doing what they shouldn't.

"All right, so where are we. What do we do here. We create reality, I said earlier. That's just about it. Sometimes we do it in fairly innocent ways, running the computations that guide a rocketship and put a man on the moon, or figuring the odds that it will rain and ruin your garden party. In cases like that, the output, so to speak, is that human beings are in closer touch with reality than before, or anyway no further removed from it. The astronaut may have no idea how he got where he got—even the people at the NASA consoles may have no very clear idea, in fact—but that's moondust under his feet: he's in touch. That's usually not how it works with computers: usually the machine takes over for reality, and as the poet says, 'You can't go home again.'

"There are two ways to put it. On one hand, the computer transforms the world—transforms it utterly; on the other, it intercedes between the human mind and the world, the 'old reality,' if you like, and just sits there, like an impenetrable fog. Let me explain. Start with how the computer transforms the world in the post office, in the Pentagon, in business, everywhere—and I don't really mean just here in the United States—there had come to be just too much paperwork and too many technical steps in certain jobs, such as automobile building, for human beings to keep up with. Along came the computer and 'saved the day'—that is, saved the status quo. If the computer hadn't come along and jacked up the existing welfare distribution systems—hence their philosophical rationales—someone might have thought of eliminating much of the need for welfare by, for example, introducing a negative income tax. But the very erection of an enormously large and complex, computer-based welfare administration created, inevitably, motivation for keeping the system as it was. No politician likes to throw away millions, even billions, of the taypayers' dollars. Welfare's a minor example, of course. The most obvious and ludicrous is our so-called military defense system—computer-built, of course—a 'servomechanism,' as the Pentagon likes to say, spread out over an area comparable to the whole American continent. You've read of it, no doubt: the SAGE air-defense system. Needless to say, once we had SAGE, we had to assume that 'they' had one too, so we had to apply our computer technology to designing offensive weapons and strategies that could overpower our own defense, that is, 'their' presumed defense, and then we had to assume that 'they' had similar weapons and strategies . . . and so on and so on, through the MIRVs and MARVs, ABMs and forthcoming GKWs . . . You get the point. Computers have changed the world into something not easy to change back from. The kids in the street yell, 'No NUKES, no NUKES!' But they've only got one hope, in my opinion: learn math, become computer freaks, learn to guess handshakes and get inside the machines. Because the people they're yelling at aren't the ones who do the thinking. The ones who do the thinking are little plastic chips."

"Wait," Craine said. "You spoke of 'handshakes.' What's that?"

"Entrance code, that's all. Every big computer has a code you have to know to get into it. You give the computer the secret handshake and it's willing to talk to you."

"And it's possible to figure these things out?"

"To some extent. It all depends. Mostly you get the code from some person who knows it—officer of the company, who's a friend of yours, for instance. You'd be surprised how careless people are about codes. Mostly, I suppose, they have so little understanding of the computers, they're unaware of the risk."

"What are the risks?"

"Theft, sabotage. A good computer freak might get into the IRS computer and erase its whole file on him, or change it to gibberish, or assign it to Richard Nixon. Or he might add new features to the central computer's program—little subroutines that amuse him or somehow benefit him. For instance, in one of the more elegant so-called computer crimes, someone as yet unidentified got into one of the big electric company computers and persuaded it that every time it rounded off to the nearest cent, it should drop the remainder in his bank account. Three million half pennies a month—that's not bad pay for maybe twenty minutes' work."

"They happen often, these 'so-called computer crimes'?"

"Nobody really knows. According to the FBI, about one percent get reported; I imagine that's just about right."

"And they pay pretty well, you say?"

"I read somewhere a while ago that in the average burglary, the take is $42.50, and with the average bank robbery the take is about $3,500. In the average computer crime—this is just in the one percent reported, within which one percent almost nobody gets caught—the take is $500,000."

"That makes it very tempting. You ever thought of it yourself, Professor?"

"Naturally. Show me a first-rate computer man who tells you he hasn't and I'll show you a liar. I worked as a teller in a bank, years ago. We used to talk all through lunch about ways of stealing money—tellers, bookkeepers, even junior officers. We thought of some really foolproof schemes, but none of us ever took a nickel, so far as I know. It's a matter of personality, motivation—satisfaction with your work, how your personal life's going . . ."

"How much would I have to know to commit a computer crime?"

"That's hard to say. It's as much a matter of native intelligence as it is your knowledge of handshakes or math or computer languages. I can tell you this: everyone down here except a few of the programmers could handle it."

"Could Ira Katz?"

"I think he'd have to have help. That's just a guess."

"I assume you're granting him native intelligence."

"No question. But I think he worked with others, mainly. More a concept man than a hacker."

"Mmm. A minute ago you said—" Craine paused, studied his pad. "I may have gotten lost, but let me ask you this anyway. A minute ago you said there are two ways computers can mess up reality. One of them you've talked about, how computers can change things that happen in the world—how in fact they can become so integral to what happens that they can no longer be, you might say, factored out."

"Exactly. In the new world they've helped create, they're a vital organ. Shut them down and you shut down the civilization."

"I understand that, I think. Tell me the second point—how computers intercede, I think you said, between human beings and the world."

"Something like this. It's oversimplified, but it will give you the idea. What people think, generally, is that the computer does what the programmer tells it to, and since it's locked in to effective procedures, it can never go wrong. That's not exactly true. The truth is more nearly that the man at the console has very little notion of what's going on in the mind of the computer. He sees lights flash on and off, and he knows it's thinking something, but he has no idea what; in fact vast hunks of the computer's thinking go on between blinks, not in the central routine of the computer but somewhere in the miles and miles of shadow."

"I'm not following."

"No, right. Look. I mentioned routines. Say we have a standard routine—that is a set of algorithmic instructions—for adding numbers. Now say one of the numbers to be added is $\sqrt{25}$. You can't add square roots in with ordinary numbers, so when we get to $\sqrt{25}$ we have to stop adding—step out of the main routine, so to speak—and move to a different routine, call it a subroutine, which is designed to do nothing but figure out square roots. The subroutine rumbles along, off by itself, until it figures out that $\sqrt{25} = 5$, at which point we 'leave' the subroutine and reenter the routine. This detour has taken us, on a slow computer, maybe a millionth of a second. So we're clear now on routines and subroutines, right?

"All right. All these subroutines you keep in the computer—they're part of its methodological memory, one of many kinds of memory. In a really complicated mathematical problem you might leave the routine and enter some sub or sub-sub or sub-sub-sub routine a hundred, two hundred, a thousand times. How does one man, in a single lifetime, program them all in, you ask me? The answer is, he doesn't—and therein lies a tale.

"It's a community effort, like the evolution of the universe. One programmer puts in the routine for square roots. Another, another day, puts in the routine for quadratic equations. Still another, another day—and so on and so on, generation on generation. The computer's gifts and capabilities grow. Not only mathematicians make use of it but also demographers, physicists, psychologists, chess players. The computer begins to make decisions for itself—decisions we're not even aware that it's making. For example: I program in simultaneous play, at random intervals, of two games simultaneously—chess and pinochle. Sooner or later the call for a chess move and a pinochle move will coincide, and the computer will have to decide, if it can, which move to make first, chess or pinochle. Does the computer jam? go crazy? As it happens, it does not. Some sociologist happens to have left in it—maybe years ago—a formula stating that chess is a game of the upper class, pinochle a game of the lower class, and another formula, or symbolic statement, to be more precise—maintaining that the lower class tends to imitate the upper: so the computer plays the chess piece first.

"Wonderful, you may say. So all the people in AI, as it's called —artificial intelligence—are quick to yell. But it seems a little odd that we should be so quick to embrace an intelligence utterly different from our own—exclusively left-hemisphere intelligence, if you will—and an intelligence we have no way to check on. Nearly all our existing programs, and especially the largest and most important ones, are patchworks of the kind I've somewhat metaphorically described. They're heuristic in the sense that their construction is based on rules of thumb—stratagems that appear to 'work' under most foreseen circumstances—and ad hoc mechanisms patched in from time to time. The gigantic programs that run business and industry and, above all, government have almost all been put together—one can't even say 'designed'—by teams of programmers whose work has been spread over many years. By the time these systems are put on line, most of the original programmers have left or turned their attentions to other pursuits. A man named Marvin Minsky's found a very good way of expressing it: a large computer program, he says, is like an intricately connected network of courts of law, that is, of subroutines, to which evidence is submitted by other subroutines. These courts weigh (evaluate) the data given them and then transmit their judgments to still other courts. The verdicts rendered by these courts may—indeed, often do—involve decisions about what court has 'jurisdiction' over the intermediate results then being manipulated. The programmer thus cannot even know the path of decision making within his own program, let alone what intermediate or final results it will produce."

"Like Darwin's universe," Craine said, thinking aloud.

"Yes, very much like that," Weintraub said. "Geological-time strata—layers on layers of program evolution; chance combinations and recombinations; occasional freak occurrences, as when some teenaged computer nut interfaces his Radio Shack with the monster and starts moving things around. And above all, of course—you're right—no Programmer, pure blind mechanical survival of the fittest."

"Interesting, all this," Craine said.

There was a knock on the door. It opened two inches and, the same moment, Professor Weintraub called, "Come in!"

The door opened more and an intense, wild-looking man poked his head in. His hair and beard were red, as unwashed as Craine's and vastly more tangled. One of the lenses in his round, steel-framed glasses had a crack with Scotch tape over it. His clothes were army surplus, or maybe the real thing—patches and stripes had been torn off the arms. He was carrying, clamped under his right arm, a large messy roll of printout. "You going to lunch, Murray?" he asked, hardly noticing Craine. His voice was oddly hoarse, and he at once cleared his throat.

Professor Weintraub raised his left arm, pushed the cuff back, and looked at his watch. With a leap of guilt, Craine looked at his own. "It's nearly quarter to three, Frank. I ate hours ago," Weintraub said.

"Oh," the young man said, not surprised, exactly, not even quite registering. "Oh," he said again; then, abruptly, "Listen, I got an incredible new feature—"

"Later," Weintraub said with a smile, raising his hand like a policeman.

"Oh, sorry," the red-head said. Now he turned to look at Craine, his expression like that of a man looking at a chimp at the zoo. "Sorry," he said. He gave a little wave and backed out, closing the door.

Craine said, shifting his weight forward, preparing to rise, "I hadn't realized how late it was getting. I've got to run. I want to thank you, Professor Weintraub. You have no idea—"

"Don't mention it," Weintraub said. "I hope it helps somehow. It's been a pleasure, actually."

"One thing," Craine said, on his feet now. "Who was that fellow?" He aimed a thumb at the door.

"That was Britt—Frank Britt," Weintraub said, and gave a just perceptible headshake, perhaps embarrassment.

"He's a programmer?"

"Very much so." He pushed back his desk chair and got to his feet, then came around to accompany Craine out. "He's what you might call a computer bum—very special modern breed." He laughed.

Though it was later than he'd thought—even if he left right now he couldn't reach Elaine Glass by quarter to three, as he'd promised—Craine hesitated. "What do they do?" he asked.

"Why, they play with computers. That's all they live for." He made a vague, airy gesture with his plump right hand. "Dreamers—mathematical loonies." When Craine went on waiting, his look still questioning, Professor Weintraub cocked his head, thought for an instant, then said: "When you talk about an ordinary engineer you're talking about a man who's, so to speak, impacted in the physical universe. What he does is ruled by its physical laws; in the end he can do only what may be lawfully done. When some device he creates doesn't work, he can't always know by his own reasoning alone whether he's on the verge of success—some small adjustment—or hopelessly lost, wandered into some closet from which there's no exit. He has to turn to his teachers, his colleagues, his books—appeal to real experience for some clue to what's gone wrong. But the computer programmer is in a different situation. He creates a universe for which he alone is the lawgiver—or at least that's his aim. And of course on a computer, it's possible to create universes of almost unlimited complexity. One may create, for example, worlds in which there's no gravity, or in which two bodies attract each other, not by Newton's inverse-square law, but by an inverse-cube law, or in which time dances forward and backward in obedience to a choreography as simple or complex as one wills. Moreover, and this is the crucial point, systems programmed in this way can *act out* their scripts. They compliantly obey their laws and vividly exhibit their obedient behavior. No playwright, no stage director, no emperor has ever exercised such absolute authority or commanded such unswervingly dutiful troops. Obviously, power like that can be addictive." Professor Weintraub shook his head again, at once quizzical and sad, and opened the door. "I'll lead you to the front office," he said. "Believe me, you'd never find it."

"Yes, thank you," Craine said. "You're right, it's quite a maze." Looking down the sterile hallway, leading to other hallways at either end, he had no idea which direction he had to go. As Weintraub turned to the right, then hesitated, waiting for him, Craine said, "So this Britt's one of the addicts."

"Very much so. They're everywhere, you know—wherever you find computer centers, which is to say in countless places in the United States and in virtually every other industrial region of the world . . . bright young men like Frank, there, of dishevelled appearance, usually with sunken, glowing eyes. They sit there at their consoles, arms tensed and waiting to fire their fingers, already poised to strike, watching the typewriter ball, staring like the gambler who keeps his eyes riveted on the dice. When he's not sitting there at the console, transfixed, the hacker—that's what they call themselves, 'hackers'—the hacker sits at a table strewn with computer printouts, poring over them like a rabbi demonically possessed by some cabalistic text. They work till they drop—twenty, thirty hours at a time. If they can arrange it, they have their food brought in to them—coffee, Cokes, sandwiches. If you let them, they sleep on cots or bedrolls near the computer—but only a few hours, then back to the console or the printouts. Their rumpled clothes, their unwashed and unshaven faces, and their uncombed hair all show plainly how little they care about *our* so-called reality. They exist only through and for the computers. Compulsive programmers. Hackers, they call themselves. They're an international phenomenon." He caught Craine's elbow as he started to turn left where they had to continue straight. "This way."

"Ah, yes." Quickly he asked, "Why do computer centers put up with them? They're not working on real projects, if I understand what you've said—"

"They're useful, that's all. They're like the 'friendly' parasites in the human body: they're not part of us, exactly, but we can't live without them. The hacker is usually a superb technician. He knows every detail of the computer he works on, its peripheral equipment, the computer's operating system, and so on. He's tolerated around the center because of what he knows and because he can write small subsystem programs very fast, that is, in one or two sessions of, say, twenty hours each. Before long, in fact, the center may find itself using any number of his programs. The trouble is—as you can guess from what I've said—a hacker will almost never document his programs once he stops working on them, with the result that a center may come to depend on him to teach the use of the programs, how to maintain them, and so on—programs whose structure only he—if anyone—understands."

"I'm beginning to understand why you called this operation what you did at the start," Craine said. "Bedlam." They were now in the first room Weintraub had brought him into. He recognized the door that led to the reception room, the secretaries' desks.

Weintraub smiled back a little distantly; Craine could feel the man withdrawing to whatever complex thought Craine's arrival had interrupted. "I suppose I haven't given you a very favorable impression of our work," he said. "The other side, of course, is that for some of us it's extremely exciting work—I can no more tell you how exciting it is, to a man like myself, to say nothing of a man like Frank Britt . . ." He reached for the doorknob but then hesitated before turning it, wanting to finish his thought. "I've told you how things can go wrong in computer work. But believe me, when they go right—" He opened the door and bowed, letting Craine go first.

As soon as they entered the reception room, they both knew in an instant that something was wrong. The secretaries both looked up at once, with an expression Craine knew but could not place, one that froze him where he stood. In Professor Furth's office—the door stood open—the young man Craine had seen before somewhere, Dennis Reed, was hunting for something in the books and papers on Furth's desk, his face solemn, squeezed shut with concentration. There was another man at his left, a gaunt, dishevelled black in glasses and fatigue cap. The minute Dennis Reed saw Craine watching him he jumped to the door and swung it shut. Something in the look of alarm, the way the boy's head jerked back, the eyes black and beady as a groundhog's switched on the lost connection. It was the boy who'd been watching him at Tully's Tome Shop—the frightened fat boy in the oversized red sweater who had been following him later in the street. He felt an impulse to rush to Furth's door right now and get to the bottom of this, but by the clock on the wall it was nearly five to three, much too late already; he couldn't get back to Elaine's even now before three, and he'd said two forty-five. And there was, anyway, this other business, the stillness in the room, like mourning.

"Professor Weintraub," the blondish secretary was saying, "have you heard?"

"Heard what?" Professor Weintraub asked. He was as still and lightly balanced as if with fright held in as when Craine had first met him.

"Professor Furth's had an accident, he's been killed," she said. "He ran his van over a cliff."

Weintraub turned his head to look at Craine, then looked past him, hardly registering that Craine was there.

"I've got to go," Craine whispered. "I'm sorry, I'm very sorry."

Weintraub, deep in thought, seemed not to notice.

Fragment Three

They had come to a gray metal door at the rear of the stacks. Weintraub opened it and waved Craine through. Ahead of them lay a seemingly endless corridor, offices on each side. Craine could not remember later who the offices belonged to. He could remember, in fact, almost none of it, only the powerful visual effects, the *strangeness* of it all. He was seeing with innocent eyes, like a child: an office where three men—two blacks and an Oriental—sat poring over a printout with the intense concentration of Chicago anarchists, all three of them wearing hats, on the table all around them coffee cups, pink plastic spoons, and sandwich crusts. Another room, later, high ceilings, flickering fluorescent lights, immense computers humming and pinging, typewriters clattering, on the floor in a corner a bearded young man on an army cot, asleep.

"You've no idea where Professor Furth is today?" Craine asked.

"None. I'm sorry. He's away a lot of course, hunting bugs and glitches in various people's software, or giving lectures at one university or another. Spends half his time on airplanes, that man, but usually he tells us in advance when he'll be gone."

"He's the general boss here?"

"Technically, yes."

He'd hit a sensitive spot, he saw, though when he looked Weintraub's face was as expressionless as ever—slightly bug-eyed, pallid as a professional chess player's, his curly hair floating along around his balding dome as if the hair and head were of a different dimension from the world they momentarily occupied. "What does he lecture on?" Craine asked.

"Doom, for the most part," Weintraub said, and smiled. "One of the two favorite subjects of computer men. The other one being how we and

only we, by our magic and clearheadedness, are destined to save the world."
He raised one forearm just enough to allow himself to raise an index finger
as a beacon. Craine glimpsed for the first time, despite the unearthly, expressionless face—perhaps it was only the shyness of an egghead—that the man
had humor in him. Craine chuckled, encouraging, and put his hat on to
free himself to work with his pipe.

"Furth, I take it, doesn't believe that only computer men can save the
world."

"No."

"And yourself?" Lighting his pipe, Craine slid his eyes at the man.

"Sometimes I'm a little optimistic—usually on Thursdays. For the most
part, no." The hand with which he'd made the beacon went to his belt
buckle, caught hold like a bat, and hung there.

"Nevertheless," Craine said, "you take all this very seriously, I can see."

"Oh yes, it's serious. Far more serious than most things—which is not
to say better." He added, as if giving the wrong impression were unethical,
"I love it."

"Tell me, Professor," Craine said, waving his pipe as if in apology,
"were Professor Furth and April Vaught at all close?"

They were passing a bank of computer screens like large television sets,
consoles below them, men and women looking up, each at his own screen,
with sunken, glowing eyes. There was a curious scent of sweat and raw
nerves, also burnt coffee and old hamburger. Panel lights flicked on and
off in seemingly meaningless patterns. Weintraub, without Craine's noticing
it, had stopped and stood watching one of the screens, his body as still as
some queerly bland figure from a wax museum. The woman at the console
below the screen was smoking a cigarette, never touching it with her fingers,
her hands poised over the typewriter keys, her eyes narrowed as if with
bitchy rage. Clearly she did not know they were there—know any of them
were there. "Come on, baby," she whispered, "you're in! you're *in!*"

Delicately, Weintraub stepped away. "Furth and April Vaught," he
said, picking up the phrase as if from some old, old memory bank. He turned
and studied Craine critically, and shook his head. "So far as I know they
never spoke to each other. He knew who she was of course; and of course
Furth knew Ira . . ."

"They're friends, Professor Furth and Ira?"

"Not precisely. When you meet John Furth you'll see why. He has enemies and allies, not friends." He smiled dimly. "But they talked some; they had certain common interests. I remember they once had a long discussion on, so to speak, computer poetry—very heated, both on the same side." He smiled more brightly, recalling it. "Ira took the position that the 'experience' communicated in true poetry is unavailable to the computer. I forget his examples—the remembered anguish of adolescent love, that may have been one of them. Or the parent's feeling when he watches his sleeping child. Furth was delighted. I think he quite literally hit the desk with his fist, he was so pleased with Ira's argument."

Craine stood puffing at his pipe, waiting for more. No more came. "What was it about it that pleased him?" he asked at last.

Professor Weintraub glanced at him, then looked at the floor. "Your question's more complicated than you realize," he said. He opened another door, nodding Craine through, then came through himself just in time to catch a blond, sallow-looking man in a light blue frock, a sort of lab coat. "Petersen!" Weintraub called. The man stopped abruptly, and Weintraub went up to him, four quick steps, asking some question Craine didn't hear. They looked together at the blond man's clipboard, then Weintraub nodded and the man hurried off in the direction he'd been headed before.

"Well," Weintraub said. He was about to say, "That's about it," and get back to his work.

"Look," Craine broke in, grabbing Weintraub's elbow. "I know you're busy, and I know it seems a waste of your valuable time, my asking all these questions, but we're dealing with a murder and the possible involvement of a personal friend of mine—Ira Katz, I mean, a man I'm sure you have some feeling for yourself. Go along with me just a little longer. All I want is to get the *feel* of this place."

"In half an hour?" Professor Weintraub asked mildly.

"I know, I know." He thought of the whiskey in the truck—his chest full of pressure, something twisting in his stomach. He was so tense, so crowded by time and the befuddling complexity of things—he must meet Elaine Glass—how much time left, half an hour?—and he must get over to Carnac—if McClaren was right he should have gone there right off—and tense for more reasons than those, of course—McClaren's suspicions, damn near had a case piled up, or so it seemed right now; Craine couldn't be sure, couldn't seem to think worth crap without that whiskey . . . He stood clinging to Weintraub's elbow, bent forward as if ready to tighten to a crouch.

"Just humor me! Believe me, I know what I'm doing! Where were we? Furth?" He began to move, pulling Weintraub along with him, half forcing him down the hallway as if he, Craine, had taken over as guide. "So why is it he hates computer poetry?"

Weintraub answered distantly, perhaps mainly out of pity. "Are you familiar with the term 'effective procedures'—or 'algorithms'?"

"I'm not sure," Craine said. "It's possible that somewhere—"

The professor held up his hand. " 'Effective procedures' are what computer programs are built of," he said. "An effective procedure is, so to speak, a set of rules that tells the player of a game, or a mathematician—or one of these computers—exactly what to do, that is, what the rules allow. Exactly. No fudging, no room for interpretation. A system as tyrannical as instinct to a bee. To put it another way, an effective procedure, an algorithm, is an inflexible, step-by-step way of doing something; for example, it may give the computer what we call a 'routine' for finding square roots. By its nature, an effective procedure assumes either the pure play of concepts, as in mathematics, or a determinist universe—you know, Leibnitz' idea that if we could know where every particle of the universe is and exactly how it's moving at any given time, we could predict the whole future of the universe.

"John Furth, as I've indicated, doesn't like the idea of a determined universe. He's a great believer in liberty, free will—all that. He's also a great believer in computers, in their place; but he doesn't want them writing poetry, or replacing the human judicial system, as many computer theorists are convinced they could and should. He doesn't want them, as he puts it, 'dehumanizing human beings'—which is to say, persuading us we ought to think lightly of intuition and emotion and be more like machines. Some people would say he exaggerates the danger—it has a suspiciously slogany sound: *Dehumanization!* But it's an interesting subject."

"I see, yes," Craine said, eagerly agreeing. (He'd have agreed to anything to keep Weintraub talking.) "He must have been shocked, finding the dead woman in his car."

Weintraub bent his head. "He was. I saw him just a few hours afterward. He was gray. Shaky. He looked like a man who's lost a great amount of blood."

"As extreme as that?"

"It was, believe me! I must say—I don't mean to be unfeeling, you know—but I was rather surprised. I don't think, if it were myself . . . But of course we all react differently to things . . . "

"If it were you, you were saying?"

Weintraub shook his head. "I don't know. It might have been exactly the same, of course. None of us knows about these kinds of things, do we."

"That's true, of course," Craine said. "No doubt a terrible shock."

Craine, leading, had accidentally brought them to a large storage room—huge cardboard boxes and, under a high window, broken things: chairs, filing cabinets, wire-basket carts, high metal stands of some kind. "This is the storage and junk room," Craine said, playing guide. He waved his pipe, authoritative.

Weintraub smiled, then started, with a nod to Craine, toward an alleyway through the cardboard boxes.

Craine asked, "Tell me, Professor, what's it all do—the center, computer work? What's the—what shall I say . . . What's going *on* here, exactly?"

Again for just an instant Professor Weintraub smiled. "Briefly," he said, "we create reality. Cup of coffee, Mr. Craine?" Economically, hardly more than a movement of one plump hand—he indicated a brown Mr. Coffee coffee maker, Styrofoam cups, cream and sugar, a group of plastic chairs. Beyond the chairs stood another double door, open, and beyond it another long hallway, offices on each side.

"Why yes, thank you," Craine said, and got out his pipe. Though it had been riding in his pocket—he had no recollection of putting it there—it was still smoking. He puffed at it, getting it going.

Carefully, with gestures as expressionless as his face, Professor Weintraub filled two cups and, at Craine's direction, added sugar and cream to one.

"I understand," Craine said as they moved toward the double door, "Ira Katz has a fairly ambitious project going."

"I imagine he does," Professor Weintraub said. "I'm not personally familiar with it, but all the programs that come through here are ambitious." He glanced absently into a room where a group of men with loosened ties sat arguing in clouds of cigarette smoke. "It's all nonsense, really—or practically all nonsense." His eyes moved left and right, halfheartedly checking the office doors as he and Craine passed with their coffee cups. Except for his legs, the rest of him, as he walked, seemed motionless, floating. "You're in Bedlam, Mr. Craine."

"I see," Craine said, and waited.

Professor Weintraub stopped, solemnly raised his cup and drank, then lowered the cup and started walking again. He gestured toward a corridor breaking off to the right. "My office is down this way," he said. As they moved toward it, he said, "What do we do here. Jesus, what a question!"

"Let me sketch in what I'm after," Craine cut in. "I just want to know what kinds of problems come up, anything at all that will help me to get some idea of what it's like to work here—for insiders, I mean. A programmer like April Vaught. The morale of the place, intrigues, disappointments . . ."

Professor Weintraub studied Craine thoughtfully with his slightly bugged gray eyes, then nodded, walking on. Before he'd figured out quite what to say, they'd reached his office. When they were seated, Weintraub at his desk, Craine opposite, Weintraub set his cup down, crossed his legs at the knees, and stared at the line where the wall met the ceiling. Framed in the window behind Weintraub's head, Craine could see the chimneys of the chemistry building.

"I myself came into computers," Weintraub said, "through mathematics. To me, computers are just large, fast calculators. They add, subtract, multiply, and so on; sort things very rapidly, by various criteria; and they remember things infallibly—in other words, they remember and manipulate formal symbols, figure out the values in a particular case of, say, $F = ma$ or $E = mc^2$, to say nothing of equations considerably more complex."

Fragment Four

The minute he spotted her waiting on the porch of her apartment house, Craine knew he was in dutch. He swung the truck into the driveway almost without slowing, then hit the brake and skidded, meaning to let her know he'd been hurrying, it wasn't his fault that he was late. It was only when he heard the gravel spitting, flying from the tires, that he realized he'd sent the wrong signal: she would assume he was drunk. Nothing could be farther from the truth, in fact. He'd jumped into the truck, turned the ignition, and jerked forward all in one crazy motion, not even thinking of taking the bottle from under the seat where it was hidden. Now as he sat bent hard over the steering wheel, his left foot on the clutch, his right on the brake, staring out the window with widened eyes as if no one could be more surprised by the suddenness of his arrival than he was, he understood that, by crimus, he'd done it this time. If she'd begun to trust him, she was finished with that now. It surprised him that she didn't turn instantly into the house, or dart down onto the sidewalk and stride away without him. She simply stood there in the porch shadows, small and furious, clutching her armload of books and staring at him, her dark eyes sharp as an Injun's. He thought of yelling something at her, taking the offensive, and thought in the same mental motion of calling out, *Sorry I'm late!* He tried to think of some lie—it was true that his watch was undependable, he thought, then backed off from the thought, somehow confused: was it or wasn't it? And all at once he understood that he'd waited too long, it was too late now to say anything, nothing to do but sit there.

Suddenly, to his astonishment, she broke free of the pillar she'd been leaning against and came hurrying down the porch steps into the sunlight and over toward his truck. Like an eager servant, he reached over to open the right-hand side door. She climbed in. She met his grin with a black-eyed flash of anger, then turned her face forward, staring out the window, saying nothing. He shifted into reverse and hurriedly, smoothly, let the clutch out.

"Do you realize what *time* it is?" he heard her ask, clear as day, though her mouth never moved.

"Yes I do," he said crossly. "I got a watch, same as you."

She shot a startled look at him, then looked forward again.

"You're only maybe fifteen minutes late," he said. Part of his mind stood back from the rest, pondering the strange possibility that he'd begun to read minds. He asked, "What building's your class in?"

"Faner," she said.

"English class?"

"Biology."

"I thought Faner was mostly for English," he said, merely to be talking; he'd never thought one thing or another about what was taught in Faner. The place was too big, he realized on reflection, to be the province of any one department.

The girl said nothing, still punishing him, or punishing him and think-ing. It was interesting, Craine mused, that she'd decided to ride with him in spite of her anger. No real choice, maybe. He was the only ride she had, and it was too far to walk; he'd seen enough to know she was something like obsessive about her schoolwork. Yet that wasn't all of it. She'd stood there waiting in the shadows of the porch like an orphan, waited some twenty minutes beyond the time he'd said he'd come; and with good argu-ment against it, when he'd come into the driveway like a crazy man, she'd decided, suddenly and sternly, to ride with him. Her skin was brown, slightly golden, as if maybe she'd spent the summer in Florida. He remem-bered—and thought, the same instant: *There it is again, memory, live and healthy, as if it were all half an hour ago*—how as a child he'd watched, fur-tively, those brown, black-haired girls with the Oriental eyes, mysterious to him as midnight. Catholics, Jews . . . He'd hardly dared speak to them. Once on a hayride, something to do with high school, an Italian girl had kissed him. She wore a perfume called Tabu. Even now when, on rare occa-sions, the scent touched his nostrils, his chest would go light.

He slowed for jaywalkers, three boys and two girls. They didn't even look up, naturally assuming he would slow for them. Aristocrats.

"Biology," he said. "You ever read Charles Darwin?"

Elaine said nothing, though her sternness had changed a little, had just perceptibly relaxed, as if she'd begun to imagine possible excuses for him, or begun to turn her arguments inward, against herself. She looked down at the books on her knees, then back up at the windshield.

"I went through a Darwin bender once," Craine said. "Every book I could lay my hands on. You aware that when he went on his *Beagle* voyage he didn't go as ship's naturalist—went as companion to the captain?"

She said nothing.

"Very interesting fact. Man named Captain Fitzroy. You see, how it was, in those days, the captain was a man of such high class he couldn't speak with the crew. Gave the first mate his orders, and that was it. All the rest of the time he was alone, even ate alone. Lot of them went crazy, like Captain Ahab. Very common. Five-year voyage, not a soul to talk to . . . Very common for captains to commit suicide, in fact—as Captain Fitzroy did, about two weeks after Darwin left him. Slit his throat, if I remember. Very strange world people lived in, back then."

Craine squinted, leaning forward, seeing clearly only now, as he told her about it, what a queer world indeed those old-timers had lived in, friendship between the classes as shocking, in fact unthinkable, as Darwin's ideas about our great-great-grandfathers and the monkeys. He imagined Captain Fitzroy alone on the bridge, hardly more than a boy—twenty-six when he set out, unless that was someone else, some other old tale—his peasant crew on the decking below him, tugging at their forelocks if they happened to meet his eye . . . the image was so vivid in Craine's mind that he almost forgot he was driving and had to veer suddenly to the right to avoid a car. When he glanced at Elaine she was looking at him in alarm. He steadied into his lane, pretending nothing had happened, then remembered to bear left for his approaching turn.

"But that's not the interesting part," he continued, pushing in the clutch, then the brake, waiting for his chance, some hint of a break in the two lanes of oncoming traffic. To their left, the campus lay as separate from the town as the world of Captain Fitzroy on the *Beagle*—buildings, trees, hedges, close-cropped rolling lawns, moss-covered boulder formations hauled in, back in the fifties, on flatbed trucks. Sunlight lay over the campus, the gold-leaved walkways, like grace. "The interesting part is that Fitzroy was a religious fundamentalist. Darwin might be his equal in aristocratic blood, but other than that, poor Fitzroy couldn't have found a man less like himself if he'd tried. Luckily Darwin was sick a lot, which made him keep to his cabin—he was sickly all his life. And also, no doubt, he was there to gather specimens, and he didn't want to ruin the chance by getting Fitzroy down on him. All the same, they had some battles, as you can imagine."

A break came and Craine made his turn, then sped up, almost reckless, making up lost time. Without a word Elaine Glass reached out with both hands, bracing herself on the dashboard. The streets through the campus were inactive, as they always were during class hours. Almost the minute the bell rang, they would clog. On the lawns, in the soft shadows of trees, students sat reading and talking, or lay asleep.

Craine said, "You can't help wondering how much influence it had on Darwin's theory—that knucklehead fundamentalism of Fitzroy's. Darwin, you know, took a very hard line on the God business. Crossed him right off. Not like Isaac Newton, who could manage both opinions, mechanistic and mystic-theological. Darwin said—softly and politely, as is the aristocratic way—'No God, brothers. Junk evolving into junk. That's all.'"

Abruptly, Elaine Glass said, "That's sick!"

"Me or Darwin?" Craine asked.

"Darwin," she said; but she was censoring herself. The tone was reproach.

There was no place to park. He pulled halfway up onto the sidewalk alongside Faner, switched off the engine, pulled the brake on, and opened his door. At once, as if materialized from nowhere, as a reprimand, a blind boy appeared and came tapping toward them, walking faster than a person with sight would walk, overcompensating, making trouble. Craine clamped his jaw and got out, let come what might.

Elaine slammed the door on her side, then saw the blind boy and cried, "Look out for the truck! There's a truck on the sidewalk!"

The boy jumped a foot, swinging his head around, first right, then left, convinced he was about to be run over. In panic, his left hand thrown out to the side, the cane in his right tapping rapidly, far ahead of him, he rushed toward the street, felt the curb and spun around and rushed, tapping, toward the wall of the building. Elaine stooped quickly, put her books down, and ran to him. "Let me help you!" He swung his face at her and said something, angry, or so it seemed from where Craine stood. She gave him some answer, calming him—calming both of them—then walked with him, cupping his elbow, around past the truck. When she released his elbow he thanked her and set about explaining something, gesturing with both hands. She nodded, answering, smiling nervously, eagerly. He continued gesturing and explaining—by the wheeling and slashing of his cane in the air, it might have been the woe of existence he was explaining—and Elaine went on smiling and nodding. Craine looked at his watch. Three twenty. This delay too, of course, she would blame on Craine. Rightly, no doubt, from a certain point of view. At last, his explanations concluded, the blind boy turned away from her and, after a last brief hesitation, went tapping down the sidewalk. Elaine turned her head to look reproachfully at Craine, then started for the entrance and the stairway.

"You forgot your books again," Craine called.

She stopped and simply stood there with her back to him. He stepped to the books, scooped them up, and hurried toward her. When she held out her arms for them, he pretended not to notice.

"Which floor's your class on?"

"Second," she said.

"We better hurry, you're twenty minutes late," he said. He made a slight movement in the direction of the door, then waited. She compressed her lips, then bent her head—in profile, her face was like the face on some ancient coin, Craine thought—and, together, they started for the entrance.

"Listen, I'm sorry if I wasn't on time," he said, not turning to look at her. "I hurried as fast as I could, scout's honor. I'm also sorry I put the truck where the blind boy could run into it. I really am. Look, Miss Glass, stop being mad at me."

"All right," she said. She glanced at him sideways and, seeing that he was watching her, gave a shrug. "So all right."

He reached out ahead of her to open the door, and perhaps against her principles, she stood politely waiting till it was open, then stepped through. "I'm also sorry about the mindless chatter about Darwin," he said as he started up the stairs behind her.

"I didn't mind. It was interesting." Whether or not she was still angry seemed impossible to tell. Ruefully, he watched how her brown-golden legs took her springing up the stairs—he, Craine, laboring behind her, winded by the time he reached the first-floor landing. By the time they reached the second, where her class was, he was ready to gag, like Royce bent over with an attack of emphysema. She went striding down the hall. He hurried, coughing into his hand, trying to catch up with her. At one of the classroom doors she stopped and stood for a moment with her head bent, listening. Craine went up to her to give her her books, his legs aching, almost trembling, from his climb. She nodded, awkwardly taking the pile.

She said, meeting his eyes and then looking away, embarrassed, "I should talk to you sometime about that thing we were talking about before, the difference between people and animals, the way we lose touch because of words—remember? I was thinking about what I've learned in analysis, and I think—I'm not *certain,* I mean, but—I think you're wrong." She turned from him to look through the little square window into the classroom.

"I'll be waiting," he said. "Anything you like, I'm your servant. Craine's Last Case. One last feeble push for humanity, and then *amen, amen.*"

She jerked her face around, her eyes very wide behind the magnifying lenses. She'd understood him better than he'd meant her to, he saw. He winked and grinned to throw her off, but her expression did not change. Without a word, she turned the doorknob, opened the door just a little, and slipped in.

Craine watched her out of sight. The professor was saying, working up interest, though she'd said it a hundred times, no doubt, "If you could put all the people in the United States on a postage stamp, that's how many rods there would be on a single retina. And as for the cells of the brain itself, if people were scaled down to the size of cells, we could hold the whole population of the earth in our two cupped hands, and there wouldn't be enough to make a brain of."

There the door clicked shut, and though he could still have heard if he were willing to strain, Craine gave up listening. He turned away from the classroom, folded his hands behind his back, and for a moment stood gazing out the large, gray-tinted window.

The sunlight fallen over the campus seemed now ever warmer, more golden, bronzing the trees, making them like trees in some noble old painting from the eighteenth century.

Fragment Five

There on the dark, quiet lawns and the shaded brick and stone entranceways where students stood waiting, inaudibly talking—they all seemed now features in some classic oil painting, fallen out of time. The Golden Age, Craine thought, and gave a little nod as if someone else had said it. Strange, downright mysterious, how placid university campuses could seem. He knew well enough that it was partly an illusion. It was here, after all, that Ira Katz made his living, full of anger and sorrow at the failure of his marriage. You could pretty well bet that once, at least, he'd loved that wife of his; no doubt believed, when first they'd gotten married, she was the prettiest creature that ever walked this earth, and the cleverest too—Wendel Davies, his chairman, seemed to think so, so to Ira, who'd loved her, it must have been all the more obvious. Emotions like that would be hard to get over: his memory of how it was at the beginning of their marriage (it was always the same, that first stage of marriage, like the first stage of a drunk), all the time love-making, night and morning and under the not-yet-paid-for kitchen table; and his memories of the hospital, when she was having their children, how she'd clung to his hand as if to crush the bones, rolling her widened eyes at him, mouth opening for a scream; and memories of moments when she'd shone and he'd been proud of her—some party where everyone was surprised at her wit or sweet modesty, whatever (more likely wit, Craine decided, studying the photograph in his mind): say she was wearing a dress she'd made herself, very tasteful, stunning, the neck perhaps a slash that showed her cleavage. There'd be no doubt, of course—against all those painfully sweet memories he carried—that their Eden had gone awry; indeed, looking back, he would see that their marriage had been awry from the beginning. Perhaps she had a jealous streak, or a sullen streak, or a mean streak, something he'd noticed—if only he'd paid attention—the first day he'd met her. There'd be no doubt in his mind that it was mainly her fault; at any rate no doubt in the part of his mind where the light was on. For all his poetry, Ira Katz was no wiser than any other poor doltish male. It was a premise with all men, Craine had long since observed, that everyone ought to feel exactly as they did; to feel otherwise was to show oneself emotionally defective—infantile, or hysterical, or cloddishly insensitive. Most men were quick to assert this premise, and proud of it. Women, who worked from the same premise, confused things by hotly denying that that was how they worked. And so they'd fought the age-old fight, tiresomely the same, from the viewpoint of the gods, generation on generation. What each of them had loved, if it had ever been love—the central mystery of the other one's being—they'd attacked with the cunning and (behind the loud skirmishing) deadly calm of professional murderers. Each convinced, of course, that he did it to save himself, not really to hurt the other—and, ironically, each one right. An old, old story. Ira Katz would have no real doubt that he'd been right to leave, in the end: she'd been killing him, he could tell himself, and very likely it was true. But ah, how terrible it must be for him now to look out at this peaceful scene, this green-golden Eden lost to him forever though he stands in the center of it! "This softness in the air," he would think, "this is how it was the night I took her to that John Wayne movie." Or, "The way the shadows are beginning to stretch out, that's the way it was the night she gave me the surprise party, the night I passed my orals." *Ah, Eden,* Craine thought, wincing and shaking his head without knowing it, *terrible, terrible place!* No man—or almost none—in Ira Katz's position could keep it entirely secret from himself that in fact it was his fault. Poet. Squeezer, poisoner of emotion, himself the ancient enemy, sly old viper. Craine would bet anything you cared to bet that even now, in his misery, what Ira Katz was writing nights was poems about his former wife, or maybe—yes, more likely—his children. "Nobody learns a damn thing," Craine muttered aloud, then, hearing himself, shut his mouth and swallowed. Restlessness, ambition, that was the enemy of marriage, always; that was Katz's sin—perhaps the girl's as well, he wasn't sure. Sin or madness. Something Elaine had said darkened the edge of his mind, then broke in—"what I've learned in analysis." Why it felt connected he wasn't exactly sure: perhaps the way the campus, in the afternoon light, had made him think of Eden, or childhood, same thing . . . Yes, anality and all that, the child's possessiveness, playing with his feces, feces symbolically transmuted into money, into time, great monuments, cities walling out Nature, Death . . . All very vague; he hadn't thought about Freud in a long time, though he remembered he'd more or less believed it as he read, in fact had seemed to remember, though of course it was impossible, nobody really remembered that far back. He'd believed ever since he'd read those books—he no longer remembered exactly which ones—that everything men did, or men and women, perhaps (he'd have to think about that)— everything they did was a fraud and a delusion, a game played against Death on a rigged roulette wheel, Death playing for the house. Music, mathematics, Egypt's cities of the dead (the brains of the corpses drained out through the nostrils and discarded as of no use), all the magnificent works of man were mere blind birds' battering flights against the roof, bluffs against Death's dull, invincible hand, a flailing of "sublimation." It was all nothing, Chartres cathedral, UNIVAC, "the shadow of a dream," as some old-time poet said. No doubt Ira Katz had read those same books. He'd refused to be persuaded, the drive to live forever too strong in him. So he'd sit up all night, intense, eyes glowing, exactly like the "hackers" Professor Weintraub had mentioned, at the computer center, and when his wife said, "Ira, aren't you coming to bed?" he'd said, "Half an hour more," lying, praying she'd fall asleep and never know if he stayed up far longer, as he intended to do, hunting for some rhythm that was the perfect music and matched perfectly the words for his sorrow or rage or sense of loss. He'd stayed up till dawn sometimes, or worked straight through, skipping a night, or maybe two nights in a row—at any rate he did that now, sometimes; no reason to doubt that he'd done it when he was married. His heart would tug from his chain-smoking, the veins in his wrists and hands would ache. He'd have to be crazy to think he was driving Death away, when obviously he was beckoning to him, waving both arms, yelling "Here! Over this way!" So all right, he was crazy: variant of the universal madness. Fooled himself by claiming he was capturing life, that is, emotion in its flow, translating time into eternity. And what was he doing? *Making things up!* Not reliving emotions and capturing them forever in the exact right words—no, making up scenes drawn partly from life and partly not, blending fact and fantasy till afterward he wouldn't know which was which, murdering the past as it really was, tearing it down like a worthless machine for spare parts. Surely he must feel some guilt over that. He could hardly forget that his feeling for his wife had been real, once, powerful—his feeling for his children no less so, perhaps. Yet he had used those feelings, changed them just slightly, for some aesthetic reason—or even if he got them exactly right (which was unlikely, but never mind) had altered them by the very act of setting them apart from the flow of things, as a beautiful young woman is one thing, darting naked from the bedroom to the bathroom, another caught forever in her flight by stiff, glowing paint. Surely no poet, not even the very finest, could help but feel to some extent a betrayer of life. If he loved his children as profoundly as he claimed, why was he sitting here sucking on his pencil while his children lay asleep in the other room? Not that poets were worse than other men; not at all. But there was no denying that poets, more than most men, were in a bad position for keeping up the helpful lie. Exact description or re-creation of feeling was their special expertise. As the chairman of Ira Katz's department had pointed out, every device in the tradition they lived by was designed for no other purpose than getting the emotion just right. So now, looking out at the soft golden sunlight, the shaded lawns of the university, Ira Katz must no doubt be pretty well aware how rotten his life had turned. He must know pretty well how his wife felt, too—careful student of emotion that he was—and how his children felt. He who had seemed their hope had proved their destroyer, he must be thinking. And what would he be thinking, given all that, about the death of April Vaught? "Dismal," Craine said aloud, then bit his mouth shut. No doubt he'd slept with her often. At any rate, it seemed general knowledge that they were having an affair. Yet she was not the first, not the only affair. So Ira Katz's guilt, in his own eyes—to Craine it hardly mattered—was darkened. That childhood self Katz had talked about was betrayed with a vengeance, then. And with her death—assuming he had nothing to do with it himself, not an easy assumption—the picture darkened still more.

All this while Craine stood motionless, staring out the window like a man in a trance, watching the sky change, dark, silvered cloud patches moving northward through the yellow, reflected in the windows of the buildings across from him, the leaves of the trees moving, inaudible to Craine, and he was thinking, despite his gloomy thoughts about Ira Katz, *Strange, how beautiful it is, how peaceful!* It was true, no mere illusion, he understood, not quite in words. It was not just that it seemed like some noble old painting, though it did, certainly; on the campus time had in some quite real sense stopped. Everyone noticed it, if only in jest. People distinguished between the campus and "the real world." It was the last playground; that might be it, perhaps. The last slow, easy breath of childhood. They came here "students" and left "workers." A grim thought. He remembered now something else he'd run into, in one of those books of Freud's, that in the unconscious *Time does not exist.* He felt through his pockets and found a pencil, then a scrap of paper. "In unconscious, no past or future," he wrote. He studied the writing, making sure he'd be able to read it when he came on it again, a week or a month from now, then folded it and tucked it in his shirt pocket. Almost at once he drew it out again, frowning, and added the words, "also sub-atomic particles, psychic experience." The last few words were very small, almost off the paper's ragged edge. He dropped it in his pocket again.

"Complementarity," he said aloud. Two whole realities in double exposure. Pastoral peace, undeniable as young love, or the childlike old scholar's endless play, up in his tower; yet in the same immortal garden, neurosis, terror, murder, Elaine Glass dreaming up her death in the colors of the Virgin, while down at the computer center . . .

He thought of Elaine in there scribbling in her notebook, then of how she'd run to the blind boy to help him and he'd almost knocked her down. What a strange marriage she was of awkwardness and grace! At once, with what felt like a massive blush, he remembered her flying toward him at Denham's tobacco store, remembered the smell of chocolate malt on her breath, and his surprise that, thin as she was, she had well-developed breasts. Quickly, Craine closed the door on that, and even more quickly he pushed away the thought of Emmit Royce.

He needed a drink. When he looked at his watch—ten to four—he was astonished and once again convinced that it must not be working; impossible that he'd stood here that long, knowing he should go down to the truck and move it, and grab a quick restorative while he was there, handy by. It came to him that he hadn't had a drink in hours, an incredible feat, he could claim, and anyone who knew him would admit that it was so—though strange to say, it seemed to him, for some reason, like nothing: he could go, if the whim took him, hours more. He wasn't even shaky, and the sweats had forgotten him. He was feeling quite unusually well, in fact, except gloomy, as he always became when he was sober. Not that he minded. Mortal gloom was the unconfessed ground of being, in southern Illinois. You saw it even in the hogs and chickens, the horses standing in fields, with their heads down, and in the Black Angus browsing in the mustardy, thistle-ridden hills or the cool, heavy shade of woodlots. It was deep in the character of the people of Little Egypt, and it infected the students in no time. Just as well. Let the people all speak the same language.

He looked down at the paperback open in his hand and frowned as if returning his attention to it, though he did not, musing instead on the idea of gloom. It was an odd thought that the dreary, philosophical gloom of Gerald Craine should be the normal gloom of Little Egypt. He was tempted to think otherwise, think something more to his own credit, but it seemed to him that the thought he'd stumbled on was sound. He would not count the young, the people who, by a sad irony, gave Southern Illinois the reputation of a party school—as if there were anything celebratory in that milling in the streets, smoking pot on curbs, drinking, dancing, knocking on the door of the mobile massage-parlor or drifting out at midnight down the county's dirt roads and weed-choked lanes toward the lakes, woods, caves, or the immense stone cliffs of Giant City. That was just the gloom of indecision and uncertainty, ambition and desire not yet harnessed to some adequate illusion. But the gloom of the crocodiles—the weedlot Baptists and mowed-lawn Methodists, farmers of hardpan, managers of banks of no significant account—that was something else again, worthy of consideration and respect. That was philosophical, not personal gloom: Lazarus' objective detachment, weighing the husk of life, tossing it in his hand, solemnly judging it: Due cause of woe. It was true, he had never been quite fair to the crocodiles. He'd heard a story once, a meeting of the Klan in some farmer's back lot. Rain had come, a soaker, and before they could escape all their Ford and Chevy pickups and sedans were stuck. They might have been there for a week, but some blacks came along with a wrecker and helped them, didn't even specially overcharge them for it. You'd think it might have led to some changes, but no. They'd been fooled all their lives by appearances: land that seemed rich—but then it cracked, or washed out from under them in a sudden roar of yellow—a gospel that seemed to promise happiness but none came . . . Even the government they'd fought wars for and paid honest taxes to had proved, in the end, one more sinister trick. Heath candy bar and Bell Telephone made a fortune on farming, while they, one by one, moved to town and gave up, to live by welfare. Therefore the crocodiles had no interest in how things seemed. They continued to burn crosses—those who were mean enough—carefully refraining from any other violence than the violence of the heart. They hardly knew what they were doing, not civilized human beings but reversions to the archaic; Craine's brothers, he thought now: gloom transformed to gesture.

Fragment Six

A door opened, down the corridor, apparently someone letting class out early. A few students came into the hall, then more, among others a blond girl Craine had seen around town before, strikingly beautiful but homosexual, real crime. Watching how she walked, legs unbecomingly solid, like a hod carrier's, head slightly forward—why would even a man want to walk like that? Craine thought—he almost missed it when Ira Katz came out, dressed in jeans and work shirt, carrying a bulging, bursting briefcase, black-bearded head cocked far to the right for balance. He was halfway down the corridor, beyond the crowd of students, when Craine got the presence of mind to go after him. Now someone else had let a class out early, and it was all Craine could do to keep sight of Ira's hurrying head and shoulders. The students around the doors where their classes had been were in no hurry to break up, talking and laughing, gossiping, complaining, making timid or bold advances in the old, old game. "That's college," Craine thought, and accidentally said it aloud as he pressed against the wall, crowding past. They should advertise that way. *Looking for a pretty girl that likes geography?* Still more doors opened, and more slow-moving students, smiling like theater people between acts, came wandering out into the corridor, massive and indefinite of purpose as cattle.

"Excuse me," Craine said, pushing past, "excuse me!" But when he came to the stairs going down and up, he couldn't tell, even when he jumped to get a look above the others' heads, which way Katz had gone. Down, Craine decided, for no good reason—indeed, when he'd gone two steps he knew he'd chosen wrong, but it was too late to go back, the crowd was all around him.

But near the foot of the stairs he saw Ira again. He'd come down after

all and was striding past the elevators, fifty feet away, moving, almost running, toward the high glass doors that led outside. "Excuse me," Craine
said, "sorry, emergency!" trying to push through. The students in front of
him looked up over their shoulders, not eager to let him pass, and moved
only a little, neither so little he had a right to be angry nor so much that
he had room to get by. When he reached the main floor, Ira Katz was nowhere to be seen. He made his way to the big glass doors, but it was clearly
hopeless. He ought to be right out there, in the wide span of sunlight between Faner and the woods, but if Ira was among those unchaining their
bicycles or moving, heads bent, into the shadows of trees, Craine was miraculously missing him.

He turned back toward the stairs and registered now for the first time
that there were pay phones over by the elevators. He crossed to them quickly—only one of them was in use—and hunted through his pockets for
dimes, then called Hannah.

"Any news?" he asked.

"You heard about the man at the computer center?"

"Professor Furth, yes. They're sure it was an accident?"

"I don't see how they can be, but I haven't talked with McClaren yet."

"Did Meakins catch up with Terrance Rush?"

"Hasn't checked in yet. I expect I'll get a call from him any time."

"OK. Listen, Hannah, I need you to take over with the girl for me.
I got some things I gotta do. All right?"

"Whatever you say, Craine," she said, less than eager.

"Make it ten minutes, then. No, on second thought, half an hour. And
bring the Bible."

"What?"

"The Bible—you know, the big white one."

"Craine," she said, then hesitated, then came out with it, "what *for?*"

"I don't know," he said. "Magic." He felt pressed, surrounded, beginning to rise to anger. Whose business was it, etc., etc. But it was an interesting question, why he wanted the thing. *Magic* was the truth. The way he
looked forward to getting it in his hands again was the way a child looked
forward to a toy or some particular suit of clothes that would change his
life—or looked forward to being four, or riding on the school bus. From
the minute he'd bought it, God knew why, it had been clear to him, at
least in the back of his mind, that there were stories he wanted to look at

again, after all these years. Purely for pleasure, he would have said: the sense of getting out of oneself. How the prophet Nathan had been so furious at Saul for raising him from the dead that he'd prophesied Saul's death in battle the next day, with all his sons. How King David had looked over and seen what's-her-name sunning on the roof. How the ghost of Jesus had appeared to the fishermen and called out, "Boys! Cast your net over there on the left!" It would not have been the same, he would willingly admit, if the stories in the book were "Rumpelstiltskin" or even Shakespeare's *Macbeth* or *The Tempest.* Tomes, tombs . . . If all books were séances, conversations with the dead, there were times—for some reason unknown to him—when some ghosts' voices cried out with vastly more urgency than others. He looked forward to getting that Bible in his hands as if he thought when he held it the light would change, become the airier sunlight of his childhood, before his mistakes. He looked forward to reading those stories—not just reading them, poring over them, boring into them, digging down and down, all his muscles snapping steel, the way you'd dig into some newly discovered great cave of the Incas—as if he thought they had a spell in them, the Fountain of Youth, such magical power as the Vedic priests, in that book he'd started, had imagined they'd worked into Sanskrit. A fool would say, "So Craine, in his old age, is hungry for religion." If it was true, it wasn't true in any sense a common fool would understand. There was something he'd known and hadn't known the importance of, and had a feeling he could maybe know again. Not life-after-death, or "walking hand in hand with God." Something those sharp-eyed, big-nosed Jews of old had known, dickering with God, dying for righteousness, carefully, carefully writing it all down—some truth, some lies, the same way other poets wrote, but with some strange ingredient that suffused the whole, crept through the parchment like the hungry, ever unfulfilled spirit of the vowels never written in the name of God.

In a word, he had no idea why he wanted it. It was an impulse that had come over him, a dowser's hunch.

"All right," Hannah said, "I'll trine remember."

He hung up, felt to see if his dime had come back, then hurried for the stairs.

It was only when he was walking down the second-floor corridor toward the room where he'd left her that Craine understood, with a jolt, the mistake he'd made. It was not that those classes had gotten out early. It was at ten minutes to, not on the hour (as he'd thought), that classes ended. He'd abandoned her just as her class was getting out, and had left her alone there for nearly ten minutes. His hand went to his coat pocket, but the whiskey wasn't there. "Damn," he whispered, hurrying more now, again and again banging his fist into his palm. He was in trouble again, more than before, he thought. She'd be sure he'd done the whole thing on purpose, and maybe in some crazy way he had. "Jesus," he whispered.

The door where her class had been was closed, and inside there was a different class. His blood ran cold, or anyway so it felt, no warmth in his body, his neck hairs rising. He jumped to the little window and pressed his eyes to the glass to see as much as he could. The teacher was now a man, short, white-bearded, waving a cigar. Craine's hand was on the doorknob, but he decided not to turn it; she wouldn't be there. *Where then?* he wondered, spinning around in panic, looking down the corridor one way, then the other. Now nausea leaped up in him, and the building swayed. This had happened before, one minute the girl right beside him, and the next . . . His mind went blank.

"Mr. Craine!" Elaine cried, "what's the matter? Are you all right?"

He turned to her, baffled. She was right at his shoulder, her hands closed on his arm. Her eyes were wide with fear.

"I'm all right," he said. "Just faint."

"You've been drinking!" she said, half angry, half pitying him. "I suspected that was it, when I came out and you were gone."

He nodded, accepting it, leaning back for a moment against the wall and gently putting his hand on hers, wearily smiling.

"Have you?" she asked, beginning to change her mind.

"I'm all right," he said, and freed her hand. "I guess it gave me a start there, when I thought I'd lost you." When he saw that she was thinking about the murderer, he said quickly, "I thought you'd decided to dump me, get some other private eye. Quite a shock to the ticker."

She smiled. "I was in the ladies' room."

"Ah," he said, and pushed his hat up with one finger. "I'd have thought of that sooner or later. No dummy, take my word for it." He straightened up from the wall and held out his arm to her, formal, like a fancy-dress escort.

She looked at his arm, then up at his face, then laughed, shaking her head, shifted her books to her left arm, and with her right took the arm he held out to her. "Thank you, sir," she said, and gave a curtsy.

"My pleasure, ma'am," said Craine, and bowed.

They made a curious couple, an objective observer would perhaps have remarked: Elaine with thick ankles and blue, pointed shoes, on her square face the smile of a girl strangely happy, also nearsighted; as for Gerald B. Craine, he walked with his chin out, his hat tipped back, his dyed-black hair hanging down over his forehead, walking not at all like an old man, just now, or a half-crazy drunkard, though it was true, an objective observer would have noticed, that his coat hung low, something bulky in the lining, and his shoelaces were not well tied.

He thought of her weightless, long hand on his arm and pondered the image of her smile inside his mind. Exactly what he was thinking he could hardly have said: something about cancer, and murder, and his peculiar sense of peace.

Fragment Seven

The room was white. There was snow outside. That was a rare thing in Carbondale. Voices coming in were like muffled bells. There were faraway voices—children playing by the street—and nearer voices—those of the attendants at the end of the corridor. Here in the sunroom there was no sound at all, though the television was on—just the picture, sufficiently in shadow that he could just make it out. But what Craine was mainly aware of—seated on the cold gray plastic couch, magazines around him, the Bible in his lap—was the dazzling winter light, so brilliant, glancing off icicles and snow, that his eyes, however long he squinted, refused to adjust. He was like a man just emerged from imprisonment in some cellar, who takes in the world by cautious peeks, then squeezes his eyes shut and sees it all again, vermilion. He was alone this afternoon, except for an old woman in the chair by the television. She sat head down, as if fast asleep, though she was not asleep, merely wilted; when she slept, she snored. Each time Craine looked, for over an hour, she was exactly the same. Then once when he opened his eyes for a moment he saw that she was raising her head, slowly, and slowly turning it, like a ghostly sunflower, more or less looking in his direction. He realized now that there was someone beside him. He looked up: a young woman—early middle-aged—a fellow patient, though not in a hospital gown like his. She wore a clean, unwrinkled white robe, expensive. A shining haze of blond hair hung, brushed and electric, to just below her shoulders, carefully fastened with a clip that glittered like a diamond.

Craine nodded, timidly, or rather bowed, a gesture grotesquely exaggerated, an observer would have said, but plainly not meant to be ironic. He drew his large feet closer to the couch, meekly offering the stranger more space. She moved away a little. On her small, stockingless feet she had pale leather slippers. Craine wished he had a drink and reached to the pocket of his pajamas, then the pockets of his robe, hunting for his pipe, unaware that he was doing it until he realized that indeed he had no pipe, nothing in his pockets but some wadded-up Kleenex, no defense against the eyes of the stranger but the Bible in his lap. He looked at her again, trying to read her face, but the brightness made her a blur. Though her face was turned slightly to one side, she appeared to be watching him, neither friendly nor, so far as he could guess, openly hostile. Watching him, though, that was the thing. It was that, chiefly, that made him aware to the bottom of his slippers that this was a woman from a different world from his. Rich, probably. He smiled, almost fiercely, and bowed to her again, then opened the Bible in his lap and put his finger down at random, preparing to read, or, rather, pretend to.

As he lowered his head she said, "Good afternoon." Distantly, coldly. A voice with an unnerving authority in it. He looked up once more, wondering in panic why she spoke to him.

"Which are you," she asked, "alcoholic or mentally ill?" The question made his heart jerk—the terrible directness. She was a teacher, it came to him; a lady professor. He should have known by the glasses hanging down by a cord, the boyish yet severe way she stood. She waited, partly turned away from him, not meeting his eyes, but expecting him to answer; requiring him to.

"You might say both," he said. Then, after a moment, making a bold leap. "Which are you?"

She turned away more and took a step toward the window as if the question annoyed her, too stupid to waste time on. Craine shrank inward. She had a cigarette in her hand, and she held it in a way that seemed to him disdainful. As she drew it toward her mouth it began to wobble violently. It struck him like a bolt of lightning that she was sick, miserably unhappy, for all her degrees or whatever, just a woman, a child. He doubted the insight; perhaps it was something else. Though she alarmed him, seemed clearly to blame him for something, he was conscious of watching her—that is, squinting blearily up in her direction—as Meakins would, full of helpless sorrow. Abruptly she changed her mind, turned to glance at him, then looked away. She stood now in front of the window, dead center, her bathrobe and hair like fire. In a voice bristling with hatred she said, "Someone committed me." She gave a sort of laugh.

"I'm sorry," Craine said.

For a long time she said nothing, ignoring him, smoking, her hand jittering like a machine. "I'm as sane as anyone," she said suddenly, as if to herself. "There's a professor in my department, lives right next door to us, he carries a clothespin in his pockets so he can always touch wood. He's fat and little. Jewish. Black suits. Brilliant mind, very famous—but let me tell you, he's a swamp. Walks down the sidewalk with an umbrella on his arm and his nose in a book, and when he comes to a corner where he has to turn right, he turns in a circle three times to the left. Never stops reading. *I'm* as sane as *that.*"

Craine nodded, noncommittal. Her words weren't really loud enough to hear, though mysteriously he'd heard them. Again she stood silent, jittering and smoking. Then abruptly she came back, taking quick little steps. "How come the Bible?" She spoke loudly now, as if she thought he might be deaf. "Are you a minister?"

Craine tipped his head and shrugged, almost cringing, apologetic. "I was a detective," he said.

"You've shifted to higher criticism?" She shouted it, flashing a smile like a razor.

Again he shrank from her. She turned, somehow offended, and walked in rage to the window. She stayed there a long time, smoking and whispering, with her back to him. He leaned forward, thinking of leaving, but he hesitated too long, and she edged back toward him, keeping her eyes from him till the last minute. Then she looked at him, frowned angrily, smiled again. "They put you here to watch me." Her index finger—the hand that held the cigarette—jabbed at him. Ashes struck his knees.

Craine shook his head. Now, for some reason, he could see her features clearly—petulant, like a child's; beautiful even in their wrong-headed fury, or so it seemed to him. Her cheeks were very pale, as if powdered. In spite of his distress, he was tempted to smile, as at a child's performance of a tantrum. Her eyes were narrowed, her shoulders pushed forward. When he failed to speak, she was checked a little, and darted her eyes away. He leaned back. She remembered the cigarette and drew it to her mouth, trembling violently again, and sucked at it. Craine said, "I'm in no condition to watch anybody. They put me here because I pretty near blew a man's head off." It was not, strictly speaking, the truth, but it expressed Craine's feeling.

"Maybe he deserved it." She liked the idea. Scent of blood.

Craine nodded thoughtfully, avoiding her eyes, and clasped his hands together. "It's a mystery."

She sucked at the cigarette again, then let out smoke through her nose and mouth in a way that showed practice, maybe practice long ago with a mirror. "Bullshit," she said, cold as ice. "Mystery." She laughed. She turned away but did not leave, stood instead staring out the window, elbows stiffly at her sides except when she remembered to take a pull at the cigarette. Craine watched her, squeezing his hands together, straining to make her form come clear; but the sunlight and snow and the whiteness of the room were, if anything, brighter than earlier. Something made him think all at once that she was crying—standing there, hands at her sides, letting tears run down her face. His mouth opened, and he thought, for a fleeting instant, of Elaine Glass. "Crying," he said to himself, a kind of whimper, thinking simultaneously of the professor and Elaine. It was like seeing the stars from the perspective of a new geometry.

A Note on the Type

The text of this book was set in a digitized version of Bembo, a well-known Monotype face. Named for Pietro Bembo, the celebrated Renaissance writer and humanist scholar who was made a cardinal and served as secretary to Pope Leo X, the original cutting of Bembo was made by Francesco Griffo of Bologna only a few years after Columbus discovered America.

Sturdy, well balanced, and finely proportioned, Bembo is a face of rare beauty, and is extremely legible in all of its sizes.

Composed, printed, and bound by The Haddon Craftsmen, Inc.
Scranton, Pennsylvania

Designed by Cecily Dunham